A BURNING EMBER
IN BLOOD AND FIRE - BOOK 2

BY KRISTINA GRUELL

KRISTINA GRUELL

TABLE OF CONTENTS

DEDICATION 9

MAP OF REDOLAN 10

    MAP OF LITHONIA 11

    MAP OF CAELDENON 12

    MAP OF PANNARIUS 13

    MAP OF THE ISLES OF THE ITHRIMIR 14

PART ONE 17

    CHAPTER 1 17

    CHAPTER 2 19

    CHAPTER 3 20

    CHAPTER 4 22

    CHAPTER 5 24

    CHAPTER 6 27

    CHAPTER 7 33

    CHAPTER 8 36

    CHAPTER 9 43

    CHAPTER 10 45

    CHAPTER 11 48

    CHAPTER 12 50

    CHAPTER 13 55

    CHAPTER 14 60

    CHAPTER 15 62

CHAPTER 16...69

CHAPTER 17...76

CHAPTER 18...78

CHAPTER 19...83

CHAPTER 20...86

CHAPTER 21...91

CHAPTER 22...96

CHAPTER 23...99

CHAPTER 24...103

CHAPTER 25...106

CHAPTER 26...111

CHAPTER 27...116

CHAPTER 28...119

CHAPTER 29...126

CHAPTER 30...132

CHAPTER 31...138

CHAPTER 32...143

CHAPTER 33...149

CHAPTER 34...151

CHAPTER 35...152

CHAPTER 36...155

CHAPTER 37...165

CHAPTER 38...166

CHAPTER 39...170

CHAPTER 40...174

CHAPTER 41...177

CHAPTER 42...179

CHAPTER 43...185

PART TWO 189

CHAPTER 44...189

CHAPTER 45...194

CHAPTER 46...199

CHAPTER 47...202

CHAPTER 48...206

CHAPTER 49...209

CHAPTER 50...212

CHAPTER 51...214

CHAPTER 52...217

CHAPTER 53...219

CHAPTER 54...222

CHAPTER 55...225

CHAPTER 56...230

CHAPTER 57...237

CHAPTER 58...240

CHAPTER 60...242

CHAPTER 61...246

CHAPTER 62...249

CHAPTER 63...253

CHAPTER 64...257

CHAPTER 65...259

CHAPTER 66...262

CHAPTER 67...265

CHAPTER 68...270

CHAPTER 69...276

CHAPTER 70...279

CHAPTER 71...284

CHAPTER 72...286

CHAPTER 73...290

CHAPTER 74...294

CHAPTER 75...297

CHAPTER 76...299

CHAPTER 77...302

CHAPTER 78...304

CHAPTER 79...306

CHAPTER 80...308

CHAPTER 81...316

CHAPTER 82...319

CHAPTER 83...321

CHAPTER 84...328

CHAPTER 85...333

CHAPTER 86...336

PART THREE 343

CHAPTER 87...343

CHAPTER 88...345

CHAPTER 89...353

CHAPTER 90...355

CHAPTER 91...357

CHAPTER 92...359

CHAPTER 93..364

CHAPTER 94..369

CHAPTER 95..374

CHAPTER 96..378

CHAPTER 97..384

CHAPTER 98..388

CHAPTER 99..395

CHAPTER 100..399

CHAPTER 101..402

CHAPTER 102..405

CHAPTER 103..408

CHAPTER 104..412

CHAPTER 105..414

CHAPTER 106..424

CHAPTER 107..428

CHAPTER 108..434

CHAPTER 109..437

CHAPTER 110..440

CHAPTER 111..447

CHAPTER 112..451

CHAPTER 113..452

CHAPTER 114..454

CHAPTER 115..457

CHAPTER 116..459

CHAPTER 117..462

CHAPTER 118..466

CHAPTER 119 473

CHAPTER 120 478

CHAPTER 121 480

CHAPTER 122 483

CHAPTER 123 490

CHAPTER 124 493

EPILOGUE 496

APPENDICES 500

THE CAST 500

CALENDAR AND DATES 506

ACKNOWLEDGEMENTS 509

ABOUT KRISTINA 510

DEDICATION

For my Mom, Dad and Bonus Dad.

KRISTINA GRUELL

MAP OF REDOLAN

MAP OF LITHONIA

MAP OF CAELDENON

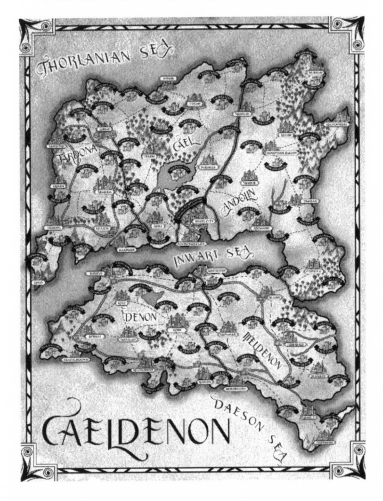

MAP OF PANNARIUS

MAP OF THE ISLES OF THE ITHRIMIR

The Prophecies of Hathor
The Archives of Ganna
Recorded: 29ᵗʰ of Minn, the year 380

The path Homeward lies in the roots of the Oaken Heart. The Branch that Flourishes From the Ashes of Fire and Death is the true Ruler of Lithonia and will Unite the Lands and Bring a Lasting Peace.

PART ONE

Late Summer and Early Autumn, the Year One Thousand and One, A.C.

CHAPTER 1

The Goddess Hestia, the Mystic of Hathor
The Temple of Ganna: Hathor
25th of Jinda

Hestia reviewed the list of priestesses that were coming into their fertile time and saw that her eldest daughter was ready to go through the sacred rite for the first time, and prayed she would conceive and birth a daughter. Hestia had seen two sons sacrificed to She Who Was, Is, and Would Always Be. Her who Hestia had been named for, when she'd given up the name she was born with to become who she was meant to be.

Hestia left her study and went to the inner sanctum, the place where the most sacred rituals were performed. Her sister priestesses were there, waiting to do the will of their Goddess Incarnate.

Hestia took her place before the silver bowl that held water from the sacred aquafer below the temple. She nodded, and one of her sisters came forward and cut her own arm, letting her blood dribble into the bowl. The sister returned to her place at Hestia's back, and all the priestesses joined hands and began to chant.

Blood and water swirled in the bowl as their Life Force swirled around her. Hestia closed her eyes and let herself drift, surrendering herself to Her. To the Goddess whose name Hestia now carried.

Hestia felt the thin barrier that separated her from the Life Force shatter, and a surge of energy and power coursed through her. She opened her eyes and looked into the bowl. The chanting behind her rose in pitch as the energy that poured toward her climaxed.

A raven formed in the bowl; a sacred sign, but also the symbol that marked the Morthan girl. The same shape that had marked her father.

Hestia would not fail like those who had come before her. She would take the Oaken Heart. She knew now that she had struck too early when she had sent Jardin to attack Harmon's Island. The time was now. She would strike the Raven Queen down, and Hestia, the Highest Priestess, the Goddess Incarnate, would rule all.

CHAPTER 2

King Garrett Morlette Morthan
Castle Endomir, Endomir: Lithonia
27ᵗʰ of Jinda

They were plotting against him again, Garrett knew it. Whispered conversations that quieted when he entered the room, bland expressions, and lip service to his face…but behind his back, he knew they were plotting.

Garrett held the trump card: their children's lives. They'd thought he would hesitate to move against them, but they had been wrong. In all the years that he had been his brother's keeper, he had learned an important lesson: fear was a great motivator.

He had ordered that all the prisoners witness the price of disobedience, even the children. He watched them as Garran Wallace was cut down from the pole he had been tied to, blood streaming from his back. Garrett had been merciful, only ten lashes—the current price for trying to flee his hospitality.

He would do what needed to be done to secure his throne. They knew that now.

CHAPTER 3

High Lord Benjamin Bennings
Bennings Place, the City of Endomir: Lithonia
27ᵗʰ of Jinda

Getting anyone out of the city without scrutiny was hard these days; getting someone connected to a high lord out was harder still. Benjamin's errand, should it be discovered by the wrong people, would be the undoing of his house. In the eyes of those who currently ruled the city—and were attempting to rule the country—it was treason, but to Benjamin, to *not* act would be treason.

The twelve-year-old boy whose shoulders this task rested on stood before Benjamin. Evan Williams was slight, a bit short for his age, with big, brown eyes and a shock of blond hair.

He was also loyal to a fault, and determined.

Evan would travel with a pair of messengers whose purpose was to draw attention away from him, the true messenger. The letter he carried would be delivered to Benjamin's wife, who would see it passed into the hands of one of his captains, who would then take it to Caeldenon, to the true Queen.

"Evan," Benjamin said, resting his hand on the boy's shoulder. "If you fall into the hands of the King's men, burn this or shred it… destroy it. Without delay."

"My lord, I won't let anything stop me from getting this to the High Lady," the lad swore earnestly.

"Heed me now," Benjamin said, bending down to his level. "There will be other chances if we fail." Though the longer they waited, the harder it would be. "Your life is more important. I need every loyal man I can get my hands on for the coming struggle."

Evan puffed up, shoulders back and head held high. "Of course, my lord."

"Good man." Benjamin clapped his shoulder. "Good man. I know you will do your best."

He watched Evan tuck the envelope into his shirt, letting it rest against his waistband. His heart felt heavy, leaving this task to a young boy. But he had the best chance, in the current circumstances.

After Evan left, Benjamin looked down at his desk, scanning the draft that he had composed before writing the formal letter now tucked safely in the boy's tunic:

To Her Majesty, Queen Lenathaina Morthan Coden,

If it were in my power to swear my fealty in person, I would. As it is, many of the high lords and much of our families are being held in the city to ensure our cooperation as the Usurper Morlette takes control of the government. I and my allies are doing what we can to slow him, but we need you, our Queen, to spearhead this battle.

To that end: my wife and our daughters are currently in residence at Seathor. She gathers supplies and troops as discreetly as possible, all of which will be at your disposal when you land. I urge you to come with all haste. Your people need you.

Ever your servant,
High Lord Benjamin Bennings

Benjamin picked up the draft and read it once more before tossing it into the fireplace. He watched the scrap of paper shrivel and curl in the flames until it was ash.

CHAPTER 4

Kenleigh Atona, Prisoner
The Temple of the Maker in White City: Caeldenon
29ᵗʰ of Jinda

Kenleigh knelt before the window of her bare chamber and watched the sunrise.

She wore a gray robe, her red hair was bound and covered with a matching head scarf, and her feet were naked. She was a prisoner, considered a runaway acolyte and a breaker of the most solemn oath. She was a woman not trusted to keep her word.

Three weeks ago, when Kenleigh had given herself up to High Priest Tadaemeric, she had been unsure of which way the hammer would fall; she was still unsure.

She had come during the weekly open supplication, when the citizens of the city were free to come forward to ask for prayers or blessings from the priests of the Maker. She'd stood in a line before the High Priest for hours. When at last it was her turn, she'd knelt before him and held her hands up, as if in prayer.

"Holy Father," she'd said, her mouth dry and her hands trembling, *"I am an acolyte. I was taken from the Holy Island, the home of our Maker, and held against my will, unable to return. I wish to redeem myself and seek mercy and sanctuary."*

Silence greeted Kenleigh's confession. Even those around her, standing before the other priests, went silent. All watched, waiting to hear what the High Priest would say.

She waited as well.

Kenleigh had then been taken to the High Priest's study, and there, she'd told him the whole of her story. How she was taken from the shores of Maker's Island while she walked alone on the beach. How she'd been beaten, starved, and raped. She told him of the other women with her, and gave him the letters from Gira and Realain, and one from the Queen, written in secrecy, telling of Kenleigh's rescue—but not of her own kidnapping and imprisonment. She gave her oath that what Kenleigh said was the truth.

With some sorrow—or so he'd said—the High Priest had followed the word of the holy law, and 'imprisoned' her…in a set of rooms with lovely wall coverings and a nice rug, a real bed, a table and chairs, and a chest to store her clothing, which had been retrieved by his servants from White Castle.

Soon, though, the other priests had argued that she must be treated as a prisoner and not a guest. So, with more reluctance on his part, she had been moved to this chamber: a stone room with no wall or floor coverings, and the only furniture a thin pallet on the floor, and a table that held a jug of water and a wash basin.

She was taken every other day to bathe in the bathing chamber, and every four hours to relieve herself. Other than that, she was left alone, with a prayer book as her only companion. Left alone to think and to wait.

A week ago, letters had arrived from the island; a priest from her home temple would come with her mother and brother to identify her. If she was who she claimed, a trial would be arranged.

That the journey had been undertaken so quickly showed the severity of her situation. She thought the fact that the Queen had been inquiring after her welfare had something to do with the speed in which things were progressing. She only hoped the Queen's influence would extend to the trial as well.

At the moment, Kenleigh felt little hope that she would live to see many more sunrises.

CHAPTER 5

Dowager Queen Mellina Morthan
Indayon Ocean, passing the Stones
1ˢᵗ of Rison

Mellina stood on the deck of the *Echo*, the wind whipping through her hair. Hair that had been almost completely black just months before, but was now streaked with silver. Lines that had shown only faintly on her face were now deeply furrowed, her violet eyes had lost their brightness, and whatever beauty she had possessed was now gone.

The changes had started slowly, but the night her son King Richard had died, she had aged overnight.

As she watched the waves, the scene unfolded before her once more, just as it did when she dreamed: Richard, her first-born, choking his wife, her thighs streaked with blood. He had beaten her, killing their child in the process, before strangling her. She was dead—Mellina could see that even if Richard could not. And his half-brother Garrett, her late husband's bastard, lay on the floor bleeding, broken, and unconscious.

In Richard's fury, he had not heard his mother enter, had not heard her close the door behind herself. She had picked up a pen knife from the desk in the corner of the sitting room and stepped up behind him...her baby, her first-born. The child that had tied her to a man she had grown to despise.

She grabbed a handful of his hair, and that was when he'd snapped out of it. Still, she jabbed the pen knife into his throat, and yanked, tearing it across his windpipe.

He clutched his throat, blood gushing from between his fingers. He turned to look up at her, and she read his last word on his lips, but he could do nothing more than gasp:

"Mother."

24

Sara Parten, Mellina's best friend—really her only friend, since her sister had died in childbed—was with her on the ship. Sara had been her chief lady-in-waiting, her confidant, and her savior from the moment Mellina became queen.

Sara's quick thinking had been what saved Mellina, when she'd found the Queen Mother clutching the hand of her dead daughter-in-law, next to her son's lifeless body. Sara had taken Mellina by the hand and led her to her room, where she had comforted her briefly and then bade her to clean herself up while Sara packed bags for them both. Sara had then gone to the one person she knew they could trust, High Master Tam Gale.

Master Tam had supplied them with money—not from the treasury, as, sooner or later, the missing gold would be noticed. Instead, he had given them gold from his private stash. And while they'd finished packing, he had gone down to the kitchens himself and come back with a large parcel of food, enough for three people to travel for two days.

Mellina had known of the pass through the southern mountains that led to a rocky beach too small to be of use or interest to anyone. The children had never been told. Only she, her mother-in-law, and Master Tam knew of it. Her late husband had known, of course, and his brother had as well.

Mellina and Nikkana had been taken to the entrance shortly after their marriages to the King and his brother, Prince Matthew. Lenathaina would have never known of it, but Richard would have been shown upon reaching his majority, and his wife with him.

He would not have that chance now. That also meant that Garrett did not know of it.

They had taken horses, sure-footed mountain ponies, and ridden through the night, their only company and protection a lone groom. When they reached the pass, riding with pole lamps had been no problem; no one could see them.

Shortly before dawn, they had stopped for a few hours to sleep. The groom did not ask any questions, he just cared for the horses and then made his own pallet not far from them. He knew who they were, of course, and that they were running from something, but he did not press for information.

They had only slept a few hours before rising to make a hasty breakfast, then they spent the rest of the day in the saddle. They had camped that night and risen early the next morning. Sometime after noon, they'd ridden into the small port town of Earnest Point. They sailed on the evening tide, taking the first ship bound for Caeldenon.

Thankfully, the *Echo* was accustomed to taking on a passenger or two, so the accommodations were not horrible—though nothing like what they were used to.

Sara came to stand beside Mellina, lacing her arm through the Queen's. The auburn-haired woman was taller than Mellina; she had eyes the color of good whiskey, and wore a hat to protect her peaches-and-cream complexion from the sun.

Mat, the young groom who now knew the whole of their story, stood on Mellina's other side. The young man was fair-skinned, with light brown eyes and hair. His features were bold...too bold for him to be called handsome, but he was a good-looking lad. Smart too. He had gathered the severity of their situation quickly.

On their second day at sea, Mellina had sat him down and told him everything. Once she'd finished her tale, he'd bobbed his head and said, *"Begging your pardon, Queen Mellina, but the King was a wicked man, and we all knew it. I'd seen him strike Queen Maratha myself. We all had. And of course there were the poor serving girls..."*

He'd trailed off, not quite meeting Mellina's gaze. Then he'd cleared his throat and continued.

"Some may call it wrong, but I don't. When a dog goes rabid, you got to put him down." He bobbed his head again and excused himself from her presence.

Mat's words went through her like a knife. Since then, he had been at her side day and night, acting more guard than groom.

CHAPTER 6

*Queen Lenathaina Morthan Coden of Lithonia, First
Princess of Caeldenon
White Castle, White City: Caeldenon
2ⁿᵈ of Rison*

Whatever the High King's opinions on the matter of
Lenathaina's presence and that of her young cousin, the High Queen
had made it her mission to see the child protected and distracted.
Jane was currently with the younger children in the royal classrooms,
being instructed on philosophy.

Lena's ladies sat around her like a flock of doves. They all wore
shades of white and gray, sometimes with black piping or ribbons,
but everything was devoid of color. They would stay in formal
mourning for three months before gradually shifting back to brighter
hues. The exception to this palette was Ellaemarhie, Lena's
Mael'Hivar Galvana, her blood-sworn sister—a woman that would
give life and limb to protect Lena. Ellae was dressed in black from
head to toe, like all the *Mael'Hivar*.

Lady Rachel Malick and Princess Fenora Tearhall were seated
side by side as they discussed the funeral and burial traditions of
their respective homelands. The two women were striking in their
own ways: Rachel had honey blonde hair that hung down her back in
waves, with alabaster skin and hazel eyes, where Fenora had skin the
color of honey, and mahogany hair that was artfully arranged in a
mass of braids atop her head, above dark blue eyes. Fenora was the
taller of the two, with angular features.

Victoria, who had been unusually quiet since they'd left Rose
Hall, sat in the corner with a letter in her lap that had just arrived
from the Dowager High Queen. Rachel and Fenora had read theirs
before continuing their discussions, but Victoria's had seemed longer
in length, and to leave her with much to think about.

Lena's missive from the formidable woman had been brief but sweet—for her—reminding Lena to have courage and hold to her convictions.

The stack of letters that had been delivered that morning was as large as it had been when Lena returned from captivity and the embassy informed her that her cousin, King Richard, had been murdered.

She had received several reports on the takeover of Endomir, and more than a few veiled questions regarding her own intentions, along with letters of condolence from various members of nobility, both from home and from Caeldenon.

A few of the notes that had come from supporters in Lithonia had pointed out that one person had motive and opportunity to kill her cousin, and that man was currently sitting on the throne that was rightfully hers. The boldest among those had offered their support to her, and shelter when she came to claim what was rightfully hers.

So far, those promises had only come from minor or middling nobility; she had yet to receive anything from any of the high Houses. Though she knew from other reports that every major House had had at least one heir taken into captivity by her bastard cousin, Garrett.

Lord Kieran Rainsmere entered the study. He was Lena and Gavantar's *gandine*—a role that combined steward, butler, and secretary, but was not seen in the same light as being a servant.

Being a *gandine* was an honor, and many children of lower nobility took the role on gladly. Some were trained for it from childhood in hopes of snagging a place in a higher house.

Rainsmere had made his allegiance to Lena and her husband Gavantar very clear when they had come home from what many assumed was their wedding trip. He knew the truth of it.

"Your Majesty?" He bowed and came to stand beside Lena. "There is a *person* outside, waiting to speak to you."

Lena felt more than saw her ladies shift their attention to Rainsmere.

"A person, you say?" she asked, moving a sheet of blank paper over the letter on her desk. Those she had read were already filed away in the locked drawer of her desk.

"Yes, Your Majesty," Rainsmere said, looking peeved. "He says that he can only speak about his errand to you."

Lena arched an eyebrow, "Well, by all means, bring him in and let us hear what he has to say for himself."

Rainsmere glanced to Ellae, who had been sharpening her sword and dagger across from Lena. At her nod, he left the room and came back a few minutes later with a travel-worn man dressed in a dark brown suit of modest origins.

The visitor knelt before Lena and bowed his head before holding out a package wrapped in a blue and green scarf that portrayed wolves, nose-to-nose in profile, at the corners.

She recognized it immediately and reached for it, but Ellae got there first. The *galvana* took the package and opened it, despite the protests of the man kneeling before Lena.

Lena laid a hand on his shoulder to quiet him and watched as Ellae unwrapped the bundle. She pulled out a box and opened it before handing it and the scarf to her.

The box held a very familiar ring, a round emerald flanked by triangular cut sapphires: the ring given to High Lady Angela Montgomery when she married Magne Montgomery.

To Lena's knowledge, she had never seen Angela without it on her finger.

Also in the box was a large, square-cut, pale blue stone.

A blue topaz, she thought.

"I have seen you before," Lena said to the man.

"Yes, Your Majesty. I am a footman for His Grace, High Lord Magne Montgomery. I travel with his Lordship's family no matter where they are in residence. Second footman, ma'am. I have served you at dinner more 'an once." He was shaking with a combination of fear and awe.

"Thomas?" Lena asked, almost sure of his identity; she had a good mind for names and faces.

Thomas beamed, blushing that she would remember him. "Yes, Your Majesty. His Grace sent me with the High Lady when she left the city a'fore the troubles." He ducked his head again, "He sent as many of us as he could without drawing attention."

He pulled a letter from inside his coat pocket and handed it to her with a sidelong look at Ellae. "I was told to put this in your hand, as it would explain many things."

Lena took the letter and nodded to Rainsmere. "Lord Kieran will take you to get something to eat while I read this."

"I thank you, Your Majesty."

She glanced at the ring, and Thomas saw this.

"Her Grace said you should hold on to that until you could give it back to her proper-like." He bowed again and let Rainsmere lead him from the room.

Lena slipped the ring on for safekeeping. It fit on her right hand—the place where, one day, she would wear the ring her uncle, King Charles, had worn all her life.

Fitting, since she was sure that what she held was the first pledge of support from a high House.

She opened the letter, her hands trembling slightly, and began reading.

24ᵗʰ of Caro, the Year 1001

To Her Royal Majesty, Queen Lenathaina Morthan Coden in White Castle, Caeldenon, from Her Grace, High Lady Angela Montgomery at Black Hall, Lithonia

My dear friend, for I hope I can still call you such, even in a formal letter, for if anything were ever a formal plea, a formal offering of aid, this would be it.

I must lay out the facts before anything. Garrett has seized the throne and taken hostages of every noble house currently residing in the city. As the season was not yet at an end, nor had the House sessions been closed, he had the choicest options for captives. All three of my sons have been taken. My girls were with me, as Magne and I had decided it was best if one of us was outside Endomir should things sour.

Neither of us could have foreseen how bad things would get, or we all would have left.

The man delivering this letter, and my own ring to offer assurances that this indeed comes from me, (and what dark times do we live in that such assurances are needed?) is a trusted servant. Anything you send back with him will arrive safely, or he will burn it before being taken. Use him as you will, but please respond, I beg you.

My House and all our resources await your call. On behalf of my husband, I pledge our undying loyalty and fidelity. You have many friends and supporters here, but there are just as many enemies or those who fear for loved ones. I need not tell you this, but I cannot help but worry for you and for our cause.

Enclosed is a Script Stone, of which I possess the mate. Please be sure you trust the Master that you choose to receive messages from it. I will carry its mate with me, on my person. Should you choose to make use of it, I will pass on any messages you send gladly.

We are, as we have always been, your friends... and now your obedient servants.

> *Angela Montgomery*
> *High Lady of House Montgomery*

Rachel came to stand at Lena's shoulder, and Lena handed her the letter. She heard Rachel gasp sharply.

"Stephen, Travis, and Derek," Rachel said quietly.

"All three of them?" Victoria asked. She was now reading over Rachel's shoulder, hand over her mouth.

"Yes, damnit." Lena kicked the drawer where her correspondence was locked away. "Magne is a very influential person, so the Usurper needed a solid hold over him. He's even taken little children. The youngest is six-year-old Merrie Long."

Lena had been keeping a list of those who had written, and their imprisoned relations. She would have to add three more names to that list now.

She stood and walked to the window, where Fenora joined her. The Princess put an arm around Lena's waist and rested her head on Lena's shoulder.

"We stand ready," Fenora whispered in her ear "Where you go, we will follow. We will fight at your side, my lady. We cannot let this madman hold sway over your people."

"It is a heavy burden," Lena murmured. "One I never thought would be mine."

"But it is." Fenora held her tight. "You have seen worse, lived through worse, and *alone*. You won't be alone this time."

Lena took comfort from the woman's embrace. She felt Ellae at her back, and Rachel and Victoria joined them, looking out the window and toward the harbor.

She was not alone. Whatever she had to face, these women would stay by her side. To the end.

CHAPTER 7

Edwin Murphy, Secretary to the King
Castle Endomir, Endomir: Lithonia
2ⁿᵈ of Rison

The 'King' was at yet another meeting with Montgomery, trying to get the High Lord on his side—something that Edwin highly doubted would happen, but having three of his sons in their custody was keeping him in line. For now.

Edwin could feel Garrett slipping out of his grasp. The King had promoted him from valet to his secretary but insisted that his private correspondence be left unopened. Edwin searched Garrett's office regularly to make sure no one was influencing the bastard away from him, but he rarely had a chance to get into his private rooms alone.

On the pretext of delivering papers, Edwin slipped past the guards and quickly rummaged through Garrett's personal desk. He found a stack of old letters from his mother, neatly tied by a fraying green ribbon, a few letters from his father, mementos from his childhood and young adult years...

Edwin was about to give up, when he shifted a book, and the smell of sandalwood filled the air. A letter had been hidden beneath a leatherbound journal.

He flipped to the last few pages of the journal to make sure Garrett had written nothing new before picking up the letter.

Garrett,

I know that you fear reversing your current stance
will make you weak, but my friend, that you must
hold onto young children to keep your throne
makes you look like both a bully and a coward. Let
them go and stand on your own. You have wit,

33

courage, and tenacity. Use your inborn skills to
your advantage. Do not be like your brother. Do
not become a monster, I beg you.

I will meet you in the woods off the southern side
of the Royal Mile, near the oak grove, at half past
ten, and we can discuss this more.

I remain your most devoted,
Brian Chiswick

Chiswick had been a fop and a card sharp in the days of the old
King, but had come to his majority and taken up his responsibilities
with his family. Edwin knew his brother was one of those enjoying a
stay in the Nursery Keep, and that the Chiswicks had been friends of
Richard and Garrett as boys and men.

This wouldn't do. No, it would not.

After the workday was done, Garrett dismissed Edwin, claiming
he was heading to his room early. It was eight o'clock; early enough
for Edwin to arrive in the woods before both men.

He took a horse from the stables and headed for town, ducking
into the woods a good mile before the oak grove. After a time, he
tied the animal up well out of sight before making his way on foot.

Edwin found a position a good way into the woods and climbed
up a tree to wait.

It was over half an hour before he heard a human disturbance. A
man settled below his tree, and he heard the striking of a match,
which lit an old-fashioned candle lantern. Edwin checked his
pocketwatch, turning it to catch the light from below: Garrett wasn't
due for half an hour.

The sound of a cork popping, and the scent of wine, came from
below.

Ah, Chiswick is settling in for a wait.

Well, Edwin was done waiting. The letter didn't seem like it was
an opening gambit, but a continuation of previous communications;

it was time for that to stop. He had his orders from the Mystic: destabilize the throne and breed distrust. If they were fighting one another, they would not see the Hathorites coming.

He touched the place inside himself that let him manipulate the Life Force that was inside all living things. With it, he fashioned a rope of energy and dropped it over the head of the interfering git below. He snapped it closed around Chiswick's neck and jerked it upward, watching the man kick and thrash for several minutes.

He felt the moment the meddler's life left him… a sweet, sweet feeling.

Edwin sucked in the energy that left Brian Chiswick, and let the rope dissolve. Chiswick fell to the ground, reeking of shit and piss, and Edwin climbed down the tree and made his way back to his horse, gleefully imagining the King's expression when he found his friend.

CHAPTER 8

High Prince Evandar Coden
White Castle, White City: Caeldenon
4ᵗʰ of Rison

Evandar considered Lan, who sat at one end of the conference table, spinning an opal Script Stone like a top. It was an annoying habit of his elder brother's, turning *everything* he touched into a toy. As a boy, it had been fun; as a man, watching him play with a magical artifact made Evandar's wame curdle.

Lan was an Arch Master of the Ithrimir, one of the people who taught and governed those who could touch the Life Source that lived inside all things. He had sent a question through the Stone to the Ithram's Council on the Isles of the Ithrimir, and was waiting for a response while Evandar and Gavan continued to debate.

Maelynn and Samera sat across from them, heads together, whispering quietly.

"If we back the Princess and Morlette wins, we've made an enemy," Evandar said yet again. "We are already angering him by keeping Lady Jane, who he claims as his heir."

His *Mael'Hivar Thane*, Deldemar Lynn, leaned between Evandar and his eldest brother Gavan, and set a glass of wine before him. Gavan's Andamar Rynear did the same for his *thane* before the pair moved back to the corner that the five *Mael'Hivar* had taken over as their own.

"A pussy-footed, backboneless fop," Gavan snorted, taking a sip of his wine. He was a bear of a man, tall and heavily muscled, with bright green eyes, and golden skin and hair. "I won't ally with a man who would take children hostage to hold his throne nor will I send him another child to lock up. Lady Jane stays with Lenathaina, as her father wanted. If he can't hold it on his own steam, he shouldn't sit his arse in it."

Maelynn laughed, and Samera covered her mouth to hold her own back, but both women looked as if they agreed with Gavan.

His wife, Samera, gave him a look he knew well; he wasn't going to get his way, and should accept it.

She looked tired, her gray eyes slightly swollen from sleep deprivation. Their fourth child had been born two weeks ago, and Samera was nursing the babe herself. Little Fadean looked like her mother, olive-skinned with eyes that Evandar was sure would remain gray. She even had a shock of amber hair.

"Be that as it may, the fop has nominal control of the city... where our embassy is," Evandar reminded everyone.

Maelynn and Samera sobered slightly, and Lan stopped spinning the damn Stone.

Gavan sat back before saying, "Our embassy has a Master seated firmly in place, and twenty guards. The Fop is a coward, he wouldn't storm it—even if we support Lenathaina.

"Besides, us backing her doesn't mean we will send an army with her. And him attacking our people would mean an all-out war, in which we would call upon our allies. He won't provoke me so far, knowing that it would mean the armies of the United Kingdom and Thynn at his doorstep."

"Be that as it may," Evandar continued.

"*Be that as it may*, we should have the girl in here," Gavan countered and motioned to Maelynn. "Could you?"

Maelynn rose, followed by Samera, and the pair inclined their heads toward Gavan and left the room with their *galvanas* at their heels.

"Why not send a servant?" Evandar muttered, leaning back.

His biggest fear was this Lithonian mess dragging them into a war while they were still fighting off Hathor on their northern shores. Caeldenon was always his first priority.

"For an advisor, you are pretty dense," Lan said, still watching his Stone. Like Evandar, Lan was tall and lean with tawny skin, hazel eyes, and reddish-brown hair, though Evandar's was darker. "She may not be a sitting monarch, but she could still be the next Queen of

Lithonia. Until a decision is made, you must treat her with the same respect you'd treat any other ruler."

Evandar was about to retort, when the Stone glowed.

Lan did something to it and pulled a sheaf of papers toward him. The Stone began pulsing again, and he scribbled whatever it was telling him with practiced movements, eyes on the Stone, and pen flying across the page.

Everyone else was silent as the Arch Master transcribed in shorthand and then told whoever was on the other side of the Stone that the message had been received.

After, Lan took out a fresh piece of paper and translated the message.

Gavan shifted in his seat and tried to wait patiently while Lan finished writing and then went back to read and reread the message, checking for mistakes.

"Well?" Gavan asked finally. "What do they have to say?"

Lan cleared his throat, "The Ithram won't get involved with the succession. Morlette-Morthan has requested a new Master be sent to him, as the former advisor to the Lithonian throne has 'resigned his position' and left."

Lan glanced up. "Interesting, seeing as most of our reports are saying that entering or leaving Endomir is strictly monitored. Was Master Tam allowed to leave?"

He shook his head and returned to the missive. "The Ithram is putting him off for now. Master Tam has checked in with them and the Council and is well, but either he hasn't given his whereabouts, or they aren't sharing them with me.

"Basically, it is up to us to decide if we will support her or not." He passed the letter to Gavan, who read it twice before handing it to Evandar.

When he reached the end, Evandar said, "I want to speak with the girl. She has been keeping to her rooms—understandable, with all she has been through, and then losing her uncle and her friend and finding out her aunt is missing."

He didn't mention the cousin whose death made her a queen. No one who had met him would miss him.

"Gavantar says she doesn't mean to let Morlette have control of her people, but I want to hear from her," he concluded.

It was another twenty minutes before Maelynn and Samera returned with Lenathaina, Gavantar, and their combined *Mael'Hivar*. Thankfully, the chamber was large, so the influx of people didn't make it overly crowded.

The *Mael'Hivar* all bowed before moving to join their fellows. Samera inclined her head toward Evandar, then she and Maelynn took their seats. Lan shifted to sit beside Evandar, leaving the end of the table open.

Gavantar bowed to his father, but Lenathaina faced Gavan calmly, hands lightly clasped before her, and met his gaze, monarch to monarch.

Gavan watched the raven-haired young woman for a long moment before gesturing to the seat at the end of the table. "Would you care to have a seat, Your Majesty?"

Lenathaina was delicate-featured and beautiful, with curling, black hair piled atop her head, sandy skin, and startling, violet eyes. A thin scar on the side of her neck served as a sharp reminder of her recent kidnapping and imprisonment.

Lenathaina gave Gavan a small smile and inclined her head in thanks before taking the seat.

Gavantar let out the breath he had been holding, and sat to her right.

"Sir," Evandar said quietly, turning to Gavan.

Gavan held up his hand. "Let her speak."

"Thank you, Your Majesty," Lenathaina said. "I know that there has been some confusion and perhaps concern on the matter of the Lithonian throne. While the Usurper Morlette may maintain he has documents signed by my late cousin supporting his right to rule, even if those documents existed, they would be invalid."

She clasped the table before her, her voice steady. "I know there are claims that my uncle was coerced into signing the succession forms that named me heir after my cousin, but I know that to be untrue."

Gavan leaned forward. "How can you know that, lass?" he asked quietly, gently. "You weren't there to see it."

"I know because it isn't the first time those papers were been signed," Lenathaina replied smoothly. "I saw the previous version myself, and have seen a copy made of the latest version by those I trust. The difference is that Morlette and Jane were acknowledged as illegitimate children but *not* as part of the line of succession. Had my uncle wished it so, he would have made it so. He may have been ill, but he wasn't feeble-minded."

She continued, "The last time a bastard was legitimized and added to the succession, it ended in a civil war. Because of that, and my uncle's promise to my aunt, he would not have changed his mind. Besides, without the House signing off on a bill, the succession could not be changed. So even if my cousin *had* signed papers, they would not be valid."

"When was the previous version made?" Gavan asked.

It was clear that the bulk of this conversation was between the two of them now.

"When I was fifteen. I saw it put into the royal courier's hands, and heard the order of delivery myself." Lenathaina drew a breath. "I even watched the couriers mount their horses and ride with a contingent of ten guards a piece."

"A piece?" Gavan asked, leaning forward. "How many were there?"

"Two. One bound for Hardcastle, the previous seat of the Lithonian throne and government, which still serves as a depository of royal papers and as royal estate." She laid her hands flat on the table. "By law, all official documents must be filed both in the archives at Castle Endomir and in the archives in Hardcastle."

"Where did the second go?" Gavan asked.

A slow smile spread across her face. "To Maker's Island, to the vault of the High Priest, where I assume a copy of the newer will and decree resides as well. Perhaps not to Morlette's knowledge."

She clasped her hands before her on the table. "So, as you see, Your Majesty, there is irrefutable proof not far away that will confirm that *I* am who your current alliance is lawfully with. I am sure Master Lan can verify these details through the Masters that serve on Maker's Island."

She pushed back her chair and rose, inclining her head toward Gavan. "I will leave you to confer with the High Priest, and I will likewise seek out the same confirmation. Then we can meet again to discuss the matter further."

Lenathaina headed for the door, and Ellaemarhie, grinning, met her there and opened it.

Gavantar rose slower behind her, gave a small grin of his own, and shrugged. He had his father's coloring and height, but had a leaner build. "I will remind you that you are the ones that picked her for me."

With that, he followed his wife out of the room.

Gavan stared at the closed door for a long moment before he struck the table with his fist and began laughing. He pushed back his chair and rose before addressing his brothers.

"The two of you, draft a politely worded request, blow as much smoke up their skirts as you feel is needed, and ask the High Priest for confirmation of the contents of the will, and see if a copy can be sent to Her Majesty here." He headed for the door. "I have a meeting with Elindger."

Evandar was surprised to hear it; nothing had been on his schedule regarding the King of Andolin.

He and Lan rose to join their brother, but Gavan waved his hand at them. "Pool and cigars. Nothing formal."

Maelynn and Samera followed the King out, heads together again, and Evandar and Lan were left on their own.

"Those two are plotting," Evandar said, still looking at the door where his pregnant wife and his sister-in-law had vanished.

"They are women. In their blood, I suspect," Lan said, pulling a clean sheet of paper toward him. "Let's get this letter drafted. I will have to go to my office to send it, as I only have the Stone for the

Ithram with me." He nodded to the opal on the table, which, when it caught the light, shifted to orange, blue, and yellow in turns. It had a large capital 'I' inside a diamond engraved on it, like the ring that Lan wore on his right hand

"We can't fight this war for her, you know," Evandar said, settling down to the matter at hand. "No matter what she or Gavan thinks."

"No, we can't. But according to our treaty with Lithonia against the Hathorites, we can give her aid and legal sanctuary, if her claims are true."

Lan filled his pen with fresh ink and gave a snort as he continued, "Thankfully, we have an official abbreviation for 'Your Exalted Holiness, High Priest and Holy Father, Clemet'. All the smoke I am going to be blowing is going to exhaust me on transmission."

CHAPTER 9

Lord Randal Bennings
Castle Endomir, Endomir: Lithonia
5th of Rison

Garrett had installed the prisoners in Nursery Keep the day guards had taken them from their homes or clubs or wherever they'd happened to find them. The walls of the keep, originally meant to keep the young heirs of the throne safe while they played, were now lined with armed guards holding rifles. What had once been a place of carefree fun had become a prison.

Randal had made a habit of walking in the garden a few times a day, making notes of when the watch changed, and the frequency of the patrols. The children distracted the guards; the nannies let them run wild in the gardens in the late morning, and all the screaming and screeching drew their eyes. If Randal were to try and escape, this would be the best time, when the young ones were at play.

Nodding to the patrolling guard, Randal turned and headed toward the kitchens. He passed a few older prisoners: a grandmother, the wife of a minor lord, and the favored uncle of another. It sickened him that Morlette kept children and grandparents. Someone had to do *something* to raise resistance. Without Randal's own life as ransom, nothing would hold his father back from doing so.

Inside the keep, there were fewer guards. They mostly monitored the border walls and the walkway that connected the castle and the keep, preventing escape; they didn't really care what the prisoners did inside the walls.

Randal made his way into the kitchens, where Mistress Thompson reigned as queen.

"Lord Randal! Here to fill your belly a bit more?" she asked as she placed a small bundle on the table and winked. "Had your snack all ready. Off with you, lad."

With a grin, Randal picked up the napkin-wrapped bundle. "You are a treasure, Mistress." He gave her a salute as he left.

Without looking inside, he knew the parcel held hard cheese, apples, and crusty rolls... even some cured meat, if she had managed to get it unnoticed from the big kitchen. All foods that a man could eat on the move.

Mistress Thompson took great risks, but as she had told him one evening, she was a Queen's woman through and through.

CHAPTER 10

Shan Alanine Fasili
River Keep, Southern Region: Pannarius
5th of Rison

Alanine lounged at the head of the women's table in the family dining room, her sister Nijah to one side, and Princess Lynear to the other.

Lynear was the niece of the Empress, may the Light ever favor her, and a distant cousin of Alanine's. She had been sent to be Alanine's guardian—even though she was almost eighteen—owing to the circumstances of her parents' deaths, and Alanine's lack of education.

Lynear was thirty-seven and an unmarried scholar. Alanine had expected her to be dull at best and oppressive at worst but instead she was… fun. Mother had been unwell for a long time, and hadn't had time for Alanine or her siblings. They had been left to the servants, their tutors and to their own devices.

Lynear was different. She took meals with them, played tiles, stones, and even taught them Lithonian card games. While Alanine's siblings took lessons with their tutors, Lynear took her to her mother's study, now Alanine's, and began teaching her how to manage the estate.

Alanine knew she wasn't ready to be *Shan* in name and deed yet, but with Lynear's help, she could feel herself getting closer.

Sevinc, Alanine's *hassana*, also sat in on many of these meetings and helped sort through the masses of confusing notes and accounts. The old woman had been handling the brunt of the paperwork and correspondence since Alanine's mother fell ill. Her illness wasn't spoken about, nor was Father's suicide, or the guests that had left at the same time.

Guests. That was what her father's playthings had been called—or, the man she had *thought* was her father. Her and her siblings weren't supposed to know about them, but the servants gossiped, and she was very good at staying quiet and listening.

The rumors that swirled were that the man pretending to be her father had unnatural leanings, and when Cousin Isra found out about them, he had been shamed into ending his life.

Alanine's own shame for what her mother had done under that man's influence was bone-deep. He'd defied the laws of gods and woman, using his twisted magiks to warp her mother's mind. Alanine remembered Maevis being kind and loving when she was little. As she grew, her mother had slipped away from her, and now she knew why.

Cousin Isra had stayed with them until Lynear came. Alanine had liked the Arch Master, and her husband, despite their... affliction. They were honest.

Isra had sat Alanine down and told her that the man pretending to be her father had poisoned her mother, and that he had committed suicide rather than face justice. Isra and her husband then explained that he'd used dark magiks taught by the Hathorites to take her real father's appearance, and neither of them were sure how long ago that had been.

Isra was sure it was after Alanine was born, but she suspected that Nijah might be that man's natural child, and possibly her fourteen-year-old brother, Namar.

Her cousin also told her that the man had kidnapped women—among them, Mother's cousin, First Princess Lenathaina. Isra had said that, as head of her house, Alanine had the right to know the truth, and she expected her to be strong enough to bear it; however, it would be up to her to tell her siblings.

For her part, Alanine decided that hearing it at seventeen was hard enough; fourteen and twelve was too young to deal with such things.

She had spent her eighteenth birthday in mourning for a mother she had barely known and a man that hadn't been her father at all.

She had then written to Queen Lenathaina, for she was now the rightful ruler of Lithonia, even though the old King's bastard was trying to take the throne. She had apologized for her father's actions and offered her condolences on her own losses. She knew she was one of the Queen's heirs, so it seemed prudent to make her acquaintance and offer her support. After all, it wasn't the Queen's fault Alanine's mother was dead.

And if she were honest, her life had improved greatly since her mother and the imposter died

CHAPTER 11

High Master Jillian Prather
White Castle, White City: Caeldenon
6th of Rison

Jillian stood at her office window, watching the display below. The barbarian woman and the Usurper Queen were at it again, playing with their swords. With the blessings Mystic had given her, Jillian could end Lenathaina's life with a touch, and none would be the wiser.

If I could just get close enough...

The fawning masses were watching from the sidelines, the men shouting encouragement. Some even seemed heartened by this unseemly performance.

This sort of display revolted Jillian. She wanted nothing more than to wrap her hands around that slim, brown throat, or sink her dagger into the girl's soft stomach.

She shook herself from her fantasies and smoothed her features to blandness again. It would not do to give herself away just yet.

Jillian gripped the windowsill and turned to look toward the other end of the courtyard; the Prince and his man were at it as well, shirtless in the frigid autumn air. She shook her head in disgust and turned away, heading for the corridor.

She made her way through the maze of hallways and staircases, down to the courtyard. There, she found a place at the edge of the crowd and watched the two women.

The little Queen's curling black hair was plastered to her face with sweat, and the blonde warrior woman's clothes stuck to her back. They were winding down, slowing.

They exchanged a few more blows, and then at some unseen signal, the pair stopped and handed the practice blades to a waiting page. A second servant offered towels, and the women took them before walking back toward the castle, lords and ladies falling in around them as they walked.

It took all of Jillian's resolve not to pull her dagger when the Queen passed her with a smile, the sleeve of her tunic brushing the sleeve of Jillian's robes.

Jillian would die if she made a move, but the Mystic offered sweet rewards in the afterlife to those who had pleased her.

Orders were orders though, so she stayed her hand. For now.

Back in her office, she closed the door and bolted it before taking down the Script Stone that that was attached to the Mystic's Keeper. She touched it, imbuing it with her energy and transmitting the pattern of light pulses that would indicate she wished to make a report.

A few moments later, the person on the other side indicated readiness.

She began sending her prepared missive detailing the state of affairs here: the little Queen's determination, the High King's reluctance to acknowledge her claim publicly, the contention over Jane.

Most of Jillian's information came from Lan, but some was from Lenathaina herself—fortunate, since Lan was saying less and less.

Several minutes passed before the reply came. Jillian took up her pen and quickly wrote down the message before signaling back that she had received. Once the exchange was completed, she deciphered the code.

The Raven must return to her nest, and the Sparrow must stay with you. More to come.

CHAPTER 12

Vera Martique
Clearwater Place, City of Endomir: Lithonia
7ᵗʰ of Rison

"Where is Magne?" Vera asked as she poured Benjamin a coffee.

They sat in the parlor where a small table had been set up for an intimate breakfast after a thoroughly enjoyable evening spent in one another's company. Magne had been due to join them, but Vera hadn't seen any sign of him.

"He sent word that the King wanted to see him again," Benjamin said, pointing at an open letter on the table. "He will most likely be left cooling his heels for a bit before Garrett actually sees him. I bet he's going to be on about the Council needing to ratify his rule again. He has been even more unsettled lately." He leaned back in his chair and stretched his long legs.

Benjamin was a tall man, with broad shoulders, green eyes, and a ruddy complexion. His short brown hair was still in disarray from bed.

"I am surprised so many are holding firm with their heirs in Garrett's possession after what he did to the Wallace boy," Vera said, picking up a piece of fleshy, sweet bright orange fruit and popping it into her mouth.

The slightly floral scent always reminded her of her mother. Aidiyah had mangoes for breakfast every day of Vera's childhood, with thick, tangy yogurt and a cup of the musky sweet tea that she preferred.

"And I think we are all unsettled," she added. "No one is quite sure why or even how Brian Chiswick was killed. On top of that, it's more than a little suspect that Garrett is the one that found him, claiming to have seen the lantern from the road…"

"I agree. There is doubt among the Lords that he could've seen Chiswick's lantern, and curiosity at why the King was out of the castle with just two guards."

Benjamin added a little milk to both their coffees, and a spoon of raw sugar to Vera's. "As to the pressure being put on the Council... it is hard. I worry for Randal." He cleared his throat painfully; Randal was his son and heir. "He isn't one to sit still and wait, but after Garran Wallace..."

Vera reached across the table and squeezed his hand.

Beth, his wife, had charged Vera with taking care of her husband. Benjamin had wanted Vera to go with Beth when she'd left the city, but Vera had refused, so the High Lady had made them promise to look after one another.

Vera had many clients, but the Bennings were the closest she had ever come to a relationship. She knew that they both wished to make their... relationship... more defined, but with everything in chaos right now, it was easier for Vera to have the freedom to use all her tricks for their cause.

After the dust settled, though, Vera thought it would be time for the commitment she had put off for so long.

Benjamin turned his hand to lace his fingers through hers, and brought her hand to his lips. "Do you have plans this evening?"

"One of my agents is due to report, but otherwise, I am free. Everyone seems to be holding their breath at the moment." She let hers out slowly. "It is hard to plan parties or evenings at the theater when so many loved ones are imprisoned in the Nursery Keep of Endomir."

"Then I shall return for dinner," Benjamin said, kissing her fingertips.

* * * * *

Benjamin left after breakfast to see to his affairs, and Vera spent her day going through reports, entertaining guests, and dealing with her household.

The restrictions put on Jasper's Keep regarding who could pass had caused panic in the marketplace, which in turn had caused unnecessary shortages. But Garrett wasn't stupid enough to take hostages *and* let the city starve; people were simply scared, and scared people often reacted in strange ways. As such, farmers were being allowed through to restock dwindling shop supplies, so one of Vera's special friends had made sure that her staff had gotten their pick of his shipment from his estates—after guards had searched it for hidden messages, of course.

Aside from farmers, those who could come and go included townspeople, and family members and retainers of the nobility. It was the heads of houses themselves that were restricted. Unless a lord swore fealty to the Usurper, he could not leave... and every family now had at least one person in the Usurper's care.

Many lords and high lords had sent their wives and daughters back to their estates, causing the season to end early for the first time since Matthew Morthan, and many others, had died on the battlefield of Harmon's Island. In result, Endomir was becoming a town of roosters with very few hens, so the brothels were making money hand over fist.

Benjamin wasn't one of those frequenting the brothels though. He was loyal to Beth and to Vera alone and spent his nights either working with the other high lords or with Vera, as he did that evening.

They had a simple meal of roast duck in curry with flatbread and pickled vegetables, after which they moved to her private sitting room upstairs.

When Vera's agent came, she excused herself and met him in her office.

"Mistress Vera," Samuel Thane said with a bow.

He had dark brown hair and light gray eyes; a good-looking man, but not so attractive as to draw unneeded attention. His rounds as a lamplighter kept him trim and fit and allowed him to walk unmolested through the city.

He reached into his coat pocket and handed Vera a small sachet of letters that had been tied with twine. "Marie sends her best wishes."

Vera took the bundle and sat down at her desk. "Anything she passed on verbally?"

Thane took his usual seat. "Some of the guards are starting to get uncomfortable with the number of children that are locked up; others… their baser sides are coming out." He leaned back in the chair. "Some enjoy taunting the little ones and making them cry, and it is making a few of the older hostages act rashly." He arched an eyebrow. "A few of the young men got roughed up when they tried to dress down a guard."

"Anyone I know?" Vera hoped to the Maker it wasn't Randal.

"The Grey lad," Thane replied. "I will try to get more information when I go see Marie again in five days—that's her next free evening. I will stop by beforehand to get anything you might want to send her."

"How is she holding up?" Vera asked, trying not to seem worried.

Thane gave her a rueful smile. "She is enjoying being in the thick of it. Don't you worry about Marie."

Vera nodded and dismissed him before reading the brief report, which only expanded on what Thane had said.

Hopefully, the sympathetic guards can be exploited.

She shuddered at the descriptions of those who were enjoying tormenting their charges, but was pleased to see that names and descriptions of the offenders were listed.

Perhaps I can do something with that?

Along with the report were a few short letters from Randal and the Montgomery boys; they were the only ones Vera trusted enough to allow Marie to reveal herself to. She took the letter from Randal back upstairs after locking everything else into her desk and locking the door of the study.

Benjamin read his son's account eagerly and let out a sigh. "He is well and claims he isn't doing anything foolish. He asks if I have instructions, anyone I want him to speak to while he is confined."

"Do you think that is wise?" Vera asked as they walked from the sitting room to her bedroom.

"No. The best thing he can do is keep his head down and avoid doing anything rash," Benjamin said, stripping off his clothing. "I will update Beth on his well-being tomorrow." He bent down to kiss her. "But for now, let's go to bed."

"Tired?" Vera teased as she unbuttoned her gown.

"Not at all," he said with a grin as he pushed her hands aside and took over unfastening her buttons. Once he had pushed the green velvet off her shoulders, it slid to the ground to pool around her feet.

He kissed her neck as he unhooked her corset. Vera shivered in his arms, her breath coming faster.

"Cold, my dear?" Benjamin asked as he blew on her neck.

"Freezing," she murmured. "Perhaps you should take me to bed."

"In due course, love."

Vera's corset joined her gown, and Benjamin set to work removing her petticoats, shift, and the rest of her underthings. When she finally stood before him naked, with her dark hair loose around her in waves, he picked her up and carried her to the bed.

"This is terribly unfair," Vera complained. "I don't have a stitch on, and you are still fully clothed."

Benjamin grabbed her wrists, pinned her hands above her head, and grinned down at her. "All is fair in love and war, so they say."

Before she could think of a rebuttal, his mouth was on hers, and she no longer cared about fairness. She liked this. Liked him taking charge of her.

His other hand moved between them, and at that moment, she wouldn't have cared if the city were on fire; in that moment, all she cared about was that she was his. Completely.

CHAPTER 13

Mael'Hivar Galvana Lady Ellaemarhie Lindal
White Castle, White City: Caeldenon
8ᵗʰ of Rison

Ellae laid down on the marble slab in the bathing chamber, naked as the day she was born, and let the attendant rub sweet almond oil, scented lightly with violets and sandalwood, into her sore muscles.

She and Lena had been up before the sun and out in the private practice yards used by the royal women of the house, as was their habit. After a series of stretches and exercises, they had sparred for a good half hour before moving on to archery practice.

Their daily sessions took up a good two hours of the morning, and were always followed by a soak in the bathing chamber and a light massage.

Lena lay on her table, lilac and orange blossom filling the room as her maid Cara rubbed oil into her skin, frowning as she gently massaged the scarred flesh. While she had been in captivity, Lena had been beaten, whipped, and repeatedly cut. Her back, rear, and the backs of her legs were a web of thin, pink lines.

Rachel sat on a stool as she read out the schedule for the day; Lithonians who were in White City for business always made a point to call on their Queen in exile, and she received those guests before luncheon. The mornings were spent on correspondence with her supporters back home, and her afternoons and evenings on her duties as First Princess... though, she had been given some leeway with those, as she was in mourning.

Rachel had already had her own time in the practice yards and gotten dressed for the day—she, Victoria, and Fenora often rose with Ellae and Lena, but did not work as long as they did—so while Ellae and Lena dressed, Rachel went to inform the maids that they would be ready to eat soon.

Lena wore a gray day dress, this one cut in the Caeldenon fashion, with a white interlace pattern at the hem and neckline, and a white, tooled leather belt. Ellae wore black leggings and tunic over a white shirt, but her warrior's braid, which was woven into the ornate braid that she usually wore her hair in, now sported the silver and lavender stripes of the First Princess, along with the green and blue of the Lithonian throne.

Breakfast, which was served at nine o'clock, was a hearty affair. While Ellae tucked into fresh fruit, eggs, sausage, and griddle cakes drenched in butter and syrup, Lena had a bowl of porridge with cream and berries. Her ladies ate and chatted to themselves as the Princess read over letters marked as personal by Rainsmere.

Gavantar and Galwyn came in smelling as if they too had been freshly bathed and oiled. Gavantar kissed his wife before picking up a plate from the sideboard and serving himself; Galwyn kissed the side of Ellae's neck before snaking an arm around her to steal a sausage from her plate.

She smacked his hand, and the ladies laughed.

Soon, everyone was sitting down and either eating, talking, or looking through their own mail.

Lena had been so quiet going through her letters that it was startling when she said, "Oh, well isn't this something?"

Everyone paused in their actions and conversations.

Finally, Gavantar asked, "What's that, *namir'ah'namira*?"

His heart of hearts.

"A letter from my cousin," Lena said, raising her eyes to meet Gavantar's. "*Shan* Alanine Fasili."

A stunned silence greeted this pronunciation, and Lena smiled slyly as she began reading aloud.

"Dearest Cousin and Queen, I send you my warmest greetings and hope that this letter finds you and your family well. I regret that we were unable to meet when you were in Pannarius; more than that, I regret the deplorable actions that brought you to my home. I hope

56

that you will not hold the sins of the father against his daughter, for I only desire to serve you as your humble and obedient ally and kinswoman."

Rachel snorted, and Lena smiled at her before continuing.

"If I or my house can do anything to aid you as you take your place as the rightful ruler of Lithonia and the head of the House which we are both descended from, you have but to ask. I remain forever your cousin and servant, Alanine Fasili."

Lena handed Rachel the letter to read for herself before saying, "That was well-played."

"Yes, it was. Very clever of her," Victoria said, taking a sip of her tea. "What will you do?"

"A tricky question, that," Lena replied.

"What are the three of you talking about?" Ellae asked, taking another forkful of eggs. "Sounds like she really wants to help you... despite—"

"Despite the fact that the man posing as her father kidnapped Lena and poisoned the *Shan's* mother, and the girl lost both her parents because of it?" Gavantar scoffed. "Sounds like a trap to me."

"A political trap," Lena agreed, "and a clever one. Help is mine for the asking, but to gain it, I must acknowledge her place in the line of succession."

"Her father kidnapped and beat you, and now she wants you to say she is your heir?" Ellae asked, bewildered. "Come to it, how does she think she is?"

"Because she technically is." Lena looked at her teacup as if she wished it had more than tea in it. "She is descended from one of Charles the First's children; he had four. The first line went extinct when the first child died, and the second was born with the Gift. I am descended from the only son, of whom I am the last legitimate heir born without the Gift. But through the female line, Alanine Fasili is the heir of the second sister, and third child... though, on two counts she could be blocked. She wasn't born on Lithonian soil—however, excluding her on that count could be dangerous—*and* she follows religious teachings that are not accepted in Lithonia."

"Why would excluding her if she wasn't born in Lithonia be dangerous?" Ellae asked, trying to follow the twisting maze of the Morthan line.

"Because it would mean that if I took the throne and I had a child in Caeldenon, that child would not have the ability to inherit." She took a deep breath. "Likewise, anyone wanting to cause trouble on this side of the water could try to exclude a child born in Lithonia."

Gavantar gripped her hand.

"You could have her on the religious point," Victoria said. "I am pretty sure there is an obscure law supporting that."

"And I am sure if she doesn't know it now, she will soon, and would profess to convert if needed." Lena huffed. "Of course, the legitimacy of her conversion would always be in question."

"You said that the first Charles had four children... what of the last?" Galwyn asked, spearing a sausage.

"The fourth line currently holds the title of High Lord of Sounton, Keeper of the Western Shores, and his name is Marc Eddening. His son, Lord Owen, is a friend of mine. In fact, many thought my uncle would marry me off to him."

"Why didn't he?" Galwyn asked practically. He looked just like his twin, Fenora, with angular features, mahogany hair, blue eyes, and honey skin. He was taller than his sister, taller than Gavantar too, and heavily muscled.

"The Morthan line is dying off. At the time, it was only Richard, Brandon, and me with the name. He didn't want the line to move to Eddening, as the senior Marc doesn't quite hold to the same ideals as my late uncle." Lena sighed and took another sip of her tea.

"I am glad he passed over Eddening, even if it was for purely selfish reasons." Gavantar cut a bite of his griddle cakes and offered it to Lena.

She wasn't eating nearly enough; her constant worry over her aunt and Lady Sara, not to mention her country, was robbing her appetite.

She took the bite and then turned her attention to the package before her that had accompanied the letter. Inside it, she found a note and a bracelet.

Ellae could see three silver charms separated by three colored stones: an oak tree, an oak leaf, and an acorn, with an emerald, a sapphire, and a brown diamond in between.

Lena read the note to herself and then aloud.

"My great-grandmother was given a bracelet like this when she left Lithonia, and it has been passed down from mother to daughter until it reached me. I had a second made to match the first, for you."

"Have it checked out by Lan," Gavantar suggested, finishing his breakfast. "Just to be safe."

He stood and kissed the top of Lenathaina's head. "I have a meeting with the Lord *Mael'Jadhar* of our guard, and some other things to do. I will see you at dinner."

He and Galwyn made bows to the ladies; Galwyn topped his with a cheeky salute to Ellae, and then the pair were off.

Lena slipped the bracelet into her pocket, looking thoughtful, and picked up her mail. "I have some work to do. You are all free to do as you wish."

Ellae quickly finished her breakfast and followed Lena into the study, where the Queen would fight battles that Ellae could not help her with.

CHAPTER 14

Lord Randal Bennings
Castle Endomir, Endomir: Lithonia
9th of Rison

A bottle of wine and a deck of cards were among the best ways to disguise a meeting between a group of young men.

Randal was the oldest, at twenty-five. Stephen Montgomery was just a few months his junior, and his brothers were two years younger.

Derek and Travis, the infamous duo; pranksters and gamblers, but good men. Their mother would countenance nothing else.

Stephen was courting the eldest of Randal's younger sisters, and would likely be his brother-in-law in due course. Their families were close; their mothers were cousins, and both sets of parents had long hoped that a marriage would bind them even closer.

Well, we're certainly close now, locked up together.

Randal and Stephen were rooming together, and so were the twins.

The group had made it a habit, in case a random guard decided to stroll through the keep, to play cards and drink in the evening, in one of the smaller parlors—or at least pretend that was what they were doing.

That night, Stephen had found Randal's stockpile of food and asked what he was up to; Randal had decided to be honest. If he could trust anyone, it was the Montgomerys.

They all agreed that if they weren't locked up in here, their fathers could make serious moves to block the tyrant on the throne. But they wouldn't be able to get away easily without being seen. Even then, where would they go? Their family homes weren't an option—they'd be found before dawn—but if they could hide out for a bit, then Marie, the agent of Randal's parents'... *mistress? lover?*

companion? could get word to Madam Vera. And Randal *knew* she could arrange something.

"We have enough food to keep us a mite," Stephen said quietly. Then he smirked at his brothers. "As long as you two can understand rationing." He was a copy of his father, tall, lean, and bald, with dark brown eyes.

"Ha ha," Travis said. "You were the one always leading us into the kitchen in the small hours." He and Derek looked more like their mother; they were shorter than Stephen, with chestnut hair and hazel eyes. All three brothers had their father's height and trim figure though.

"Enough," Randal interjected, wanting to stop the brothers before their banter got them off track. "Alright, let's go over this again. The nannies take the little ones out to play for the last time in the evenings after their early supper, and they come in just before dusk."

Stephen picked up the thread. "And we've had a quiet word with a few of them, and they have agreed to keep them out a bit longer the night of the dark moon." He took a sip of his wine.

"So no drinking that day." Travis rolled his eyes. "We're to stash our sacks in the kitchen woodshed."

"Then pick them up separately and meet at the north postern," Derek continued. "And use the key Marie filched for us."

"Right," Randal said. "The nannies will get the little ones caterwauling, and that will pull the guards' attention. With luck, we can get out unseen."

"With a *lot* of luck," Derek amended, a note of fear in his voice.

"If any one of us is caught, the rest run. Even if *one* of us escapes, it will help the cause," Stephen pressed. "If you get out the gate, run and don't look back. No matter what."

They all nodded gravely, and the men spent the rest of the night drinking in silence.

CHAPTER 15

High Queen Maelynn Coden
White Castle, White City: Caeldenon
10th of Rison

"Your Majesty!" Valeran, their *gandine*, came into Maelynn's sitting room, kinky black hair standing on end. His clay skin was ashen, and his gray eyes were wide with shock.

"Valeran, whatever is the matter?" Maelynn asked, turning from her writing desk.

Emerlise had come to her feet when the door opened, but upon identifying their visitor, had returned to her seat, her book open in her lap. Her flame-haired *galvana* straightened her uniform. Em had copper skin and pale gray eyes. She towered over Maelynn and was whipcord thin.

"The Dowager High Queen, Your Majesty," Valeran said. "She has arrived with the *Duc ah* Kilmerian, Lady Cressa, twenty *Mael'Hivar,* and the Dowager's household."

"I'll be damned," Maelynn whispered.

"You will be if her rooms aren't in order," Em quipped before turning to Valeran. "Where is she?"

"In the Gold drawing room," Valeran said. "She has summoned Queen Lenathaina, First Prince Gavantar, and the Queen's ladies."

"Bloody hell," Maelynn said, rising. "Send for the High King and then see that her apartments and the guest barracks are readied."

Maelynn and Em left the apartment, headed for the Gold drawing room, and she sent up a silent thanks for Valeran's foresight. The Gold room was the largest, so at least it would not be overcrowded.

Her flame-haired *galvana* straightened her uniform. She plastered a smile on her face as a servant opened the door, and walked in with Em at her side.

"Mother Arrysanna!" Maelynn effused, crossing the room to kiss her cheek.

The Dowager's skin was the color of old teak and soft as parchment, but her eyes were sharp. Like Maelynn's eldest daughter, Aeleonna, she had had silver hair all her life, which matched her eyes.

"Your *gandine* is well-trained," her mother-in-law said, "but you needn't have come so quickly. I want to speak to my granddaughter-in-law."

"Of course I came to greet you, Mother Arrysanna." Maelynn turned to greet her brother-in-law. "Hello, Baerik."

Baerik was standing by the window, and gave Maelynn a slight bow. He was as tall as his brothers, with ocher skin, dark gray eyes, and curly black hair that fell to his shoulders. He was slender in the hip with a well-muscled frame. Gavantar was built the same way.

He opened his mouth to reply, but the door opened again.

Maelynn glanced at the door and saw Gavantar and Lenathaina come through. She looked back to ask Baerik where Cressa was, and saw something she had not seen on his face in many years: love and joy and a smile that was as sweet as honey.

He quickly put his stoic mask back on, and she saw Lady Victoria flushing prettily and ignoring Baerik.

*Well, **that** is an interesting development.*

Mother Arrysanna allowed Gavantar and Lenathaina to kiss her cheek in turn, and then shooed them off. Mother rose—something she rarely did for any of her children—and greeted Lenathaina's ladies. She exchanged quiet words with Rachel and Fenora before allowing them to kiss her cheek, and then turned to Victoria.

After a moment, the pair were still speaking quietly, and one look from Mother when Maelynn stepped forward to greet Gavan, Evandar, and their *thanes* when they entered the room was enough to tell her that it was a private conversation.

Further proving the fact, Mother Arrysanna held up a hand to her first and third-born children, halting them while she finished speaking to Victoria. Even Gavantar and Lenathaina looked perplexed at this exchange, but Baerik was pointedly looking out the window.

At last, Mother allowed Victoria to kiss her cheek, and she greeted Gavan. "Well, my son, this is quite a tangle, isn't it?"

She allowed Gavan to kiss her cheek and escort her back to her chair. Footmen arrived with tea, and they all sat down. As soon as the beverage was served, Maelynn dismissed the servants.

"We can handle it," Gavan assured his mother, taking a sip of his tea. His gold hair was swept back like a lion's mane, and the red and gold strands of his warrior's braid stood out starkly.

"Of course you can. But another sharp mind is never amiss when fools get up to mischief." Mother rapped her fan on the arm of the settee, then addressed Lenathaina, "What is your plan, child?"

"I have been ordered to return to Lithonia with Lady Jane, and hand her over to Garrett." The lack of a title for her cousin hung in the air. "I will do the former, but not the latter."

"You will give yourself over to this man?" Mother asked.

"I will remove that man from my throne," Lenathaina responded sharply. "Not only am I the rightful heir, but I refuse to allow someone who would kidnap children to secure a claim to rule my people."

"Very sensible of you," Mother Arrysanna nodded. "And what army do you plan to accomplish this with?"

"I have assurances of support from several noble houses," Lenathaina said calmly.

That was good to know; the girl had kept her own counsel, and was holding things close to the vest.

"I plan to go as well, Grandmother," Gavantar added.

Gavan pressed his lips together and drew in a sharp breath, which Gavantar pointedly ignored.

"Maker knows we can't stop you from following, but you have to go as her husband and not the head of an invading force," Mother cautioned, taking a sip of her tea.

"Gavantar and Lenathaina will only take the *Mael'Hivar* that legally must accompany them, but their blood-sworn will be instructed to bring the First Prince and First Princess back—against their will, if they must—should the danger become too great." Gavan's grip on his cup was so tight that Maelynn feared for the porcelain.

"Nonsense," Mother admonished. "If you allow them to go, you must accept the risk. And truth be told, the girl is right: she is the heir to that throne, so you cannot deny her the right to fight for it. And Gavantar has already proven he will follow her to the ends of the earth, so short of imprisoning him, you won't stop him from going either." She set her cup down and turned back to Lenathaina. "What will you do with Lady Jane?"

"That has not been decided yet," Lenathaina admitted stiffly.

It had been a point of contention in the household. Maelynn wanted to keep the child here, but Gavan feared the political fallout if Lenathaina's attempt to regain her throne went against her.

"I will take her," Mother said. "She and Cressa get on so well, they will be a distraction for one another." She smiled at Lenathaina.

"Why does Cressa need a distraction?" Maelynn asked, looking from Baerik to Mother Arrysanna.

Mother ignored the question. "You intend to take your ladies?" she asked Lenathaina.

"Yes," Lenathaina said, smiling at the women fondly. "Rachel and Victoria demanded that they come, and Princess Fenora has commanded me to take her."

Baerik's shoulders stiffened, and he put his cup down. "Is that wise?" he asked, speaking for the first time.

"I will need attendants, and I understand that you are responsible for their excellent fighting skills." She inclined her head toward him in thanks. "And we will have the *Mael'Hivar* and my own countrymen protecting us."

"They have a little training, yes," Baerik allowed, his voice rising. "But they need years more before they will be ready for something like this. I really think you should leave them here, where it is safe."

"Baerik," the Dowager said warningly.

65

"I will not be parted from my Queen," Rachel retorted. "Not when she needs me."

"Nor will I," Victoria said pointedly, looking at Baerik directly. "I will go with her."

"Mother, why does Cressa need distracting?" Maelynn said again, turning back to Mother Arrysanna.

"Because her father will be in Lithonia," Arrysanna said simply.

The silence in the room was deafening.

It was Lenathaina that finally turned back to the Dowager and asked the obvious question.

"Why will he be in Lithonia?"

"Gavantar needs a second to command the *Mael'Hivar* and help oversee military matters. You will have your own people in Lithonia, of course, but another skilled general could not hurt," Mother reasoned, patting Lenathaina's hand. "And he will keep Gavantar from doing anything foolish, which will ease my son's stress." She smiled at Gavan.

"And of course, Baerik isn't about to let his wife go into danger without him." Mother picked up her teacup and smiled like a cat who had been in the cream and did not care who knew.

She took a long, slow sip. "I do hope you will let me see my newest granddaughter, Evandar," she said to her stunned third child.

Evandar nodded, speechless.

Victoria put her cup down with shaking hands; Baerik closed his eyes briefly before moving to stand behind her.

He laid a hand on her shoulder and leaned down to whisper something in her ear. Fenora covertly squeezed her hand, and then Victoria, hands still shaking, slipped a chain off her neck.

The silence in the room was deafening as she slid the gold ring that had apparently been tucked into her bodice onto the third finger of her left hand.

Baerik looked across the room to his brother. "I owe you an apology and must ask for your forgiveness. As head of our family, I should have asked your permission before I wed."

Gavan set down his teacup and shifted uncomfortably. He looked at his Mother, who was still calmly sipping her tea. She'd known about this and she had sought Victoria out as soon as she could.

Maelynn could see the questions in his eyes. How long had she known? Did she approve?

"Well, uh… yes," Gavan agreed, shifting again. "You have observed all the forms?"

"We handfasted," Baerik replied. "At Rose Hall. We did not think it appropriate to have a formal ceremony, considering Queen Lenathaina's situation at the time."

"I see. If Lenathaina would like to accept your help?" Gavan looked to Lenathaina, who was having a quiet conversation with Gavantar.

She turned to Gavan and nodded. "We would be pleased if the *Duc ah* Kilmerian would join us."

"And you wish to go?" Gavan asked his brother.

"I gladly offer my nephew and his wife my services," Baerik said, his hand still on his own wife's shoulder.

His wife!? Maelynn still couldn't wrap her head around it.

"Then it would be prudent to observe all the forms before you depart," her husband was saying, "as I assume you plan to share a bed?" Gavan pointedly looked at the couple in question.

Victoria blushed furiously, but defiantly stared back at him. "Just as you would share your wife's bed, I expect my husband is eager to return to mine."

Gavan and Baerik both blushed, but Gavan nodded. "Yes. Well."

"It can be arranged for the day after tomorrow," Maelynn inserted.

"But before any other preparations go forth…" Victoria slipped off the settee and crossed the room to kneel before Lenathaina.

Lenathaina leaned forward, taking her friend's hands; the dark head and the light touched foreheads, and a whispered conversation was had.

Only random words could be heard, "*Sorry*," "*Need not ask forgiveness,*" "*Love him,*" "*Of course*," "*So happy…*"

When they broke apart, Victoria moved to stand by Baerik, and Lenathaina inclined her head toward Maelynn.

"Well then," Maelynn said to Baerik and Victoria. "We should meet later to discuss the ceremony."

As everyone rose to congratulate the couple, another thought crossed her mind.

Where in the bloody hell is the pair going to sleep?

CHAPTER 16

High Master Tam Gale
White Castle, White City: Caeldenon
11th of Rison

While traveling, Tam had worn a nondescript suit of brown tweed. It may have been a century or so out of style, but it was serviceable. When he arrived in the city, he took a suite of rooms in a well-to-do inn for himself and his apprentices, and sent his best robes down to be cleaned and pressed.

He almost sent a letter requesting an audience with the Queen, but decided it would be better to seek one in person. He knew Mellina wouldn't be far behind him; he had sent her through the pass, but had gone out the front gates himself, hoping any pursuers would come after him.

None had.

Tam and his apprentices had taken a ship from Seathor after staying at the home of High Lord Bennings, having taken a package to his wife. Tam was less likely to be stopped than anyone else who may have tried to leave Endomir, so Bennings had asked if he could send a package with him, and he had agreed.

And now… Tam was getting ready to greet his new Queen.

He straightened his robes and buckled the tooled white leather belt with its Ithrimirian buckle, which matched his ring. One apprentice, Ellis Braithwaite, had polished the ring and handed it to Tam; the other, Babak Kareen, helped him into a white cloak that was edged in silver and white, like his robes.

Tam surveyed himself in the mirror. His white hair was cut short and neatly brushed; he had aged in the last year, the lines around his dark brown eyes were deep, and his skin looked like crumpled parchment.

"Ellis, Babak, I will return soon, or someone will come for you," he said, pulling his cloak around him.

"How will we know they come from you, Master?" Babak asked, trepidation and fatigue clear in his voice.

Both men were in their late thirties and had rarely been away from the Isles since they'd first arrived when they were six years old. Babak was Pannarian, and his family had disowned him—which happened more often than not when a Pannarian child manifested the Gift. He'd had beaded black braids when Tam first met him, but had shorn his head since, deciding they took too much upkeep. He was copper-skinned, tall, and had the most startling amber eyes, almost orange in some light.

Ellis was of average height, with ivory skin and light brown hair and eyes. Both young men lacked confidence in themselves out in the real world.

"I will send this with them," Tam said, touching his ring. He gave them both a reassuring smile before leaving.

He asked the innkeeper if he could borrow a horse, but was instead given instructions to something called a bus, which turned out to be a very large carriage pulled by draft horses. It had a multitude of windows and doors, each with a step to make it easier to climb aboard.

He paid the driver and was handed a slip of paper. thoughtfully, he took a seat at the front of the bus.

They made several stops as they wound their way through the city. Tam admired the architecture; even the humblest homes had porches and balconies, most of which had plants lining the rails. Finer homes were inside walled complexes with guards posted at the gates, and some of the shops sported what looked like apartments above them.

In the residential blocks, he could see green spaces between the free-standing houses; it looked as if they had both gardens for pleasure and to feed their small communities. There were also complexes with flags that had the sigil of Caeldenon, a sword and shield with a single rose on it surrounded by a ring of thistle blossoms, in tandem with other sigils: a female silhouette against a full moon, wolves, and others, all on a field of black. Black-clad figures, like those that had come with the High King for Queen Lenathaina's wedding, could be seen entering and leaving the complexes.

Tam also saw chapter houses for his people, the Masters of the Ithrimir. Healers, scholars, counselors, hunters, teachers, warriors, and crafters. Everyone but the Purple Mir, the spell-weavers, who were reclusive at best.

White City was a truly welcoming and diverse city. Every shade and shape of person could be seen, and all the languages of the free world were spoken openly.

The bus took him over a bridge to the far side of the city, where six castles stood in a half-circular row, with plenty of space between them. The carriage stopped between the largest of the castles and one made of deep red stone.

The driver turned in his seat. "This is your stop, High Master." He tipped his hat to Tam, who opened the door and climbed down, bowing slightly in return.

The driver pointed toward the larger castle; a huge edifice made of the same glittering white stone as the walls of the city. It was three times the size of Endomir—and that was saying something.

"That is the one you want. Best of luck."

He clicked his tongue at the horse and flicked his reins, and the bus began trudging forward.

Tam turned to face the castle and began walking up the long drive.

He presented his credentials to the guards at the gate, and again to the steward at the door. He was then led through a maze of corridors and up a grand staircase, made of polished blond wood with stone railings, and down another maze of corridors.

He had to present his documents three more times; each time, once they were reviewed, the guards or stewards bowed, and his guide, a young man in red and white livery, led him on.

Eventually, they reached a set of doors with a thistle bloom and a red rose intertwined. The guards flanking them wore black, as all the others had, and had gold swords embroidered on their right arms.

Once again, Tam presented his papers from the Ithram, stating his name, rank, and Mir with the Ithram's seal—a large 'I' inside a diamond, surrounded by a ray of color representing each Mir. They were a little faded, but he had not been back to the Isles in some time.

The guard opened the door, and Tam stepped into an antechamber. Four doors and a hearth were spaced around the round chamber, with chairs and small tables between them. A desk sat center stage, in front of a wiry man who looked to be about thirty years of age. He was bronze-skinned, with deep brown hair and green eyes.

When he saw Tam's robes, he rose, and the guard handed the man his papers. The man bowed and dismissed the guard before reading his credentials.

His eyes widened and he handed them back, bowing deeper. "I am Lord Kieran Rainsmere, *gandine* to the Queen and the First Prince. Her Majesty has spoken of you many times, High Master Tam, with great fondness," the assured him. "If you will allow me to take your cloak, you can have a seat while I inform the Queen of your arrival."

"I thank you for your warm welcome, Lord Kieran."

Tam took off his cloak and handed it to the young lord before taking the seat he had indicated. Lord Kieran hung the cloak on a rack and then went through the third door, closing it behind himself.

Lord Kieran came out quickly and ushered Tam into a stately yet comfortable sitting room that was furnished in creams, pale green, and gleaming dark wood. Lady Rachel and Lady Victoria, along with two other women, were in the room with Lenathaina, who stood before a large settee, smiling.

All the women, save one, wore day dresses in various shades of gray with white trim in the Caeldenon style. The final woman stood beside Lenathaina and had a long, silver-gold braid with a warrior's braid threaded through it, her skin the color of ripe wheat, and eyes a bright turquoise. She looked like a warrior and was dressed in black.

Tam bowed formally. "Your Majesty, I have come to offer you my services as your court advisor and healer, the same services I provided your uncle, grandfather and great-grandfather."

"My dear Master Tam." Lenathaina held her hand out to him. "Of course, I will gladly accept your offer."

Tam took her hand and kissed it formally before rising. "I am glad to find you looking well."

And she did look well, though not like the woman that had left Lithonia; she looked older, as if she had been through some great trial and come out the other side changed forever. She was not dressed like a Lithonian woman, either... instead, wearing the layered dresses of her new homeland that allowed greater freedom of movement.

"Yes, well, it has been a trying time, but I am glad to have you here." The Queen sat down and motioned for Tam to sit.

The other women found seats of their own as he sat with Lenathaina.

"Do you know what has happened to my Aunt and Lady Sara?" she asked with some urgency.

"I do." Tam had known she would ask this question, so he'd had time to think about his answer. "They should be only a few days behind me. I cannot say more, as it is Queen Mellina's place to tell you her tale."

Lenathaina looked as if she would argue, but after a moment, gave him a slight nod. "Where are you staying?" she asked instead.

"I and my apprentices have rooms at an inn," Tam replied.

"I will speak to my husband, but I am sure we can accommodate you all here." She glanced at Rachel and the woman dressed in gray who he did not know as if asking a question.

"If the apprentices don't mind sharing a room for now, then we can manage. Jane can sleep with Victoria until Victoria moves into her new apartment," Rachel said, smiling at the young woman.

Tam did not know Lady Victoria very well, but she had seemed like a sweet and well-mannered girl when he had met her in Lithonia.

"Why is Lady Victoria moving out of your apartments, Your Majesty?"

Victoria blushed slightly but held her head high. "I am moving into my husband's."

Tam stared at the small slip of a girl, dumbfounded.

"Victoria is to wed the *Duc ah* Kilmerian tomorrow," Lenathaina interjected. "And we are very pleased for her. He is the youngest brother of the High King."

"I see," Tam said, mentally trying to put the facts together. If he wasn't mistaken, the *Duc 'ah* Kilmerian was the half-brother of the High King by his second wife, while the first one was still living.

He knew that things were different here, but he wondered what the Lady's family would say, and if they would deny their support to Lenathaina's cause because of the slight.

It's too late to stop things now, if the wedding is tomorrow.

"Would you like to go back and retrieve your apprentices, or shall I have Lord Kieran do that for you?" Lenathaina asked, changing the subject. "If you think they will be agreeable to the accommodations, that is."

"They will be agreeable, Ma'am," Tam replied, but before he could accept her offer to have the lads sent for, the door to the sitting room opened again.

First Prince Gavantar entered with his black-clad shadow and two young girls, one of which was Lady Jane Grey. The other girl had ocher skin with curling, black hair and dark blue eyes.

The two of them together, Jane with her cream skin and light brown hair and eyes, and the other girl with her dark beauty, was a lovely picture, especially as they held hands and skipped to the settee where Victoria and Rachel sat, then threw themselves into the ladies' laps, giggling. The girls were dressed in leggings and tunics with sandals, of all things.

Victoria wrapped her arms around the dark-haired girl and kissed her forehead fondly.

"Who is the man, Mama?" the girl asked, pointing at Tam.

Tam nearly choked, but Victoria smiled down at the young girl.

"This is High Master Tam. He is to be Queen Lenathaina's advisor. How do we greet a Master, girls?" She raised a brow at both children.

The girls scrambled off the women's laps, and both curtsied. "How do you do, Master Tam?" they said in unison.

Tam rose and bowed formally. "Very well, I thank you, ladies. And who do I have the honor to address?" he asked, even though he knew Jane well.

"The Honorable Lady Jane, cousin to the Queen of Lithonia," Gavantar said, joining in the fun. "And Lady Cressa Forrester-Coden, daughter of the *Duc 'ah* Kilmerian."

He crossed the room and offered his hand to Tam. "It is good to see you again, Master Tam. I hope your journey was pleasant?"

"As pleasant as can be expected, circumstances being as they are." Tam took the young First Prince's hand and shook it. "The Queen has kindly offered myself and my apprentices a place in your household." He waited for his reaction.

"You have two aides, if memory serves?" Gavantar turned to Lenathaina and Rachel. "If my wife can't manage rooms here, I can speak to my mother. I know there are some empty apartments, even with Grandmother and her entourage in residence."

"I think we have sorted it out, but Master Tam may appreciate some space and a study to himself?" Lenathaina turned to Tam, waiting for his opinion.

Tam weighed the options, knowing Mellina and Sara would soon be here, and Lenathaina would want them close. "If a small apartment could be arranged, it would allow me more room to teach my students without being underfoot."

"Excellent. I will go speak to Mother. I am sure by the time you have arranged things with your apprentices, everything will be in order."

Gavantar kissed Lenathaina's cheek with obvious affection, and he and his shadow—Tam thought his name to be Galwyn, but he wasn't sure—left.

"If your steward could arrange transportation for me back to my inn and arrange something for my lads, I would appreciate it," Tam said after the Prince left.

All things considered, it might be best if he prepared them in person for this blended court.

CHAPTER 17

King Garrett Morlette Morthan
Castle Endomir, Endomir: Lithonia
11ᵗʰ of Rison

It was late and Garrett was drunk. Again. Maybe he was more like his brother than he wanted to admit, but sleep had become a stranger since he had found Brian Chiswick dead in the woods.

There had been whispers that he had done it, that Brian had been plotting against him instead of with him. It didn't matter that there was no proof, nothing to point blame his direction; Garrett had been the one to find him under mysterious circumstances, and that was all most people needed to decide he had done it.

Lord Alfred Chiswick, a retainer of High Lord Mitchel Parr, had demanded the release of his other son, Brad, to console him and his wife in their grief. Garrett had granted it, though Murphy had argued against it and railed at him afterwards.

The man was forgetting his place, but he knew far too much for Garrett to rebuke him too harshly.

To top it off, the Council was still refusing to ratify his rule. Only Parker spoke up for him, and that with some reluctance. He wanted his precious heir back before he campaigned on Garrett's behalf; Garrett wanted him to campaign first, so they were at an impasse.

Someone had unearthed an older copy of his father's will that acknowledged Jane and him but clearly stated that they would not take part in the succession, only be left an inheritance. That, along with the fact that Richard hadn't had the power to change a law, nor the right to leave him a place in the succession in his will, was making the Council stand strong.

Only the fact that Garrett had the guard mostly on his side kept him on his unstable throne. Those who had refused to support him were removed from service; the more vocal ones, imprisoned. Those he had bought had friends that could be bought too, and they were swelling the ranks.

The fact that he mostly left them on their own to guard as they saw fit was another advantage as it made it a more attractive position. As long as they didn't kill anyone outright, Garrett didn't care how they kept the peace or the prisoners in check.

However, if things didn't start going his way soon, he was going to have to take a harsher stance.

Lenathaina had had everything he should have had his whole life: she was his father's beloved child, she had the love of his stepmother, she was the darling of the court, she had been Master Tam's pet student. Everything in life had been handed to her on a silver platter, but Charles had been *Garrett's* father. He was Charles' son. He even looked more like the late King than Richard had, with his dark brown hair and blue eyes.

He had the right to rule by birth; his cousin wouldn't take his throne from him.

Though Garrett would bet his last shirt that Tam had run to her, and even now the pair of them were plotting, scheming. But he would win over the Council... by force, if he had to.

CHAPTER 18

Princess Fenora Tearhall
White Castle, White City: Caeldenon
12th of Rison

Even though the Lithonian court was still in formal mourning for the deaths of both King Charles and King Richard, Lena had insisted that Victoria should have a traditional Lithonian wedding gown and Fenora thought that she looked beautiful.

Three seamstresses had worked into the small hours to complete a gown worthy of a *Ducessa*. The azure blue garment was made of shimmersilk, purchased by the Dowager High Queen at her insistence, and trimmed with silver lace and shimmer-thread, which had been a gift from Lena. Tiny owls were hidden in the silver vines that trimmed the hem and bodice of the gown, the sigil of Victoria's father's house.

Victoria wore her light brown hair atop her head in a mass of braids threaded with seed pearls. As a married woman, she did not wear a maiden's lock—and she was quite cheeky about it.

Lena had given over her own dressing room and kicked Gavantar out, so the ladies had free rein. Each of them had a hand in preparing the bride, taking turns helping Cara Sanders, Lena's maid, decorate Victoria's hair, buff her nails, and get her into the elaborate gown.

Martingale, the Dowager's maid, and Kellingswith, the High Queen's, arrived with gifts from their mistresses. The High King, High Queen, and the Dowager had come together to present Victoria with a gift to show her how welcome she was in the family, and to provide her with jewels appropriate of her new rank.

Baerik's house colors were red and green, and his sigil was a hawk with a red rose in its talons on a field of green, so it wasn't surprising when Victoria opened two black, lacquered boxes to find a necklace set with emeralds and diamonds, along with a matching bracelet, earrings, and tiara.

Victoria was breathless, but Lena stepped forward to admire the quality.

"It is an exquisite set," the Queen said, lifting the necklace from the box and placing it around Victoria's neck. "They must favor the match highly to send such jewels."

Fenora bent forward to look, and gave Victoria a smile. "They are from the Royal Collection. I have seen the Dowager High Queen wear them many times."

The stones were the same shade of green as Victoria's eyes, and stood out against her alabaster skin.

"They must be a loan, then," Victoria said, still in awe.

The outing of her secret and the whirlwind arrangements for her second wedding ceremony had taken up so much of Victoria's time that Fenora doubted she'd had time to think about, much less process, the change in her circumstances.

"A gift," Martingale said with a smile.

The older, gray-haired woman was of an age with the Dowager, but had the vitality of a much younger woman.

She took the tiara from the last box. "These jewels were made for Lady Elyria Forrester-Coden when she became the old High King's *kessiana*, by my lady. They have been held in trust by her for many years, and my lady has decided that they should now be yours to pass on to your daughter when it is time."

With practiced hands, she arranged the delicate tiara, which complemented the azure gown, in Victoria's hair.

Finally, the two maids excused themselves, and the other ladies finished dressing while Victoria nervously sipped tea.

Ellaemarhie lounged in the corner, safely out of the way of 'the madness,' as she called it, drinking her own tea. Fenora watched as Ellae's eyes settled on Victoria.

"Surely, you haven't got jitters about the wedding night," she teased. "I mean… by the way that man looks at you, he's had a taste and he is hungry for more."

Victoria blushed furiously, and Lena shot her *galvana* a very pointed look.

Victoria admitted, "I am nervous that word of this will reach my parents before I have the ability to inform them myself." She lifted her chin a fraction of an inch. "I have no regrets when it comes to my choice of husband, but I do not wish to fall out with my family over our hasty nuptials."

"You won't. I will make sure of it," Lena said, letting Sanders make last-minute adjustments to her gray silk gown. She wore a set of diamond jewelry, sticking to her current palette of gray and white.

Fenora and Rachel were likewise attired, but Fenora could not wait for the mourning period to be over, just over a month and a half from now. If they had only been mourning the Queen's uncle, she would not have minded, but Rachel had told Fenora all about Richard, and it sounded as if a nastier man had never drawn breath.

They had shared many stories of their childhood, Rachel and Fenora, nestled in their cocoon of blankets in one another's beds. Fenora looked forward to the day when they no longer had untold stories from their pasts, only shared experiences.

She was pulled from her dreamland by her lover's touch as Rachel repined a lock of Fenora's hair that had fallen from its arrangement. They shared a look, both wondering if a day would come when they could publicly celebrate their union. As it was, they intended to speak to the Queen about a private arrangement, something like the handfasting that Baerik and Victoria had done. Once they got their nerve up.

"We are going down," Rachel said with a smile.

The Silver Ballroom, which was the smaller of the two but still a massive room, had been arranged to host the wedding. Rows of chairs had been set up, with a place at the front for the priest. The High Priest Tadaemeric, in fact. Quite an honor, but as Baerik was the son of a High King, it was fitting.

Rachel and Fenora took seats in the third row. The Dowager, looking proud—as a mother should—sat in the center of the first with Ladies Cressa and Jane. The High King and High Queen sat to her right, and Queen Lenathaina and First Prince Gavantar to her left. High Prince Evandar and his wife were in the second row with Masters Lan, Jillian, and Tam, but the children of the High King and High Prince Evandar were scattered between the second, third, and fourth rows.

A few other people, some of the men that served under Baerik, and Cressa's grandparents and uncle—the family of his late wife, Hira—had also been invited.

Fenora wasn't surprised to see Lord Renath Mellan and his wife, Lady Ceralaen, the *Marque and Marquessa ah* Fall Haven, and their son Lord Kenalan. Baerik had had a good relationship with them before his wife died, and had continued it after, making sure Cressa saw her other grandparents as often as possible.

A hush came over the room, and Baerik stepped out of a side door looking every inch the *Duc*. He was in the formal military dress worn by the Coden family: a white uniform with fitted breeches and a knee-length jacket that had slits from waist to knee on both sides. Across his chest was a gold-trimmed red sash lined with medals, and his curling, black hair fell to his shoulders. The uniform contrasted his ocher skin in a very pleasing manner.

Fenora had always thought Baerik handsome, even if she didn't care for men in her bed.

Before everyone had a moment to catch their breath, Victoria entered from the other side of the room. When Baerik saw her, his face lit up; likewise, Victoria glowed like a candle.

It was obvious that it really was a love match, and not a rash decision made in the heat of lust. Even the High Priest smiled at the obviously sincere feelings of the couple before he began the ceremony.

"Marriage is a sacred covenant given to us by the Maker, in His wisdom, so that we do not have to walk through this world alone. When one finds the person that they are meant to share their life with, it is only fitting that they stand before their family and friends and promise to love, honor, and respect one another."

He of their hands. "You each have your own strengths and weaknesses and, in all things, must strive to do what you can to uplift each other."

A collective, "Amen," came from the occupants of the room.

"Baerik Aden Forrester-Coden, do you swear to love, honor, and respect this woman?" Tadaemeric asked, putting Victoria's hand in Baerik's.

"I do," Baerik said, his eyes on Victoria's.

Hidden by the folds of their skirts, Fenora took Rachel's hand and squeezed her fingers.

The High Priest continued. "Do you swear to bring all that you have and all that you are to this marriage, to give freely of the gifts the Maker has bestowed on you, and to endeavor to lift up your wife when her own weaknesses cause her to stumble?"

"I do," Baerik promised again.

Tadaemeric smiled fondly at him and turned to Victoria. "Victoria Jean Wallace, do you swear to love, honor, and respect this man?"

"I do," Victoria said.

Fenora thought she saw Tori squeeze Baerik's hand.

"Do you swear to bring all that you have and all that you are to this marriage, to give freely of the gifts the Maker has bestowed on you, and to endeavor to lift up your husband when his own weaknesses cause him to stumble?" the priest asked.

"I do," she said again.

High Priest Tadaemeric wrapped his hands around Baerik and Victoria's clasped hands. "As this couple has already sworn a blood vow, our short ceremony is concluded, so I give you the blessing of the Maker, the Creator of our world, our holy Father, and pronounce you husband and wife. You may kiss the bride."

He released their hands and smiled as Baerik kissed his wife.

"I present the *Duc* and *Ducessa* '*ah* Kilmerian."

To Fenora's great surprise, she found herself crying.

CHAPTER 19

The Goddess Hestia, the Mystic of Hathor
The Temple of Ganna: Hathor
12th of Rison

Over a thousand years ago, Hestia's people settled in Hathor, a land of scorching days and freezing nights, with poisonous and venomous creatures and unforgiving terrain: mountains and jungles, sandpits that can swallow a man whole. They came with what they could carry, in battered ships and canoes. Many of the faithful died, and with every body they gave to the sea, they cursed those who'd banished them from their homes, Lithonians and Pannarians both.

When the Priesthood of the Maker came into its full power, all followers of Hathor and her daughter Hestia were banished from Lithonia on pain of death.

While some in Pannarius still worshiped them, Hestia was seen as a goddess of hate and evil, and Hathor was only good for protecting the dead. Many of their true believers in Pannarius had come to Hathor, once the land was settled, to fulfill the mission of their goddess. The people who'd inhabited the land before them were savages and became their slaves.

The settlers named their new home Hathor after the mother of their Goddess, whose sacred name was only spoken by priestesses. When one became the Mystic of Hathor, they shed the name they were born to and took them name of the Goddess Hestia, meaning all deeds done by the new Mystic were done in the name of all who came before her.

There was no way to make a name for yourself or to leave a legacy, save to leave your people stronger than they were before you came—and Hestia planned to leave them stronger than any who had come before her.

A series of messages lay on Hestia's desk, all received by the Consort that oversaw the Shrine of Stones, where all the Script Stones for her servants in the field or priestesses on missions were kept. Two of the Consortium were on duty at all times so no message was missed.

She had reports from Lithonia, Caeldenon, Thynn, the Isles of the Ithrimir, and Pannarius. Now that the traitorous cow that had taken out Jardin—one of the sons of the Hareem that had spent the better part of a decade subverting the Oaken line in Pannarius—had left the girl alone, one of Hestia's daughters was close to making contact with her.

The girl didn't have the Blessing, but Jardin had been secretly teaching the boy to control his abilities.

She read a message from one of her pet Masters saying that she was having trouble getting information out of her intended; disappointing, but not a barrier to moving forward. The Master was useless to Hestia for the moment.

She had ideas… but it wasn't yet time to cause further chaos in Caeldenon. Events in Lithonia were moving apace; the city was crumbling from within.

She looked at the wall across from her desk, where the Holy Prophecy, given by their Goddess to the second Mystic of Hathor, had been carved into the stone.

The path Homeward lies in the roots of the Oaken Heart. The Branch that Flourishes From the Ashes of Fire and Death is the true Ruler of Lithonia, and will Unite the Lands and Bring a Lasting Peace.

The meaning had been debated for hundreds of years, and many believed, as Hestia did, that the branch the prophecy spoke of was the line of Maevis Fasili. Pannarius was often called the land of fire, and the Red Priestesses worshiped the goddess who had power over life and death.

The prophecy had been made centuries before the Morthan House, whose sigil was the oak tree, had taken the throne.

In the years since, they had worked to bring about the prophecy. The time was ripe. Their hour was coming. Lithonia would be awash in blood and fire, and her people would take their rightful place and *they* would bring the lasting peace.

The oak sapling born in the cinders will deliver the faithful to their glory.

That prophecy had come from another source. Hestia knew that it was incomplete. One day, one of her servants would retrieve the full prophecy. She felt it held the key to everything.

CHAPTER 20

Lady Victoria Forrester-Coden, Ducessa 'ah Kilmerian
White Castle, White City: Caeldenon
12ᵗʰ of Rison

Their second wedding celebration was vastly different from the first, but both had been special in their own way. Victoria would always count the evening that Mother Arrysanna had witnessed their vow as the day that she truly became Baerik's wife.

A lavish meal had been laid out, and the additional guests that had been invited for dinner and dancing had all taken time to congratulate her and Baerik. Lord Renath, the *Marque 'ah* Fall Haven had even danced with Tori twice, and both he and his wife professed their happiness to have her as part of their family.

It seemed like a dream, a fairytale. She only hoped that her family would forgive not being part of the ceremony. They would have a celebration of their own when they got to Lithonia.

At half past nine, Mother Arrysanna announced that it was time to retire. Tori and Baerik took Cressa with them, and went to their apartment for their first night as an official family.

Tori helped Cressa change into her nightgown, even though the nanny was there. She wanted as many of these moments with her new daughter as possible before they left for Lithonia.

In the morning, she and Baerik, along with his former in-laws, would go to the registrar's office and file the paperwork registering their marriage and Victoria's adoption of Cressa.

"I am not sleepy!" Cressa complained as she climbed into her bed.

"It is far past your bedtime, *namira*," Baerik said, pulling her covers up. "And you are the only *dinalall* up."

"Am not!" Cressa protested. "Jaemi is still up."

"Jaemi is almost a man and not a child," Baerik countered, kissing her forehead. "To bed with you."

"I want a story," the little girl pouted.

Baerik opened his mouth to speak, but Tori laid a hand on his arm.

"I still need to take the pins from her hair. I will tell her a story while I finish getting her ready, and then," she turned to the little girl, "she will sleep, yes?"

"Yes, Mama," Cressa said, her dark blue eyes full of love and trust.

Baerik kissed Cressa on the forehead again, and then kissed Tori lightly on the lips before heading for the door. He looked over his shoulder and smiled at the pair of them before leaving and closing the door behind him.

"Now, what story do you want tonight?" The past two nights, since their secret had come out, Cressa had requested that Tori tuck her in.

The girl had always had the love of her father and grandmother, but she had been without a mother for a long time. Tori had worried that the child would resent the intrusion, but Cressa had quickly attached herself to Tori.

Their time together at Rose Hall had helped, she was sure.

"I want a Lithonian one," Cressa said, making room for Tori to sit down.

The girl had wanted her hair done like Tori's for the wedding, so her black hair was piled on top of her head in a mass of curls. As Tori took the pins out and laid them on the bedside table, she began the tale.

"There was a young girl who was greatly favored by her father. They spent much time together, discussing books and philosophy and plays. He doted on her, but he didn't believe in spoiling."

"He sounds like Papa," Cressa said with a sigh.

"He does, doesn't he?"

Tori picked up the silver-backed hairbrush and slowly brushed out Cressa's black curls as she continued.

"The girl asked her father for a horse. A real horse. She had a pony, but she wanted a horse fit for the woman she was becoming. Her father said that she would have to prove she was ready for the responsibility. Girls could let stable lads care for their mounts, but a woman had to take a hand in caring for her animal."

"That definitely sounds like something Papa would think up," Cressa said, snuggling down into the covers.

Tori laid down next to her, careful not to dislodge her own tiara, and put an arm around Cressa.

"So the father told her that if she cared for her pony every day for a month to the head groom's satisfaction, she could get her horse. Now, this was in winter, so it was cold, snowy. Some days, the girl had to walk through falling snow and on icy paths, but she did as her father asked, and cared for her pony on her own."

"Did she get her horse?" Cressa asked, cuddling close.

"She did. A fine roan gelding, sixteen hands high, named Brutus." Tori smiled fondly.

She hoped her father would bring the gelding from their estates. She would prefer a familiar mount.

"Do you think your Papa would like the father in the tale?"

"He would," Cressa said with a sigh. "Papa thinks I should work for things too."

"I have to agree with him. I have learned valuable lessons from having to work for a reward or freedom," Tori said, stroking her hair.

"Will Papa get to meet the father in the story?" Cressa asked, suppressing a yawn.

"He will, and I hope someday, you will as well. That man is my Papa."

Cressa smiled at that. "I wish I could go to Lithonia with you."

This had been an often-expressed desire.

"It isn't safe. Not now." Tori slid out of the bed and tucked the sleepy child in tighter. She kissed her forehead. "Goodnight, *namira*."

"Goodnight, Mama," Cressa said, turning to curl up on her side.

Tori left the little girl and walked down the hall to the room she would share with Baerik when they were in residence at White Castle. The apartment wasn't as large as the one Lena shared with Gavantar, but it was more than enough for her small family.

She walked through the chamber that had small rooms to either side for a *thane* and *galvana,* which neither of them had, and to the door opposite that led to their private sitting room.

Baerik was waiting for her there in his faded dark green, silk dressing gown. He held out a hand, and she crossed the room to sit in his lap.

"I dismissed your maid," he said, kissing the side of her neck. "You will have to settle for me tonight."

Tori slipped her hand inside his dressing gown and laid her hand over his heart. He didn't wear a sleep shirt, and the curly, black hair on his chest tickled her hand.

"It isn't *settling*." She leaned down to kiss him.

He stood, cradling her in his arms, and carried her to their bedroom. "I am glad to hear it, wife."

He laid her on the bed and began removing her jewelry and clothing in a way that no maid would ever dream of doing.

While Baerik's hands were busy with buttons, hooks, and laces, Tori removed his sash with its medals, then she too began working at buttons and laces.

His mouth was on her neck, his breath hot on her skin. Tori gasped as his tongue rasped against her neck.

When they were both finally naked, her jewelry on the bedside table and their clothes haphazardly piled on the floor, Baerik pinned her to the bed, his body atop hers.

"Are you happy, my love? Truly?" he asked.

"I am, Baerik. Happier than I thought I could ever be," Tori replied. "And you?"

"I never thought I would love again, but then you came into my office with your dagger." He grinned and bent his head to nip at her ear.

Tori squirmed under him. "You didn't answer my question."

90

"Yes, my Ducessa, I am happy. When this war is over, I can't wait to take you to our home so we can start our family." He shifted slightly, and she could feel him throbbing against her. "But for now… we can practice. You have been drinking your tea?"

Tori nodded, unable to speak.

She arched her hips in invitation, and Baerik grinned down at her before he slid home to claim her once again. His wife in every way.

CHAPTER 21

Dowager Queen Mellina Morthan
The Docks of White City: Caeldenon
13th of Rison

Mellina's entire life had been spent in Lithonia, before she killed her son. So stepping off the boat in White Harbor, surrounded by glittering white stone, with men and women speaking various languages and dressed in a variety of clothing styles, was almost overwhelming.

She saw tall Pannarian women dressed in trousers and tunics with beaded braids down their backs, Thynnian men with their hair cropped short or in oiled curls that rested on their shoulders, men of Caeldenon with their warrior's braids, and women in their dresses cut for movement and comfort.

She felt out of place and uncultured.

Captain Aidan of the *Echo* helped Mellina down the brow and gave her a polite bow. They had given false names, so he thought Mellina and Sara were sisters, coming to visit a brother who had done well for himself. "Do you have lodgings, Madam Gale?"

"We have directions to our brother's home. We just need to find transportation," Mellina said with a smile.

"Your boy can flag down a cab, or you can walk to Kaen Street, to the bus stop on the corner."

The captain appraised Mellina and then looked to a place at the end of the pier set aside for waiting carriages. "I am surprised your brother isn't here to meet you ladies," he said with a note of suspicion.

"He is very busy," Sara said, taking her arm. "Come, Beth. It will be another adventure."

"What did you say his name was again?" Captain Aidan asked, taking a step forward. "Happens I know most of the merchants in the city. Perhaps I could have one of the company carriages drop you at his home."

Mat stepped between the captain and Mellina. "'Twon't be needed, Cap'n. Me and the ladies will be right fine." He turned and grabbed Mellina's other arm, and he and Sara marched her to the line of cabs.

"Don't forget that you must check in with immigration, Madam Gale, Madam Hart," the captain called after them with an odd smile. "I must hand over your details myself, and you wouldn't want them to have to come find you."

Mellina was nearly sick on the cobbles, but nodded.

Sure enough, there was a booth at the end of the pier, next to a small, official-looking building before the waiting line of cabs, with several officials and four guards.

Mellina looked at Sara. "What do we do?"

"Tell the truth, I suppose. I wouldn't want to end up in prison for falsifying information," Sara said with a frown.

It wasn't required in many smaller ports in Lithonia to show credentials to purchase a ticket, nor to board a ship—though that was changing in some places—but it was to enter a country.

All Lithonians were issued a certificate of birth as babies, and at the age of fifteen—or sooner, if they traveled abroad—they filed with their government offices for credentials. These stated name, year, and place of birth, as well as parents' names, a brief physical description, and title, if applicable. When one married, they were required to update this information with their spouse's details, and update again if that spouse died.

Mellina pulled the small, hard-scale folio from her handbag and saw Sara doing the same. Mat pulled a disreputable-looking leather wallet that had seen better days from his pocket, and Mellina made a note to get him something a bit more durable.

A tall, olive-skinned man in a dark brown suit stepped up to the window of the booth. "Credentials, please." His tone implied he spoke the words many times a day and they had little meaning to him.

Mellina gathered everyone's folios and handed them over, clasping her hands before her to stop them from trembling.

The official began mechanically recording their details, starting with Mat. When he got to Sara's, his eyes widened, and he paused to look at Mellina's before continuing.

"Queen Mellina, forgive me."

He turned to someone inside and barked an order, and soon, Mellina and Sara were installed in chairs inside the small building, being served tea and cakes while their documents were processed.

Once the official business was over, Mellina asked sweetly, "Would it be possible to get transportation to White Castle?"

"A carriage is being brought around as we speak, and a messenger has been sent up to tell the First Princess of your arrival, Ma'am." The official, a Mister Harkin, bowed again.

Moments later, they were helped into the carriage with their meager belongings, and sent riding off through the city.

Sara was in awe, but Mellina was too distracted by the fact that she would soon have to confess her crime and throw herself on the Queen's mercy.

* * * * *

They were met at the entry by no fewer than a dozen courtiers. Their greeters all bowed formally, and a broad-shouldered man in a gray suit stepped to the front of the group. He had skin the color of reddish-brown clay, dark gray eyes, and black hair that flowed to his shoulders.

"I am Lord Valeran Heather, *Nielam Gandine* to their Majesties High King Gavan and High Queen Maelynn Coden."

A second man stepped forward. "And I am Lord Kieran Rainsmere, *gandine* to First Prince Gavantar Coden and his wife, Queen Lenathaina."

Lord Valeran motioned a pair of footmen forward. "They will take your luggage while you meet with their Majesties, and see to your servant."

"I'm staying with her," Mat declared, drawing himself up to his full height, which wasn't much taller than Mellina.

Lord Valeran looked at Mellina, and when she nodded her assent, he directed the servants to take their bags, not commenting on the lack of trunks and so forth.

"Might I ask if High Master Tam Gale is in residence?" Mellina was surprised when her voice did not quaver.

"He is, indeed, Queen Mellina," Lord Kieran said as Lord Valeran offered her an arm. Kieran performed the same service for Sara.

Mellina wished that the ship had had better washing facilities available, as she was quite sure they stunk.

They were led up a set of glittering stone steps carpeted in crimson, and down a corridor to a pair of gilded double doors. Lord Valeran nodded to the black-clad warriors who stood guard, and they opened the doors, bowing their heads slightly.

Mellina was trembling; Lord Valeran supported her as he walked her to the center of the room.

She was there: her Lenathaina. Prince Gavantar was by her side. The High King and High Queen, a tall elderly woman with silver hair and teak skin, sat on a settee with a folded fan in one hand, and Lady Victoria, of all people, sat with a very handsome man with ocher skin and black hair.

A variety of the black-clad men and women that shadowed the Royal Family were around the room, engaged in various quiet activities but alert to every movement.

When Mellina entered, everyone rose.

Lenathaina crossed the room and took Mellina into her arms, and Mellina nearly wept, both with joy to see her, and out of fear that Lena would shortly reject her.

"I am so glad that you are here and safe," Lena said, holding her tightly. "But why did you go into hiding? Did you fear Garrett would use you against me?"

Mellina drew back. "I went into hiding because I killed your cousin, my son." She pulled away from Lena's slack embrace. "And

I am here to throw myself on the mercy of the true Queen of Lithonia." She fell to her knees and bent her head in supplication.

"I'll be damned," Mellina heard the old lady say.

CHAPTER 22

Lord Randal Bennings
Castle Endomir, Endomir: Lithonia
13th of Rison

The day had arrived, and all their preparations were in place. It was time. Each of them had slept as late as they could, even though their nerves were high, in anticipation of spending most of the night awake and on the run.

Randal was sitting under the shade of a willow tree, his sack hidden in the shrubs behind him, watching a pair of nannies play with their charges. The sun was getting low, and the guards atop the wall were ready for their shift change and their dinner, so they were not paying as much attention to the ruckus below as they had been earlier in the day. They knew that the young ones would be put to bed soon and everyone else would be heading into dinner.

Randal saw Stephen not far away, speaking to a young lady, and the twins were playing jacks with a pair of young boys. He slipped into the bushes when he was certain no one was paying attention to him, and signaled the nannies.

One leaned down to whisper in the ear of the little girl she was tending, and the child nodded. The other nanny then whispered to her charge, and both girls stood and ran off. Moments later, one began shrieking as if the other was trying to do her in.

The attention of the guards became riveted as the two children began tussling on the ground. More children came to watch the fight, and a few joined in. Soon, most of the prisoners outside were gathered around the mass of small, seething bodies, trying to pull them apart.

The guards were still egging on the little scrappers as Randal and his friends made their way through the overgrown garden and toward the north gate that was hidden behind a wall of ivy.

Randal had oiled the lock the day before, so the old key made little noise as he turned it. They slipped out one at a time and locked it behind them, then turned and ran full tilt for the woods.

"Hey!" someone called behind them.

The guards, remembering their jobs, had returned to watching both sides of the walls, and had seen them.

"Run!" Randal shouted.

He found himself glad that he and his father regularly sparred; he was in decent shape. His friends were less fit, and panting behind him. Then a shot rang out.

"Stop, you fucking shitfaced fuckers!" a guard called.

Randal risked a glance over his shoulder and saw that all four guards lined the wall, their rifles ready, and the twins were struggling to keep up.

He put on a burst of speed, only half a mile from the tree line.

Another shot.

Randal pushed himself as hard as he could.

Another.

Randal heard shouting, but he was too far away to make out the words.

He burst through the tree line, well aware he was now out of range. With all his will, he urged his friends on as he gasped for air. Stephen was almost out of range of the rifles, but Derek and Travis were not.

Derek stumbled and fell, and Travis ran on a few steps before he realized his brother wasn't with him.

All four rifles went off just as Derek was coming to his feet.

Randal couldn't say which guards made the lucky shots, but he did see the blank expression on Derek's face when one bullet took his friend in the back of the head and came out his right eye. A second must have taken him in the back, as the front of his shirt blossomed in a pool of red.

"Derek!" Stephen called, turning to see his brother fall as he made the tree line.

Travis turned to see his twin on the ground, surely dead, and ran back to him. Randal and Stephen dropped their bags and hurried to drag him back.

"He's gone," Stephen sobbed. "Gone. We have to go. They will send horses after us."

Randal grabbed the bag that Derek had dropped and dashed the tears from his eyes as he helped haul Travis to safety.

Once inside the tree line, they headed north, into the mountains. They would have to stay clear for a few days before they could make the rendezvous.

CHAPTER 23

Queen Lenathaina Morthan Coden of Lithonia, First Princess of Caeldenon
White Castle, White City: Caeldenon
13ᵗʰ of Rison

The room spun around Lena briefly, and everything went fuzzy around the edges.

Gavantar grabbed one arm and Ellae the other, and the pair helped her back to her seat.

"Send for Master Tam," Gavantar said to Ellae.

She nodded and stepped out the door to send a servant on the errand, and was back at Lena's side before she could protest.

"I am fine," Lena said, eyes on her aunt.

She heard a whispered conversation at the other side of the room, and Jaedinar, one of the High King's *Mael'Hivar Thanes* slipped out the door.

"You murdered Richard?" she asked hoarsely. "Why?"

"He killed Maratha and nearly killed Garrett," Aunt Mellina said, still kneeling on the floor. Lady Sara and a man Lena didn't know stood behind her like guards. "By the time I came into the room, Maratha was already dead, and the babe she carried as well. He had beaten it out of her. But he was still strangling her."

Lena heard Maelynn gasp and the Dowager take in a sharp breath.

Her aunt continued. "I should have done it sooner, when I found out what he was doing to that poor girl behind closed doors." She was shaking, pale, and looked visibly ill; Sara laid a hand on her shoulder.

Lena exchanged a look with Victoria and Gavantar; they had heard the rumors here, but she hated to believe that Maratha had been hurt so badly. Maratha had been a prisoner as much as Lena had been in Pannarius, but no one had come to her aid.

"Why not turn him in to the authorities?" Gavan asked, pulling a cigar from the inside pocket of his jacket. He was eyeing Aunt Mellina with a calculated look.

"Because I didn't want to chance him hurting another person." She tilted her chin up. "And I gave him a far cleaner death."

"Why not just remove him from the throne?" Lord Baerik asked, leaning forward.

"And you are?" Aunt Mellina asked, sounding every inch the queen she had been for so many years.

"Allow me to introduce my brother," Gavan said, gesturing to Baerik. "Lord Baerik Forrester-Coden, the *Duc 'ah* Kilmerian. I believe you know his wife, Lady Victoria Forrester-Coden, the *Ducessa 'ah* Kilmerian."

Aunt Mellina's eyes widened a fraction, and she nodded. "Pleased to make your acquaintance, *Duc*," she said to Baerik before turning to Victoria. "And to see you again, *Ducessa*."

The silver-haired Dowager rapped her fan on the arm of her chair. "Up you get, child, and come have a seat," she commanded Aunt Mellina, who hesitated for a moment before taking the offered place next to the woman.

"My mother, the Dowager High Queen Arrysanna Coden," Gavan said, sighing.

This was turning into a bad comedy play.

Before anyone else could speak, Masters Tam and Lan entered the drawing room. Both men bowed to the room at large; with so many monarchs and Dowagers in the room, bowing to each would be akin to a workout in the practice yard.

Lena eyed Master Tam coolly, and he had the decency to blush. There had been plenty of time for him to tell her all of this and instead, he let the story play out here.

"It was her story to tell," he repeated softly.

He began walking toward her, but she held up a hand.

"I am fine," Lena said sharply.

"May I inquire what this meeting is about?" Master Lan asked tactfully.

The Dowager smiled, obviously in her element. "The Dowager Queen Mellina killed her son after he almost killed the wastrel now sitting on Lenathaina's throne, beat his wife, caused her to lose a babe, and then strangled her to death. The only fault I see is she didn't take out the Usurper while she was at it."

Master Lan stared at his mother open-mouthed, and then bowed to Aunt Mellina. "Arch Master Lan Coden, at your service, Queen Mellina." He found himself a seat and pulled out his pipe.

"Addressing the *Duc's* question about removing Richard from the throne," Mellina said at last, "I and others were working on that. A delegation from the Isles of the Ithrimir was on its way to evaluate his sanity. If we could have proven he was unstable, which he obviously was," she still looked as if she were in shock, "we would have been able to remove him. There was no other mechanism, short of civil war, to do so."

Masters Tam and Lan nodded their agreement; both would have studied Lithonian law as part of their training.

"He could have been held after the murder, it is true," Aunt Mellina admitted. "But after the way Maratha was killed, I think her father would have found a way to take Richard out himself, and he would have had help. Taking a knife to my son's throat was... swifter. And that way, none of the guards had to endure his abuse."

Something the Dowager had said moments ago seemed to connect. "What Usurper ?" Aunt Mellina asked.

"Garrett Morlette," Lena answered curtly, then continued with an edge to her voice, "Despite your paltry... explanations, Richard's death has thrown Lithonia into a civil war."

She could feel Gavantar urging her through their link to be calm, but ignored it.

"If he had been imprisoned and tried, there could have been a smoother transition. Instead, we have children locked up, and heirs held hostage so Garrett can secure the throne for himself."

Mellina covered her mouth with one hand. "What?"

Master Tam interjected. "Garrett produced what I believe to be false, and unequivocally unlawful, documents saying that Richard made him his heir and it was what Charles wanted. To secure the throne, he then took hostages from every noble house, high and low, and now has them imprisoned in the Nursery Keep."

"Maker forgive me," Aunt Mellina whispered.

"The question is," Gavan said, turning to Lena, "what to do with her? She has confessed to murder—regicide, at that, and prolicide to top it off."

Lena turned to Master Tam.

The Master said, "She would have to be tried before the House of Lords. Once a verdict is found, Queen Lenathaina has the ability to pardon her, but she does have to be tried first." He looked from Aunt Mellina to Lena. "And she can't be tried until the situation in Lithonia is taken care of. Until then…"

"She needs to be held until a trial can happen." Gavan sighed.

"For now, she needs some strong, well-sugared tea, a bath, and bed," the Dowager declared, coming to her feet. "I will see to it and make sure she doesn't take to the heather."

She turned to Aunt Mellina. "Come, child," she said with something close to kindness in her voice as she whisked Mellina off before anyone could argue.

Gavan turned to Lena. "I think it best if we keep the details of her confession between us for now."

"I agree," she said, feeling exhausted.

Maelynn stood. "It may not yet be time for luncheon, but I think we could all do with a stiff drink."

A few of the *Mael'Hivar* chuckled, and Maelynn went to order luncheon and whiskey to be brought to the sitting room.

Once the food and drinks had arrived, Gavan raised a glass of whiskey to Lena.

"I will say one thing. Life is never dull with you around, daughter." He smiled and took a drink.

Lena took a drink of her own and silently agreed.

CHAPTER 24

High Lord Marc Eddening
Sounton House, The City of Endomir: Lithonia
14th of Rison

Marc's butler let High Lord Ellis Parker into his study.

While not generally the most appealing specimen, the High Lord's pale skin was downright pasty, and there were large bags under his eyes that spoke of a sleepless night.

News of Derek Montgomery's death had spread rapidly the night before, after King Garrett had had his body delivered to his father's front doorstep with a note saying that if Montgomery didn't return his other sons to the King, they would be returned to him the same way his youngest son had been.

Garrett hadn't even had the decency to have the boy cleaned up, rumor said.

The other two Montgomery sons and the Bennings boy were still on the loose—and good for them. The search would keep the would-be-King busy. But the fact that Garrett had actually killed one of his captives, even if the boy was trying to escape, had cast a dark cloud over the city.

When Parker had requested this meeting, Marc had hesitated briefly. He knew Parker had been seen with Garrett before Richard had been murdered, and Marc still believed it was Garrett who had blood on his hands... not that Richard was anything to mourn, but still.

Personally, Marc didn't mind the chaos that Richard and Garrett had brought to Lithonia; it was making achieving his own goals and the goals of those he worked with easier.

He rose to greet his guest, offering a hand. "Parker."

"Eddening," Parker replied hoarsely.

They shook, and Marc resumed his seat. Parker took the seat across from him and stared out the window blankly for several minutes before turning back to him.

"Bloody awful business," he said at last.

"It is," Marc said, steepling his fingers and looking at his guest. His salt and pepper hair hung lankly, and his suit looked slept in. "I would think it even worse for any who might have encouraged people unsuitable for their current roles to take what didn't belong to them."

Parker winced; Marc's words had struck a nerve.

"Yes," he eventually agreed. "I never thought he would do something like this, you know."

"You just thought he would keep *me* from the throne." Marc arched a brow.

Parker was quiet again, then finally said, "I thought it would keep Lenathaina from the throne. She, Bennings, and Montgomery are in each other's pockets so deeply. Add in Collins and Harmon…"

"And she could pass just about anything she wanted with little work," Marc replied. "Yes. It wouldn't have been so bad if she and my son had hit it off, but there we are."

Parker looked as if he thought that match might have been worse, but changed the subject.

"The fact is that few want to see a woman with a foreign husband on the throne—or a woman at all, for that matter. Unreliable creatures, women."

Well, it wasn't any big secret that Parker and his wife Leanne did not have the happiest of unions. Rumor had it that his youngest didn't resemble him so much as she resembled another High Lord.

"What is there to do now?" Marc asked bluntly. "He is on the throne, and he has our children and heirs locked up in a heavily guarded keep."

"If enough of us band together with our combined guards—"

"He will outright *murder* those he has hostage," Marc interrupted. "If we need proof of that, we only have to go look at Derek Montgomery's body."

Parker winced again. "What do you suggest?"

"We can start by you telling me what you and Morlette discussed before he stole the throne," Marc said, leaning back in his chair.

Parker looked out the window for another long moment before turning back to Marc. "I forged the letter that said Charles wanted to put him in the line of succession," he said bluntly. "And promised that Rendon and I would stand behind him."

It took a moment for that to sink in, and when it did, Marc leaned forward. "You forged King Charles Morthan's signature on a document that may well have started a civil war?" he asked coldly.

"I did, but whatever punishment you deem necessary can wait until we get you on the throne in place of that bastard," Parker said, meeting and holding his gaze.

Marc stared back at him before nodding. "You have a deal."

CHAPTER 25

Kenleigh Atona, Prisoner
The Temple of the Maker in White City: Caeldenon
14th of Rison

Kenleigh had been moved back to her original quarters following the conclusion of her trial. Five priests, including the High Priest Tadaemeric and Father Beauregard from her home temple, had sat in judgment during the private trial. At one point, those few priests allowed to listen in on the proceedings, as well as Kenleigh's family, had been excused as Queen Lenathaina's letters were read aloud to the court.

Since hearing of Kenleigh's pending trial, she had written again, offering to come in person if needed, to speak on Kenleigh's behalf. Likewise, the First Prince, Prince Galwyn, and Lady Ellaemarhie had written their own accounts, only sparing the details of the Princess' capture and torture.

The final touch it seemed, was a letter from the High King himself, stating he had heard all the details of her capture, imprisonment, and rescue, and knew that justice would be served, and Kenleigh would be freed.

And she was.

After the trial was over, Kenleigh had been returned to her rooms, and all the things that Queen Lenathaina had sent to her had been appeared again. She bathed and dressed in a light blue gown, and had dinner with the High Priest, Father Beauregard, and her mother and brother.

After dinner, it had been suggested that she and her family go to her rooms for a private reunion.

Wine had been brought, but the servants withdrew to leave them in peace. To give herself something to do in the awkward silence, Kenleigh poured each of them a glass, and then sat down on the settee while her mother and brother decided if they would actually speak to her.

They had yet to say anything directly to her, or offer any kind of impression that they were glad she was alive and now free.

"Why did they send us out during most of the testimony?" Kenleigh's older brother, Nathan, asked brusquely. He picked up his glass of wine and took a healthy swallow.

"Because it was testimony giving in confidence by other people who had witnessed my captivity or had also been victims," Kenleigh said, sipping her wine.

Her mother snorted.

Kenleigh looked much like her, though her mother's red hair was shot through with silver, and her creamy skin was lined with age, but her green eyes were still as clear as Kenleigh's.

Nathan was bulky, built like the blacksmith he was, his skin weathered and tanned, and his hair a few shades darker than Kenleigh's.

"I wonder just what kind of confidential *testimony* you gave?" Mother asked after a long silence.

Kenleigh felt her face grow hot. "And what is *that* supposed to mean?"

"That you are a shamed and fallen woman, and a disgrace!" Nathan nearly shouted, spraying wine as he did so.

He had drunk his fill at dinner, and was already more than tipsy.

Kenleigh stared at him in shock. "How am I a fallen woman?" she asked, voice shaking. "I was kidnapped, tortured, and raped, yet I still held to my faith. I still did my devotions."

"None of that matters," her mother said quietly. "You were promised as a chaste wife to the Maker, and your vows have been broken, no matter your willingness. You are a disgrace to our family and will not be welcomed back to the island." She glanced at Kenleigh's gown, noting the fine cut and cloth of the blue silk dress. "I suggest you sell some of your finery before you have to resort to selling yourself."

Something inside Kenleigh nearly broke. She was being blamed for the actions of a depraved man, for what *he* had done to *her*? She was deemed at fault? By her *family*?

Mother rose, and Nathan set his glass on the table before pulling out a dagger and setting it down as well.

"Do the decent thing. Cleanse the taint from your honor," he said.

"I hope to see you in the next life, but I will never again see you in this one," her mother said, and they both turned their backs and left her chambers.

*****

Kenleigh spent the night at the table, looking at the dagger and drinking the wine. She fell asleep just as the sun was rising, her head pillowed on her arms next to the knife her brother had gifted her to end her life.

She woke some time later to a hand on her shoulder, shaking her awake. One of the acolytes was looking from Kenleigh to the knife, concern clear on her face.

"You have visitors, miss," the young woman said, moving the dagger away from Kenleigh before quickly crossing the room and letting in two women.

Princess Fenora Tearhall surveyed Kenleigh, the empty flagon of wine, and the dagger, and clucked her tongue. "We feared as much," she said before turning to the acolyte and sending her for some tea.

When she turned back, she gently informed Kenleigh, "The Queen wanted to send for you last night, but the High Priest said you were with your family. Then he sent word early this morning that they had left. Without you."

Kenleigh's head was fuzzy from the wine and lack of sleep, so she only stared at Princess Fenora, dazed.

Lady Rachel Malick crossed the room, her honey hair loose down her back. She pulled open the curtains and poured a glass of water for Kenleigh. "We will have you sorted shortly, dear, and on your way home," she promised, brushing the hair from Kenleigh's face.

"I have no home," Kenleigh said hoarsely.

"But you do," Princess Fenora said, smiling reassuringly. "The Queen has offered you a place in her home. Didn't you get her letters?"

"I have been held prisoner in isolation," Kenleigh said, watching Princess Fenora rummage through her closet.

The woman shot Kenleigh a look over her shoulder that said no one had known the details of her captivity. Shock and anger were clear on her face. "She has asked that you join her household as a friend and advisor."

Kenleigh sat stunned as Princess Fenora pulled a pale green dress from her wardrobe.

"This will do for now. I am sure that between us, we can rustle together enough gray until something can be made for you."

"Grey?" Kenleigh asked, feeling slightly overwhelmed at the rapid change in her circumstances.

"We are in mourning for the Lithonian king," Lady Rachel answered, coming back with a bowl of steaming water, a cloth, and a towel. "He is no great loss, but the formalities must be observed."

It was then that Kenleigh noticed both women were dressed in layered gray dresses in the Caeldenon fashion. One, with light gray over dark, and the other, dark over a very pale gray with hints of white embroidery.

"I see…"

She thought she did. Mostly.

"We will get you cleaned up enough to get you to the castle, and then you can have a nice soak and a massage," Princess Fenora said soothingly. "We… understand. What you have been through."

Lady Rachel laid a hand on Kenleigh's shoulder. "You aren't alone anymore." Her tone matched the Princess'.

It took a moment for Kenleigh to understand the implication of their words. Then she drew a shuddering breath, and a hoarse sob broke loose from somewhere inside her.

She buried her face in her hands and cried.

When she felt the arms of both women embrace her, she truly understood that she had joined a new sisterhood; one that no one should be a part of, but that she had become an unwilling member of nonetheless.

CHAPTER 26

Shan Alanine Fasili
River Keep, Southern Region: Pannarius
15th of Rison

Princess Lynear was visiting with her sister, who had come with letters from the Empress, may the Light ever favor her, so Alanine would be receiving her visitor alone.

It still felt strange to be using her mother's private audience room as her own, but she did her best to look as if she felt in control and comfortable in her new position. Alanine's *hassana*, the small and elderly woman that had cared for her mother's and grandmother's estate since it was created, made sure Alanine was settled before she went to get her guest.

Her *hassana*'s thin, beaded, black braids were streaked with silver, and her red-gold skin was wrinkled, but she still walked with a sure stride, her black eyes missing little. She quirked an eyebrow at Alanine as if she saw something that wasn't quite up to standards before letting herself out, the skirts of the pale brown wrap dress that was her uniform snapping with each step.

Alanine checked her appearance in the mirror once more and saw that a few of her auburn braids had come out of their elaborate arrangement.

Her skin was lighter than the *hassana's*—a light coppery tone instead of the rich red-gold, thanks to her Lithonian blood—and her eyes were a clear and startling blue, a feature that often attracted attention.

Princess Lynear wanted to present Alanine at court in the spring, and had promised that all the Shans, and maybe a few of the lower Princesses, would be fighting to arrange Alanine's marriage to their sons.

The idea of binding herself to a man with little to no interaction beforehand wasn't exactly appealing.

Alanine had read many novels imported from Lithonia, Caeldenon, and even Thynn, and envied the way those girls mixed with young men, and flirted and danced. In Pannarius, unmarried men were kept cloistered to curb their naturally wild nature. Women, both married and unmarried, met for dances in the cities, but those events were often reserved for them alone. Their societies segregated to the extreme, not only by gender, but by station and education.

Alanine finished fixing her hair and returned to the pile of cushions padding the couch that sat directly on the floor. She arranged her red silk wrap dress and took a sip of the crisp, sweet wine her mother had loved to calm her nerves.

The *hassana* entered and prostrated herself on the floor, her first fingers and thumbs forming a triangle on the ground before her.

The triangle represented the Trimunave in Pannarius, the High Priestess, Senior Imperialist, and the First Mother—the leaders of the factions that dictated the rules all Pannarians lived by. At their center was the Empress Eternal, Alanine's third cousin.

The woman with the *hassana* copied her movements fluidly, prostrating herself beside her.

"Rise," Alanine said, proud that her voice didn't shake, and she sounded authoritative.

Both women obeyed, and then *hassana* said, "It pleases me to introduce *Shan* Alanine Fasili." She spoke to their visitor, a woman with lightly tanned skin and brown hair. Her features were bold but pleasing. "*Shan*, this is *D'Khan* Castia Marn."

Alanine gestured to the lounging couch opposite hers. "Please, be seated. I am interested to hear what has brought you to me."

D'Khan Castia Marn, who was tall and slender, seated herself on the lounger and artfully arranged her modest green wrap dress. She waited until Alanine dismissed the *hassana* before speaking.

"Your father and I had many common friends, so I knew him in passing. On behalf of those I work with, I wanted to come and offer our sympathies at the news of your parents' deaths and offer whatever aid I can."

Alanine barely managed to control her features at that statement.

She knew her imposter-father had acted in a manner that was unbecoming of a Pannarian man, so to hear that he had been friendly with a woman was shocking.

D'Khan Marn smiled knowingly. "Your father had special blessings from our Goddess that he had to keep hidden. Your mother resented him and his blessings. It is a shame she never came to embrace all that could have been hers."

"And what is that?" Alanine asked warily.

She didn't dare ask if this woman knew that the man she spoke of had not really been Alanine's father. She and Isra had agreed that the fewer people who knew about that, the better.

"The everlasting life that is given to all who faithfully worship She Who Was, Is, and Will Always Be," *D'Khan* Marn said, leaning forward with a fervent look in her eyes. "She whose name is so sacred, it is only spoken by those who devote themselves to being Her priestess. The daughter of the sacred Hathor."

"You mean the Red Priestesses?" Alanine asked, trying not to recoil. "Those who worship death and the afterlife?"

She did not say the goddess' name, for to say it was to summon her.

The serene, brown-eyed woman held out her hands in supplication. "She is so much more than you have been taught."

Alanine appraised her for a long moment. "Many things are often more than they seem," she said finally.

D'Khan Marn smiled again, but this time, there was something dark in it. "Did your father ever tell you of the blessings our Goddess bestowed upon him?"

Alanine took another sip of her wine to buy some time as she studied *D'Khan* Marn over the rim of the glass. "I did not spend much time with him, I fear. He was always otherwise occupied, and it seems that many of his preoccupations were of an unsavory nature." She let the statement hang in the air for a moment. "He did spend much time with my brother, *Holire* Namar."

The other woman smiled greedily, as if some gift had fallen into her lap. "Yes. The young *holire* was likewise blessed by Her with holy gifts. The Consort gave him lessons in its control by order of our Mystic, the mother and incarnate form of our Goddess."

Alanine scoffed. "Incarnate form of the goddess?" she asked. "Impossible."

D'Khan Marn hissed. "Do not speak such profanities."

"*D'Khan...*" Alanine warned. Her title was of the third station, putting her well below nobility—let alone a person related to the Empress herself. "I think you forget yourself."

The woman drew a breath as if to cool her anger. "Of course. You are not accustomed to our ways, nor have you had the ability to learn our holy teachings." She smiled charmingly again. "I would like to offer my services to allow you a chance to learn your birthright, and to instruct your brother in further control of his Blessing."

Alanine paused for a long moment, dread filling her heart. "What sort of blessings does my brother have?"

"In this country, it is called a curse, but to our Goddess, it is her truest Blessing, only bestowed on those she deems worthy." The woman's intense look had returned, and she leaned forward. "As your father was and your brother is. If I cannot teach him to harness it, at best, he will be sent away to those blasphemous Ithrimirites; at worst, he'll be outright killed."

Alanine remembered her cousin Isra and her husband; even if their affliction was disconcerting, both seemed like good and kind people. At least, they were not fanatical, as this woman seemed to be.

She thought it best to consult with Isra and have the Master come back to see Namar. She knew she had gone to court to speak with her sister, the Empress.

"I will consider your offer and write to you with my response," Alanine said at last. "Where can you be reached?"

D'Khan Marn studied her for a long moment. "I have much business in the area, but I will return in a week." She rose at the obvious dismissal. "But do not mistake me, the life of your brother may well depend on your response." She bowed formally and let herself out of the room.

Alanine watched her go, she went cold with fear.

She withdrew to the inner chamber of her suite of rooms and began drafting an urgent request to Cousin Isra. River Keep was a three-day train ride from the city; if an audience could be gained swiftly, she and her husband could be here before *D'Khan* Castia Marn returned.

For some reason Alanine could not identify, she did not want to face the woman alone again.

Still, she decided against telling Princess Lynear about the outlandish meeting. While she believed she could trust the Princess, she didn't want to risk her bundling Namar off to the nearest Masters' outpost to be shipped off, maybe never to be seen or heard from again.

CHAPTER 27

Samuel Thane
Castle Endomir, Endomir: Lithonia
16th of Rison

Two and a half days had passed since the murder of Derek Montgomery and the escape of his two elder brothers and Lord Randal Bennings. Not wanting to tip anyone off, Samuel stuck to his prearranged time to meet Marie on her evening off. The guards were testier than usual but let him pass, and he took Marie into a woodshed on the pretext of a quick swive.

Samuel kissed her roughly as he closed the door, but as soon as they were alone in the dark shed, he broke it off and put his mouth to her ear. "Have you been getting any trouble?"

Marie hesitated before speaking into his ear, "Nothing I can't handle." She was a beautiful woman with dark hair, black eyes, and skin with a golden undertone.

Samuel sighed and leaned his forehead against hers. "Say the word, and I will get you out of here," he whispered.

"Not yet," Marie whispered back. "I am still needed here."

She loosened her stays a bit and pulled out a piece of parchment that had been wrapped in waxed paper to protect it from moisture. "Take this to Mistress Vera," she said, and then, "I have seen them make a few people turn out their pockets."

Samuel sighed, knowing only a few places on his body that wouldn't be thoroughly searched when he left the castle.

Marie tactfully turned her back while he dropped his trousers and hid the wax-wrapped parchment in a place that rarely saw the light. He heard her titter at his struggles.

"Hush," Samuel hissed. "You're supposed to sound like you are in rapture, not getting tickled."

He pulled up his trousers and pinned her to the wall. "Now. Be a good girl and act like you're getting fucked."

*****

An hour later, after being roughed up by a guard and interrogated about his prowess and his lady's charms, Samuel arrived at home. He waited another two hours before making his way to Mistress Vera, making sure he had not been followed.

Once there, he was ushered into her study, where he presented the document, its wax wrapping having been removed in his apartment and burned, and waited for her to read it.

After a long moment, she set it down.

"Do you know what it says?" she asked.

"I could not help but read it once it was removed from its protective wrapping."

Samuel held up a hand when it looked as if she would ask. "You do not wish to know, Mistress Vera."

The letter had not been from Marie, but from Lord Randal, detailing where he and his friends could be found a few days from now.

Getting to them would not be easy. Getting them into the city would be even harder. Getting them out of Endomir through any traditional means would be impossible. That left them going over the mountains in the fall, where temperatures already left the higher peaks covered in snow, or hiding them somewhere in the forest or the city.

Mistress Vera appraised Samuel for a long moment before nodding. "I don't want to send you, I have someone else in mind. But I will have to figure out where to hide the Boys."

She would tell him more or she wouldn't.

"At your next meeting, I want you to order Marie to come back here. I think it might be best to get her out of the city," she said after another long moment.

"I offered to get her out tonight," Samuel admitted, watching her.

"Your offer and my order carry different weight," she said finally. "Go get some sleep."

Samuel bowed and left the study, knowing that, order or not, if Marie thought there was a job to do, she would stay and do it. No matter the cost.

CHAPTER 28

Queen Lenathaina Morthan Coden of Lithonia, First Princess of Caeldenon
White Castle, White City: Caeldenon
17ᵗʰ of Rison

Lena was pleased to see that the invitation from High Queen Maelynn to have tea with her and the Dowager High Queen was a politely worded request instead of an instruction. Maelynn had always been kind and welcoming to Lena, but she knew sharing a home with an exiled monarch who happened to be your daughter-in-law couldn't be easy.

Only Lena's company had been requested, so she left the apartment with Ellae as her sole attendant shortly before three in the afternoon.

When they arrived, one of the *Mael'Hivar Naheame* stood guard—this one with a red shield on her right arm, which marked her as one of the High King's personal legion. She bowed her head to Lena and nodded to Ellae before opening the door for them.

Both the High Queen and the Dowager were waiting for them, their *galvanas* situated at their own table with a place set for Ellae, who gave Lena a slight bow and joined her fellow warriors, while Lena took her seat with the Queens and wondered if this was to be a social visit or a battle.

After the social niceties had been observed, tea had been poured, and sandwiches and cakes had been passed out, Lena broached the most delicate subject in the room— or rather, the lack of her presence.

"How does my aunt fare?"

Dowager High Queen Arrysanna snorted. "You could come to see her for yourself," she retorted, taking a bite of her sandwich. The scent of perfectly cooked beef and the sharp bite of peppercorns filled the air.

"I have been rather occupied," Lena replied smoothly, taking a sip of her tea.

"Occupied with deciding what to do with her, more like," the Dowager said with a knowing smile.

"Mother Arrysanna, play nice," Maelynn warned before turning to Lena. "Mother and I have been discussing your aunt's situation," she said gently. "It would not be safe for her to return to Lithonia until she can receive a fair trial. If she accompanied you, her life would surely be forfeit, should anyone find out what she has done."

Lena nodded in acknowledgment. "There are some places I may be able to leave her once we arrive, but yes, ensuring her safety and deflecting questions about why she was in custody could prove... difficult." She could not help but let a little acidity slip through at the end of her statement.

"No one is saying that she couldn't have gone about things better, child," the Dowager cut in. "But your cousin deserved worse than he got."

She rapped her ever-present fan on the arm of her chair to forestall any remarks Lena might have. "We have spent some time talking, the two of us. I have heard in some detail the things he did; more from that pet Master of yours. The matter will have to be addressed, but fairly, and when cooler heads can rule the day."

The woman leaned toward her. "You aren't there yet. All you can see is how a tangled mess has been made worse by her killing a monster."

Lena was stunned into silence, taken aback at how easily the Dowager had divined the mess inside her heart and mind and cut to the quick.

They left her with her thoughts while they continued eating, watching, and waiting for her to compose herself.

At last, she asked, "What do you propose?"

Maelynn and the Dowager smiled at one another.

"That your aunt be given in to Mother Arrysanna's custody on her estate in northern Denon, Trahelion Manor. She will ensure that, when it is time for a trial to take place, your aunt will be delivered to your desired location. To everyone else, we can put out the story that she is recovering from her many losses."

"And what does High King Gavan think of this plan?" Lena asked warily.

"My son will think what we tell him to think," the Dowager said with another smile.

"My dear, sometimes these things are best left to us women," Maelynn said. "We will have everything arranged and set into motion between the three of us before he has time to wrap his handsome head around the issue."

"I would want it in writing, the agreement," Lena ventured, warming to the idea.

"Of course. A treaty between monarchs would be appropriate," Maelynn replied smoothly, taking a bite of cinnamon-dusted cake.

"But what if the High King refuses to sign?" Lena asked, finally taking a bite of a salmon and dill sandwich.

"Child, leave my son to me on this one," the Dowager said, patting Lena's hand. "Now, about dear Jane."

"I remember you offering to foster her with Lady Cressa," Lena said, waiting to see if that had changed.

"Yes," the Dowager said. "Cressa will worry overmuch about her father and new mama, I fear, without companionship." Victoria, with the blessing of Lord Renath Mellan, the *Marque ah* Fall Haven and the father of Lord Baerik's late wife, had formally adopted Cressa in the Caeldenonian fashion the day after the wedding. "And it would likewise keep Jane safe."

Lena nodded and took another bite of her sandwich, enjoying the delicate flavors. She swallowed before warning, "My aunt is not fond of Jane."

The Dowager pursed her lips. "You may trust that I will not see the child abused in any way—even from your aunt," she said sharply.

Lena studied her for a moment and then nodded. "I trust you. With both matters." She paused. "Might I ask what became of the young women I left in your care?"

Realain and Gira had been captives of the man posing as Amir Fasili, along with Kenleigh, the young acolyte that had come back to White City with her. The pair had been left with the Dowager.

"I made arrangements with King Trenant Mycium of Thynn, who of course is my son-in-law, and both young ladies have been returned to their homes, where they were welcomed with open arms," the Dowager said kindly. "And I understand that Miss Atona is now in your charge?" she asked curiously.

"She is," Lena said sadly. "It seems she was *not* welcomed home with open arms. After what she has been through, she deserves rest... but more than that, she deserves a choice when it comes to the next stage in her life."

Maelynn nodded, and the Dowager appraised Lena with a thoughtful and approving expression.

"If she would like, she is welcome to join us. If nothing else, she can help with the little girls." Her tone was kind, with none of its usual sharp edges.

Lena inclined her head. "I let her rest when she first arrived. Fenora and Rachel have been making sure she gets settled and has everything she needs to feel at home. I have a meeting scheduled with her this afternoon."

The other two women exchanged a knowing look before Maelynn said, "I can think of no one better than those two to look after her." Her tone was pained.

Lena knew about Rachel, but that Fenora might know something of what Kenleigh had been through was a surprise.

She nodded, a lump in her throat.

While she had been physically abused to the point that she thought she might die, and her body still bore the scars of that time, no one had possessed her body in the way that she knew they had with Rachel and Kenleigh.

"I will speak to Miss Atona and see what she wants," she said finally. "I know I will have your support when I tell her that, whatever life she wishes to have, we will provide whatever she needs."

Both women nodded gravely.

They turned the conversation to lighter topics as they finished their meal, and Lena realized not only had they treated her—a twenty-one-year-old woman who had not even sat on the throne she claimed, and had not been crowned a queen—as their equal, but more than that, *she* felt it to be true.

*****

Lena had little time to refresh herself after tea and before her meeting with Kenleigh Atona.

Ellae was uncharacteristically silent as Lena sat at her dressing table while Sanders arranged her hair.

Lena had changed into a Caeldenonian evening gown with capped sleeves and a high waist, cinching just under the breasts, of pale gray trimmed in seed pearls. She would be glad to put off gray and return to colors. While she genuinely mourned Uncle Charles, it was hard to do so for her cousin.

When Sanders finished, Lena gave her a smile and sent her to check on Jane before turning to Ellae.

"What are you thinking?" she asked.

The golden-haired warrior stroked her customary braid thoughtfully. "I worry that some will think you are harboring a murderess instead of seeing that you are making sure she has a fair trial, and that will put an additional target on your back," she said frankly.

It was, after all, her job to assess the threats in and around Lena's life.

"But I think it is the best choice, all things considered. Just another thing to keep in mind." She smiled reassuringly.

Lena nodded and rose, shaking out her skirts. "Thank you for your counsel."

She found that she preferred the Caeldenonian cuts, but she knew that once she was home and seeking her throne, she would have to lean more toward the tightly-laced stomachers and wide skirts that the Lithonian people preferred—at least at the start. She must not be seen as an outsider, but as a daughter of Lithonia, returning home to her people.

"On to my next engagement," Lena said, heading for the door.

Ellae put a hand on Lena's shoulder to stop her. "You need to slow down. Between our sessions and your duties, you hardly give yourself a moment to rest, and I worry."

Lena met her gaze briefly before looking away. She was exhausted, but she didn't sleep well. Instead, she used her constant flurry of activity as a distraction, not just from the situation in her homeland, but as a mechanism to keep her from thinking of her time in Pannarius as well.

"I will think about it."

It wasn't the first time her *galvana* had said something, nor was she the only one to express concern.

Lena left the bedroom and stepped into the small sitting room that adjoined it. They had only just sat down when Fenora brought in the flame-haired former acolyte.

Both women curtsied, and Lena motioned for Kenleigh to sit.

"Thank you, Fenora," she said in dismissal.

Fenora gave Kenleigh a reassuring smile before leaving the small sitting room, closing the door softly behind her.

Lena turned to Kenleigh. "Are your rooms alright?" she asked, taking her hand.

"They are more than alright, Your Majesty. You have been very generous, and I cannot thank you enough," Kenleigh said sincerely.

"No need to thank me," Lena said, squeezing her hand. "You offered me comfort when I was in a dark place, and I do not forget it."

Kenleigh nodded, remembered pain flitting across her face. "When I found out who you were, I thought we would all be put to death according to Pannarian law, but instead, you were the instrument of my salvation, and I will never forget that."

Tears were in her eyes, and Lena felt them gathering in her own as well.

She cleared her throat and tried to ignore the painful lump that had formed there. "Be that as it may, we need to discuss your future."

A shadow of fear entered Kenleigh's features, so she quickly continued, "You have many options. You are not being set adrift."

"Options, Ma'am?" Kenleigh asked, confused.

"You have been offered a place as a companion to my young cousin Lady Jane and the granddaughter of the Dowager High Queen Arrysanna, Lady Cressa, while I return to Lithonia to settle matters there. Or you may stay with me—though that path may not be safe, nor will it be tranquil."

Ellae leaned forward to interrupt. "It will be outright dangerous, lass," she said quietly but with care. "Our lives will be in danger more than once, and it is possible you will see more than one bloody battle, so think carefully about your answer."

Lena nodded her thanks to her sister, the woman sworn to put Lena's life before hers, before turning her gaze back to Kenleigh. "Or you may choose a different path. You could marry… we would provide a dowry and help find suitors. Or if there is some training you want, if you want a quiet life away from court, the Dowager, the High Queen, and I are all committed to helping you on whatever path *you* want *your life* to take."

Kenleigh looked overwhelmed, as if she never could have imagined having a choice in her life again.

Considering how long she had been captive, Lena understood.

"You don't have to decide now," Lena said quietly as she stood and pulled Kenleigh to her feet. "Take the time you need. Speak to Fenora and Rachel, if you like."

Ellae laid a hand on Kenleigh's shoulder, as she had done to Lena not so long ago. Kenleigh gave her a watery smile, and Ellae said, "Don't worry, she seems to turn the life of everyone she meets upside down." She grinned at Lena. "You get used to it."

CHAPTER 29

High Lord Benjamin Bennings
Bennings Place, the City of Endomir: Lithonia
18th of Rison

The past five days had been agony. A petition to the King to allow Magne to have his son's cremated remains sent to his family's elm grove had been put forward in the House of Lords the afternoon after Derek's death.

The unanimous and almost immediate passage by every lord in attendance had persuaded Garrett to allow Derek's ashes to be escorted to his ancestral home by no more than four guards. If any of the '*guards*' were found to be Magne's missing sons, or Benjamin's, they would be executed on the spot.

Other than the letter that had been delivered to Vera, he had heard nothing from the boys—and unless they were captured, Benjamin didn't think they would until the proposed rendezvous.

To shield the woman he loved only second to his wife, Benjamin hadn't been back to see Vera since she'd received the letter.

He understood the boys' motives in escaping, he really did; little held him and Magne back from fighting against the Usurper now. He had no doubt that if they were captured, the guards would kill them on the spot—a thought that made his blood grow cold. But as long as they were free, Benjamin's and Magne's hands were no longer tied.

A few of the nobility, emboldened by their sons' daring, had begun to seek out Magne and Benjamin and ask after their plans. Neither he nor Magne had said anything that could put them in danger, but Harold Harmon, High Lord of Harmon's Island and the Watcher of the North, had come right out to tell Benjamin that he had already sent his pledge to the true Queen.

Harry's second son, Nate, was held in in the Nursery Keep, his eldest had been left at home in command of his father's forces.

Harmon's Island had not been left without a Harmon in charge in two hundred years, bar the few weeks that it had been run over by the Hathorites.

Additionally, Lord Samuel Collins, who was the Queen's great-uncle, and Benjamin's vassals—Lords Proudmourn, Prather, and Payne—along with Montgomery's Lords Highland and Southernby, had come to say they had done or would do the same.

It made Benjamin wonder how many others had done so, but he wasn't willing to go door to door to find out.

Every high lord had up to three lesser lords in his county that would, in time of war, march under him. In the past, those lords would have even come to a high lord for judgment on disputes, and paid tithes to them, but times had changed... and much for the better.

Those old bonds still held in some areas, and the ancient fealty that once dominated all had shifted to a different, but still productive, relationship. There will still deeply rooted ties between a high lord and his vassals, but they were no longer subjugated to them. Loyalty and friendship had forged stronger bonds.

Benjamin had spent the day consoling Magne, whose grief was magnified by his Link with Angela. He had contacted her immediately via Script Stone to let her know what had happened to their youngest son; Benjamin knew because he had been by his friend's side while he composed the message.

Magne's anger and pain were moving him toward recklessness, and Benjamin feared for what he would do.

For himself, Benjamin was now composing a letter to his wife with instructions for people to contact. She was well-placed to speak to the merchants and guild masters in Seathor, and to move their preparations forward.

He knew Lenathaina would come for them, and they would need to stand ready when she landed.

His study was well-lit with gas lights, comfortably furnished, and smelled of cigar smoke. It was a cozy room, one that his father had furnished.

He wondered what his father would think of the current situation, but had no need to ask; David Bennings would have never allowed a tyrant to sit on the Lithonian throne.

He glanced down at the letter, reading the words he had written, and wished yet again that his family had two Masters, as Magne and Angela did. It would be much safer to communicate that way. As it was, their Master, Nathan Zane, was with Beth and the girls—something that Benjamin was very glad of.

18th of Rison in the Year 1001

My Darling Beth,

I think it is time to approach the Guild Masters of Seathor and to begin recruiting more forces as quietly as possible. The weapon stores that you have already secured may not be enough to arm the men we need to both protect Seathor and to give the Queen the men we owe her in times of war.

Continue to be cautious, but you must, my love, deliver what we owe to our liege.

I have had some assurances here that others will be with us when the time comes. If you or our other friends get news from Caeldenon, please have it transmitted securely. Such news would bring heart to our endeavors, especially after our recent blow.

Derek was a good boy, if a wild one. I will miss him.

My love to our girls. Remind them to stay strong. And my unending love to you, my dearest girl.

Love,
Ben

He put the letter in an envelope and slipped it into the top drawer of his desk before locking it. The key went into his pocket, and he went downstairs to the library for a book to take to bed. He had just taken the last step off the staircase when someone pounded on the front door.

Kern, his butler, opened the door and was roughly pushed aside by several guards. An officer dressed in the House Morthan colors stepped to the fore and handed over a sealed parchment.

"I have orders to search the premises for the wanted fugitives."

Benjamin took the warrant, which had been signed and sealed by King Garrett Morlette Morthan, authorizing the search for Randal Bennings and Stephen and Travis Montgomery or any proof of communication from them.

"This means nothing. His rule has not been ratified, so he has no legal right to issue such orders," Benjamin said bluntly, tearing the paper in half.

The guard grinned in a way that was mildly unnerving, as if he had hoped for such behavior. He jerked his head at a pair of rough-looking guards behind him and said, "Search him."

Kern started inching out of the room, most likely heading for help, but another guard seized him as well. They were thrown against a wall, their persons and clothing searched.

Kern had only the items he always carried: his watch, a box of the new matches that Vera favored, and his keys. Benjamin had emptied his pockets when he came in from spending the day with Magne, but he still had the key to his desk, which the guard handed to the officer.

"You are under arrest for denying the authority of the true King of Lithonia," the officer said to Benjamin before turning to his men. "Take him to the city's holding cells. I will stay behind to search the house with the rest of the men."

The officer turned back to him and bowed mockingly. "I will see you later, Your Grace."

*****

In the early hours of the morning, Benjamin was pulled from his cell and marched into a small room with a table and two chairs; fetters had been placed on his wrists. He was left waiting for some time before the officer that had arrested him entered the room again.

"I didn't get a chance to introduce myself, Your Grace." The man used the same mocking tone he had before. "I am new to the city, you see, but I find I like my new job quite well. I am Captain Bain Roan, and the King has put me in charge of the investigation to find your missing son."

Benjamin did not reply.

Roan smirked. "See… I hoped at best I would find the escaped prisoners hiding out in your home, or at worst, something to lead me to them." His smirk changed to a satisfied grin as he pulled a piece of parchment from his pocket, and Benjamin's stomach sank. "But I didn't think I would find proof of outright treason."

Benjamin still said nothing.

"The King has seen this and has kindly asked me to convince you to tell us about these 'assurances' you've gotten and who they come from." Roan took off his jacket and laid it on the back of the chair before whistling sharply.

Two more guards came in, already in their shirt sleeves, and Roan began rolling up his own. "Now. Would you like to comply with the King's request, or do you need persuading?"

They had proof that Benjamin had been working for the Queen, but he would give them nothing else. No matter what.

"I will comply with no order or request that isn't issued by the true ruler of Lithonia, Queen Lenathaina Morthan Coden."

Roan's eager grin came back. "I was hoping you would say that."

He jerked his head at the other guards, who rounded the table, and each took one of Benjamin's arms. Roan pushed the table aside and walked around him once, slowly.

And then the blows began to fall.

CHAPTER 30

Samuel Thane
Ashbury Avenue and Clearwater Place, City of Endomir:
Lithonia
20ᵗʰ of Rison

Samuel arrived for his shift at six o'clock sharp, as he did four evenings a week, but when he stepped into the supply room, he was greeted with silence.

He moved toward the equipment rack to get his satchel and pole, and the supervisor stepped out of his office.

"Thane, a word," he called gruffly.

When Samuel entered the office, Gene Vorn's portly form was seated behind his desk.

"Have a seat," he said.

Samuel did, nervous but not letting it show. The last time he had been called to this office, it was for a promotion... but then, Vorn had been jovial and had had a bottle of whiskey on his desk. Right now, he was far from jovial and not a drop of whiskey was in sight.

"What can I do for you, sir?" he asked.

"Can you tell me why you were seen kissing a man after your shift on the seventeenth of this month?" Vorn asked.

Samuel felt his face flush, but not in embarrassment. "I don't see what that has to do with anything. As you say, I was no longer on duty."

Vorn colored and nearly sputtered, "It is my business because you work for me, and this organization doesn't approve of... of..."

"Open-mindedly accepting that people can love who they want?" Samuel offered.

"Vulgarity!" Vorn shouted, spittle flying from his mouth. "So, you don't deny it?"

Samuel sighed. "You wouldn't be asking me if you didn't have proof."

"It was reported to this office by *two* individuals," Vorn said, his color still high. "And one claims they have seen it happen on more than one occasion."

He pulled an envelope from his desk and tossed it at Samuel. "That's what you're owed. A copy of the report was sent to the house that employs your dirty little friend too. Good luck finding a job— you won't get a reference from me."

Samuel felt like he would be sick as he picked up the envelope and shoved it into his pocket. "Damn you, sir."

"You're the one who is damned," Vorn retorted with a smirk.

Samuel did his best to casually walk out of the office and through the supply room. Most everyone had left on their rounds, but those still in the building stared as he walked by, some with looks of pity and others with disgust.

He hurried down the sidewalks and streets until he reached Ashbury Avenue. He turned down the alley behind the houses, walked up to the servants' entrance of the Caeldenon Embassy, and rapped on the door.

The cook, a stout woman with gray hair and hickory skin from Caeldenon, looked Samuel up and down. "Come on in, lad."

She dusted her hands on her apron and led him into the servants' hall, where Jack was seated at the table with a glass of wine in front of him.

"Your Excellency?" the cook said to the other man at the table.

The ambassador had ebony skin and black shoulder length hair, and was dressed in a dark gray Caeldenon military uniform. He looked up at Samuel with a sympathetic smile. "Ah. Are you our Jack's partner?"

"I…" Jack looked up at Samuel, heart in his brown eyes. It was clear he had been crying.

Samuel steeled himself. "I am, my lord." He walked around the table and laid his left hand on Jack's shoulder, and extended his right to the ambassador of Caeldenon. "Samuel Thane."

"Jaeryn Lyss, *Marque 'ah* Rollan and ambassador for His Majesty, High King Gavan Coden of Caeldenon." The *Marque* shook Samuel's hand and gestured for him to take a seat. "Our Jack has had a trying day, and by the looks of you, yours hasn't been better."

He poured Samuel a glass of wine and handed it to him. "Jack says you are a lamplighter?"

"I was," Samuel sighed. "I was just sacked."

Jack turned to him. "Never!"

"There are some small-minded people in this world, and it seems that the current political climate has given some an excuse to be nastier than usual," *Marque 'ah* Rollan said, taking a sip of his wine.

"Who caught us out, and why'd they report it?" Samuel asked, taking a sip of the dark red wine.

He had been expecting something cheap, since his lordship was freely pouring it for his servant and a recently sacked lamplighter, but it was actually a decent vintage. If Samuel wasn't mistaken, it was an Andolin red, northern region.

"My mother," Jack muttered, raking his fingers through his blond hair. "She came by to drop off a package a few days ago, and saw us." He blushed. "Seems she told my father, who came asking around a few houses here to see if anyone else had seen anything *unsavory*, as he called it. They bribed a maid down the way that I didn't want to go with to file a complaint."

He took a huge drink of his wine before continuing. "Said if I didn't swear you off, they would disown me. Tried to get His Excellency to sack me too."

The *Marque* snorted. "I told you I don't care who you swive, lad. Just do right by one another."

This bold and shocking statement got a nod of approval from the cook, who was still standing over them like a mother hen. "Do you have a place to go, lad, if things get rough?" she asked Samuel gently, shooting the *Marque* a pointed look.

"Yes," the man added sadly, "if they have spoken to your employer, then your landlord is likely next. So if you need a place to stay or employment, we can work something out. Who you love isn't something you should be punished for."

Samuel took a breath, still in shock at the acceptance of the Caeldenon people. "I have someone I can talk to who might let me stay with them if I need to, but I don't have family in the city."

"Take Jack with you. I have given him the night and tomorrow off," the *Marque* said, standing up. "And if you need a place to stay, you can come back here. We have plenty of rooms."

He gave them a stern look. "But no sharing unless you two want to talk about some kind of commitment. You aren't *Mael'Hivar*, after all, so do things properly."

He waved for them to stay seated and left the servants' hall. The cook also left the room briefly, and came back with bowls of rich curry and flat bread.

"You lads eat up before you go about your business." She touched Jack's cheek and patted Samuel on the shoulder before heading back to the kitchen.

*****

An hour and a half later, Samuel and Jack were hastily packing up Samuel's personal possessions as his landlord stood in the doorway. The furniture came with the apartment, but most everything else was his. A loan of a handcart had been given, but Samuel had to give over two golden oaks as a surety that he would return it—which was enough to buy a new cart three times over.

Samuel and Jack pushed the cart through the lamp-lit streets to Clearwater Place, noticing that doors and windows were shuttered tightly on every street they passed. Even the taverns and clubs looked deserted. Samuel took them around to the back door, leaving the cart in the back courtyard, and let himself into the kitchen.

Loren, the cook, looked him up and down and set a kettle to boil. "Who is your friend, Sam?"

"This is Jack," he replied, sounding as exhausted as he felt. "Is Mistress Vera in?"

"She is in her study." Loren turned her gaze to Jack. "I will take care of this one while you attend to your business."

Samuel left Jack in her capable hands and headed for the study. He knocked twice then waited until he heard her call, "Come in," before opening the door.

Mistress Vera looked haggard and exhausted. Samuel knew that High Lord Bennings had been arrested, and he was a good friend of Mistress Vera's.

He sat down, and she looked him over.

"Rough day?" she asked. Then she narrowed her eyes. "Shouldn't you be on your rounds?"

"Jack's mother saw me kiss him, and got some reports filed. I have been sacked from my job and kicked out of my apartment," Samuel said bluntly, remembering that just two months ago, she had warned him to be careful.

Mistress Vera sighed. "And Jack?" She rubbed the spot between her eyebrows.

"Disowned from his family, but the Caeldenon people seem to think we've done nothing wrong, so he still has his job. They offered to find me something, if I need a place to go."

Samuel looked at her, waiting to see if he *did* need a place to go. After all, this would compromise his ability to spy.

Mistress Vera shook her head. "I have a room going spare, and you're welcome to it. We may have to change your position, but… we will figure it out." She gave him a tired smile. "Tell Mrs. Fitz to set you up."

"Jack is here with me. Can he…uh…" Samuel didn't know quite how to ask.

"Stay the night?" Mistress Vera prompted. "Of course. You should take every chance you get to be with the ones you love. If you learn nothing from me, learn that."

Samuel had never seen her so shaken, so melancholy. He reached out to squeeze her hand. After she squeezed back, he rose and went to find the housekeeper.

CHAPTER 31

Arch Master Lan Coden
White Castle, White City: Caeldenon
21ˢᵗ of Rison

Lan's mother, Maker bless her seemingly eternal self, could be a lot to take. His father had been the spare heir, never expected to take the throne, and thus, for most of his youth and early adulthood, had been left to do as he pleased.

Dominaris Coden had been raised to be his brother's advisor, as Evandar was for Gavan, but when his elder brother, Bael, was killed in a hunting accident, Dominaris had been thrust forward. Bael's wife had given birth to three sons, but only one had lived, and he'd been born with the Gift.

Father's first wife had died in childbed, the child with her, and it wasn't until Father had taken the throne that Lan's grandmother, Zephier, had pushed him to marry. Father had let her do the picking, and Lan's mother, Arrysanna, had been all but sold into marriage by the junior branch of the Mycium House of Thynn in a bid for power.

Mother had only been fifteen when she married Father, and they had Lan's brother, Gavan, a scant ten months later.

Lan knew his mother in a way that his brothers, and perhaps his sister, did not. It wasn't until he had gone to the Isles of the Ithrimir that he truly began to understand her.

Mother wasn't one to lament the hand she had been dealt in life aloud, but in her letters to him—and further, in journals that she had passed into the care of the Ithram for Lan to read when the Ithram deemed him ready—Lan learned more of her, and of duty, than he ever could have at her feet. Mother let the veil down in her private writings in a way that she never did in person, and the fact that she had shared that with him was a treasure.

Even if there were days that taking her on in person required a stiff drink.

But lately, dealing with his mother was far preferable to dealing with the woman he loved. Perhaps it was the years apart, or the fact that Jillian was settling into a position that required her to balance her duties as a Master with those of family, or perhaps she had spent too much time with Master Tam, who served as healer, advisor and teacher to the Morthan family—even if he was only trained for one of those mirs.

Things worked differently here; unless Jillian was pulled in to consult, the conversations that Lan had with his brothers on state matters were private.

As part of their training, Masters were taught to understand the roles they were trained for, and told that any family, organization, or government they might choose to serve would have different expectations. They could accept those or they could choose to work elsewhere.

Throwing tantrums over not getting information that wasn't pertinent to their job didn't get them anywhere, and worse, made them look a fool. And Jillian had made herself look like a fool more than once recently.

The separation enforced by the Order before the marriage of two Masters was making more and more sense. It wasn't that Lan no longer loved her, but since they had returned to Caeldenon, he was struggling to like her. It wasn't that Lan no longer loved her, but since they had come back to Caeldenon, he was struggling to like her.

Their apartment was one of six on the family's private living floor. Gavan and Maelynn had one, as did Evandar and Samera. Gavantar and Lenathaina, Mother, and Baerik and his new wife— which was still something to wrap his head around—had their own apartments, and now so did Lan and Jillian. There was also a large and small sitting room, as well as a dining room just barely large enough to seat the whole family in the shared space between all the apartments. Guest apartments were on the floor above, where Lenathaina's Master Tam now resided.

Lan was tempted to go speak to Tam, but instead, made his way to his apartments for dinner.

The door was decorated with a simple border of interlacing knotwork and flanked by a pair of *Mael'Hivar Naheame*. Though Lan didn't qualify for his own *thane,* every apartment on this floor, and every corridor or passage in the castle, was guarded by either his brother's Red Shields or Gavantar's Gold Swords.

Lan nodded to the pair, acknowledging their salutes as they opened the door, and braced himself for another night of discord.

Jillian had already changed out of her white robes and into a pair of tan leggings and a green silk shirt, and her dark blond hair lay loose on her shoulders.

Her amber eyes found Lan's, and she smiled sweetly. "Evening, my love. I thought we would have a simple meal this tonight, if that suits?"

Lan couldn't help but smile back; perhaps she was adjusting after all, and he had nothing to fear. "That sounds fine." He kissed the top of her head. "I will get changed and meet you in the dining room."

While not as large or ostentatious as Gavan or Gavantar's apartments, the rooms allotted to Lan and Jillian were still far more than they could need by themselves. Lan hoped that one day, the spare rooms would be filled with the sounds of children and grandchildren, but for now, it was just the two of them.

His footsteps echoed on the stone floor as he walked into their chambers and shed the uniform he wore when serving in his official capacity. Dark blue trousers with a matching open-fronted jacket that flared at the hips, a dark red vest, knee-high black boots, and a creamy, butter-soft linen shirt completed the outfit. His belt had the symbol of the Ithrimir. The belt, along with his ring, marked him a Master; the colors of the suit, red and blue, marked his mirs.

When Lan came into the dining room, he wore a loose pair of green sleep pants and a matching tunic. His reddish-brown hair was cropped into a mass of short curls that he knew stood on end from his habit of running his fingers through them while he was thinking.

He dropped another kiss on the top of Jillian's head and sat down across from her.

It was a simple dinner of soup, crusty rolls, strong cheese, and fruit, with a flagon of chilled wine.

Lan poured for them both and asked, "How was your day?"

"Dull," Jillian retorted, taking a spoonful of her soup. "The family is healthy, so I did a few checks on some of the household staff." She shrugged. "And I have been catching up on the family histories left by High Master Andric."

"Perhaps you could finally slow down and spend time on your interests, my love," Lan suggested, taking a sip of his soup. "After all, you have spent your life studying, or working in hospitals. It might seem strange at first to take it easy, but it also might be a blessing."

Jillian gave him a cool look. "I may have primarily studied healing, but I do wish your brother would understand that I have many other skills and fields of knowledge."

Lan sighed, resisting the urge to rub his temples. "He knows, Jill, but he has plenty of counselors. My brother Evandar is his chief military advisor, and he has representatives from the government, as well as representatives from each providence that he meets with weekly, and that is on top of the Kings themselves. You may be well versed in Lithonian court matters, but Caeldenon and her providences are a vast tangle that takes years to learn. You have only been here for a few months. You aren't ready for a council chamber, or even to deal with the round table in my brother's office."

"*Perhaps,*" Jillian growled, pushing her chair back, "if you and your precious brothers would let me in even to just *listen*, my understanding would grow faster." She stood, hands on her hips, and continued. "Every other member of this family has duties but me. I want to know why."

"Jillian," Lan took a deep breath, struggling to keep his temper. "We haven't even married yet… you know that counts for a lot here.

We are getting many allowances because of the circumstances, but a lot of things will be on hold until we are married."

Jillian scoffed. "In the vaunted progressive Caeldenon, marriage is still something that matters."

Lan thumped the table with his hand. "Yes! Honor and commitment matter here. I have no idea why you have been resistant on setting a date, but until that happens, you will not be given familial duties."

He pushed back from the table. "And another thing, I know you have attempted access to my personal office. I won't have it, Jillian. I won't have snooping and sneaking to get what you want. My brother will bring you in on information that *he* wants you to consult on when *he* is ready. Try sulking a bit less and becoming part of the family that you seem so eager to help steer. Maybe when you act like part of it, we will treat you like part of it."

"Maybe if you would tell me why Queen Mellina is here, quartered with your mother, I wouldn't have to *snoop*," she spat back. "I haven't even been granted leave to visit her."

"She is convalescing after her many losses in the past months and is seeing no one." Lan repeated the party line, but for some reason he didn't feel guilty about the half lie. "She is seeing few people."

Jillian stared at him and shook her head. "There is so much you are keeping from me, Lan."

Lan spoke, not knowing where or why the words came from his mouth, but knowing there was truth in them. "Not nearly as much as I think you keep from me. Goodnight." He turned on his heel and left the dining room.

He would sleep in one of the spare rooms. He didn't have energy to deal with her for another moment.

CHAPTER 32

Vera Martique
Harding House, City of Endomir: Lithonia
22ⁿᵈ and 23ʳᵈ of Rison

The number of times Vera had come to this house could be counted on one hand, and she had never come through the front door.

This time, she had presented her card and been shown, with an obvious display of disapproval by the butler, to a sitting room to await his lordship's pleasure.

Lord Samuel Collins had once had dark hair, owning to the Tardonian blood in his line—the same blood that gave Lenathaina her raven hair and startling purple eyes. Samuel's eyes were gray with flecks of that same purple, and he had fair skin as well—the reason Vera's wasn't so out of place in Lithonia, despite her Pannarian grandmother.

He dismissed the butler as soon as he entered the room, and waited until the door had closed.

"I ordered tea," he said stiffly.

Vera rose. "I am sorry to disturb you, but some things can't be put into writing at present, and I am in need of a grave favor." She curtsied deeply, eyes on the floor, and said quietly, "You must know that my need is great to come here and beg anything of you."

"I have never known you to beg a damn thing of anyone, girl, or to take an easy life when freely offered," Grandfather retorted. "Sit down and tell me what mess you've gotten yourself into."

Vera did as instructed and sat down in the wing-backed chair across from him. "You know that a quiet life in the country as a minor lord's wife would have never suited me."

"It would have been better than... what you do now," Grandfather said, turning red with embarrassment.

"I think we both know that appearances can be deceiving," Vera replied quietly.

"Be that as it may... your appearances aren't the best. I just wanted more for you..." Vera was surprised to see him looking a little emotional. "A home, a family. Love."

"As you loved your wife?" she asked tartly.

"As I loved your grandmother," he said sharper.

Vera sighed. "Would it help any to know that I have found my own sort of love, and it is why I am here?"

Grandfather sat forward. "If you're happy, then yes." He took her hand. "What can I do?"

Vera took a deep breath. "Let three young men enter your home late tonight and hide them."

He gave her a long, searching look. "That is a dangerous game you are playing."

"You're right, and it would be dangerous for you to help me, but I can think of no place less likely for the Usurper to come looking for them than here." Vera held her breath, waiting for his response.

"Still working hand in hand with your cousin, then?" Grandfather squeezed her hand. "Good. It will be a proud day when our girl takes the throne."

"It will be." Vera squeezed back. Then she said seriously, "But for now, I need to keep those who would follow her alive."

"I trust my people," Grandfather said. "I can put them in the guest wing that is never used, but they will have to keep the curtains closed and stay to their chambers."

"Of course," Vera said, gratitude clear in her voice.

Her heart ached for Magne and Angela, but she couldn't lose Randal; she had to keep him safe for Ben and Beth.

Grandfather gave her a hard look. "I imagine you have ways of getting things out of the city, if not people?"

Vera studied him for a long moment. "I do."

"If I got letters to you, could you see they get where they need to go?" he asked, studying her just as hard.

Vera nodded.

"Will I see you this evening?" he asked, almost hopeful.

"I don't think so. The fewer of us moving, the better," Vera said. "But when this is over…"

"Yes. It is time to put the past to rest," he said quietly.

*****

Being a woman of ill repute came in handy at times. For instance, none of the guards Vera passed had any reason to question her being out late; so long as she endured their lewd comments, pinches and awkward caresses, and flirted… she could go where she pleased.

Not that it didn't make her stomach churn to allow it, but sometimes one had to look at the bigger picture.

Vera made her way off the road and into the woods, passing the hunting lodge that she had often met with Lenathaina in, and riding a few miles further. Her tin lantern gave just enough light for her to see the trail and little else.

She came into the clearing marked on the map that Randal had sent, and waited. Fifteen minutes passed, and all the while, she could feel eyes on her.

Finally, the three ragged young men cautiously came out of the trees, looking worse for the wear, but alive and whole.

Vera slid off her mount, and Randal threw himself into her arms, shaking.

"We haven't much time," she warned, squeezing him fiercely before turning to do the same to Travis and Stephen. "It is a long walk back to the city."

"The city?" Stephen asked, sounding confused. "We had hoped to be on our way out of Endomir."

"Garrett has increased the guards and even sent some of his own men to Jasper's Keep to make sure that no one who shouldn't gets through."

Vera pulled packets of dried meat and cheese from her saddlebags for each of them—she was sure they hadn't enough food to keep them going—and each man quickly wolfed down his portion.

"Before we go…" She looked at Stephen and Travis. "Derek's body was cremated and has been sent to your mother." She laid a hand on each of them. "I wish I could send you there as well. Whatever your motives, you boys have set a fire in the city. None thought Garrett would go so far and now that he has, more are emboldened to work against him."

Travis sniffled wetly; Derek had been his twin, his other half.

Vera turned to Randal. "Your father has been arrested for treason," she told him bluntly. "While guards searched his home for you lot, they found letters implicating him as a supporter for the Queen. That is all I know."

Randal was shaking, his face red with fury. "If I turn myself in—"

"It wouldn't matter," she interrupted honestly. "The letters were damning enough on their own."

She wiped her eyes and turned to pull leather flasks from her saddlebags, partly to hide her face. "We have a long walk. I will take you to the edge of the woods, then you will follow my directions to a farm where you will meet my man. He will get you into the city."

"Where are we going?" Stephen asked, taking the leather flask. He opened it, and the scent of good whiskey filled the air.

"Lord Samuel Collins is going to hide you in his home," Vera said.

The three men exchanged a look.

"Why?" Randal finally asked.

"Because I asked him to. That is all you need to know."

Vera took the reins of her mount, and they set off, following the path back.

She had left the city as the sun was setting, but it was well past midnight by the time she reentered. She had drilled the pathway into their heads, and the directions she and her grandfather had agreed on.

Either way, she would hear from Grandfather in the morning.

Vera approached the city alone, looking pleasantly disheveled, and paused at the gates to the city.

"Evening, Mistress Martique," Guard Captain Tollard said, grabbing her horse's halter as she came to a stop.

Vera smiled down at him. Tollard was one of those so enamored with his own looks that he thought everyone else was too. Reddish-brown hair and dark green eyes, with chiseled features. He was tall, muscular, and imposing. "Evening, Captain Tollard."

The other five guards at the gate turned their attention to them, and she urged her horse forward a few steps, drawing them inside the walls completely.

"Did you have a pleasant ride, Mistress Martique?" Tollard asked as his hand creeped under her skirt to wrap around her ankle. His tone implied that he wasn't just talking about the horse.

She managed to keep her expression controlled, though she wanted to kick him in his smiling face. "I did." Vera made herself return his smile. "I am quite fond of my mount." She patted Darrington, her horse, who was trying to shift away from the captain—as anyone with good sense would.

Several of the guards chuckled and nudged one another.

Tollard slipped his hand a little higher. "Perhaps some time, we could go out for a ride." He leered, "If you were properly satisfied with your mount, you wouldn't need to go through so many stallions."

His fingers dug into the back of her calf. "And making friends in the right places might benefit you. Your current protector is in no position to be of any help to you right now."

Vera nearly lost the contents of her stomach. *He is speaking of Benjamin.*

If these louts thought him her protector, then others would as well. Some knew her real trade, but others assumed the wealthy of the city bought time in her bed.

"I will keep your generous offer in mind, Captain," Vera said, smiling again. "For now, I need to find my bed. I am rather tired."

The captain caressed her leg once more before letting her go.

She rode her horse down the gas-lit streets, hoping Jack had found the young men and would soon be leading them through the small gate used by farmers who brought in milk in the early hours of the morning. It was left unlocked and open for use so those who lived in the city could see to the herds that they kept in the fields to the south.

Jack had taken old slouch hats, scarves, and coats and met the young men near a local farmer's barn to get them changed. They would come through the gates in pairs with the milk carts, and with luck, none would think they were more than they appeared.

Prayer had not been something Vera indulged in often in her life, but she found in recent days, her pleas to the Maker were unceasing.

CHAPTER 33

High Lord Benjamin Bennings
Castle Endomir, Endomir: Lithonia
23rd of Rison

The Master leaned back to examine his work. "There is some scarring, I fear. Some of these were left too long."

Benjamin grunted and looked at his face in the mirror. There was a thin line in his right eyebrow where it had been split. "All things considered, Master, I don't think it will matter much."

The Master winced and nodded before glancing at the door. "Are there any messages I can send for you?" he asked quietly.

Benjamin studied the Master for a long moment and shook his head. He knew that the man wasn't Garrett's personal Master, but he didn't know him well enough to trust him. "Nothing, but I thank you for the kind offer. I have left letters for my wife and children in the care of the King. If he denies me a last word to those I love, he will answer for it in the next life, if not this one."

The Master nodded solemnly. He was a young man, for his kind, but compassionate. "I can walk with you," he offered.

Benjamin hesitated but then nodded. "I would be grateful for a friendly face beside me."

The Master touched his shoulder lightly. "I will be outside."

Benjamin shaved, for the bruising and cuts from the beatings he had received had made that impossible before now, and finished dressing. A black suit, a silk shirt, and fresh linens had been fetched from his home.

He would go to his execution in style.

A priest had come to hear his confession and, on his oath of office, had taken the true letters for Benjamin's family.

Damnation was a serious thing for a priest, so he didn't think the priest would risk it. Besides, they could only kill him for treason once.

The guards came shortly after he had finished his preparations, and he was escorted, with the Master by his side, out of the room he had been held in at Castle Endomir.

The procession was quiet, the only sounds the armor and weapons of the soldiers clinking. A pavilion had been constructed outside the castle gates, but the Usurper wasn't even there, coward that he was. The members of the House of Lords had assembled, however.

Benjamin mounted the steps and defiantly looked out into the crowd as the order was read.

"High Lord Benjamin Bennings, you have been convicted of treason against His Majesty King Garrett Morlette Morthan." It was Murphy, the lackey of the Usurper, reading out the unlawful decree; the man looked giddy. "Therefore, you have been sentenced to death. Have you any last words?"

"Long live the Queen," Benjamin said loudly.

Several men in the crowd met his gaze and nodded, but no one spoke. Magne looked as if he would stand, come to Benjamin's side, but Benjamin shook his head slightly, and Magne stayed seated, tears in his eyes.

"Then kneel and take your punishment," Murphy said, stepping back.

Benjamin let the executioner guide him into place, and then he laid his head on the block. He closed his eyes and sent every bit of love that he could through the Link that had bound him to his wife for many years.

Then he heard the *swish* of the axe.

CHAPTER 34

High Lady Beth Bennings
Seathor Hall, Port City of Seathor: Lithonia
23rd of Rison

Angela had sent Beth a messenger as soon as she had heard of Benjamin's arrest. Two days with two mounts had seen the man here, nearly dead of exhaustion, and his horses with him. That had left Beth three days to wait and worry.

She pushed on... Speaking to the captains of the Bennings Guard. Putting forward orders for rifles, armor, and housing for their new recruits. She had made sure that word got out that her husband had been arrested.

It was becoming quite clear that Garrett only held Endomir, and he only held that because of the hostages he kept.

It was time to turn the tide.

Beth was sitting with Captain Elkhart when it happened. Her bond with her husband was not as strong as Magne and Angela's, so at this distance, for a feeling or emotion to come through, it had to be extremely powerful.

And the burst of love Beth felt was the most powerful it had been in the whole of their marriage, and then... it and everything else was gone.

CHAPTER 35

Shan Alanine Fasili
River Keep, Southern Region: Pannarius
24ᵗʰ of Rison

Alanine and Lynear were having a breakfast of thin pancakes made of rice and coconut with a delicate egg curry, along with a pot of floral tea, while they went over the schedule for the day. Alanine was to meet with some local guild mistresses to discuss their current needs, and Lynear wanted to make sure she was up to date on the statuses of each business.

Often, these meetings just reminded Alanine how much her mother had failed her education, and how much she resented the imposter for that.

They were moving on to the proposed tax cuts that had been asked for when her *hassana* rushed into the room, not even pausing to prostrate herself, before bursting into sobs.

"Namar, he is gone!"

Lynear looked up at the tiny woman. "What do you mean he is gone?" she asked sharply.

"His room is empty," the *hassana* panted. "The guard was found dead in a cupboard!" She looked from Alanine to Lynear, eyes begging them to fix this. Sevinc loved Namar.

Alanine and Lynear came to their feet and rushed down the stairs to the second floor of the keep. Servants and guards were milling outside Namar's room. Nijah was being held by her nanny down the hall.

The crowds parted for them, and Lynear and Alanine stepped into the room. Two guards prostrated themselves until Lynear bid them to rise, then one handed Alanine a slip of parchment.

She opened it and read the short message: *You should not have sent for the blasphemous whore.*

Alanine handed the note to Lynear and said, "Clear the room."

The guards scrambled to follow her orders, closing the door behind them.

"What does this mean?" Lynear demanded. She held the paper in her lap, and the star tattooed on her hand to mark her as a woman of the Royal House was stark against her copper skin.

"When your sister came to visit, I met with a woman," Alanine said, shifting guiltily.

"Someone came for a grief-visit, yes?" Lynear said, sitting on the end of Namar's bed. "The *hassana* told me."

"She did, but more than that, she started going on about her goddess—she who the Red Priestesses serve—and said she wanted to come here and teach us of them, as our father followed her." Heat suffused Alanine's face.

Lynear spit at the mention of her 'father'; they did not speak of him, lest they summon his evil shade. "Unholy speech, that," she hissed. "Why didn't you tell me, child?"

Alanine winced at her tone and her words, then whispered, "Because she said that... *that man* and my brother had the Curse, and she could teach him to control it. I didn't want you to send Namar away, so I messaged Cousin Isra."

Lynear shook her head. "I would have waited for *Coralie Banar* and the Empress, may the Light ever favor her, to make that decision." She looked down at the paper and then at Alanine again. "So, this woman has taken your brother, you think?"

Alanine nodded.

"Well." Lynear put the paper in her pocket and stood. "We will double the watches so nothing happens to you or your sister." She looked around the room. "I will send a swift courier to the palace and make sure *Coralie Banar* is on her way."

She took Alanine's face in her hands and kissed her forehead. "I know you acted out of fear for your brother. *Coralie* will make this right." She pulled back to look Alanine in the eye. "But you must trust us."

"Should we cancel the meetings today?" Alanine asked, unsure how she could go on with things as usual.

"No. We can't let on that anything has happened. I will speak to the *hassana*," Lynear said, heading for the door. "We must keep this quiet until *Coralie Banar* tells us what to do."

Alanine nodded and wrapped her arms around herself, wishing she were holding her brother instead.

CHAPTER 36

First Prince Gavantar Coden of Caeldenon
White Castle, White City: Caeldenon
25th of Rison

Gavantar and Baerik were sitting in the office that had been given to Gavantar when he became First Prince. It was off the same corridor that housed his parents' and uncles' offices—a sign of the importance of his role in government.

Baerik was nursing a whiskey after having been torn to shreds by his young wife in front of forty or so *Mael'Hivar* and a handful of servants. He had made the mistake of suggesting once more that his she stay safely in Caeldenon while he helped Lenathaina regain her throne.

"Feeling better?" Galwyn asked helpfully with a cheeky grin.

Baerik grunted. "I didn't know she had such a vast knowledge of the Old Tongue," he murmured, taking another sip.

"Vast and colorful," Gavantar mused, sipping his drink. "I think you need to concede this fight with as much grace as you can muster."

Baerik snorted. "You think I am stupid enough to suggest she stay here again after that? I will just have to make sure the stubborn woman has a damn guard. Almost makes me want to take a *thane* so she can have a *galvana*."

Since Baerik was not a prince, he didn't have to take a *thane*, though he could if he wished, as the son of a high king. But for Victoria to have a *galvana,* he would first have to exercise his right.

Baerik would have to initiate the process himself, as it would only be forced to take a *thane* if he inherited the throne, and he could only inherit if all the descendants of Dominaris Coden's first marriage died—something unlikely to happen, as prolific as the Codens were.

Gavantar laughed. "Yeah. I know that feeling. Though sometimes, I think *galvanas* get them into as much trouble as they keep them out of it."

"On the bright side," Galwyn interjected, "we are entitled to an extra ten *Mael'Hivar* with the *Ducessa* coming. So twenty each for Gavantar and Lenathaina leaves ten for you and Victoria each."

Baerik nodded and pulled the list of candidates to accompany them to Lithonia forward again. "True…"

Three loud knocks cut off whatever Baerik might have said next.

Galwyn answered the door and stepped back to admit the sleek form of Under-Sect Commander Alysse Mahone. Her curly, cropped, red hair had just a touch of gray that had not been there before the Battle of Keltonmere and the loss of her daughter, but her green eyes still held fire, and her copper skin was smooth as a girl's, belying her age.

She gave Galwyn a slight bow of the head and then saluted both Gavantar and Baerik, with her right fist to her heart and a deeper bow of the head. "My Prince, Your Grace, Prince Galwyn."

"Commander," Gavantar said, standing to cross the room and shake her hand.

"Rumor has it that you are preparing a little expedition," Mahone said with a smile.

"We are," Gavantar nodded, not surprised that she had heard. The *Mael'Hivar* grapevine moved quickly.

"Have you finalized your choices?" Mahone asked, sitting across from Baerik.

"We had, but since the *Ducessa 'ah* Kilmerian is now definitely coming, we have an additional ten spots," Gavantar said. He poured her a small whiskey before taking a seat.

"Ah, yes." A slow smile spread across the commander's face. "I heard that she has quite a sharp tongue." She took a sip of her whiskey.

Baerik grunted. "Like a spell-forged sword."

Gavantar laughed.

A spell-forged sword was a weapon made by the crafters of the Masters of the Ithrimir; it never dulled, and was one of the sharpest weapons known to man.

"Well then. I would like to request to be considered for a spot, with a couple of my girls," Mahone said, looking from Gavantar to Baerik.

Baerik shifted. "At the moment, we are only looking at Gavantar's Gold Swords. As his personal guard—"

"Ah. But what about yours? Or your wife's?" Mahone put her drink down and leaned forward. She turned to Gavantar. "Besides, I owe you a debt, and I would like to be able to pay it."

"I don't feel you owe me any debt, Alysse," Gavantar said quietly.

"You let me have my vengeance and then you helped me see my daughter on her final journey," Mahone said, voice choked with emotion. "So let me help you sit that pretty wife of yours on her throne."

"Even a handful of the *Lynene 'ah Hanal* would be a useful thing…" Baerik considered.

"Very useful. And easier to hide among the women, in places men might not be welcome," Galwyn added, leaning back in his chair.

Mahone smiled and took another sip of her whiskey, watching Gavantar.

They had history, Alysse and Gavantar. She had been with him at his first battle when he was sixteen—had pulled him out of a mess, in fact. He trusted her with his life, and she knew it.

More, Gavantar trusted her with Lenathaina's life.

"Okay," he nodded again. "Yourself and four of your women. I will let you have the pick."

Mahone grinned. "Might I make a suggestion, My Prince?"

"Of course," Gavantar replied.

"Make the last five *Zandair Gelines,*" she said seriously.

Baerik and Gavantar exchanged another look.

The *Zandair Gelines* were a small, exclusive sect of elite Sharp Shooters, the best the *Mael'Hivar* army had. Every member was a deadly weapon. Gavantar would have to clear the request with his father, as well as the one about the *Lynene 'ah Hanal,* also known as the Daughters of Night.

Baerik nodded, and Gavantar sighed.

"I will speak to my father. Considering our history and your volunteering," he said to Mahone, "I think he will have no objection to a few of the Daughters coming. I am not sure about the *Zandair Gelines,* though. I will go find him and send you word."

Mahone laughed. "I will wait right here with the *Duc* in case I have to argue my corner with His Majesty." She turned to his uncle. "Besides, I want to hear more about this *Ducessa* and how she wooed the mighty Baerik Forrester-Coden, Hero of the Battle of Gelandine."

Baerik groaned, and Gavantar chuckled.

* * * * *

Time with his wife when they were both awake was rare these days, and usually centered around meals with their personal household or with the extended household of his parents, uncles, and grandmother, so finding themselves alone before dinner, and in their private sitting room with only Galwyn and Ellae for company, was a pleasant surprise.

"I think Baerik and I have our contingent picked out," Gavantar said, putting his arm around his wife and propping his feet on the padded footstool. He was exhausted. "And between the two of us, we have put everyone through their paces."

"Gold Swords only?" Lena asked, stretching slightly.

"No. We have five Daughters of Night, and Father has given me permission to approach the Sharp Shooters and ask for five of them. Baerik will have control of the contingent, under me," Gavantar said, checking the time.

They had about ten minutes before drinks with his family.

Lena nodded, taking it all in. "Is he more settled about Victoria coming?"

Galwyn and Ellae snickered.

"He is. Besides, her rank granted us ten more *Mael'Hivar*." Gavantar smiled as he kissed Lena's temple. "And he got quite the tongue-lashing the last time he proposed her staying here to protect Jane and Cressa."

"In the practice yards," Galwyn put in helpfully.

"She has earned much respect from the female Gold Swords," Ellae laughed. "She has been spending time sparring with some of them, and expanding her vocabulary."

"In colorful ways," Galwyn smirked, tugging Ellae's braid. "In both Common and the Old Tongue."

Lena chuckled. "That doesn't surprise me, she has been sitting in the observation decks of the House of Lords from the time she was fifteen."

She snuggled up to Gavantar and relaxed. Through their Link, he could feel her exhaustion and how much this brief pause in activity was needed.

"Her keen mind was what drew me to her," his wife admitted. "Her spirit only cemented my choice of ladies."

"She really is a special one," Ellaemarhie said gently.

"Quite," Lena agreed.

A soft knock interrupted the conversation.

Galwyn walked down the short corridor from the sitting room to the entry of the suite where he and Ellae had chambers, and answered the door. He came back with Lord Kieran and Master Tam, who both looked grave.

Lena made to rise, but Master Tam waved her down, taking a seat himself. Lord Kieran leaned against a wall with his arms crossed over his chest.

"One of my friends in Lithonia has been in contact with me today to share the most recent developments there, Your Majesty." Master Tam rested his hands on his knees. His skin was wrinkled, and his hair a pure white.

Gavantar wondered how much longer Lena would have his support.

She sat up, and Gavantar felt her mentality shift through their Link; no longer a wife relaxing with her husband, but a queen, ready to face whatever obstacle came next.

She nodded for Tam to continue.

"On the 13th of Rison, Lords Randal Bennings, Stephen, Travis, and Derek Montgomery escaped the Nursery Keep," Master Tam began. "The younger of the twins, Derek, was shot and killed as he fled. The other three young men are still at large."

Gavantar felt the wave of grief that came over her, though outwardly, she remained composed.

"On the 18th of Rison," Master Tam continued, "High Lord Benjamin Bennings' home was raided in hopes of finding the missing captives or information of their whereabouts. Many consider the warrant that ordered this raid to be void, as Garrett's rule has not been ratified by the Council, and the legality of his situation is still undetermined. However, during the raid, information was found proving Lord Bennings is covertly supporting you."

The old man's eyes rested on the girl he had helped raise. Sadness filled his entire face. "He was executed outside the castle on the 23rd, on the grounds of treason."

"May the Maker bless his soul," Lena whispered, fighting back tears. "I must write to Beth and Angela."

"Not only that, Your Majesty… I must urge you to move your plans forward," Master Tam pressed, leaning forward.

Behind him, Gavantar could see Lord Kieran nodding in agreement.

Lena stood and walked to the window, which faced the city and the harbor beyond. Gavantar could feel her emotions raging, and knew the effort it took for her to stay calm.

A long moment passed, and she nodded. "I will speak to the High King and see how quickly we can advance things. If the Usurper is now killing my supporters, I must go to them."

Gavantar's heart clenched with a mix of pride and fear. "Baerik and I will make our final selections in the morning and do our part to get everyone ready."

"And you know your ladies are half-packed," Ellae offered quietly. "We all stand ready to serve."

Gavantar felt the burden settle on his wife, and swore he would do all he could to share it. She was still struggling with all that had happened in Pannarius; she rarely slept a full night, and often had nightmares that she refused to talk about.

Not that Gavantar had room to complain, there. He didn't talk about his either.

"It is time to go in for drinks," he told her gently. He turned to Master Tam. "If you would join us so we can fill my mother and father in on the details?"

"Of course, Your Highness," Master Tam said, standing to bow formally.

Before they left the apartment, Gavantar saw Lena pull Rachel aside to share the information. The two women embraced briefly, but the look of determination they shared spoke volumes.

As they walked through the corridor, Rachel and Fenora had their heads together, whispering. Gavantar had noticed in the months since they'd come to Caeldenon that the pair had formed a strong attachment—one he wondered at.

Gavantar often caught Galwyn studying his sister and the Lithonian Lady, too, as if he suspected something but was waiting for Fenora to tell him in her own time.

Most everyone was already in the drawing room when they arrived. Mother kissed Lena's cheek fondly, and Father kissed the top of her head, as he did when greeting his own daughters.

Mother and Father, as well as Evandar and Samera, believed that even the young children should be included in these family dinners, so the room was bustling with activity and conversation. With twenty-four mixed family members, including Rachel but excluding Grandmother and Queen Mellina, plus ten *Mael'Hivar,* Miss

Kenleigh, and Master Tam and his apprentices, the room was pleasantly warm, but not crowded, and full of love.

Gavantar heard Lena quietly ask his parents for a word after dinner, while shooting a significant look at Evandar and Lan. Father nodded and said something Gavantar couldn't hear, and Mother squeezed Lenathaina's hand before moving to speak to Samera.

Gavantar grabbed a glass of wine for himself and Lena, and they sat down on one of the settees, where they were immediately converged on by 'the little people,' as his younger siblings and cousins were referred to as. Jaeminderiel was the eldest of this contingent at fifteen, though the youngest of the Tearhall siblings.

Jaemi was officially Gavantar's parents' foster son, as all of his siblings, had been at one point or another, save the eldest, owing to the circumstances of their parents' deaths and the hostile environment that had reigned in the Tearhall family, thanks to King Taemendred, Galwyn's eldest brother, and his wife Queen Caralain.

Lilithe and Takanar, Gavantar's younger cousins, and siblings Landon, Evan, and Oldonna rounded out the group, which had taken Cressa and Jane into their tribe. The mock battles and games that they played often filled the residential corridors, practice yards and courtyards with chaos and noise.

Jane now took her rightful place at Lena's side, and the little people regaled them on their latest escapades, which it seemed included a nocturnal raid of the kitchens.

Gavantar felt his wife relax again, happy to share in this time and set her burdens aside for a few minutes. Jane scooted closer, and Lenathaina put an arm around her young cousin, and he felt her love for the child.

Sooner than Gavantar might have wanted, dinner was announced by his parents' *gandine*, Lord Valeran, and they all filed out of the drawing room and down the hall to the large family dining room.

For the sake of sanity, the young people held court at one end of the table, with the adults at the other. Conversation floated up and down the table as first a clear soup, and then a light salad of the last of the greens were served. The main course was a garlic-crusted rack of lamb, with roasted carrots and a creamy mushroom rice, paired with a Tardonian red wine. To finish the meal off, they had a lemon and berry tart.

When dessert was concluded, Gavantar's mother and Aunt Samera exchanged a look, and Samera rose.

"I will take the ladies through." She smiled at Jillian. "I had wondered if we might discuss some concerns I have about our refugees, Jillian?"

Jillian gave Lan a sharp look before leaving with Samera. Fenora, Rachel, Victoria, and Kenleigh followed the other women out, along with Master Tam's apprentices.

The little people likewise rose and ambled out of the dining room, kissing their parents goodnight. They would soon be collected by their various nannies and taken to their parents' apartments to get ready for bed.

That left Gavantar, Lena, his parents, his three uncles, and Master Tam.

The men began lighting pipes and cigars, while the servants served port and sherry for everyone. The elderly Master related his information again, and this time, the alcohol helped it go down better.

When he had finished his tale, Lan turned to ask, "Source?"

"Another Master and a trusted friend," Master Tam said, meeting his gaze. "In the service of one who is a staunch ally to the Queen."

Lan nodded, accepting this answer with no outward reservations.

Father turned to Lena. "Does this change anything for you?" His tone was sympathetic but not overly so. It was a fine balance between the relationships of father and daughter-in-law and allied monarchs.

"We would like to move our plans forward as soon as possible," Lena said, looking from Father to Uncle Evandar.

Gavantar knew the current hold-up was pulling enough ships to transport the sixty *Mael'Hivar*, and the assorted weapons, supplies, and mounts, as well as Lenathaina's court.

Evandar looked at Father. "The second ship is pulling in on the twenty-ninth. Could have it turned around by the first of Xavar."

That gives us six days, Gavantar thought.

Lena nodded. "That would be sufficient. Your aid and support during these times will not be forgotten," she assured Father, sounding like the Queen she was.

Father chuckled. "Don't forget, when all this is over, we'll have another treaty to work out." He patted her shoulder. "The line of succession might get a little muddled with all this."

Lena inclined her head, giving him a small smile. "A treaty I look forward to bargaining over, Your Majesty."

CHAPTER 37

King Garrett Morlette Morthan
Castle Endomir, Endomir: Lithonia
26th of Rison

Walking through the halls of the castle was becoming uncomfortable for Garrett. Every turn he took, people were either staring at him or avoiding his gaze. It reminded him of the looks Richard had gotten, and it left him with a sick feeling.

Was he turning into Richard? He didn't rape the serving women or beat anyone for no reason. The hostages that he held were to help secure the kingdom and bring peace. To keep Lenathaina from making Lithonia another providence of Caeldenon.

Murphy continued to assure Garrett that he was in the right, doing the best thing for the country, but then why did so many work against him?

He was the late King's son, a rightful heir. What did it matter that his mother had only been King Charles' mistress and not his wife? Garrett was the seed of his body. His blood. His child in a way that Lenathaina could never be, no matter what he or she wanted.

Even Parker seemed to have abandoned him, coming with reluctance whenever Garrett summoned him, and offering no solid show of support. Only Murphy stood by his side, and he would need more than a secretary to hold Endomir, let alone the country.

Murphy thought Garrett should make more arrests, or perhaps take out the reluctance of the high lords to move to action on their family members in his care. He knew some of the newer guards had few scruples and would enjoy making examples of the more... troublesome prisoners.

He was doing this for the good of the country; the Maker would forgive any measures he had to take to watch over His people. *Garrett's* people.

CHAPTER 38

High Queen Maelynn Coden
White Castle, White City: Caeldenon
26ᵗʰ of Rison

A pair of Gavantar's Gold Swords opened the doors to her son's apartment, and Maelynn stepped through, Emerlise behind her. Maelynn held a long package, wrapped in oiled leather and tied with a dark blue ribbon, in her arms.

Lord Kieran Rainsmere, a nice young man who had turned into the perfect *gandine* for the young couple, rose and bowed. "Your Majesty," he said formally. "How may I be of service to you?"

Maelynn smiled at him. "If Queen Lenathaina is in, I would like to speak to her."

"Of course," Lord Rainsmere said. "I will let her know you are here." He gestured to the chairs before disappearing through one of the doors off the circular antechamber.

He returned quickly and escorted her and Em into the sitting room.

Lena rose and smiled. "To what do I owe the pleasure of this visit?" She glanced at the package in Maelynn's arms before meeting her gaze.

Maelynn had to admit that Lena's eyes held a startling directness at times.

She walked to the settee, nodding at Ellaemarhie as she did, and sat down with the package in her lap. Em wandered over to the younger *galvana* and took a seat, and the two began a quiet conversation.

"I have something I would like to give you," Maelynn said, gesturing to the seat next to her.

Once Lena sat down, Maelynn transferred the package over to her lap. The young Queen arched a black brow at the weight of it and began untying the ribbons and unwrapping the leather.

Inside was a sword with a filigreed hilt and guard, light ribbons of gold threaded through the silver; the pommel was set with a brilliant blue sapphire. The scabbard was tooled in gold and silver, with sapphire thread in a swirling, feminine design.

Lena stood and pulled the sword from its sheath to reveal a finely made weapon with a keen edge. She looked at Maelynn and asked, "Spell-forged?"

Maelynn nodded. "A gift from Gavan," she added, admiring the weapon, as she had so often. "Though, one that has rarely seen use. We both agreed that you needed a queenly weapon at your side." She smiled at her daughter-in-law. "And a token to remind you of your new home, and that all our prayers and wishes go with you—though we wish we could be at your side as well."

Lena swallowed hard and re-sheathed the sword. She set it on the table and leaned down to wrap her arms around Maelynn. "I wish I could take you with me, to have the counsel of a mother and another Queen," she said quietly.

Maelynn returned the embrace. "I have no doubt that in all things, you will make the best decisions possible, daughter."

The sound of a door opening startled them apart, and Maelynn looked up to see the young former acolyte standing in the doorway that led to the smaller sitting room Lena's ladies used.

The red-haired girl hesitated and then curtsied. "I am sorry to interrupt, Your Majesties." She began backing away. "I will come back later."

"Come in, child," Maelynn said with a welcoming smile.

The young woman had been through much and needed all the support they could offer.

And love too, she thought.

Kenleigh hesitated again, and Lena smiled in invitation.

"Please do come in and admire the gift my mother has brought me."

It touched Maelynn to hear that endearment from Lena. She moved to make room for young Kenleigh, who dutifully admired the blade.

"Was there something you needed, Kenleigh?" Lena prompted quietly.

The young woman drew a breath and nodded. "I have been thinking of our conversation... about my options," she ventured.

Both Maelynn and Lena nodded.

"While I appreciate the offer of going off into the world, I don't think I want to do that. Not right now. I don't want to marry at the moment—maybe not ever—and to take up a trade, I would be on my own, and I don't want that either."

Kenleigh looked at them both to take in their reactions, and they gave her encouraging looks, so she continued.

"That leaves going with you into the Lithonian war, or staying here. And while I am grateful for all that you have done for me," she hastily assured Lena, "I think I would enjoy spending time with the little girls here."

Her sentence trailed off quietly, and Lena took her hand.

"I think that sounds like a wonderful plan. There is much you can teach Jane and Cressa—not to mention my aunt." Lena gave her an encouraging smile. "I think it would be good for you and for them."

Maelynn offered her own smile. "And I think you and my mother-in-law will have many interesting talks. Don't be fooled by the Dowager's bark, she has a kind heart."

Kenleigh smiled gratefully at them. "Thank you, Your Majesties." She slipped off the settee and curtsied again before letting herself out.

Maelynn turned to Lena. "You did a good thing, bringing her here," she said with pride.

Lena sighed. "I wish I could do more for her, I really do."

"Giving her time and space to allow her wounds to heal, and offering choices in the direction that her life will go is a big step to her recovery."

Lena nodded, lost in a darkness of her own.

Maelynn remembered yet another young woman who had been abused, and by those who should have loved her. Giving her the freedom to make her own choices and the ability to stay away from her abuser had helped so much.

Lately, Maelynn had seen a change in her, and thought she had finally found a kind of peace.

Her attention once more on the woman beside her, she put an arm around Lena, feeling her eventually settle against her, letting someone else briefly take on her burdens and take care of her.

She was so much, for so many people, but for a moment, Maelynn allowed her to be a daughter with her mother.

CHAPTER 39

Dowager Queen Mellina Morthan
White Castle, White City: Caeldenon
27ᵗʰ of Rison

Mellina paced the small sitting room as she awaited Lenathaina's visit.

Her niece had only been to see her twice in the last week and a half, and both visits had been short. The first had been to tell Mellina that she was to stay in the Dowager High Queen's apartments and see no one without Lena or the Dowager's permission. The second visit was to tell her that she was to be put into the old lady's custody on one of her estates while Lena dealt with the situation in Lithonia.

The implication that Mellina had made things worse was strong.

Mellina had finally gotten the servants to stop referring to her as 'the Dowager Queen Mellina'. She hated the term. She used to be Her Majesty the Queen, but that was now Lena's title. She was simply Her Majesty Queen Mellina, or Queen Mellina. 'The Queen' was now and would always be Lena.

For a brief moment, Mellina had been the Queen Mother; she supposed she would be the Queen Aunt now… if Lena didn't disown her outright.

At last, Lord Braen, the Dowager High Queen's *gandine*, opened the door. "Queen Lenathaina Morthan Coden of Lithonia."

Lena nodded to the *gandine* as she passed him, her black-clad shadow behind her.

Mellina had asked during Lena's first visit if they could speak without the golden-haired woman, but the suggestion had been sharply dismissed.

Mellina had to admit that, despite their current strained relationship, she was immensely proud of Lena.

The Queen was dressed in a silk day dress of dark gray with black embroidery, in the Lithonian style, her curly, black hair coiled atop her head and studded with silver pins that winked in the light.

Lena sat down and motioned for Mellina to do the same. The woman with her—Ellaemarhie, Mellina believed she was called—sat down in a chair in the corner.

Mellina could feel Ellaemarhie's green eyes on her, but she didn't look her way.

Best to pretend she's not there.

"You will be leaving for Trahelion Manor in two days," Lena announced. "As discussed before, you will be in the custody of the Dowager High Queen Arrysanna Coden."

Mellina nodded. "Yes."

"She has agreed to take this on to spare you the danger of the trip to Lithonia, and the consequences should anyone find out what you have done," Lena continued, resting her hand on the arm of the chair she sat in, as if it were a throne. "You will remain there until such time as a proper and fair trial can be arranged."

She sniffed. "I can't commute a sentence or pardon you until you are tried, but others might not hesitate to inflict their own brand of justice. Much can be said against Richard, but he was still a king. Your crime could carry a heavy sentence."

Mellina took a shaky breath. "Yes. I know. And I know I have made more problems for you, but I only sought to keep him from hurting more people."

Lena's eyes blazed. "And had you sent for the guards, they would have seen the dead body of the Queen, and held Richard until the Masters arrived to evaluate him," she said with more than a little heat. "And the Council could have taken things in hand under Magne until I arrived."

Mellina resisted the urge to squirm in her seat.

What Lena said was true. If Mellina had not acted out of turn, Lithonia wouldn't be starting a civil war, nor would Benjamin Bennings and Derek Montgomery be dead.

"Now," Lena said, seeing that her words had made their point. "About Jane."

"What about Jane?" Mellina asked warily.

The little girl flitted between most of the apartments on this floor with Lady Cressa, the Dowager's granddaughter by her husband's bastard. Mellina understood that there was a difference in the situation for the Dowager, but how she could treat Baerik like a son and his daughter like a grandchild was beyond Mellina's understanding.

"Jane will be going with the lot of you as the Dowager's ward." Lena leaned forward as she ordered, "And you will treat her with kindness and compassion."

Mellina sat back in her chair. "The whole point of her coming here was so I wouldn't have to deal with her."

"Well, you wouldn't be here if you had made different choices, so you will just have to accept the situation with as much grace as you can muster." There was just a hint of sarcasm in Lena's tone, and the golden-haired woman snorted from her seat in the corner.

Mellina nodded stiffly.

She would just avoid the child. No need to worry about being rude if she never saw her.

"Miss Kenleigh Atona will also be accompanying you, as a companion to you and the young girls. I have given her permission to share the details of how we met."

Lena settled herself in the chair once more. In a kinder tone, she said, "She is in need of love and acceptance, too, but I think you can find solace and comfort in one another's company. She is a kind soul, and I expect you to treat her well."

Something about her expression when she spoke of the young woman—who, rumor had it, was a former acolyte of the Maker, but now a favored guest in the castle—gave Mellina pause.

At last, she nodded, deciding she would speak to the girl once they settled in the Dowager's manor.

The conversation lapsed, and then Mellina asked, "When do you leave?"

Lena hesitated, and in that pause, Mellina saw just how much of Lena's trust she had lost.

Finally, the Queen said, "On the first."

Mellina nodded and looked toward the window. "I haven't told you how I escaped Endomir."

When she looked back at Lena, she could see by the expression on her niece's face that, with everything that had happened, she had not thought of it.

"You haven't," Lena confirmed.

So, Mellina told her of the pass through the mountains—the one Lena would have been told of, had she been crowned in Lithonia. It was her right to know, and whatever use she made of the knowledge was her right as well.

Mellina recounted the directions turn by turn, and when she was done, she pulled out the crude map that she, Sara, and Mat had put together. The man was a good hand with a pencil, and she thought he had done a fair job.

"It is not easy going," Mellina warned. "You can't take a horse or even a large party. We used ponies."

Lena studied the map, nodding. "But a small force of trained warriors…" she murmured, thinking aloud.

Finally, she shook herself and looked at Mellina. "I thank you for this."

"You are the queen of Lithonia. This knowledge is yours by right," Mellina said simply.

Lena nodded and rose, and so did Mellina. With some hesitance, Lena kissed her cheek before turning to leave.

"Will you see me off?" Mellina asked as Lena's hand closed on the doorknob.

Lena glanced over her shoulder, past the woman that was her shadow, and nodded.

CHAPTER 40

High Lady Beth Bennings
Seathor Hall, Port City of Seathor: Lithonia
29ᵗʰ of Rison

Six days after the death of Beth's husband, his cremated remains were delivered to her, along with a letter from His Majesty Garrett Morlette Morthan.

It was the captain of their house guard that delivered the plain wooden box and parchment envelopes sealed with the royal blue and gold wax. Rage was clear on his face.

"His last words were for our Queen, Your Grace," Captain Townsend said, kneeling before Beth. "'Long live the Queen.'" The grizzled officer looked up at her, eyes blazing. "I will say them too. Long live Lenathaina Morthan Coden, the true Queen of Lithonia."

Beth's throat was tight with tears, and she gave Townsend a jerky nod, bidding him to rise. Her daughters, Anne, Jane, Mary, and Sara stood behind her with her youngest, James, and her pregnant daughter-in-law Lissa. Beth clutched the rough wooden box to her chest, a poor vessel for so great a man.

"I don't know where Lord Randal is," Townsend continued, letting his voice grow loud enough for the assembled staff and soldiers that filled the courtyard of the Hall to hear. "And I don't know what those letters there say, but I will tell you this, Your Grace."

He pulled his dagger from his belt and took a step forward. He kissed the tang of the blade and knelt again, offering Beth the hilt. "I swear by my hope of life everlasting, on my honor, that I will faithfully serve you as my liege Lady and through you, serve our great Queen. Never shall I raise my hand in rebellion against you or her, and if I do, I ask you to pierce my heart with this blade."

Silence filled the courtyard.

Beth turned and handed the box to her eldest daughter, Anne, and then turned back to Townsend. She took the dagger and kissed the tang before returning it to him hilt-first. "I accept your pledge and promise to always treat you and yours with fairness and justice."

For the space of ten heartbeats, the silence continued, and then the courtyard erupted into cheers.

The men who had faithfully served her husband and family formed a line. Townsend took up the place to her right, and Master Zane took the one to her left, holding the parcels that contained the letter from Garrett, and another parcel that had been smuggled from the city by a priest who'd carried the last words of a husband and father to his family.

Beth stood on the steps of the Hall as one man after another knelt and swore to follow her and to see Lenathaina on the throne.

She never faltered, only pausing when Zane made her take a sip of water, before taking the next man's oath.

The sun was setting when the last man had sworn. Word had spread through the city, and Beth could hear her people outside the gates.

A hastily erected platform was made in the space just outside the castle walls, and Master Zane climbed it and opened the parchment from Garrett. He murmured words and moved one hand in a pattern, and a shimmering, clear circle appeared in the air before him. When he spoke into it, his voice rang loud and clear he read out the words that had been sent to Beth.

"*By order of His Majesty Garrett Morlette Morthan, son of the late King Charles Morthan and rightful King of Lithonia—*"

Boos and angry shouts filled the air, and Zane had to pause until the crowd quieted again.

"*High Lord Benjamin Bennings has been put to death for his treasonous activity. Randal Bennings is stripped of his rank and will no longer have a place in his family's line of succession.*"

The crowd roared, and Zane raised a hand and sent a shower of blue sparks into the air, which stunned them into silence.

After a stern look, he continued.

"If the child that Lady Lissa Bennings carries is a male, he will take his grandfather's title. Otherwise, Lord James Bennings will inherit. I hereby order both Lady Lissa and Lord James to come to Endomir as royal wards."

Zane drew a breath. "It is signed, *King Garrett Morlette Morthan."*

Beth mounted the platform and took the parchment. "Do you have any matches, Master Zane?" she asked calmly.

Master Zane held out his hand, palm-up, and a small ball of flame appeared there.

Beth turned her gaze to the crowd and held the decree over the flame. When it had caught, she dropped it to the cobbles in front of the platform.

"That Usurper has lit a blaze he cannot contain," she called out. "We will not bend!"

Cheers and cries of support filled the air.

"Lithonians do not suffer tyrants!" she declared.

More cheers.

"Long live the Queen!" she bellowed, then let the cries of support wash over her.

"Queen Lenathaina!"

"High Lady Beth!"

"We stand with the Queen and our Lady!"

Tears ran down her cheeks, but she stood firm and resolute. She would lead her people in her husband's place.

CHAPTER 41

Queen Lenathaina Morthan Coden of Lithonia, First Princess of Caeldenon
White Castle, White City: Caeldenon
29ᵗʰ of Rison

Lena kissed Aunt Mellina's cheek and gave her a brief hug. She didn't know when she would see her again and wanted to part on amicable terms. "I hope you are able to make the most of this time," she said as Aunt Mellina climbed into the carriage.

Aunt Mellina nodded stiffly as Jane and Cressa climbed into the second carriage with Kenleigh. Jane was still dressed in gray, mourning a half-brother that, thank the Maker, she had never really known. Cressa wore a pair of brown and pink dresses, and Kenleigh dark green and pale blue. The red-haired former acolyte seemed to be enjoying the company of the young girls.

Lena had said her goodbyes to the girls and Kenleigh, both privately and here, but she blew Jane a kiss nonetheless. She ignored Aunt Mellina's pinched look and turned to the Dowager.

"Don't worry," the Dowager assured her, her eyes twinkling. "I will have everyone in hand."

Lena could not help but smile at that. "I have all the faith in the world that you will." She kissed her on, not one, but both cheeks.

"Write to me as often as you can," the Dowager said as she squeezed Lena's hands before climbing into the carriage. "My counsel is yours for the asking, child."

Lena rejoined her husband and his family on the steps, and they all waved as the pair of carriages moved off.

The final agreement between Lena and the High King had been signed just the day before, promising that Queen Mellina Morthan would be held in trust by the Dowager High Queen Arrysanna Coden until such time as the Lithonian people had accepted their new ruler. At that time, Mellina would be returned to Lithonia for trial.

Until then, an agreed upon sum of money would be paid for her maintenance, and she would be confined to the grounds of Trahelion Manor under guard by the *Mael'Hivar*. Gavantar's cousin, Taemos, would be temporarily taking his uncle's place as head of the Dowager's *Mael'Hivar*. Lena knew that he was trying to prove himself to his parents and to his aunt and uncle so he might be able to seek his cousin Aeleonna's hand in marriage.

Once the carriages had driven out the front gate, the family turned to go back inside. Maelynn gave Lena a reassuring smile, and she took a deep breath, for now letting go of the burden of her aunt and her crimes.

CHAPTER 42

Princess Fenora Tearhall
White Castle, White City: Caeldenon
29ᵗʰ of Rison

Fenora's stomach was a bundle of nerves as she and Rachel walked down the corridor on Gavantar and Lenathaina's side of the apartment and knocked on the door to their suite.

Ellae answered, wearing a faded red dressing gown loosely belted over cream sleep pants and a tunic, and looked the pair of them over with a discerning eye. She gave them a slow smile and stepped aside. "We are just having a drink. I am sure they would be happy for you to join us."

The *galvana* led them into the comfortable sitting room. The same redwood that had been used throughout most of the castle was predominate in this room too, as was the pale green used in other areas of the apartment. Accents of lavender, for Denon, and rose for Cael, gave the room a feeling of spring and growth.

"Evening, Fenora," Gavantar said from a settee.

Lena sat next to him in her violet silk dressing gown with a stack of letters in her lap. She rarely ceased reading, writing, or otherwise preparing for what would happen when they landed in Lithonia.

Both Gavantar and Galwyn, Fenora's twin, wore dressing gowns as well over their sleep clothes.

Rachel hesitated beside Fenora. "We didn't realize you had already retired," Fenora's darling girl stammered, blushing. "We can come back another time."

"How often did you, Maratha, and I lounge about in our nightclothes, playing cards and drinking into the small hours?" Lena teased. She set the stack of letters on the table and gestured for her oldest friend to join her.

Rachel sat next to her, and Fenora took a seat beside her brother, who gave her a one-armed hug. Ellae poured Fenora and Rachel a whiskey before sitting on Galwyn's other side.

"Not to discourage further late-night gatherings, but I am surprised to see the pair of you this late in the evening," Gavantar said, taking a sip of his whiskey.

It was only just past ten. Fenora knew from Rachel that in Lithonia, they had often stayed out until midnight or later, but that was a different life… one that didn't have early morning training sessions that often started before the sun had risen.

Rachel blushed again and said, "It is often hard to get a moment to speak to the pair of you without an appointment."

Lena inclined her head, her raven braid falling over her shoulder. "Things have been busy lately and, often, Gavantar and I spend our days going in opposite directions, it is true." She touched Rachel's hand lightly. "But you need only ask if you wish to speak to us. You are a priority in our lives, I hope you know."

Rachel nodded and then looked at Fenora. They had discussed how they should proceed.

"When I came into your service," Fenora began, looking at Lena; the Queen turned her gaze to Fenora, but left her hand laying lightly on Rachel's. "I made it clear that I did not wish to marry or form a romantic attachment."

"Your words at the time were, 'There is not now, nor shall there be, a man I am interested in sharing my bed with,'" Lena supplied, encouraging Fenora onward.

It was Fenora's turn to blush; she hadn't thought Lena would understand the implication there, but if she had ever been naive, she wasn't now. "Right. Well."

"How is it that you wish to move forward?" Gavantar asked, looking from Fenora to Rachel.

Fenora nearly choked on the sip of whiskey she had taken as she realized that what she thought was one of her great secrets was known to at least everyone in the room.

"We want to take our time," Rachel said, meeting his gaze. "But we also would like to be able to turn away unwanted advances. We are at war, effectively, and would like to have something to mark the commitment that we intend to make to one another in due course, when it can be a time of celebration."

She turned to Fenora, hazel eyes blazing. "We understand that there may be difficulty with the King of Cael," she turned back to Lena, "And likewise, our sort of relationship isn't something openly flaunted in Lithonia. I know you can't fight battles on every front…"

"No one should have to fight a battle to love who they love," Lena said, squeezing Rachel's hand. "But when the time comes, and you are ready for that battle, I will stand behind you."

Fenora hastily wiped away the tears that trickled down her cheeks and felt her brother wrap his arm around her again.

Galwyn kissed her temple and said, "And I will fight your corner too."

"And my parents will as well, I know it," Gavantar said, meeting Fenora's gaze. "No matter what, we won't allow you to go back to Cael or be under Taemendred's power again."

His tone was soft and full of sympathy, and Fenora thought the fragile thing inside her that shielded what she thought to be her secrets would break.

She knew that the High Queen had known what had happened to her when she had gone home at eighteen to be presented to the court in Cael, but she had hoped no one else had known.

"Taemendred wrote to tell me to make you come home for good, after your visit for your eighteenth birthday. Some of the things in his letter… I didn't like them." Galwyn held her tighter. "I was already *thane* to Gavantar, so he had to come with me when I spoke to the High Queen," he explained, then drew a shaky breath. "She made me swear I wouldn't kill him."

Fenora nodded, still stunned.

Gavantar interjected, his deep voice soothing. "I think it wise for the pair of you to take time courting one another. After all you have been through," his gaze moved to Rachel, "and some of it so recently, and all that is ahead of us... It makes sense to move forward slowly. You both have wounds that are healing, and you need to be whole within yourselves before you fully commit to one another."

Fenora laughed, a little shaken, and asked, "When did you get so wise on matters of the heart?"

"I am a married man now," Gavantar teased. "I know everything there is to know."

Lena snorted softly and elbowed her husband, and the group's solemn mood shifted to one of easy laughter.

Rachel leaned against Lena and whispered something to her, but Fenora didn't need to know every thought Rachel had or word she said; she trusted in the love they shared.

She had worried that, with everything going on, Lena would drift away from her oldest friend. Marriage took some people that way. But Lena had also been through as much, and more, than Rachel and Fenora had been through, and now she was fighting for her birthright.

It was, Fenora thought, a bit understandable that she hadn't had as much time for Rachel of late.

"A courting bracelet would send the message." Ellae had been silently listening to the conversation, but seemed to want to get back to the women's original request. "It sends a loud enough message here in Caeldenon, and it wouldn't take much work to send rumors through the nobility in Lithonia. But you'll have to dodge questions if you don't want to reveal who's courting you." She grinned; Ellae loved a good mind game.

Gavantar and Galwyn were nodding.

"And, not that I think either of you would change your mind, it has the advantage of being non-binding." Gavantar held up a hand before Rachel's outrage could erupt. "Which means that you could use the excuse of continuing a private courtship without disclosing your intended, as you are still undecided."

"Ah, as Victoria did," Rachel realized.

Lena nodded, smiling. "But if you do have a secret wedding, let us in on the fun. The Dowager had her share already."

Rachel and Fenora looked at one another, and Fenora wondered if the love she so clearly saw on Rachel's face showed on her own.

"We promise you a full part in any shenanigans we get up to," Fenora said, turning to Lena.

"Excellent." Gavantar stood. "Knock those back, and I will open something special."

He vanished into the bedroom, and everyone quickly finished their drinks.

When he returned, he peeled red wax off a pale brown bottle. "High Lord Montgomery gave this to me in Lithonia."

"Oh, he makes a wonderful whiskey," Lena said wistfully. "Aged in charred cherrywood barrels."

Gavantar poured them all a healthy drink before setting the bottle down. Then he raised his glass and looked from Fenora to Rachel. "May I be the first to wish you both a long and happy life together."

Everyone took a sip of the rich, slightly sweet liquor.

Fenora wasn't sure if it was the alcohol or the happiness, but she felt like she was floating.

*****

An hour later, when they returned to their side of the apartment, Fenora and Rachel slipped into Fenora's bedroom and closed the door. Some of Rachel's things were spread about the room, just like Fenora had things in Rachel's room.

Fenora pulled her lover into her arms and kissed her, letting all her passion, love, and the tumult of emotions that had overwhelmed her in the last hours flow out in that kiss.

When they finally broke apart, Fenora rested her forehead on Rachel's.

"I do love you so," Rachel sighed.

Fenora smiled. "I love you too, lass." She twined her fingers in Rachel's and pulled her deeper into the room. "What do you think about us sharing a room?"

Rachel hesitated. "What about the servants?"

"It isn't an unusual arrangement, unmarried women giving one another comfort. None would think anything of it until we make it clear what we are to one another," Fenora reasoned.

Rachel wrapped her arms around Fenora and rested her head on her shoulder for a long moment, and then... she began unbuttoning Fenora's gown.

She hadn't done that before—initiated intimate relations.

Fenora didn't push. She let Rachel undress her in her own time. And in her own time, Rachel pulled Fenora into their bed and showed her that she was truly ready to take their relationship forward.

CHAPTER 43

High Lady Angela Montgomery
Black Hall on the eastern shore of Lithonia
30th of Rison

Angela opened the letter from her husband with shaking hands in the privacy of her bedroom.

Two of her daughters sat vigil in the great hall, watching over the polished walnut box that held the ashes of their brother, as the family, their servants, and soldiers and people from Brayman, the city that their ancestral home was in, filed in to pay their respects to the kindest prankster that had ever graced these halls. Her middle daughter, Adeline, was on the Isles of the Ithrimir, and would have to be told of her brother's passing soon.

My Love,

Never did I imagine that Garrett would take things this far, or that our sweet boy would die at his hands. I am thankful that you were spared the sight of what the monsters that the Usurper calls guards did to him, for it will be forever seared into my mind. Instead, you can remember the unruly child that loved to play jokes, gamble, and make those around him happy.

I cannot leave the city, for I refuse to swear fealty or offer any support to the man who holds the nation hostage. I have had word that our sons are well and safe for now, as is Randal. If you can get word to Beth, it may be a balm to her.

And write to our Queen. The time for action has come. We need her.

Keep yourself safe, and whatever happens, know that in this life or the next, I will be at your side again. You are my heart. We are two halves of one soul.

Love,
Magne

Angela set the letter on her bedside table and stood to look out the window. The courtyard was full of people waiting their turn to pay their respects. She would sit her own vigil tonight, in private.

She walked out of her chambers and down the stairs, taking the servants' passages to avoid the mourners, and went into Magne's office. General Silas Hall was waiting there with Arch Master Brian Mulgrew.

The two men could not have been more different. General Hall was sixty with gray hair and dark brown eyes. He looked as if he had been put out to dry in the sun: whipcord lean and deeply tanned. Master Brian was most likely the same age as the general, but looked to be in his late twenties, thanks to his Gift. He was a bit softer, very pale, with wise blue eyes and a shock of blonde hair that gave him a permanently startled appearance.

The two men had been in quiet discussion, but when Angela entered the office, they rose and bowed.

"Your Grace," they murmured.

"Please, sit," Angela said wearily, taking Magne's customary seat.

She had lost weight, her curves were not as full as they had been a month before, and her chestnut hair and creamy skin had dulled. Grief and fear were taking a toll.

Both men complied, waiting for her to gather her thoughts.

After a long moment, she said, "I need word sent to High Lady Bennings that her son is alive and safe for the moment. Then inform the Queen what has happened here. We need to know what she wants us to do."

Both men nodded, accepting her words; Master Brian began taking notes.

"And we need to call a muster," Angela said, addressing General Hall. "To our vassals, or their wives. We need the men and supplies they owe us in time of war. We must begin training for whatever comes next."

"Your Grace," Master Brian said, eyes resting on her with compassion. "You understand that this will be taken as an act of war?" he asked quietly.

She met his gaze, and he melted a little from the heat he felt there. "When Garrett took my sons hostage, when he shot my boy, he started this war. I will play my part to see it ended, and if there is justice in this world, I will cut that bastard Garrett Morlette's heart from his chest myself."

The two men exchanged looks and nodded.

"Any other orders, Your Grace?" General Hall asked.

"The walls are to be fully manned here in the castle and the city," Angela said, rising. "We need to prepare for all contingencies.

Lithonia will not come under the rule of a tyrant. If Lenathaina won't come, I will lead the march myself."

PART TWO

Autumn, the Year One Thousand and One, A.C.

CHAPTER 44

Shan Alanine Fasili
River Keep, Southern Region: Pannarius
1ˢᵗ of Xavar

Cousin Isra stalked into Alanine's private sitting room in a swirl of green wrap dresses over brown leggings, her beaded braids clicking madly. The expression on her face was enough to make Alanine sink back into the couch.

Isra took one look at her, and her face softened slightly. "I understand, child, after all that you have been through that it is hard to trust anyone."

Alanine moved to prostrate herself, but Cousin Isra waved her back onto the low couch; Lynear too.

Cousin Isra sat down beside Alanine and wrapped her arms around her in a comforting gesture that was unexpected. "I don't know if we can find Namar," she said truthfully. "But for now, my concern is for you and Nijah and Lynear." She turned to Lynear. "A friend of mine will be coming to stay with you."

Lynear looked puzzled. "With me?"

"You will assume control of this estate for the foreseeable future," Cousin Isra told her. "I will be taking both Alanine and Nijah to El Manteria, and my sister and I will decide what to do next. It is clear that they are not safe here."

Isra's arm was still around Alanine, and strangely, it was the safest she had ever felt in her life, despite—or perhaps because of—Cousin Isra's affliction. Alanine knew that as long as she was with Isra, no one could harm her.

Funnily enough, she felt safer with Isra than she ever had with either of her parents; although, knowing one was a magi that stole faces, and the other was drugged and under his control, that made sense.

"What type of friend will be staying with me?" Lynear asked with caution, though both Alanine and Lynear knew the answer to that.

"A fellow Master... a man you will treat with respect. He is a learned scholar and warrior, and I can think of none better to keep you and this household safe," Isra said, and it was clear that there was no room for arguments. "Arch Master Hassim Bertoth."

Lynear's mouth dropped open for a fraction of a second. The Bertoth family was in the same tier as Alanine's, a step below the Imperial Family. She inclined her head and smoothed her skirts. "As you wish, Aunt."

Alanine could not tell if hearing that the man was a Bertoth had helped any, but the idea of treating a man with respect was an odd one. Though, Lynear had perked up when Isra had said the Master was a scholar; Lynear loved discussing history.

Isra gave Lynear an ironic smile and turned to Alanine. "Let us go tell Nijah of the adventure she has before her."

Alanine and Isra found twelve-year-old Nijah with her tutor, who was quickly dismissed.

Nijah had become skittish and clingy since Namar had been taken, only taking comfort from her nursemaid, the *hassana,* or Alanine. Nijah often crawled into Alanine's bed at night, and only fell asleep while Alanine stroked her long, black hair.

Alanine sat beside her now and took her hands. "I have some wonderful news," she said, trying to sound cheerful. "We are going to visit the Imperial City."

"Is it because the bad people took Namar? Are we going to get him back?" Nijah asked, her large, brown eyes wide with fright as she looked from Alanine to Isra and back again.

"Yes, child," Cousin Isra said, sitting on her other side. "We are leaving to protect you from the bad people. I cannot promise to get your brother back, but I do promise to try." She stroked Nijah's back softly. "Now, if you will go to your rooms and put together a special bag of the things that you love most, I will have your nurse gather some clothing and other things. Your sister and I have much to do before we leave in the morning."

Nijah turned to Cousin Isra and threw herself into the woman's arms.

Alanine saw tenderness on Isra's face, and reminded herself that Isra was a mother as well as a Master; she had two children of her own, though Alanine knew they had rarely been to Pannarius.

The love and compassion she saw in Isra's face made her wonder why so many thought those that could use the powers that she could were cursed. She knew that elsewhere in the world, few thought those called Masters of the Ithrimir were bad people.

She also wondered where this journey would end, and if they would get to meet Cousin Isra's children who lived on the Isles of the Ithrimir.

Once Nijah had been sent on her way, Isra turned to Alanine.

"I will do all that I can to get your brother back, but I fear for his life," she said with sincerity. "I do swear to you, whatever happens, I will have vengeance for the wrong done to our family, and I will see you and your sister safe. I can't say when or if you will be able to return to your home, but safety and vengeance... *that* I can promise you."

Alanine met the black gaze of the woman who was her kin and nodded. "I will ask no more than that. Vengeance for my brother, and safety for my sister."

They met Lynear in Alanine's study, and Master Isra drew up the papers that would effectively give Lynear complete control of River Keep until Alanine returned. Alanine signed them, and so did

Lynear and Isra: Lynear in acceptance of the burden, and Isra as a witness.

The *hassana* was called in, and Master Isra explained what was going to happen.

"I will come," the wizened old woman said.

Isra shook her head. "You will be needed here. Princess Lynear will need your help."

"*Hassanalan* can help Her Highness." *Hassanalan* was the assistant to the *hassana*, the one trained to succeed her. "She knows everything I know. I will come with the girls."

Isra looked to Alanine, who nodded.

"She can help care for Nijah. She loves and trusts Sevinc like a mother."

Isra turned to the older woman. "Do you have clothing that isn't your uniform?"

Sevinc nodded.

"Pack those. You will travel as a companion to the girls. We leave in the morning."

The *hassana* left the study, and Isra turned back to Alanine.

"And it is time that you go pack too. I am not sure when or if we return, or when we will reach a place where things could be sent to you."

Alanine pushed back tears and left the study, heading for her rooms.

Someone had already had a small travel trunk and a satchel delivered. She went through her rooms, packing her jewelry and the mementos that meant the most to her, as well as her clothing, tooth powder and brush, soap, oils, and her hair box, which had beads, a comb and brush, her spare hair wrap for sleeping, and everything else she would need when it was time to re-braid her hair.

She changed into a sleep shift and packed away her dresses, then she sat down at her dressing table and picked up the small vial of oil that she had left out. She would pack that and her other hair wrap in the satchel, which held clothing for the journey.

She poured a small amount of the liquid onto her fingertips and massaged it into her scalp between the braids. After, she wrapped the silk scarf around her braids, and once it was secured, she crossed the room and sank into the low bed.

She looked around the chamber that had been her mother's and then briefly hers before blowing out the candle.

CHAPTER 45

Lady Victoria Forrester-Coden, Ducessa 'ah Kilmerian Aboard the Wind Hawk, the Docks of White City: Caeldenon
2ⁿᵈ of Xavar

Tori had spent a good deal of time with Cressa at Rose Hall and grown very fond of her—especially as her relationship with Cressa's father became more serious, and Tori realized that, at some point, she would be a mother to the little girl.

Baerik and Tori had met with the parents of his late wife, Hira. Lord Renath Mellan and Lady Ceralaen, the *Marque and Marquessa ah* Fall Haven, had welcomed Tori with open arms. Baerik had apparently told his former in-laws of their handfasting soon after, so Tori had been less of a shock to them than she had been to everyone else.

They had agreed to the adoption with the traditional clause that they retain their places in Cressa's life and that Tori would do all she could to honor their daughter's memory.

While nominally done for form's sake, Tori found that her feelings for the young girl had rapidly grown, and in return, Cressa had already begun to cling to her. Tori was often requested to read stories, to come watch her and Jane in the practice yard, to listen to the two girls—who acted as if they had always been together—recite their lessons or discuss whatever the Masters had taught that day.

The Dowager employed a Master of the Yellow Mir, a teacher, as well as a Master of the White for healing, who also taught the girls about traditional medicine and botany. While they had been in White Castle, with eight children in residence, the combined strength of all the Masters employed by the High King and High Queen and the Dowager had been put to use.

The High King arguably employed the most Masters of a single house in Caeldenon, if not the world. His own brother, Lan, was an Arch Master of the Blue and Red, meaning he was a counselor and advisor, a master of law and politics, as well as a trained battle warrior. Jillian, of course, was a healer, and High Master Jaron Baz was a dual scholar and teacher.

The High King also employed High Master Geillis Kane, a Brown, to oversee the maintenance of the castle and such artifacts that had been made with the Gift, and Arch Master Greer, a Red who kept the High King's personal guard in shape.

Thanks to the Masters' wealth of knowledge and resources, the children of White Castle had a very well-rounded and expansive education.

Tori found herself wondering if they needed to do more along those lines for Cressa and Jane.

Perhaps hire a scholar?

Her fretting and worrying over every little aspect of Cressa's life was shocking. Tori had never been the maternal sort, but she found that she was excited and eager to help shape this child that she had grown to love so well.

But as much as Tori found herself missing Cressa as she stepped onto the *Wind Hawk* on her husband's arm, she was glad that Cressa would be here and safe.

Only this morning, a letter from Tori's father had arrived detailing her brother's recovery after the Usurper had had him strung up and lashed in the gardens of the Nursery Keep for trying to escape his false imprisonment. Father hadn't spared details.

It made Tori see red. She couldn't wait to see her family again, but more than that, she could not wait to see Garrett Morlette face the justice he deserved.

Tori had written to her parents to tell them she had news of a personal sort that she hoped to share when she arrived. She didn't go into detail; she didn't know how safe the mail was, and wasn't risking sensitive information falling into the wrong hands.

Baerik pulled Tori from her thoughts as he moved one hand to her back and took her hand with his other one to help her over the last step from the brow to the ship. Not that she needed help, but she had to admit that she liked being doted on by her husband.

As this was an official expedition, both Gavantar and Baerik were in military uniform, though both had suits with them as well. Instead of the ceremonial whites, which were also somewhere in their wardrobes, they wore the more practical dove gray and black with red trim. The fitted gray breeches, glossy knee-high black boots, and gray jacket that buttoned to the waist and flared from the hips over a black waistcoat were quite flattering—not that Tori was partial.

Both men wore their hair down to their shoulders, with the colored threads of their warriors' braids gleaming. Baerik's manservant Jorin had taught Tori how to braid the pinky-width section of hair and secure it with the first thread at the scalp before moving into the correct pattern and thickness of colors. It had to be done at least once a week, but more often if a certain person wasn't careful when brushing their hair. But Tori found she enjoyed the task.

Ahead of her, she watched the ship's captain, Charnderial Denall, greet Lenathaina and Gavantar as they boarded, and then he turned to Baerik and Tori, offering a bow that wasn't quite as deep as the one given to the Queen and First Prince, but still showed deference and respect.

"Welcome aboard, Your Grace," he said to Baerik before turning to Tori and taking her hand to kiss it formally, as he had done to Lena. "And to you, Your Grace."

Tori nearly blushed; she was still adjusting to the deferential treatment she now received everywhere she went. She had spent most of her life as the second daughter of a mid-tier lord, though a highly respected one, and then a short time as lady-in-waiting to a future High Queen, but being a *Ducessa* had jumped her status by several degrees.

Tori smiled. "Thank you, Captain Denall. I look forward to a smooth journey."

"Smoother than the one that brought you to these shores, Your Grace."

The battle at sea that had interrupted their journey from Lithonia to Caeldenon was no secret. Tori did hope that this crossing would be uneventful. They had enough chaos waiting for them on the other side.

Denall turned to a pair of cabin boys. "Please show Her Majesty and Her Grace to their cabins." He turned back to the Queen. "Your other ladies are already below decks, getting things sorted out."

"Thank you, Captain Denall," Lena said, inclining her head.

She took Tori's arm, and they followed the two lads, who were obviously eager for adventure, down the staircase that led to the state rooms, with Ellaemarhie at their heels.

They went to Lenathaina and Gavantar's suite first to see that Rachel and Fenora were in fact busy making the room into a temporary home, with the help of Sanders, Lena's maid.

Once Lena was divested of her cloak, she and Ellae went to find Master Tam, and Tori let one of the lads lead her down the corridor to the room she would share with Baerik.

After seeing that her maid Diason, who she'd acquired with her change of rank, was setting her things in order with the aid of Jorin, Baerik's manservant, Tori headed back to the deck so she could get a last view of White City to hold in her heart until they returned.

Naheame Salmeara Jinn was on deck doing the same. She was one of Gavantar's Gold Swords, and they had spent a lot of time training together in the past month. Tori enjoyed her company both on the training grounds and off. She was also sure that Baerik had asked Salmeara to keep an eye on Tori once they landed.

Tori didn't mind; she would be a good friend to have at her back.

Tori knew that Baerik was considering finally taking a *thane* just so he could make her take a *galvana*. He had made up his mind enough to bring along one of the *Mael'Hivar* that had served under him at Rose Hall for many years while he contemplated his choice.

"*Ducessa*." Salmeara inclined her head as Tori joined her, then went back to watching the bustle on the docks as the *Wind Hawk* prepared to cast off. "I have never left Caeldenon," she said after a long moment of silence.

"Not long ago, I had never left Lithonia," Tori replied, resting her arms on the rail. "And now we go to war to liberate the Lithonian people from oppression. A worthy reason for such a voyage, I think."

"Very worthy." Salmeara smiled at her and clapped her on the shoulder in a familiar gesture. "We will have to keep up your training on the voyage. Can't have you arriving to battle out of shape."

Tori returned her smile. "I wouldn't have it any other way."

CHAPTER 46

High Lady Angela Montgomery
Black Hall on the eastern shore of Lithonia
2ⁿᵈ of Xavar

Angela sat at Magne's desk and read the reports that had come in on the state of their army, something she never thought would come to be. Of course they kept a standing house guard, but an army? It had been almost two centuries since the House had abolished standing armies for a more limited house guard, while the king and government oversaw the Lithonian Army and Navy. Even the garrison at Harmon's Island were Lithonian soldiers; High Lord Harold Harmon served as a general, and was in command of those forces.

Angela took a break from reading, and stood, walking to the window. In the courtyard below, new recruits were drilling in formation while holding swords, where just days ago, they had held farm tools.

She hoped that they would be able to turn this group of young men into a battalion of soldiers that could stand their ground when being fired at.

Someone knocked on the study door, and Angela tiredly called, "Enter," before shaking off her fatigue.

It felt like a year had passed since she'd left Endomir, instead of three and a half months.

General Hall came in and bowed before setting a sheaf of papers on her desk. "The newest recruitment lists, Your Grace." His eyes moved down her body in a curious manner. "Are you aware that you are glowing?"

Angela followed his gaze to see a pale blue light pulsing in her pocket. She fished out the blue topaz Script Stone that she always carried with her, and commanded, "Send for Master Brian."

General Hall stepped out into the corridor and barked an order at the page waiting there; she could hear the boy running before the general closed the door. He looked at the Stone as if it might explode if not responded to in a timely manner.

Master Brian burst into the study a few minutes later in a panic, as though he thought someone was dying, and found the two of them staring at the topaz and then him expectantly.

"The Queen has the mate to this Stone," Angela said anxiously.

The Master hurriedly gathered supplies and sat down in the seat Angela had vacated moments before, and responded through the Stone.

She stood behind him and watched as the message came through:

HL AM,

Have set sail. Expect in Seathor around 1 Minn. Bring with me sixty warriors with supplies and horses. Stand ready and gather who you trust to our cause. Messenger should be with you soon.

QLMC

Angela's heart nearly stopped as she read the words, and then quickly penned a missive to send back:

QLMC,

We stand ready. Will await messenger. Maker Save the One True Queen.

HL AM

Master Brian sent the message through and then looked up at Angela. "Does that mean what I think it means?"

"Horses? They are bringing their own bloody *horses*?" General Hall muttered.

202

"It does," Angela said, feeling hope blossom. "We need to contact High Lady Bennings to warn her, and speed up our own preparations." She turned to look out the window again. "We need to be ready to march in fifteen days."

"As you command, Your Grace," General Hall said, standing. "I will whip them into shape in no time."

Master Brian went back to his office to retrieve the Stone linked to Beth's, and Angela pocketed the blue topaz once more. She then penned her friend a note, relaying what the Queen had said and adding that they would be marching in fifteen days.

When Master Brian came back, he held a green jasper in his hand. Angela handed him the sheet of parchment, which she had already encoded, and he sent the signal that they had a message.

Ten minutes passed before they got the reply that Beth's Master was ready to receive. He transmitted the message, and they waited again.

The reply was short and not encoded:

Thank the Maker.

CHAPTER 47

Samuel Thane
Clearwater Place and Castle Endomir, Endomir: Lithonia
3ʳᵈ of Xavar

The ciphers were finally starting to make sense.

Mistress Vera had given Samuel a pile of old letters, some outdated by a decade. They were all in ciphers, and she had told him to break them.

Not an easy task.

At first, the missives, which looked like nothing more than random jumbles of letters, did not make sense; each letter had a different code. But with practice and a few tips from Mistress Vera, Samuel was beginning to get the knack of finding different cipher groups that would help break down the message as a whole.

Words like *the, and, for,* and *was* were common, as well as letter groupings like *th, sh, ch, ing.* Once the cipher for those groupings was broken, it was a matter of time before the rest was cracked as well.

Samuel's first one took three days to break, but now he could get at least one done in a day. Mistress Vera said he had the mind and talent for code breaking.

He checked the mantel clock and saw that it was past time for him to head to the castle to meet Marie. Mistress Vera had written out an order for the woman to extricate herself from the castle with haste; Samuel didn't think she would.

He filed all his papers into the desk in the small office that he had been given, and locked the drawers before heading up to his room to quickly freshen up. Showing up to the castle covered in ink stains and looking rumpled from a day of mind-breaking decoding wouldn't do. He had to look like a man eager to see his sweetheart.

The walk to the castle was uneventful, though traffic was unusually light, owing to the fact that no one wanted to be there unless they had to.

Just a year ago, people would have strolled up to walk in the public gardens, or catch a glimpse of Princess Lenathaina.

My, how times have changed.

Samuel went to the back of the castle and waited in line with three others who were there to see family members or sweethearts that worked within, but before it was his turn, Marie walked out the gate and took his arm.

They strolled across the lawn arm in arm with their heads together.

"Are you doing alright?" Samuel asked once they were far enough away that their voices wouldn't carry.

"Bloody oppressive in there," Maria said, leaning into him. "The King is getting paranoid. Anyone who turns in their notice is suspected of working for someone who's against him. A poor chambermaid got interrogated by his goons when she said she was leaving to tend her elderly grandmother. It wasn't until they went to her grandmother's house to prove she had one that they let her go."

Samuel's stomach dropped. "Mistress Vera has ordered you to leave this posting."

Marie looked up at him, her dark green eyes tired. "I have to play this one to the end, whatever that is. To leave now would bring attention to all of us."

Samuel stopped walking and pulled her into his arms. "I could marry you," he offered.

Jack would understand... though the rumor mill would have an interesting time chewing that one over.

"It would still draw too much attention to our employer," Marie said, shaking her head.

"Keep your head low, friend," Samuel said, hugging her tightly.

"As low as I can," Marie agreed before pulling away. "Now... Eddening has had his people in the archives a lot lately. I don't know why. The Nursery Keep is restless, and the guard has been doubled there."

They continued walking, heads bent together. From a distance, they would look like lovers whispering sweet nothings to one another.

"Eddening in the archives makes me worry. I wonder what he is up to?" he mused aloud. "Why do you think the guard has been doubled?"

"The young people are getting brash." Marie snorted. "Also, I fear there will be some hasty weddings."

"Ah. Well… that will be interesting. Any alliances we should be concerned about?"

Nothing like a deflowered noblewoman to flare tempers and get blood running hot.

"Andrew Eddening and Jean Lorvette," Marie said with a sigh. "And Bernice Vectors and David Proudmourn."

"Oh hell."

Samuel wished he had a stiff drink. Both Bernice and David were married—and not to one another—and Jean Lorvette, cousin to Garrett, was betrothed to a Cromby.

"Well, we have bigger problems than cuckholds to deal with," Samuel said, "but I will keep Mistress Vera updated. Ready to head back?"

"No. Let's walk a bit longer. I need the time away." Marie smiled tiredly at Samuel. "Update me on your news."

They walked for another hour as he told her about Jack and losing his post, about Mistress Vera and his new training.

Samuel and Marie had flirted a lot over the years, but had never acted on anything. They were friends, good friends, and he was glad for it.

"I want to visit Caeldenon someday," Marie said wistfully. "It sounds so…"

"Accepting?" Samuel finished for her.

She nodded and sighed.

They turned back by unspoken agreement, and Samuel left her at the servants' gate, wishing there were a way to pull her away without drawing the attention of dangerous people.

CHAPTER 48

High Lord Marc Eddening
Sounton House, the City of Endomir: Lithonia
5th of Xavar

In the two weeks since Parker had made his confession, Marc had raked him over the coals and gotten all the details of his plot to put Morlette on the throne. Once he had all he needed from Parker, he called in Blake Rendon.

He had both men by the balls. Forgery, treason… the deaths of Benjamin Bennings and Derek Montgomery could be put on them as well. Their only hope of avoiding execution was seeing Marc on the throne. He would keep their nasty secret if he could, and if he couldn't, he would find a way to pardon them.

Parker stood by the window while Blake Rendon sat in the corner, sullenly nursing a whiskey, while Marc reviewed the figures the High Lord had brought him. The troops Rendon could personally raise: those vassals he thought he could bring to Marc's side, and what he thought they could raise. Food stuffs, weapons, and other supplies…

Marc looked at Rendon over the rim of his spectacles. "You have three mills on your estate by Two Rivers, don't you?"

Rendon grimaced and nodded. "Aye, what of it?"

Marc raised an eyebrow and looked down at the sheet of paper in front of him.

"I might be able to get more grain," Rendon said, as if someone was pulling his yellowed teeth. The last weeks had aged him; at seventy, he was one of the oldest high lords, and he looked it today. "But I can't strip my estates or the farms around them."

Marc nodded. "Why don't you see what more can be done, then? I don't want your people to suffer, but we all must tighten our belts. For the greater good."

Parker sat down. "Your brother will have command?"

"Yes," Marc replied, leaning back in his chair. "Fitting for the brother of the future king to have command in the field, don't you think?"

"Of course," Parker said hastily. "And we are honored that our men will be the first to join the forces of the true King."

"Quite honored, Your Majesty," Rendon said, knocking back the rest of his drink.

Marc surveyed them both. "I won't use that title until I am accepted by the House of Lords. The fact that I will be liberating the city from the usurping tyrant Morlette should go a long way to securing votes."

"Some will be hard to sway," Rendon said, looking uncomfortable. "My nieces are neck-deep in it. Women meddling in politics always brings trouble," he grumbled.

"Montgomery, Bennings, Collins, and their ilk are all trouble," Marc scoffed, drumming his fingers on the desk. Angela Montgomery and Beth Bennings were the daughters of Rendon's younger brothers. "But if we can sway enough of the rest, it won't matter."

It would only take a two-thirds majority to ratify changing the succession. If Marc were the one to free Endomir, if he were the savior of children and parents, well… that would be something. Having an army outside the city wouldn't hurt, either.

He had other tricks up his sleeve—ones that neither of the men in the room knew about.

"I know you have both already sent word to your own estates, and I received confirmation from my brother a few days ago. He has already begun his muster, they march in two days."

Rendon and Parker nodded, looking only mildly troubled.

Parker said, "My brother is doing the same."

"And my younger son," Rendon replied, pouring them all another round of drinks. He held his glass up. "To a successful campaign."

They all drank, and then Marc said to Parker, "I heard your niece has been stepping out with the Usurper."

"Ellen, my brother's wife, thinks it is best to have someone close to him. Janna says the King has been *sad*." Parker snorted. "I think Ellen wants to be on his good side just in case the Usurper manages to take control of the country."

"Do you think Janna would say more to you?" Marc asked.

"She might. My brother Michael hasn't told Ellen what is going on—the woman could never keep her mouth shut," Parker shook his head. "But the girl does seem to like him."

"After a crown, is she?" Marc asked.

Parker shrugged and poured himself another drink.

CHAPTER 49

Dowager Queen Mellina Morthan
Trahelion Manor, Providence of Denon: Caeldenon
6ᵗʰ of Xavar

Mellina was in the sitting room of the apartment that had been given to her during her stay with the Dowager High Queen. She was watched everywhere but her bedchamber, but at least in there, she could escape that child that looked more like her husband than any of the children she had ever borne him. Even now, with the windows open, she could hear Jane playing with the Dowager's granddaughter and another girl.

Lady Seryl Lyss was sitting with Mellina while Sara took her daily walk. Seryl was one of the young women sent to the Dowager for seasoning, had been assigned as Mellina's lady-in-waiting, along with Lady Sara.

Apparently, for those young members of royal and noble families who did not choose to serve in the Caeldenon army or in the *Mael'Hivar,* it was common for them to spend between two and ten years fostering in homes of other nobility or royalty—usually in another providence than the one they had been born in.

Often, they spent two or three years with one family, and then moved on to another. This built ties of family and friendship outside their own homes and showed them how other families lived. It also introduced them to eligible young people.

That wasn't the only difference Mellina had seen in Caeldenon. She was still shocked that the children of nobility were allowed the option to pledge their life to service—and more still, that relationships of the same sex were seen as commonplace.

A man or woman might have a duty to see their family line move forward, but premarital relations with a member of the same sex were seen as normal and post-marital ones were viewed in the same light, so long as those participating were respectful of their spouse. The Dowager had, in her own household, a married older couple serving as her ladies!

As long as heirs to a title were plentiful, people didn't care if a lady or a man chose a life partner.

It made Mellina's head spin... and it made her jealous of their freedom.

Before Charles had died, needlework had always kept her hands busy, because Maker forbid she have an opinion on anything that could be considered a man's territory. She returned to that occupation, missing the breakfasts she had shared with Magne and Tam, discussing politics and the running of the country.

They had cared for her thoughts and opinions like Mellina was an intelligent person with common sense and a brain. But now, here she was, sewing.

A useless woman who's a burden and a liability.

That was how the Dowager High Queen found Mellina: sitting in the late afternoon light, embroidering the thistle blossoms that Lenathaina seemed so fond of these days.

Mellina didn't bother standing when the Dowager entered; they were equals, despite the fact that Mellina was a prisoner in all but name.

But she was a formidable woman, this Dowager. It took all of Mellina's resolve to stay seated when she arched an eyebrow.

The old woman dismissed Seryl and took up her vacated seat. "Do you plan on ever leaving this suite for more than meals?" she asked, placing her hands on the arms of the chair in a way that made it seem a throne.

"I see no reason," Mellina said tartly, realizing she sounded petulant.

"You have every reason. Stop acting like a child," the Dowager said.

"You have no idea what I have been through! You know nothing about my life," Mellina said indignantly.

"What is it that I don't know, my dear?" Arrysanna asked. "You came to the throne young and didn't have any power? I was fifteen the day I wed a high king, and sixteen when I started churning out his babes—seven of them. He was seventeen years my senior with one wife in the grave, and didn't give a fig about me. My mother-in-law was a tyrant to boot. You have lost children? I have laid three in the ground myself. I bore four more and sent one of them to the Ithrimir, same as you sent your lad. Your husband had affairs? I raised the child of my husband's second wife as my own and thanked her for taking him off my hands. Mule-brained, stubborn man that he was, she could handle him, and I could not. You killed your son? Well… you have me there."

She pointed her folded fan at Mellina, who could not help but shrink back a little. "But from what I have heard, he should have been drowned as a pup, and the world would have been better for it. Pity he was not, but you did right in the end. A tricky bit that he was a sitting king, but there you have it.

"Now, if you are ready to stop sulking like a girl and act like the woman you are, I am sure that between the two of us and that capable girl you raised, we can figure out a way to keep that pretty head attached to that slim neck of yours."

Mellina felt like she had been hit by a ton of bricks; she could not speak, could not move.

The Dowager Queen rose and leaned down to pat her hand. "Just think on that. When you are ready to be a big girl, come find me."

CHAPTER 50

Thomas Barrow, Second Footman
Black Hall on the eastern shore of Lithonia
7ᵗʰ of Xavar

Before that upstart bastard stole the throne from Queen Lenathaina, Tom had never been farther from his home city of Brayman than Endomir. Sure, the capital was on the opposite side of the country, but it was one thing to take a train, and a whole other to get on a ship and go to a place where women wore trousers and swords, and the food was strangely spiced.

Not that Tom minded. It was good food… even if it cleaned his innards clear out.

Either way, he was glad to be home. As much as he wanted to see his Mam and Da as soon as he got off the train, he hightailed it to Black Hall. He had to see the High Lady with all haste and deliver his package to her.

Tom was shocked, though he ought not have been, to see guards lining the walls, and three times the normal amount at the gate, both for the city and the Hall. What was both more shocking—and encouraging—were the soldiers camped outside the city in rows of orderly tents.

House Montgomery was mustering for war.

As soon as Tom told the guard who he was, he was immediately taken to the High Lord's study, where the High Lady, Master Brian, and General Hall were in conference.

Tom bowed to the High Lady, who was quite the beauty, even if she was old enough to be his Mam. Her chestnut hair gleamed in the light from the window, and her creamy skin was as smooth as a girl's.

It ain't a crime to look, after all; everyone does, even though we all know she and His Grace was made for one another.

214

"Thomas," the High Lady said. "It is good to have you home." She gestured for him to take a seat next to Master Brian.

Him, Tom Barrow, sit in her ladyship's presence?

Never!

But the look she gave him wasn't one to argue with, so he gingerly sat down on the edge of the upholstered chair and waited.

"I know that your errand was a success," the High Lady began, "as Her Majesty has been in contact via the Script Stone you delivered to her."

Tom bobbed his head. "She was right queenly, Your Grace. She remembered me serving her, a-and my name too," he stammered, feeling overwhelmed at the attention. "Housed me in her own apartments the two nights I stayed there like I was some great lord. I even met the High King and Queen!"

The High Lady smiled at him fondly. "Her Majesty is quite special, isn't she?"

Tom nodded his head in agreement. "She has your ring on for safekeeping," he said, "and I know she is doing all she can to get here and help us and all."

He pulled out the package and handed it to the High Lady. "She said to give this to you directly."

The High Lady opened the package. It contained three folded and sealed sheets of parchment and a thin, wooden box. The High Lady opened the box, and with trembling hands, pulled out a medal.

"Maker preserve me," she whispered, and then laid the medal reverently aside and shuffled through the letters. "Two for Her Grace, High Lady Beth Bennings, two for me."

Tom could see that one was sealed in a sapphire and gold wax, and another in lavender.

The High Lady looked up at him, "You have done a great service for us, Thomas, but your duties aren't over yet. Go home and see your Mam and Da, and then come back. I will be sending you with my girls to stay with my sister to the south."

Knowing a dismissal when he heard one, Tom nodded and stood, bowing before he left the room.

CHAPTER 51

High Lady Angela Montgomery
Black Hall on the eastern shore of Lithonia
7th of Xavar

When Thomas left the room, Angela opened the letter sealed with lavender wax and read it. Lenathaina apologized for the burden she was putting on Angela and went on to explain that there were few outside of Endomir that she trusted. She promised to reward Angela for her faithful service and thanked her for her work on behalf of the Crown and Lithonia.

Angela handed the letter over to Master Brian and General Hall before opening the second letter, this one sealed in a swirling blue and gold that was used by the monarch of House Morthan.

She must have had it made specially for Royal correspondence.

The contents were written in very formal language, and highlighted the reason she had sent the medal that was last worn by Prince Matthew Morthan, Marshal General of the Lithonian Army, Lord Protector of the Realm.

By Order of Her Majesty, Queen Lenathaina Morthan
Coden of Lithonia:

High Lady Angela Rendon Montgomery is hereby instated as temporary Marshal General of the Lithonian Army and Lady Protector of the Realm.

This Order is in effect from the 3rd of Rison. The Marshal General shall have the authority to gather the men, supplies, and horses owed to the rightful Ruler of Lithonia in times of war on behalf of her Majesty Queen Lenathaina.

Any refusing to honor their pledges of support or to follow the Marshal General will be seen as traitors.
Lenathaina Morthan Coden, Queen of Lithonia, First Princess of Caeldenon

Angela handed the second piece of parchment to Master Brian and walked over to Magne's sideboard to pour herself a stiff glass of his special whiskey. By the time she had finished the task, Master Brian had read the parchment, handed it to General Hall, and was heading to pour himself and the other man a drink.

General Hall said, "I'll be damned."

He looked to be reading it a second time, and once he had finished, he put the parchment carefully on the desk, and rose to take the drink Master Brian had poured for him.

"If you don't mind me saying, Your Grace, the young Queen has some big balls."

Angela nearly spit her whiskey, but managed to choke it down. The slight burn and the sweetness from the cherrywood casks were enough to bring her back to herself.

"Huge ones, you have no idea," she managed.

"Any guesses as to what she wrote High Lady Bennings?" Master Brian asked.

"I can't be sure, so I won't speculate," Angela said, moving back to the desk. "She won't have heard about High Lord Bennings when she sent these." She took another swallow to force the rising tears back. "But she knew that both he and my husband were trapped in Endomir, and that High Lady Bennings would have been put in control of her husband's house, as I have been."

General Hall looked down at the parchment and touched it reverently with one finger. "I don't suppose this changes our plans much… just gives you more authority."

"Authority many will resent," Angela countered.

"Your Grace," General Hall said. "Fact is, *most* of the heads of houses are locked in Endomir. Out here, it is women and male relations running the show. You are a senior member of court, and the wife of the man who was named regent. You have a strong force of will. Use it."

"And, Your Grace," Master Brian added with a note of sympathy. "Word of what happened to your son has spread. I think you will find many of the women are with you, will follow you."

"Not just them. I am not one of those who thinks a woman doesn't have anything between her ears but sewing notions and how to care for bairns." General Hall knocked back his drink. "You can do this, and you'll have us behind you."

He clapped the slight Master on the back, almost knocking him over, and Master Brian nodded his agreement.

Angela surveyed them: her private army. They might not be much to look at, but she knew she couldn't find more loyal or braver men to stand at her side.

She cleared her throat and pushed her emotions aside. "Let's get started then."

CHAPTER 52

The Goddess Hestia, the Mystic of Hathor
The Temple of Ganna: Hathor
10th of Xavar

Hestia left the ceremonial chamber where High Priestess Razi would spend the night surrounded by three of her sisters, who would pray over the seed that had been planted inside her. The man, Consort Tarek, would be taken to the ritual bathing chambers to be cleaned from his sacraments.

She changed out of her robes and into a sleep shift and dressing gown of scarlet before removing the kohl that rimmed her black eyes. She gazed at her reflection. Her ebony skin was still as smooth as it had been a hundred years ago, and her form was still trim despite birthing six babes. But her features were too sharp to be called beautiful, and her bald head only highlighted the sharp edges.

A sparse meal of cheese, figs, and flatbread awaited Hestia in her chambers, along with a warm, spiced wine. She lounged on the low couch as her youngest daughter, an acolyte, served her meal.

She dismissed Nadia with a sharp word; even though the girl was Hestia's favorite child, she could not show it. Nadia had to fight for her place as Hestia's heir.

Kaleck, Hestia's favorite of the Consortium, and who served her personally, came in once Nadia was gone and lounged next to Hestia, putting his head in her lap to be petted and fed scraps of food.

Hestia had checked the records and knew that of her six children, he had fathered four, and all of those had been Blessed by the goddess.

"How was the ceremony?" he asked.

Hestia took a sip of her wine, contemplating. "The omens seemed favorable when I reviewed their stars, but he had trouble performing."

It had been Tarek's first time taking part in the Ritual of Joining, and some men did not like performing the sacrament in front of Hestia and the other priestesses. Other men seemed to revel in it... which honestly made it more enjoyable to watch. No one wanted a stallion that could not get the job done.

Kaleck rubbed his face against Hestia's stomach. "It isn't easy for some, but it is always an honor to be of service."

Hestia stroked his dark hair and took another bite of cheese.

A gentle knock interrupted them, and once she had called, "Enter," another member of the Consortium came into the room, bowing to press his forehead to the ground three times before he finally approached her with a scroll of parchment.

Hestia took the scroll and read the message:

Your Divinity,

The Raven should be almost halfway to the Promised Land. The Dove remains here but has been moved to a new cage. Also here is the aunt of the Raven, who is now with the Dove.
The Raven will land at Seathor.

Awaiting instructions.
Servant Jillian Prather

Hestia tossed the scroll on the table and said to the Consort, "Tell her to kill the Dove and the aunt."

She hoped that Jillian would be more successful in her post than Jardin had been. He had failed her three times.

He deserved whatever death the blasphemer gave him.

The Consort bowed again and left Hestia alone with Kaleck.

She took a handful of his hair and brought his head up so she could kiss him.

Being the Goddess had its rewards at times; she had taken Kaleck as her own twenty years ago, and he hadn't once complained. Nor had she.

CHAPTER 53

Mael'Hivar Thane Prince Galwyn Tearhall
Aboard the Wind Hawk: Indayon Sea
12ᵗʰ of Xavar

Galwyn, Gavantar, and Baerik were sitting at the dining table in the main cabin that had been allotted to Baerik and his wife. Lena had taken over the same space in her and Gavantar's room, doing her queenly things.

They had various maps of Lithonia, both ones that showed the whole country and smaller ones that only had certain sections. They had, by luck, found a Master Scholar in White City that had a passion for map making. He had set his apprentices to making copies and they had been ready the day before they set sail. One even detailed the Lithonian railways, which was what Baerik and Gavantar were currently focused on.

"If we can take control of the railway from Seathor to here…" Baerik pointed at what looked like open country right after the river, close to the Endomir basin. "Do you remember if this was open, or farmland?" He looked at both, waiting for an answer.

"Open, I think. Lena would know better," Gavantar said. "I want to say it was open for a few miles off the railway but eventually turned into an orchard."

Galwyn nodded his agreement, and Baerik continued.

"It would be a good staging area. Build some fortifications and put whatever army we have there before marching on the city. If we can maintain control of the trains, we would have a steady supply line."

"Who lives here?" Galwyn asked, pointing at two keeps near the railway line.

Gavantar squinted to read the fine print above each black triangle. "Greenbelt, seat of Lord Reynolds, and Nain's Hold, seat of

Lord Collins." He looked up with a grin. "We would have to ask Lenathaina about Reynolds, but Collins is her great-uncle, and she is his favorite niece."

"That will be helpful," Baerik said cheerfully.

He was cheerful a lot lately, but Galwyn had long ago learned that a man with a warm bed and a woman or man whose company he enjoyed was often cheerful.

"What will be helpful?" a composed voice asked from the doorway.

They had been so absorbed that they had not heard it open. Lena stood flanked by Victoria, Fenora, Rachel, and Ellae.

The way the five of them traveled in a pack reminded Galwyn of the pictures of lionesses in Pannarius, stalking prey.

The men hastily stood, and Lena crossed the cabin and kissed Gavantar on the cheek before bending down to look at the maps.

She picked up a pencil and began circling some of the castles. "Montgomery, Bennings, Harmon and all their allies are with us. So is my Uncle Collins," she said. "I think there are others who haven't been able to communicate but will rally when we land."

Baerik studied the map and nodded, thoughtful. "At the very least, we will have a sound hold of the southeast when we land, and a base of operations."

Lena nodded. "I am not yet sure where High Lord Eddening stands in all of this. If he is on our side, we should have a smooth progress to Endomir."

"And if he isn't?" Gavantar asked.

Lena pointed to a place on the map that Galwyn thought to be a day and a half by train to Endomir. "He can cut us off here."

Baerik turned his gaze back to the map and was quiet for a long moment. "Not much more we can do until we get more information."

Lena inclined her head in agreement. "I hope to have more for you soon."

She leaned down again and circled a castle labeled *Hardcastle*, three times. It had a river to the north and west, and a large city to the south and east.

"This is Hardcastle, the former capital, until my ancestor married the Ryne heir."

Galwyn remembered seeing an act of a play depicting this, before Gavantar and Lena had married.

"The Royal Archives are duplicated there, and I think they would be receptive to me," Lena said. "It could be a base of operations."

Baerik surveyed the map. "It would put us in a good position. We would only be a week's march from most areas of the country."

"Is it well-fortified?" Gavantar asked.

Lena inclined her head. "Extremely. Hardcastle has more than a few tricks up her sleeve."

"Well, then," Baerik replied. "Hardcastle it is."

CHAPTER 54

King Garrett Morlette Morthan
The City of Endomir and Castle Endomir, Endomir:
Lithonia
14ᵗʰ of Xavar

Garrett walked out of the temple, dressed in a pale gray suit with a matching cravat and white silk shirt. His brown curls had been tamed into submission that morning with a gum solution, as Murphy didn't think his wild curls looked kingly.

He had chosen Lady Janna Parker to accompany him to the temple for the commemoration ceremony of the Battle of Two Rivers, which had been the last battle of the Ryne Civil War. Janna was dressed in an elegant, dark gray, silk day dress with fitted sleeves trimmed with pale gray lace, and a matching shawl.

She had joined him on a few public outings recently. Garrett hoped that High Lord Parker would entertain a match; if he bound their houses together, the High Lord might be more willing to help Garrett.

He waved at the crowds; some people waved back, but most stared sullenly at him.

It will take time, but they will adjust to him.

He had recently had the castle make a large delivery of food and clothing to the local poorhouse to show what a kind and benevolent ruler he would be.

He helped Janna and her maid, who had come as their chaperone, into the carriage before climbing in himself. He rapped the top, and they set off.

"Did you bring things to the castle to change for the feast or did you plan to return home?" Garrett asked Janna. Her company had been one of the few things to bring him out of his melancholy after Brian's death.

"I brought things with me, Your Majesty," Janna said with a small smile. "Perhaps we could go for a walk in the gardens?"

"They aren't much to look at this time of the year. Everything is dead or dormant," Garrett said, looking her over.

She was a pretty thing, with brunette hair and blue eyes, and she carried herself well. She would make a good Queen, and the pair of them would make lovely children. If he could marry her and get her with child, the nobility might be more inclined to confirm him.

"Perhaps tea in the Royal residence?" he suggested.

Her maid, Evans, coughed politely.

"With your chaperone, of course," Garrett amended, smiling at the woman.

"Perhaps just the two of us," Janna said coyly. "If we leave the door open, it would be quite proper."

Garrett returned her smile, and their talk turned to the city and the rumors that Granger Place Theater would be opening again soon.

Back at the castle, the pair enjoyed tea in the sitting room that Garrett had occupied with Mellina and Tam not long ago. He looked forward to making new, happier memories here, and in other rooms that still held the ghosts of his past life.

Janna had just left to go to the apartment she used when staying at the castle when Murphy entered, his black hair in disarray and his brown eyes wide with shock.

"What is it, man?" Garrett asked, coming to his feet.

Murphy thrust a note into his hand. "Urgent messenger from Jasper's Keep," he panted.

Garret opened the letter hastily and began reading.

Your Majesty,

I have just received an urgent message from Lord Andrew Collins at Nain's Hold. An armed body of men is making for Endomir at a fast clip. They should arrive at nightfall. Deliver instructions with all haste.

Lord Martin Jasper
You know my damned titles

Garrett handed it to Murphy, who was still panting from his run.
The man might want to consider some regular exercise.

When Murphy finished reading, he handed the note back. "The messenger told me."

"What do we do?" Garrett demanded.

Murphy gave him an incredulous look. "You're the one who was taught about armies and ruling. What do you think? We close the damn gates."

"Right," Garrett said, not caring that Murphy hadn't used his title. "Send the order back with the messenger."

Murphy left to see to the order, and Garrett headed for his rooms to change for the feast.

He had to keep up appearances.

CHAPTER 55

Samuel Thane
Clearwater Place, City of Endomir: Lithonia
15th of Xavar

Jack had taken to spending his days off at Clearwater Place. Mistress Vera had interrogated him, quite alone, and explained their mission, and Jack was on board. He wouldn't betray secrets about Caeldenon, but anything that could help the cause of the Queen, he would pass on.

Since that conversation, he'd been splitting his time. If he wasn't with Vera, getting tutored on being a spy, he was with Samuel learning how to break codes and ciphers.

He came in early that morning, blond hair windblown. He wore a brown suit of decent cut but second-rate fabric—the ambassador paid well, but Jack tended to spend his money unwisely. He had a mug of tea in hand for both himself and Sam; Loren, the cook, had obviously decided Jack needed to warm up a bit.

Loren had taken to Jack like a mother hen, as most cooks seemed to. Tall and lanky, Jack was one of those people that always looked like he needed feeding up. He got plenty of that here and from the ambassador's cook, Denalla.

Jack kissed the top of Samuel's head. "Do you think we could go speak to Mistress Vera? There is something I overheard as I was taking His Excellency his brandy last night."

"Sure," Samuel said, locking his papers away.

They left his small office and went down the hall to Mistress Vera's. Samuel knocked and waited for her terse call of, "Enter," before opening the door.

Mistress Vera looked up from her desk and surveyed the pair of them. She wore a gray day dress, and her dark reddish hair was piled on her head—she was in mourning for High Lord Bennings, though none of them acknowledged that aloud.

"What do you want?" she asked. It looked as if she had been crying. Again.

"Jack overheard something, Mistress, and thought you might be interested."

Samuel tried not to let sympathy show on his face or in his voice. He almost succeeded, but she still shot him a look. She didn't like to talk about Bennings.

"What is it, Jack?" she asked, motioning for the pair of them to sit.

A chest sat on her desk, open. Samuel had seen one of the Bennings' guards enter through the front door early that morning, and the man had been at the servants' table when Samuel had gone to get a basket of rolls.

"When I took brandy to His Excellency and Master Jearn last night, I overheard the pair of them speaking," Jack said.

Vera sat up.

"Her Majesty, Queen Lenathaina, is on her way to Lithonia. The ambassador and the Master have been told to be ready to aid her if she takes the city, but not to intervene until she does."

A slow smile spread across Vera's face. "Excellent."

Before any of them could speak further, another knock interrupted them.

"Yes, what is it?" Vera said impatiently.

Mallard, the butler, entered with a small, silver tray bearing a note. "This was delivered by one of Lord Samuel Collins' men, Mistress. He left, saying no reply was needed."

Vera took the note and hastily opened it. She read its contents and then dropped the parchment into the hearth, which was already well ablaze.

The late autumn chill had taken hold of Endomir. Most mornings, there was a light sheet of ice over any liquid surface, and hearths burned from morning to night, with the fires only banked when all were abed.

"A force marches on Endomir," Vera said, looking up at them. "With the standards of High Lords Eddening, Parker, and Rendon."

"We are truly at war, then." Samuel felt as if he had been punched in the gut.

"We have been since the Usurper stole the throne." Vera turned to Jack. "I need you to go back to the ambassador."

She bent down and unlocked one of the drawers and began rummaging through it. She pulled out a letter and handed it to him.

It was open, so Samuel leaned over Jack's shoulder to read it.

Jaeryn Lyss, Marque ah Rollan

The person in possession of this letter is my trusted agent and friend. If she has this letter delivered to you, then she is in need of aid or has information that you need. Please meet with her and hear what she has to say. All that she does is in service to me and my crown.

Queen Lenathaina Morthan Coden
First Princess of Caeldenon

Samuel let out a low whistle.

Jack looked up the mistress. "Where do I tell him I got this from, Mistress Vera?"

"Me. Tell him to come visit me. Most people, if not all, will assume he has come for carnal reasons. I know his wife went back with the High King's party to tend to family matters."

Vera waved a hand when it looked like Jack would ask how she knew such a thing; she had a way of finding things out. "Just tell him to come."

Jack took the letter and tucked it into his pocket. Then he stood and gave Mistress Vera a small bow and let himself out.

*****

Two hours later, Jaeryn Lyss, *Marque ah* Rollan and ambassador to High King Gavan Coden of Caeldenon, was escorted into the main drawing room by Mallard.

Mistress Vera rose and offered her hand, which the *Marque* took and bowed over as if she were a great lady. Master Jearn, who had accompanied him, followed suit. Rollan wore a gray military uniform of fitted breeches, a knee-length jacket that had slits from waist to knee on both sides, and the Master, dark blue tunic and trousers.

Jack had hidden himself in the kitchens, but Mistress Vera had invited Samuel to stay with her. The ambassador had given Samuel a curious look before taking the offered seat.

"I wondered how Jack had become acquainted with you. All the lad would say is that you had information that I needed to hear," Rollan said, looking at Samuel. "And I can see that you have landed on your feet, Samuel... I am glad to see it. Jack assured me you were okay but wouldn't say much more."

Samuel gave a small bow of the head. "I have worked with Mistress Vera for many years. She made sure I had a place to stay and work to occupy me."

Rollan turned his gaze on Vera. "Very kind of you, Mistress Martique."

"Samuel has always done good work for me," Mistress Vera said. "But I did not invite you here to discuss Samuel."

Rollan pulled the letter from his pocket and returned it to her. "Are you in need of aid, or do you have information for me?"

"Information," Mistress Vera said. "An army is marching toward Endomir with men from the Houses of Eddening, Parker, and Rendon. If you have a way of getting this information to the Queen..."

Rollan looked at Master Jearn, who nodded.

"A roundabout way," the ambassador admitted. "It may take a bit."

Mistress Vera said, "I have a roundabout way as well. More than informing the Queen, I wanted you to be aware so you could prepare your home."

"You have my thanks, Mistress Martique. If I can be of service to you, let me know," Rollan replied.

"Have you had any word of the Queen?" she asked.

Rollan hesitated. "She is on her way to Seathor with the First Prince, her ladies, the *Duc 'ah* Kilmerian, his wife, and a force of sixty *Mael'Hivar.*"

Samuel didn't know who the *Duc* was, though he knew that *ducs* ranked higher than *marques*, but it all sounded impressive.

Mistress Vera inclined her head in her thanks; it was more than Jack had been able to tell them, and a sign of trust from Rollan. "The *Duc 'ah* Kilmerian would be the half-brother of the High King?"

That was news to Samuel, but he didn't know much about the Caeldenon court.

"Yes, son of the late High King's second wife, and a well-respected general in his own right," Rollan said, "He runs the house of the Dowager High Queen Arrysanna Coden and rarely leaves her side. That he comes with Queen Lenathaina says that the Royal Family is taking this seriously."

Samuel could see Mistress Vera mentally filing all this information away.

"Can you tell me how you know of this force?" Rollan asked, leaning forward.

Mistress Vera hesitated and then said, "Someone who is related to me sent word. I cannot tell you who, but I trust them. With my life."

Rollan watched her for a moment; Vera let her expression remain as open as possible. Eventually, he leaned back, and she smiled.

"It seems like we are working on the same side. Shall we work together, then?" he proposed.

Mistress Vera smiled. "We shall."

She offered her hand, and he took it.

CHAPTER 56

Kenleigh Atona
Trahelion Manor, Providence of Denon: Caeldenon
17th of Xavar

The Dowager High Queen had a soft spot for people in pain. Kenleigh had often found that people who hardly knew her could open up and share their deepest secrets and darkest fears and hurts. Things that perhaps they had never shared with another living soul.

It helped that Kenleigh had a gift for reading people and could see through the façade that most everyone kept up.

At her first meeting with the Dowager High Queen, Kenleigh told the Dowager that she used her brusque manner to keep people at a distance. The Dowager had poured them both a glass of wine and told Kenleigh how her mother-in-law, Zephier, had taken her eldest three children from her at birth and raised them as she wished until the High King Gavan was eight. By then, Arrysanna was twenty-three and surer of herself.

A large part of that sureness had to do with Elyria Forrester-Coden Rainsmere.

Elyria's first husband had died in battle against the Hathorites before the marriage had been a year old, and had come to court to receive her widow's dole—a sum of money given to women who'd lost their husbands in service to the kingdom.

Although technically owed this dole only by the King of Denon, Lord Natic Rainsmere's last heroic act had saved Dominaris Coden's cousin, so she had been summoned to court to receive a second dole and a posthumous medal of valor by High King Dominaris Coden.

While there, the young widow had taken note of the then High Queen's unhappiness and began spending time with her. The pair had become close friends, and Elyria had been the one to help Arrysanna stand up to her mother-in-law and take control of the Royal Nursery.

Dominaris, who had previously only visited his wife's chambers to get her with child, became interested in the fiery woman she was becoming. But his earlier treatment of her, and the way he allowed his mother to treat her, had left a mark on Arrysanna.

So between Elyria and Arrysanna, the pair hatched a plan. Elyria and Dominaris had much in common, and the widow actually liked the High King; more than that, his rank didn't faze her. Elyria called him out when he wasn't polite to his Arrysanna in private. The trio spent time together comfortably.

In 959, the young widow reverted to her maiden name and officially became the *kessiana* to High King Dominaris, and rose to second lady-of-the-court, pushing his mother to third. She became Lady Elyria Forrester-Coden, second wife to the High King.

Understanding Elyria and Arrysanna's relationship and the scars that the Dowager had received as a very young woman made Kenleigh understand her better. The iron-willed old lady with a sharp tongue had once been a cowed and demeaned young woman.

Her fierce protectiveness over young women who had been badly hurt suddenly made sense.

Kenleigh quite enjoyed their morning talks and the Dowager's confidences in her, but that morning, it seemed she had the problems of another woman on her mind.

Arryssanna wore a dressing gown of gray silk with large pink roses embroidered on it. Her silver hair was in a braid that hung across her shoulder and coiled in her lap, but despite the fact that she truly looked her age, her gaze was sharp.

She was in a bit of pain that morning, and had finally admitted that she would need to see the healer about the arthritis in her hip, so she and Kenleigh were taking breakfast in her rooms.

Kenleigh was sipping her and eating honeyed porridge when suddenly, Arrysanna said, "The woman needs to go outside."

There wasn't any need for Kenleigh to ask *who* needed to go outside. There was only one person at Trahelion Manor who was reclusive, and that was Queen Mellina.

"Some air and exercise would do her good," Kenleigh agreed. "Poor Lady Seryl is bored to tears. Lady Sara at least goes for a stroll after lunch."

"She is afraid to run into Jane," Arrysanna said with a sigh. "And the poor child has noticed that Mellina doesn't even look her way at dinner." She *tsk*ed and sipped her tea. "I think it irritates her that Sara is kind to all the children, Jane included."

"It is neither Jane nor Mellina's fault, the situation they are in," Kenleigh said, putting down her spoon and delicately wiping her mouth. She didn't want to chance getting anything on the pair of silk day dresses she wore. Lenathaina had seen Kenleigh fitted out like a lady, and Arrysanna had only added to that. "I will go spend some time with her this afternoon, give Seryl a break."

Arrysanna reached over and squeezed her hand. "Go after luncheon, while Sara is out."

After lunch, which Mellina had not come down for, Kenleigh went to the apartment that had been given to the Queen for her stay. It was one floor up and at the opposite end of the house. Only half of Arrysanna's court had been brought with them; the rest had stayed on at White Castle, or had been sent early to their next fostering.

Between Cressa, Jane, and Mellina, Arrysanna had enough to deal with at the moment.

Kenleigh knocked on the door to Mellina's apartment, and Seryl, one of the few wards that Arrysanna had kept with her, answered the door. Her tawny face lit up, and her whiskey-colored eyes shone at the sight of a visitor.

She smiled brightly. "Hello, Kenleigh." She stepped aside to let Kenleigh in.

Mellina was sitting at an embroidery frame. Kenleigh curtsied, and she inclined her head in acknowledgment. "How can we help you, Miss Atona?"

Kenleigh took a seat across from her at the frame without being asked. "I thought I would come keep you company, and let Seryl have a turn in the gardens. They are quite lovely."

Seryl shot Kenleigh a grateful look, but waited for Mellina to nod her permission.

Once the door had closed, Mellina turned to Kenleigh. "Why are you really here?"

Kenleigh surveyed her for a long moment, and the Queen shifted uncomfortably. Finally, Kenleigh said, "It isn't healthy to wall yourself in this room with your grief and guilt."

Mellina stared at her, stunned. She shook herself. "Who said I was guilty?"

"No one," Kenleigh said, keeping her gaze on Mellina. "But you are."

The other woman scoffed. "Why do you think that? You know nothing about me."

Kenleigh leaned back in the chair. "I don't need to know much, I see it. But I think you feel guilty because you killed your son, even though by all accounts, he was an abusive rapist and murderer. I think you feel guilty because of how he turned out, because he was a bad man."

She could see Mellina shaking, but she went on. "And you feel guilty because in killing him, you caused a lot of problems for a lot of people."

Mellina's lip trembled, and tears welled in her eyes.

Kenleigh leaned forward. "You can't do anything about that. You have lost both of your sons, and from what I have been told, you lost three children before that. You've lost your husband, your sister, and her husband, and now you fear you have lost their daughter."

Mellina buried her face in her hands. She sobbed for several minutes, and when she looked up, Kenleigh handed her a handkerchief.

"I resented my sister," the Queen said quietly. "I resented her happy marriage. I loved her husband, and he loved my sister. I grew to hate Charles as he turned from me to other women."

"Do you think he could see that you didn't want him?" Kenleigh asked quietly. "As much as you could see that he didn't love you?"

Mellina paused for a long moment, and then nodded, as if that had not occurred to her.

"You can't do anything about the past, or those you have lost," Kenleigh said, taking Mellina's hand. "But you haven't lost *everyone*. I know that it will hurt and be hard at first…"

Kenleigh could see that Mellina divined her next words before Kenleigh spoke them, and she began shaking her head.

"Think of it as atoning for the sins of your past." Kenleigh suggested, and that reasoning seemed to take root.

The Queen blanched and swallowed hard.

"You have killed one child," Kenleigh continued. "And perhaps the resentment you had for your husband colored how you ignored Richard and Garrett… but you have a chance to atone for that. You have a chance to nurture a child who has no parents."

She squeezed Mellina's hand and rose. "It is time for me to go down to the gardens with the girls. We have taken over the smaller garden, which was overgrown, and we are making it our own. Will you come with me?"

Mellina hesitated and then nodded. "Let me change," she said, rising and heading into her bedroom.

She came out a few minutes later in a plain gray dress of Lithonian design.

As they walked through the corridor, Kenleigh could sense Mellina's mounting tension. She slipped her arm through the Queen's and led her out a side door, flanked by *Mael'Hivar*, and into the gardens.

The garden that Kenleigh and the girls had taken over was on the southwest corner of the estate. Arrysanna had told her that it was once her mother-in-law's private garden, and the room connected to it had been Zephier's. When the house had been given to Arrysanna, she chose a different suite of rooms and redecorated the entire house.

The girls were already waiting for them when they arrived: Cressa and Jane, aged ten, and Nyelle, who was nine years old and a ward of Arrysanna's, her parents having died of a sickness that had swept through Rose Hall three years ago. So many had been ill that the Master had not been able to save everyone. Nyelle had no other living relatives, so Arrysanna had taken her on, and she had been raised with Cressa.

Cressa and Nyelle were unfazed by the appearance of Mellina, but Jane shrank back, looking uncomfortable.

"Make your curtsies, girls," Kenleigh said to her assembled troop.

They all made perfect curtsies, and Mellina gave them a shy smile.

"I believe we were going to clear out the weeds at the back wall and plant some rose bushes," Kenleigh told the girls. "What should we plant around them?"

"Lavender," Jane said quietly. "Gran swears by lavender. It keeps the weeds down and the roots cool."

"My rose bushes in Lithonia had lavender around them," Mellina said to Jane.

The little girl looked shocked that Mellina had spoken to her, but smiled in return.

"Lavender it is," Kenleigh said, turning to the gardener that had come to assist them. "Do you have any seeds, Neddyck?"

"Better than that, Miss Kenleigh, I have some small plants in the nursery." Neddyck tipped his hat. "I will go fetch them."

Ned strode out of the garden, and Kenleigh turned back to her crew.

"Right, weeding."

They all donned aprons and picked a spot along the back wall to begin. Kenleigh was pleased to see that Mellina took the space next to Jane.

They worked on in silence for some time, Ned bringing carts of supplies, and gathering the weeds to haul off.

Kenleigh was about to suggest a break when Jane called out, "Kenleigh! Look at this!"

The four of them gathered around the chestnut-haired girl to look at her discovery. She had unearthed a young tulip.

"What a clever find," Mellina said to Jane. "Perhaps a pot could be found, and you can put it in your bedroom window."

Jane smiled at the idea, and Ned went off to find a suitable pot.

The other girls went back to their patches, hoping to find a treasure of their own, while Kenleigh left Mellina to help Jane dig up the young tulip.

It wasn't much, but it was a start.

CHAPTER 57

High Lord Magne Montgomery
Montgomery House, City of Endomir: Lithonia
19ᵗʰ of Xavar

Word had spread through the city that Marc Eddening, Ellis Parker, and Blake Rendon had an army camped at the Gates of Endomir. When Eddening had sent a note asking for a meeting, Magne had been reluctant but finally agreed.

The house was oddly quiet with Angela and the girls gone and the boys in hiding. In these circumstances, it was unsettling. Derek and Benjamin's deaths were a heavy weight on him... one he bore alone, with only Master Simon for company. Though, knowing that Stephen and Travis were safe, unreachable, helped some.

He wanted to hug his boys, and thrash them for not being careful and patient. Most of all, he wanted to lay his eyes on them and know that they were truly safe and alive.

Most nights he ended up in Derek's room with a glass of brandy. He often fell asleep in the wing-backed chair that faced his bed. This happened so often that the servants had begun lighting the fire in Derek's room and leaving a blanket on the chair.

It would be some time yet before he might see his living sons. For now he had to act as if he had no idea where they were or if they were alright while he lived with the ghost of the one that he lost.

Willis, his butler, let Eddening into the drawing room at half past ten in the morning.

Eddening shook Magne's hand. "Sad business. I know I sent a note around at the time, but I wanted to say again that I am sorry for your losses. To lose your son and your best friend so close together... and to not know where your other boys are..." He let his last words trail off and looked at Magne with an open expression, as if urging him to confide.

240

"I am sure they have found a cave or something to hole up in. My sons are resourceful," Magne said confidently, sitting down and gesturing for Eddening to do the same.

Willis came in and laid the table for tea before excusing himself. Magne rose and poured himself and his guest both a cup, taking his black and leaving Eddening to add what he liked to his—which turned out to be a liberal amount of milk and sugar.

Once they had both sat back down, Eddening decided to get down to business.

"I am sure you have heard about the men I have rallied to help push the Usurper off the throne."

"Is that what they are here for?" Magne asked mildly.

"What else would they be here for?" Eddening asked, trying to sound surprised as his plum face flushed.

He was on the heavy side, his vest straining over his paunch, and his pale hair was thinning. Magne didn't know why he didn't just shave it, like he did.

"So you can take the city and the throne for yourself," Magne answered blandly.

Eddening sputtered, affronted. "I only want to free those poor people that have been taken captive. Including my own son!" He set his tea down and leaned forward. "And make it safe for yours to come out of hiding. Morlette has no right, and more, no training or ability to run this country. It is *you* that failed to keep him from the throne," he accused.

"It was me that was taken prisoner in front of every lord in the city, and none, not even you, stopped Morlette as he had me cleared out of my office and escorted from the castle."

Eddening blushed at that and picked up his tea to have something to do. "Well, he had our children, our relations."

"He still does," Magne said as he eyed Eddening with something close to suspicion as he took a sip of his tea. "It seems that the only thing that has changed is you have Parker and Rendon in your pocket somehow."

Magne set his cup down. "What hold do you have over *them*? Not so long ago, they were whispering in Morlette's ear. He still seems to think he has Parker on his side. After all... it is Parker's niece on the would-be King's arm. So my question to you is this: do you really think Parker is on your side?"

Eddening shifted uncomfortably. "I do, yes. Now, will you help me get Endomir out of this mess?"

"What do you want of me? I am no longer regent," Magne retorted, watching Eddening.

"Many still think you should be," he said. "If you back me, Jasper might open the gate, against Morlette's orders.

"And if I back you and you decide to take the throne as soon as you enter, it will look like I support you as king," Magne said candidly, still watching him.

Eddening flushed.

"I thought that was the way of it. Let me be blunt." All traces of friendliness were gone now. "Lenathaina Morthan Coden is the only ruler I will bow my head to. It is to her that I will swear allegiance to, and none other."

Eddening rose, and Magne followed.

"It seems we have nothing else to say to one another, then," Eddening said at last.

"It would seem not," Magne agreed.

Eddening inclined his head and left without another word.

CHAPTER 58

King Garrett Morlette Morthan
Castle Endomir, Endomir: Lithonia
20th of Xavar

Janna had been removed from the castle by her mother, 'for her safety,' Lady Ellen had said. And some of the guards had deserted their posts once word of the advancing army had spread through the city.

Murphy had called Garrett a weakling and a coward, and the unassuming, short, slender man with light brown hair somehow looked terrifying as he'd stood over Garrett, berating him.

Garrett had begun to notice that when Murphy was around, he felt a sense of fear and urgency. When they were apart, that fear began to lessen. He had tried to send Murphy away, but his secretary reminded him that he alone knew the depths that Garrett had gone to in order to steal the throne.

Earlier that evening, Murphy had come to tell him that Eddening had been to see Montgomery. No one knew what had come from the meeting, but Murphy thought it was time to make an example of Eddening's heir, time to put a stop to their disrespect.

He left Garrett with a pen and paper and told him to write the execution order, but Garrett hadn't.

Instead, he waited until well after dark and packed a satchel. He knew he still had clothing stored in the place he was bound for, so he only took things he couldn't replace: letters from his mother and father, a few mementos from his childhood, his father's cravat pin, and the ribbon Janna had given him. Then he'd snuck down the back stairs like the thief he was.

Father was right to always go to Lenathaina first. To trust her more. She's the one all this belongs to. She is the one meant to rule. I am meant to be behind the scenes, nothing more.

Maybe if he hadn't let others push him to take what wasn't his, Lena would have trusted him to be her right hand. That was what he had been raised for: second place.

*****

It was an hour before dawn when Garrett entered the kitchens of Havencrest Manor.

Matilda, the plump cook, looked up from the bread she was kneading and gave Garrett a sad smile. "Oh, Master Garrett. What a mess you have gotten yourself into."

She cleaned her hands off on a towel and rounded the scarred table to wrap her arms around him. The top of her head barely reached his chin, but her embrace was comforting, almost motherly.

Matilda had been his mother's cook, and when Father had opened this house for him and Richard, Father had let him bring Matilda from his estates. She had helped raise him until his mother died and he had come to Endomir.

He couldn't remember how tall his mother had been, but in that moment, he liked to think that her embrace would have felt like this: a place of safety and love.

CHAPTER 60

High Lady Beth Bennings
Seathor Hall, Port City of Seathor: Lithonia
20ᵗʰ of Xavar

Beth stood on the castle steps, her white skirts whipping around her in the crisp fall breeze. Behind her, all four of her daughters, her daughter-in-law, and her youngest son, James, stood in a line, dressed in shades of gray. Master Nathan stood to her left, and Captain Townsend to her right. The man had rarely left her side since swearing allegiance to her.

Her generals were all in the fields to the east of the city, where a sprawling army camp now lay. Angela's men would now be joining hers, but her best friend and cousin was entering the gates of Seathor Hall.

"Welcome," Beth said, walking down the steps.

She and Angela met halfway between their parties and embraced one another. Angela wore a pale gray riding dress; like Beth, she was in mourning.

"Thank you," Angela said, gripping her fiercely. "The welcome from the city!" she said in awe.

Beth had heard the cheers from the castle, as Angela's party entered the city.

"They are for our Queen," she said, slipping her arm through Angela's and leading her up the stairs toward her family.

Angela greeted each of Beth's children and her daughter-in-law, Lissa.

"You didn't bring Henriette and Claire?" Anne asked, looking for her friends.

"They have gone to my sister Gia's." Angela kissed Anne's cheek. "You are welcome to go too." She looked at Beth. "She has room for all the girls and James."

245

"I won't go," Lissa said, her hand on her pregnant belly. "I am either the wife of the next High Lord, or possibly the mother." She rested her hand on James' shoulder. "And failing that, the sister. I will do my duty to this House." She was slightly taller than Beth, and had straightened her back so she looked down on her mother-in-law. She had red hair, green eyes, and angular features.

She would be strong enough for whatever came, Beth was sure of that.

"And I am not going anywhere until I know where Stephen is," Anne said, meeting Beth's gaze.

Jane, Mary, and Sara started to add their protestations to Anne's, but stopped when they saw the look on their mother's face.

Beth turned to Angela. "The younger three can go to Gia. I will need Lissa to run things here in my absence, and Jane can assist her."

"What of Anne?" Angela asked as they walked through the massive oak front doors.

"Anne will come with me," Beth said, and she heard her daughter mutter a prayer of thanks.

"We will have need of her," Angela said.

They all made their way into the main drawing room. Angela's Master Brian and General Hall were with her, and Master Nathan and Captain Townsend had followed them in. The drawing room was pleasantly full.

"Master Brian?" Angela prompted, holding her hand out to the man.

The Master pulled a pair of envelopes from the satchel he carried, and handed them to Angela, who in turn passed them to Beth.

Beth looked at the seals: one lavender, and the other, the sapphire and gold of Morthan House.

"Do the lavender first," Angela directed, sitting down on one of the settees.

Beth opened the letter sealed with lavender wax and read it quickly.

The note was short: an apology for the burden that Lenathaina was placing on Beth, and her thanks for all she was doing. She sent her love.

Beth tucked the note into her pocket and opened the second with shaking hands.

By Order of Her Majesty, Queen Lenathaina Morthan Coden of Lithonia:

High Lady Angela Rendon Montgomery is hereby instated as temporary Lady Admiral of the Lithonian Navy.

This Order is in effect from the 3rd of Rison. The Lady Admiral shall have the authority to gather the men, supplies, and ships owed to the rightful Ruler of Lithonia in times of war on behalf of Her Majesty Queen Lenathaina.

Any refusing to honor their pledges of support or to follow the Lady Admiral will be seen as traitors.

Lenathaina Morthan Coden, Queen of Lithonia, First Princess of Caeldenon

Beth looked up from the letter and met Angela's eyes. Angela then pulled the medal of the Marshal General of the Lithonian Army from her pocket, and pinned it to her dress.

"I imagine she didn't have the medal of the Lord Admiral with her. She likely only had this one because it was a memento of her father's."

"I'll be damned," Lissa said, sitting down rather hastily. All the color had left her normally rosy complexion.

"We all will be if we don't win this war," Angela murmured, shooting Lissa a concerned look.

Beth sat down next to Lissa and handed Master Nathan the letter.

As he read, his red eyebrows rose. "Well. This is interesting."

"Do we know when she arrives?" Beth asked.

"Seven days, by my estimation, but I planned to let her know that we arrived today, via Script Stone," Angela said. "I can ask when they think to make landfall."

"Do we know how many they have with them?" Beth couldn't help but wonder where they would put everyone.

"Sixty of those black-clad warriors, along with their horses, as well as Lenathaina herself, and her husband and ladies, I would imagine," Angela recounted. "I am sure we can put some of the warriors with the army."

Beth nodded.

She was coming. Lenathaina was coming, and soon... the war would truly begin.

CHAPTER 61

Queen Lenathaina Morthan Coden of Lithonia, First Princess of Caeldenon
Aboard the Wind Hawk: Indayon Sea
21st of Xavar

Lena sat at the table in her sitting room on the ship, poring over the list of lords that had sent their pledges of loyalty, and noting who wasn't on that list: Eddening, Rendon, Parker, Parr, and Maceon— though Garn Wallace, who was Rendon's man, and Gerald Grey, who was Parker's, had sent their letters.

She had a lot of Houses behind her, but not enough. It would not be smooth sailing.

She stood and walked to the window and looked toward the horizon. They were passing through the Stones, and once they were on the other side, they could pick up speed safely.

A knock on the door pulled her from her thoughts.

"Enter."

Master Tam came in; the topaz Script Stone that linked her with Angela was pulsing in his hand. He bowed to Lena and to Tori, who was her only attendant at the moment, as Rachel and Fenora were sparring with some of the female *Mael'Hivar*.

Tori had been reading the notes they had all compiled, speculating about the lords who hadn't declared their allegiances. Eddening's silence was concerning. They had had reports from Vera stating that Parker and Rendon had been in Garrett's company a lot before Richard had been killed, so she suspected that the pair were on Garrett's side, though she knew they hadn't thrown support behind him in the Council chamber yet.

It was all a tangled mess.

"Ah, Master Tam," Lena greeted, giving him a tired smile. "I see I have a message waiting." She motioned for him to take a seat at the table.

"Good afternoon, Master Tam," Tori said, moving some of her papers aside to make room for him.

"Good afternoon, *Ducessa*," he said with a warm smile.

Lena suspected he had had reservations about Tori's hasty marriage, but his time with Baerik and his observations of the couple had changed his mind.

Anyone who saw them together could see how much they loved one another, and Baerik had a keen mind and had taken Lena's cause on as his own.

The white-haired Master turned back to Lena. "You do have a message, Your Majesty." He set the Stone on the table, found a blank piece of parchment, and picked up Lena's pen. "With your permission?"

"Of course," Lena said, standing beside him. She was eager to see what Angela had to say.

Tam touched the Stone and did whatever it was that Masters did to indicate that he was ready for the message. The Stone began pulsing with a complex pattern of light, and he began writing, never taking his eyes from the Stone.

> *QLMC*
> *Have arrived in Seathor and delivered letters to HL BB. We are happy to serve you in any way we can. Request approx. arrival of your ship.*
> *HL AM*

Tam looked up at Lena and awaited her instructions.

"I believe at our current pace, we will get there on the 27th... the 28th at the latest," she said, looking down at the note.

Happy to serve.

She had known they would be on her side before she had ever gotten their letters. With the Bennings and Montgomerys, she had a real chance.

"Thank goodness. We will be out of mourning by then," Tori said, looking up from her list. "I think there is a dark blue day dress that would be fitting."

"I should take a white shawl, though, to show respect for the loss of Benjamin and Derek," Lena said, feeling the heaviness of those losses.

Garrett would pay for them.

"Send those dates to Angela," she said to Tam, turning back to the window.

Less than a week, and she would be back in her homeland.

One step closer to the throne.

CHAPTER 62

Shan Alanine Fasili
Atar Palace, Imperial City of El Manteria: Pannarius
21st of Xavar

Alanine prostrated herself before Empress Hourina Palin, may the Light ever favor her, alongside Isra and her husband Amir.

They had arrived in El Manteria a week and a half ago, and this was Alanine's third audience with her Imperial cousin. The Empress had invited Alanine and Nijah for a family dinner in her private residence.

"Rise," the Empress said in her low, sultry voice. Her beaded braids were streaked with silver, she had a fine web of lines around her gray eyes, and her skin was the same caramel as Isra's.

The two women were strikingly similar, though Isra, who was the elder sister, looked young enough to be Hourina's daughter. Thanks to her Curse, Isra aged at a much slower rate than the average person.

Alanine came to her feet and watched the Empress embrace Isra. Hourina was tall and slender and held herself like a much younger woman, even though Alanine knew she was well over sixty. Hourina hugged Amir next, as if he were a much-loved member of the family.

In her time at the Atar Palace, her views on the Masters of the Ithrimir had changed. To her great surprise, she discovered that the Empress had a secret Master of her own: High Master Kamala Nalime. She dressed like a Pannarian noble woman, and even the High Priestess treated her with respect.

After Hourina released Amir, she turned to greet Alanine as well.

"I have someone I would like you to meet, Cousin." Hourina said, steering Alanine to the men's side of the room.

Women could cross to the men's side, but they could not cross to the women's without being summoned.

A tall young man close to Alanine's age prostrated himself until Hourina bade him to rise. His beaded black braids hung halfway down his back, and he had sienna skin and bright blue eyes. He was handsome, well-formed and pleasing to look at.

"This is my grandson, Aram."

Alanine smiled politely. "Hello, Aram."

He bowed over her hand. "It is pleasing to meet you, *Shan Fasili*."

"Stop matchmaking, sister," Isra scolded. She touched Amir's hand before he went to sit with the Imperial Consort, Rami.

Hourina laughed and touched Alanine's cheek. "Such a beautiful and intelligent young woman."

Alanine blushed and joined the other women. Dinner was served as soon as they made themselves comfortable.

The first dinner course was served, triangular pastries filled with spicy potato or lamb, with a variety of yogurt or fruit and vegetable dips. Goblets of red wine and glasses of water were served all around, then the servants withdrew.

Isra turned to Hourina. "I have been thinking…"

"That rarely bodes well for the rest of us, sister," the Empress said with an affectionate smile.

Isra snorted. "It might be wise to move Alanine and Nijah to a place where there are more Masters. These Hathorites can move among us so easily because Masters cannot. It will be easier to protect them with more than just Amir, Kamala, and myself."

Alanine's heard skipped a beat, but Nijah was down the table, in conversation with one of Hourina's granddaughters and not paying attention. That was most likely for the best.

"You want to take them to the Isles?" Hourina asked, taking a sip of her wine. She wore what Alanine thought of as her 'Empress Face'; that face hid all thoughts and emotions.

"They would be safe among my children," Isra offered.

Hourina was silent for a time; her adult daughters were watching their mother, waiting for a sign of her thoughts or mood.

Isra took another pastry and bit into it, seeming content to wait.

At last, Hourina said, "I think not. The High Priestess wouldn't approve of such a move. She becomes more comfortable with the Ithrimir, but to send the girls to the Isles would leave many with the impression that they have the Gift."

Alanine noted to herself that the Empress didn't call it a blood curse.

"And should they want to come back," Hourina added, "many might not accept them."

It took all Alanine's will to speak up in this company, but it was her fate they were deciding.

"I wrote to Queen Lenathaina, offering her my support. She wrote me back."

She felt every eye in the room on her.

Isra asked, "What did she say?"

"That she would welcome my help," Alanine replied, meeting the Arch Master's eyes.

Isra turned back to her sister and arched an eyebrow.

Hourina lifted her chin. "Do you think it wise?"

"I have met Queen Lenathaina," Isra said; no one spoke of the how or why. "More than that, I have spent much time with her husband. They are honorable people."

"And I am her heir, in all technicality," Alanine put in. "I can't bring her aid, but I can stand by her side as she fights."

"A war isn't a place for a child," Hourina considered, looking down the table at Nijah.

Isra followed her gaze. "Which, along with the reasons we previously discussed, is why I think Nijah would be better off with my children on the Isles. At least until Alanine decides what path she wants for her life."

Alanine knew what 'reasons' she spoke of. She, the Empress, and Isra had met alone, and Isra had explained that she believed Nijah was the natural child of the man who had killed Alanine's true father and that Namar most likely was too. The Hathorites had already come for Namar so it wasn't unreasonable to think they would come for Nijah too.

"That is for Alanine to decide. She is the head of her family," Isra said, looking at her.

Hourina inclined her head. "She is." She too turned to Alanine, who sat on her left. "What do you want to do?"

Even Nijah had heard her name enough that she was now looking at her sister.

Alanine met Nijah's gaze. "Sister, would you like to go stay with Cousin Isra's family while I forge a path for us?"

Nijah looked nervous to have so many eyes on her. "Could *hassana* come with me?"

"Of course," Alanine said with a smile.

"There is much you can learn on the Isles," Isra told her young cousin gently. "The non-magical lessons are open to all, so you could go to those and explore the island. My Sari is your age, and she does not have the Gift. I think you could be fast friends."

Nijah nodded, and Alanine saw Hourina's granddaughter, Jani, touch her hand lightly in comfort.

"And you would join Queen Lenathaina?" Hourina asked Alanine.

"I think so," she said, looking to Isra.

"We will see Nijah settled at my home on the Isles, and then I will escort Alanine to the Queen," Isra stated, turning to the Empress. "If you agree, sister?"

Hourina nodded. "I think Alanine has chosen wisely."

CHAPTER 63

High Lord Magne Montgomery
House of Lords, City of Endomir: Lithonia
22ⁿᵈ of Xavar

Magne sat in his seat as Speaker in the House of Lords. Every man who had the right to a vote was present, save Morlette. The tension in the room was thick.

All the captives had been released, and in the excitement, his sons Stephen and Travis, and Randal Bennings, had quietly come out of hiding.

His sons had collapsed into his arms and cried like they had not since they were children. Having them home and in his arms made it easier for Magne to begin to heal.

But Randal would never have that healing, and now he sat in his father's former seat, white-faced with fury.

The day before, when it had been discovered that Morlette had fled, the Council had met, arranged the release of the captives, and all save Eddening, Rendon, and Parker had voted to reinstate Magne as Regent until Lena arrived.

That morning, Eddening played his hand. He stood on the floor of the House and said, "Where is she? This woman you would call Queen is nowhere to be found. King Richard was killed three months ago—plenty of time for Princess Lenathaina to come to our aid. We have been left on our own, our children and our parents locked up. Abused. Killed. Where was she then?"

He didn't give anyone time to respond. He was puffed up, red-faced. Righteous in his disdain for an absent leader.

He blathered on. "She was in comfort and safety in another country, doing nothing to aid us—as she is now! We need a king, not some woman who comes and goes at another man's bidding."

"Who's going to take the throne, then, *you*?" Harmon cackled. "You have an army at the gate! You claim to be our savior, but you are a bully, just as Morlette was."

Magne thought Eddening would have an apoplexy right there on the floor, but Parker stood up and clapped him on the back. "High Lord Eddening was the only one willing to take the risk and gather a force to come after the Usurper. Even though his son was hostage, he moved against him, unwilling to allow a tyrant to rule Endomir."

"He moved for his own gain and was willing to risk his son for the throne," High Lord Maceon retorted. "We all know Eddening has been gathering support to put himself in line after the last descendants with the Morthan name... even though the Fasili girl has a better claim."

Lord Nicholas Payne stood up. "It is neither here nor there, at the moment, whether Eddening or Fasili has claim. Lenathaina Morthan is next in line, and that is down in law." He stabbed a finger at Eddening. "You can't get past that!"

"But where is she?" Eddening demanded again.

"Five days from Seathor," Magne announced.

The room became still.

He stood, and raised his voice. "The Queen is five days from Seathor, where she will meet my wife and the mother of High Lord Randal Bennings."

"I am sure she is bringing that foreign husband of hers," Eddening sneered. "I would bet anything she didn't come until he let her."

Magne and Harry Harmon laughed at that, and Harry said, "You don't know the Queen if you think she was waiting on any man's permission. Think, Eddening. She had to gather ships and supplies and confer with her ally, High King Gavan Coden." He arched an eyebrow at Eddening. "She couldn't just ride a damn horse across the ocean."

"Mark me, whatever you say, she will have that barbarian Prince whispering strange ideas into her ear. Women were meant to be wives and mothers, to run their house and the nursery," Parker railed. "They weren't meant to rule over men."

"Sit down, Parker," Maceon scoffed. "Just because your wife runs circles around you doesn't mean that every woman isn't trustworthy. Perhaps if you had spent more time at home and less in the brothels, she wouldn't have had to turn to others for support."

Eddening and Rendon each grabbed Parker by the arm to hold him back, and Magne banged his gavel, shouting over the commotion.

"Order!"

When some semblance of decorum had been regained, he said, "I can't believe I am having to do this, but we will put it to a vote. Those who are going to support the rightful Queen of Lithonia, move to the right... those who oppose her rule, to the left."

He had basically asked the traitors to declare themselves, and everyone knew it.

Some quickly moved to the right: Collins, Harmon, Reynolds, Jasper, Harmon the Younger, who was his father's vassal, and Fraser and Kent. Magne's own Highland, Southernby, and Lorvette, as well as Randal Bennings and his Payne, Prather, and Proudmourn.

And then there was a pause.

Rendon, Parker, and Eddening moved to the left, and at a slower pace, most of the lords under their purview did as well: Gordon, Avery, and Harewood, who all followed Eddening, and Parker's Malick and Cromby, but Grey turned his back and walked to the right, followed by Rendon's Wallace. However, Rendon's other vassals Dorn and Gregory went to the left. Vectors and his lords stood and, to the man, crossed the room to stand with Randal and the other supporters of the Queen.

Vectors had aged a decade in the months since his daughter had been killed. He wanted answers. He wanted vengeance.

Maceon finally stood and walked to the right, his three lords, Parten, Greer, and Broome with him. He looked at Eddening. "This is what King Charles wanted, Eddening. We can fight about who comes after her once we have healed Lithonia's wounds."

Eddening stared daggers at him but said nothing.

All eyes turned to Parr and his three men; the only ones left undeclared. Finally, Edward Long turned on his heel and went to stand with those to the right. Parr was counting the numbers and weighing his options. Dale and Norrington turned to the left, and at last, only Parr remained.

Refusing to look at his Dale and Norrington, Parr walked to the left. "If she had married a good Lithonian man, I would have stood for her. But you saw those Codens, with their black-clad soldiers. Who says she won't bring masses of them and make us a vassal state?"

Magne shook his head. "She would never do that," he said quietly.

Parr stood his ground.

With a sigh, Magne began to tally the counts. "Twenty-six for Queen Lenathaina."

He ignored the grumbles from the left.

"And thirteen against, with two absentees." One being Morlette, and the other, Lenathaina herself. "Those who stand for the Queen have the majority."

Without another word, Marc Eddening stood and left the House. All of those who had stood with him followed.

Jasper turned to Magne. "Lord Regent, what are your orders, sir?"

Magne took a deep breath. "Do not let that army cross into Endomir, but open the gates for any who wish to leave. Double the patrols." He stepped off his dais and looked up to the balcony where Lenathaina should be sitting. "And find Morlette."

CHAPTER 64

High Master Jillian Prather
White Castle, White City: Caeldenon
22nd of Xavar

Jillian knocked on Lan's office door and waited for him to call, "Enter!" Then he walked in, all smiles.

She had been particularly sweet the last week or so, to throw him off the scent. She had finally decided how to get to Trahelion Manor. After that, she was sure she would have to run for it.

She had spent three solid days messaging back and forth with the Mystic, who had finally agreed that removing the child was worth Jillian leaving her post. After all, Jillian hadn't been able to learn much. She would be more useful elsewhere.

The message had been clear: she had failed her prime directive, and the only way to atone for that was to remove the child.

"This is a pleasant surprise," Lan said as he came to his feet. He walked around the desk and kissed her.

Jillian was glad that her days of pretending to love this man were numbered. Soon, she would be in Hathor with the Mystic.

"I had an idea that I wanted to discuss with you," she told him after she returned his kiss. She sat down on the settee near the window and waited for him to join her.

"Oh?" he asked, hooking a finger around a lock of her hair and twirling it.

She hated that he was so touchy. So affectionate. It took all her willpower not to strike him.

"Yes. I thought I might go visit your mother to discuss the wedding. Between the two of us, we can arrange something small and informal." Jillian smiled sweetly. "Perhaps at Trahelion Manor or Rose Hall? Considering Queen Lenathaina and the Prince's situation, it would not be right to have a lavish wedding, but I think you are right, it is time to move things forward. I truly want to be part of the family."

The jubilant smile that bloomed across Lan's face was almost laughable. Somehow, she managed to return it.

"I can't tell you how happy this makes me, Jillian." He wrapped his arms around her, and she could feel emotion come off him in waves. He pulled hack to look at her, his hazel eyes bright.

Is he about to cry?

"When will you go see Mother?"

"I have nothing going on, and I am sure I can be spared for a day or so here, so I thought I would leave this afternoon." She tried to sound like an eager bride-to-be.

"Would you like me to come with you?" Lan offered.

"No." She tried not to sound panicked. She would never get away if he were there. "I think your mother and I need some time together to get to know one another."

He gave her a rueful grin. "Mother is more bark than bite. She really does have a soft side; she just hides it well."

As well as I hide my true self.

The woman was a harridan.

"I look forward to seeing it." She stood and kissed him again. "I will speak to your brother and go pack."

He grabbed her hand and kissed it. "You really have made me the happiest man, Jillian."

CHAPTER 65

Dowager Queen Mellina Morthan
Trahelion Manor, Providence of Denon: Caeldenon
25ᵗʰ of Xavar

Mellina and Jane were in the small walled garden that Kenleigh had taken over with the little girls. Sara sat on a bench against the manor, reading. It was just the three of them and two of the *Mael'Hivar* women, who sat playing a game that involved small, metal objects and a little ball that bounced.

The goal of the game seemed to be to bounce the ball and grab as many of the little metal pieces as possible before the ball hit the ground again. Mellina wasn't fooled; she knew even though the women seemed absorbed in their fun, they were aware of everything around them.

This was the first time she had taken Jane with her to the gardens without Kenleigh or the other girls. Kenleigh was in attendance on the Dowager, who was entertaining Master Jillian, who had come to discuss her upcoming wedding. Cressa and Nyelle were with Cressa's grandparents, who, it seemed, were regular guests of the Dowager. As Nyelle had been raised with Cressa for some time, the *Marque and Marquessa* often took the little orphan on rides with them.

The most shocking thing was that it had been Mellina's idea to take Jane to the gardens. Kenleigh had smiled when Mellina suggested it, and the Dowager had flashed a rare, approving look.

It was well into autumn now, and they were pruning the rose bushes. The first killing frost had come the week before, and the gardeners had been hard at work since, preparing the many acres of walking paths and flower beds for the coming winter. Kenleigh had told them to leave this small walled garden alone, that they would care for it.

It had been a long time since Mellina had taken a hand in tending plants, but she found the knowledge and skills coming back quickly. She also found the time outdoors cleared her head and boosted her mood.

"Aunt Mellina!" Jane called, sounding distressed. She had gotten her sleeve stuck in a bunch of thorns.

Mellina rushed to her side and began disentangling her gently.

They had decided that 'Aunt' would be the best title for Mellina for now. It was better than 'Queen Mellina'; less rigid and formal.

"Oh, your sleeve is torn," Mellina said, checking to make sure she hadn't been cut.

"Do you need assistance?"

Mellina turned to see Master Jillian standing in the entrance to the garden.

Mellina stood and dusted the knees of her gown. "She just tore her sleeve. We can easily mend that." She gave the Master a cordial smile; she hadn't spent much time with Master Jillian when she had lived in Endomir, and found it curious that she would seek Mellina out.

"I should look, to be sure," Jillian said, moving toward Jane.

Something about her expression, the eagerness there, made Mellina uncomfortable. The Master also had a satchel with her, which was odd.

Why would she need a satchel to move about the manor?

"Truly, she is fine," Mellina said firmly, letting some of her old queenly voice come back. She stepped in front of Jane, and something dark crossed the Master's face.

"You know King Charles liked to err on the side of caution when it came to his children." Master Jillian's voice had a sharp edge to it, as if she were trying to cut Mellina.

Once, that might have worked... but the hair on the back of Mellina's neck was standing now.

The blonde-haired Master's tone and demeanor had also attracted the attention of the *Mael'Hivar* guards, who had abandoned their game. The two black-clad women, one fair and one dark, were standing now, hands resting on the hilts of their swords.

"The child is fine. I have made sure of it," Mellina said, standing her ground. "It is time for us to get ready for tea. If you will excuse us?"

The guards had taken a few steps toward them, moving between the Master and Mellina, sensing her discomfort.

Master Jillian sighed as if annoyed, and raised her hands. Two lines of blackness shot from them and went to the guards standing before Mellina.

The women crumpled to the ground without a sound.

Mellina screamed and turned to pick up Jane. She didn't know where the strength came from, but she managed easily. She ran toward the manor, knowing she could do nothing to stop the woman, but refusing to stand by while she killed Jane.

Something hit Mellina from behind. Searing pain covered her legs, and she fell to the ground, her body still shielding Jane.

The last thing she saw was Sara, her best friend, standing like a vengeful spirit, a white rope of energy in her hands.

She heard the Master screaming, and then the pain overtook Mellina, and she passed out.

CHAPTER 66

High Queen Maelynn Coden
White Castle, White City: Caeldenon
25th of Xavar

Maelynn and Gavan were seated in the main sitting room of their apartment with Em, Andi, and Jaed when Valeran let himself in, looking pale.

"High Prince Evandar and Master Gedry are here to see you, Your Majesties."

Maelynn exchanged a look with her husband and said, "Bring them in."

Master Gedry was one of the Masters employed to monitor their vast network of Script Stones. He was a non-descript man with skin the color of driftwood, shorn black hair, and black eyes.

He and Evandar both bowed before Master Gedry handed Gavan a folded sheet of parchment.

His expression went from shock to stunned disbelief. "Do you have the Stone to Trahelion Manor with you?" Gavan asked Gedry hoarsely as he handed Maelynn the parchment.

"Of course, Your Majesty," Gedry said, pulling out a dark green Stone.

Evandar sat on the settee and buried his face in his hands. His Thane, Deldemar, moved across the room to speak with Andi, Jaed, and Em.

Maelynn opened the parchment with a sense of dread.

HK GC,

M Jillian Prather killed two Mael'Hivar and attacked QMM and LJG. Jane sustained minor injuries. QM seriously harmed. Has lost part of both legs. LSP captured MJP, later aided by me. MJP currently drugged and held captive. Pls reply w/instructions.

AM BR

Maelynn looked up from the page, feeling she same shock she saw on Gavan and Evandar's faces. "Why?"

"We won't know until we can speak to her," Evandar said. "What should we do?"

"Have her brought here," Gavan said, shaking his head. "We will need to contact the Ithram." He turned to look at Master Gedry, the question plain on his face.

"We are bound by the laws of the lands we enter," Master Gedry said, rubbing a hand over his cropped head. "We must contact him, but ultimately, I believe he will leave the decision in your hands, Your Majesty."

Gavan nodded, feeling the weight of the burden settle on him.

Jillian had committed murder, and there were harsh punishments for those who took another life outside the field of battle.

"LSP... is that Lady Sara Parten?" he asked, looking at Maelynn.

"I don't know who else it could be," Maelynn mused. "Though..." She looked at Master Gedry.

"It isn't unheard of, though rare. As long as she could control it without bringing attention to herself, the secret could be kept." Gedry shook his head. "I will have to report the use of magic ..." He sighed. "I don't know what will happen."

"We will deal with that later. As far as I am concerned, Lady Sara deserves a damn metal. I just hope Queen Mellina will be alright." Gavan rubbed a hand over his face.

"Someone has to tell Lan..." Evandar said.

Maelynn folded the note and put it in her pocket. "I will do it."

Gavan and Evandar exchanged a look and then nodded. Their brother wouldn't take this well. He loved Jillian.

Gavan sat down at the desk in the corner, and Maelynn left the apartment with Em by her side.

"Are you alright?" Em asked quietly. She ran a hand through her short, red hair.

Maelynn found, as she always did, the presence of the tall copper-skinned woman a comfort. She drew strength from her.

"No," she said truthfully. "But I don't have time to let myself be anything other than strong. Lan will need me. Gavan and Evandar will need me." She drew a shuddering breath. "Mother may even need me. And poor Mellina and Jane…"

Em wrapped an arm around her as they continued walking. "You know I will be by your side, whatever comes."

"And I know the debt that I owe you can never be repaid." Maelynn grasped the hand on her shoulder.

"My life for yours," Em said, squeezing her tightly once more before letting go. "And I have never regretted it."

The walk to Lan's apartment didn't take long. Maelynn let herself into the room where a *gandine* would usually have an office; Jillian had refused Maelynn's offer to find someone to run their household. She hadn't thought much of it at the time, but now… she had to wonder if the blonde Master had more nefarious reasons for refusing to follow tradition.

She knocked on the door to the sitting room, hoping she wouldn't have to wander too far into the apartment to find him.

"Come in," Lan called.

Maelynn opened the door, and Em followed, looking around the room to assess their surroundings. She took a seat in the corner, and Maelynn sat next to Lan.

He wore gray sleep pants and a matching loose shirt, and his short, reddish-brown curls were unruly—as usual.

He smiled at her. "To what do I owe this pleasure?"

Maelynn took a deep breath, and whatever Lan saw on her face made his smile falter.

"Is everything alright?"

She pulled out the piece of parchment and silently handed it to him before laying her hand on his arm, lending him whatever strength she could.

As he read, his expression shifted from shock and bewilderment. He read it again, and again before finally looking up. "No. This can't be right." There were tears in his eyes.

"Gavan is having her brought here. We will hear what she has to say," Maelynn said quietly.

"But... murder?" He couldn't seem to wrap his mind around it.

Truthfully, Maelynn couldn't either.

"You must have courage, brother," she said quietly.

Lan looked at her, and reality began to set in. Jillian had committed murder. The laws were clear.

"Leave me. Please," he said hoarsely.

Maelynn rose and gently squeezed his shoulder before letting herself and Em out.

Lan's sobs broke the silence before the door had closed.

CHAPTER 67

Kenleigh Atona

Trahelion Manor, Providence of Denon: Caeldenon

26ᵗʰ of Xavar

Kenleigh watched Arch Master Braxton Rivers examine Queen Mellina. She still had not regained consciousness. Lady Sara was asleep on a chair in the corner of the room, next to the hearth, and Jane lay at the foot of the bed, sleeping fitfully.

"How is she, Braxton?" Arrysanna asked quietly from her place by the door.

"I think she will wake soon, Your Majesty," Master Braxton said, just as quietly. Like the Dowager, Braxton was teak-skinned with gray eyes, though his hair was closer to gold than silver. He was tall and lean with a calm demeanor.

"Is there anything else that can be done?" Kenleigh asked, looking down at the dark-haired Queen.

Mellina had hardly stirred since she had been brought to this room, the suite connected to the gardens that had been so lovingly tended. Arrysanna had decided it would be best to have her on the ground floor, as Mellina could never climb stairs again.

"Continue to keep her warm and feed her water and broth." The golden-haired Master moved toward the door, and Kenleigh followed. "You have done an excellent job with all three of them."

Jane and Sara had refused to leave Mellina's side.

With her secret finally out, Sara had confessed that her parents had hidden her Gift and had an uncle teach her to control her abilities. She had been her parents' only surviving child, and they hadn't wanted to lose her. As there was no law stating a child *had* to be sent to the Ithrimir, when Tam had discovered her abilities when she had come to them as a young widow, he had continued her training in private.

"I feel helpless," Kenleigh confessed.

"We all do, child," Arrysanna said, her eyes on Mellina.

"What has been done with Master Jillian?" Kenleigh asked. She had not left Mellina's side, so did not know what was happening elsewhere in the house.

Arrysanna pursed her lips. "Arch Master Haden has taken her to White City. My son commanded it. However, I would have gladly slit her throat here and been done with it."

Kenleigh found herself agreeing with the Dowager, despite her previous religious training. "Is moving her safe?"

"I drugged her and provided Master Haden plenty of the potion to keep her unconscious," Master Braxton said, "And there are twenty guards with her. She is also bound. If she cannot use her hands, she cannot cause harm."

Kenleigh nodded, though she knew little of the mysteries of the Gift.

"If my son doesn't see fit to execute her, I will do it myself." There was barely suppressed rage in Arrysanna's voice.

A small sound, not quite a moan, came from the figure on the bed.

Master Braxton rushed to Mellina's right side, and Kenleigh and the Dowager went to the left. Jane sat up and rubbed her eyes. The girl's light brown hair had been braided but was now disheveled, and her brown eyes were red-rimmed. Behind Master Braxton, Sara came to her feet and nearly pushed the golden-haired man aside.

Slowly, Mellina opened her eyes, blinking slowly as things came into focus. Her eyes searched the room until she found Jane, and the sound she made was somewhere between a whimper and a sob.

The little girl threw herself on Mellina, who wrapped her arms around the child.

"Come, Jane, let the Master examine her." Arrysanna tried to pull the child away, but Jane only clung to Mellina tighter.

"She is fine, Your Majesty," Master Braxton said. "I have already examined her. I just need to ask some questions."

Mellina nodded, still looking around the room. When she found Sara, she let out a sigh and held her hand out to her friend, who took it.

"Do you know who you are?" Master Braxton asked, not taking the Queen's hand from Sara's, but pressing his fingers to her wrist.

"Mellina Morthan," she said hoarsely.

"And do you know where you are?" he asked, releasing her wrist.

Mellina looked around the room, which would be unfamiliar to her. "I think I am in Trahelion Manor."

"You are, child." Arrysanna laid her hand on Mellina's shoulder. "We have moved you to a new room."

Mellina seemed to be concentrating on something, then she took a shuddering breath. "I can't feel my feet."

Jane began sobbing quietly; Mellina held her tighter.

"The damage was... extensive," Master Braxton hedged, looking down at his patient. Kenleigh could see he was struggling to stay composed. "The magic she used was dark... nothing she could have learned from the Ithrimir."

Kenleigh saw Mellina process this information.

The woman shifted slightly, trying to move her legs, and let out a hiss of pain.

"Try not to move. I have healed you as much as I had strength to, but I will have to do another session tomorrow. The wounds are stitched for now…"

Master Braxton looked as if he felt he had failed, but Kenleigh had seen what had been left of Mellina's legs when they found her. Nothing could regrow a limb.

"Tell me," Mellina commanded, stroking Jane's back.

"You have lost your right leg from the knee down, and the left, right at the knee," Master Braxton said matter-of-factly.

"Do not blame yourself, Master," Mellina said, her voice shaking. "I am sure you did your best."

He bowed his head, and his long, blond hair swung forward to conceal his face.

"And you are unharmed?" Mellina asked the child in her arms.

"Aside from some scrapes and bruises, Jane is fine," Arrysanna said softly. "Thanks to you." She looked up at Sara. "And Lady Sara."

Mellina squeezed her friend's hand, showing no shock at Lady Sara's role in the events. "And Master Jillian?" she asked coolly.

"Has been sent to my son to deal with," Arrysanna said.

Mellina nodded, looking around the room. The décor was a century out of date and heavy on decorative flowers. Her shock to find such a room in a house owned by the Dowager was evident.

"This was my mother-in-law's room," Arrysanna explained. Then she smiled. "I will put you in charge of redecorating." She squeezed Mellina's shoulder. "First, you must rest. Master Braxton?"

"Yes, Your Majesty?" the Master asked, looking at his mistress.

"If you could come with me? We should let my son know that Queen Mellina is awake," she said, turning to go.

Once the Dowager and the Master left, Kenleigh turned to Jane. "Let's take you for a bath and a change of clothes."

She held up a hand to halt the little girl's protests. "We will come right back, if that is okay with Queen Mellina."

Mellina stroked the girl's hair and nodded. "Sara can help me freshen up too, and we can have dinner in bed."

Kenleigh and Jane left the room. No sooner had the door closed, they heard Mellina sobbing.

Kenleigh picked up Jane, who had started to cry again, and carried her to her room.

CHAPTER 68

Queen Lenathaina Morthan Coden, First Princess of Caeldenon
Seathor Hall, Port City of Seathor: Lithonia
27th of Xavar

Sanders and Lena's ladies took greater care preparing her for her arrival than they had on her wedding day.

The dark blue day dress was nowhere near as ornate as her wedding gown had been, but every pleat had been twitched into place twice; Cara had put her hair up and taken it back down at least three times; Rachel had changed her mind on what shawl would be more appropriate before settling on a dove gray trimmed in white lace; Diason, Tori's maid, was flitting around Tori as Tori flitted around Lena.

Finally, Lena said, "Enough!"

Everyone stilled, and then Sanders said, "I think you look perfect, Ma'am."

Lena nodded her thanks and moved toward the window.

It had been decided it would be best for her to wait to go topside until after the ship had docked. But she could see the walls of the city now, and Seathor Hall on the hill at the city's center.

She was glad to be entering Lithonia after the mourning period for her cousin had ended.

Rachel and Tori flanked her, and the three of them watched as the ship pulled up to the pier, and the ropes flew off the ship to be caught by dock workers.

Someone knocked on the door, and when Fenora answered it, Gavantar, Baerik, and Galwyn were on the other side.

"Ready?" Gavantar asked.

Lena nodded and crossed the room. Gavantar offered her his arm, and she took it until they reached the deck.

Half of the *Mael'Hivar* went down the brow and flanked it, fifteen to one side and fifteen to the other. She had discussed it with everyone aboard: she would go first, with Ellae and the rest would follow.

She saw them: her loyal friends and now servitors. Angela and Beth. One dressed in pale gray, and the other in pure white, mourning son and husband, respectively. She walked down, head high but heart heavy. Ellae was five paces behind her, a shadow, as she was meant to be.

Lena reached the pier and stood, waiting to see what her reception would be.

First, Angela and Beth, as well as her daughters Lissa, Anne, and Jane, dipped into deep curtsies with their heads bowed. And then in a wave, every man, woman, and child that had arrayed to greet her—what seemed to be half the city and garrison—all bowed and curtsied.

Lena's breath caught, and she had to fight back tears.

Beth stepped forward and said in a loud, clear voice, "Seathor gives welcome to Queen Lenathaina Morthan Coden!"

The cheers were deafening.

Lena raised a hand and waited for silence before saying at last, "And your Queen is thankful for that welcome, and profoundly sorry not to have been able to receive it earlier."

Her tone was solemn as her eyes rested on her friends. "I cannot bring back those that have been lost at the hands of the Usurper, but I promise you this: justice will be served!"

The cheers came in a flood, and she stepped forward, offering her hand first to Beth, as Lady of the City, and then to Angela. Both women curtsied again and kissed her hand.

She heard the sound of many feet on wood, and turned to see her husband, Galwyn, Baerik with Victoria on his arm, Fenora and Rachel, and lastly, Master Tam and his apprentices.

"You have left Lady Jane behind, Your Majesty?" Beth asked, and it was so odd for Lena to hear her friend address her so formally.

"She has been left in the care of the Dowager High Queen Arrysanna Coden, along with the daughter of the *Duc* and *Ducessa 'ah* Kilmerian," Lena said. "I thought it safer to have her far from home, and she and Lady Cressa have become attached to one another."

"I am glad that she has found a friend," Angela said.

"I am as well. She is well-loved and well looked after." Lena turned as Gavantar joined them. "I am sure you remember my husband, First Prince Gavantar Coden."

Both women curtsied, but not as deeply as they had for Lena.

"A pleasure to see you again, High Lady Bennings, High Lady Montgomery." Gavantar bowed over both women's hands in turn. "I am sorry for both of your losses, and will do what I can to see your husband and son avenged."

This statement seemed to please both women, as they gave Gavantar approving nods. Then they turned to greet Lena's ladies.

"Lady Rachel," Beth said, kissing her cheek before turning to Tori. "And Lady Victoria." She kissed Tori's cheek as well.

"Actually, it is Lady Forrester-Coden now," Gavantar said with a slight smile in his voice.

Both women looked at him in shock, and Gavantar gestured for his uncle to step forward.

"May I introduce my uncle, Lord Baerik Forrester-Coden, the *Duc 'ah* Kilmerian and husband to the *Ducessa*, Lady Victoria Forrester-Coden?"

They had also decided against trying to hide or delay announcement of the nuptials. They only hoped that they would get to meet with Victoria's family before they heard of it from another source.

Beth grinned broadly. "Harry is going to have a field day with this. Many congratulations, my dear." She kissed Tori's cheek again, and then Angela took her turn congratulating the couple.

"And this is my other Lady, Princess Fenora Tearhall," Lena said once the excitement had died down.

When all the introductions had finally been made, they got into the fleet of waiting carriages and rode through the city. The streets were lined with people all cheering for their Queen and the High Ladies. It gave Lena hope.

When they arrived at Seathor Hall, Beth led them into the larger drawing room, which was already laid for tea.

Once Lena was seated with a cup of tea in hand and a small plate of sandwiches on a table beside her, she asked, "What news do you have of Endomir?"

Angela and Beth exchanged a look, and Angela finally said, "The Usurper is missing."

"What do you mean *missing*?" Master Tam asked, setting his tea down.

"I mean no one knows where he is, and many of his personal items are gone," Angela said.

"And Eddening, Parker, and Rendon have an army outside Endomir. You won't get past them without a conflict," Beth said gravely.

"I see," Lena said. "So they have declared against me?"

"They have." Angela reached to grip her hand. "Five days ago, in the House of Lords… with ten others."

Lena did the math in her head. "So twenty-six lords and high lords are with me?"

Beth and Angela nodded.

"Magne sent a list of who is on what side," Angela assured her. "For now, there has been no open conflict, but, as you can imagine, things are very tense in the city."

"And the captives?" Lena asked.

"All released," Beth said. "My son Randal was in hiding, but has now taken his father's seat in the House."

Then she is the Dowager High Lady Bennings, and Lissa is now the High Lady—though she seems to be allowing her mother-in-law to still take the lead.

"And Stephen and Travis are well?" Lena asked, turning to Angela.

The chestnut-haired woman nodded. "They are. Both have written to me, though Anne got a longer letter from Travis." She smiled at the eldest Bennings girl.

Lena nodded. "I would like to meet with you and your generals as soon as possible to solidify our plan."

"Of course," Beth said, coming to her feet. "They are already here, waiting to greet you."

Lena put her tea aside and stood; everyone else followed suit. "Let's have them in, and then we can get down to the matter at hand."

Beth left the room and returned with three men. "Your Majesty, may I present General Landgrave, who has command of those men who owe fealty to my son; Captain Townsend, who has command of my house guard; and General Hall, in command of the Montgomery forces."

Each man bowed when introduced, Townsend looking almost reverent.

"Do you have someplace we can use to begin discussions?" Lena asked.

"I have had the smaller ballroom set up with tables and so forth." Beth turned to Lissa. "Would you like to see the ladies settled, daughter?"

High Lady Lissa came to her feet, not quite as gracefully as Lena had seen her move in the past.

For a moment, Lena let herself imagine what it would be like to be in an advanced state of pregnancy, but quickly pushed it aside.

There will be time for that later. After the war.

Lena nodded to her ladies to go with Lissa; she knew they would soon have a wealth of information for her. The three of them were experts at finding out things that Lena needed to hear.

Then she followed Beth and Angela, and was in turn followed by Ellae, Gavantar, Galwyn, Baerik, the generals, and Master Tam, who was in conversation with two other vaguely familiar Masters.

True to Beth's word, the smaller ballroom had been set up with a long table and several chairs.

The Dowager High Lady walked to the head of the table and laid her hands on the back of a chair. "This seat is for you, Your Majesty."

There was a stillness in the room as Lena walked toward it. Gavantar joined her there and pulled the chair back so she could take her seat. Once she had done so, the others sat down.

Gavantar sat to her left, and Angela and Beth to her right. She felt Ellae at her back, as always, and drew strength from that.

"Let's start with the list of who has declared against me," Lena said, sounding more confident than she felt.

CHAPTER 69

High Lord Magne Montgomery
Castle Endomir, Endomir: Lithonia
28th of Xavar

One of Magne's first acts as reinstated Regent was to let go of all the new guards that had been hired by Morlette, and to rehire—or, in some cases, release from prison—those who had been in the guard under the late King Charles.

This had been a popular move with those both in the castle and the city, as the guards under Morlette had been less concerned with protecting the citizens of Endomir and upholding the law, and more concerned with breaking it. Most people were still too nervous to attempt to leave the Bowl, with an army camped on the other side of Jasper's Keep.

The cold had taken a firm hold. Soon, snow and ice would start to make travel difficult. He wondered how the Queen planned to get to the city… and past the army, once she arrived.

That his Angela had been named Marshal General and Lady Protector of the Realm, even in a temporary capacity, made Magne proud and fearful in equal measure.

He walked to the window and looked out onto the grounds. A legion of gardeners was hard at work protecting the prized rose garden of Endomir. Every color and breed of rose in the known world was represented here; something that had taken the Morthan family two hundred years to accomplish.

He was in Charles' study, which had briefly been occupied by Morlette. With the help of Harry Harmon and Caleb Vectors, Magne had gone through all of the Usurper's papers, looking for clues on where he might be or what his plans were.

They had found the will and the letter supposedly from Charles, talking about his wishes to make Morlette his heir, and the signatures on both documents had been compared to documents in the Royal Archives. They were close, but forgeries, all three men agreed.

On top of those, they had found documents in Morlette's study and in the office of his secretary that outlined the plan they had executed to take control of the castle. It wasn't clear which one of them had concocted it, but both had been instrumental in taking the hostages.

Magne very much wanted to get his hands on Edwin Murphy, but the man had gone to ground shortly after his Master had.

"Lord Regent?" a familiar voice said from the door.

He turned to see Harry Harmon.

"No need to be so formal, Harry," Magne said, gesturing to the seat in front of the desk.

Harry took it, and Magne sat down behind the desk.

"What can I do for you?"

"Well, it's what I can do for you," Harry said, sitting forward. He was a large man, all muscle and brute strength, with short, brown hair that was starting to gray, and blue eyes.

Magne had known Harry since the two were young men new to the city.

"What's that, Harry?" he asked, curious.

"Let me help Jasper with the patrols," Harry requested. "My boy has a good hold on things up north, and you know I sent most of my family home after Morlette took hostages. All I have with me is my daughter Isadora, and she is ready to lead a patrol herself."

"I know I am regent, but I don't want to overstep into Jasper's authority."

Magne stood and walked to the sideboard to pour them both a whiskey. Once he had handed Harry his, he sat back down.

"I already talked to him," Harry said, taking a drink. "He said he could use the help."

Lord Marvin Jasper had control of the soldiers that patrolled the basin of Endomir. He was the first and last line of defense. The City Guard had its own structure, but ultimately fell under Jasper.

The Castle Guard were all Morthan guards, but the structure had been stagnate for years and had never seen any real action, so it had become a joke. Magne had asked Jasper to oversee its restructure and also take a hand in cleaning up the mess that Morlette had turned the City Guard into.

"If he wants the help, you have my consent and my blessing," Magne said, glad to have the mess off his plate. He had enough trouble as it was.

"Did you hear what happened this morning?" Harry asked, downing the rest of his whiskey.

"About Parker and Vectors' men getting into it?" Magne asked.

At Harry's nod, Magne said, "I did. Officially, I had to fine them both, but I paid Caleb's myself."

Caleb Vectors had lost a daughter to this war already; in truth, her and her child had been the first casualties. Magne had offered to have her cremated remains put in the royal oak grove, as was her right, but Caleb and his wife Giselle had elected to take her home. Only Caleb had come back from that trip. Giselle and his other children had stayed home, so Morlette had never had a hold over him.

Caleb had kept quiet since, wrapped in his grief, but now he was determined to see his daughter's friend take her rightful place. It was a fire in him.

"This city is a pot on an over-stoked fire, Magne," Harry said, looking troubled. "Any minute, that pot is going to boil over."

CHAPTER 70

High Prince Evandar Coden
White Castle, White City: Caeldenon
28ᵗʰ of Xavar

Gavan and Evandar had decided it would be best to speak to Master Jillian without Lan, at least to start. Lan had rarely left his rooms since the message had arrived from Trahelion Manor.

Thankfully, word had come that Queen Mellina lived, though she was struggling to come to terms with her missing limbs. Gavan had already set Valeran to making quiet enquiries for the best wheeled chairs available. The Gift could heal many things, but not *all*, so there were still those in the world that needed such devices.

Evandar hoped that regaining some of her mobility would help the Queen. Though she had committed a crime of her own, no one deserved to be hurt as she had been. And that she had sustained the injuries protecting the child of her dead husband and his lover… well. The woman had redeemed herself. At least in Evandar's eyes.

Three Masters of the Ithrimir and High Priest Tadaemeric were in the room with Evandar and Gavan when Jillian was carried in by two *Mael'Hivar* and escorted by two more Masters. Once she had woken, she had attempted to free herself, swearing to kill the Masters that held her. She had been silenced since.

The blonde-haired Master had been changed into simple leggings, a shirt, and a tunic for her journey to White Castle, and had declined to put her robes back on once she returned to White Castle. She had also declined to eat, drink, or speak beyond making threats. In the end, Masters had been forced to *make* her eat and drink.

Evandar did not ask how.

Jillian glared at Gavan as she was put in a chair facing him and Evandar. Their *Mael'Hivar*, Jaed, Andi, and Deldemar, stood behind them; all three had pistols trained on the woman.

"Do you know why you are here?" Gavan asked, green eyes on Jillian. His golden hair was brushed back, mane-like, and his expression was ferocious.

She looked as if she would not answer, but then finally said, "Because the damn Lithonian bitch can touch the Life Source and I didn't know it."

Her words and tone were so starkly different from the way Jillian usually spoke, Gavan and Evandar exchanged a look. This was not the woman they knew.

"You are here because you killed two of my soldiers and tried to kill Queen Mellina Morthan and Lady Jane Grey," Gavan said after several moments. "Why did you do this?"

"My actions are no affair of yours. Let me go, and I will leave your damned country forever," Jillian said, staring daggers at him.

"I am afraid the laws say otherwise, child," Tadaemeric said. "You have not only broken the laws of this country, but of the Maker himself. Murder is a grave sin."

Jillian's hot gaze turned on the priest, and Evandar was impressed that the old man didn't shrink from it. Instead, he observed her coolly.

"Your kind are nothing but charlatans and blasphemers peddling lies," she said fervently.

Tadaemeric tilted his head and looked at her. "Unlike Hestia?"

Something visceral came over Jillian's face, and she struggled against her magical bonds, nearly coming out of her chair. "Don't you say Her name!"

Most of the eyes in the room turned to the priest, save the *Mael'Hivar* and the Masters keeping Jillian contained.

He watched Jillian curiously. "You are the first Master that I have met who has been turned to the cause of that would-be goddess," he said. "But you all have the same turn of speech when confronted. You all claim it is we who are in the wrong, instead of those who seek to destroy anyone who does not share their faith."

Jillian snorted. "And where did we get that idea?"

"History a thousand years old is no excuse for you to try to kill a child," he stated firmly before turning to Gavan. "Your Majesty, she is a Hathorite. It would be prudent for you to inform the Ithram of this. If one has been turned…"

"There may be others," Gavan finished, his eyes on Jillian, who was smiling in a disturbing way.

"You will never find us all," she taunted. "We will see Her will done."

"And what is her will, child?" Tadaemeric asked, cocking his head again.

Jillian closed her mouth, refusing to speak.

"More than one of your kind has tried to infiltrate the sacred home of the Maker, and they have failed. In the end, they all out themselves, or fail in their attempts to do whatever the woman who thinks herself a *goddess* sends them to do," Tadaemeric said blandly.

The expression on Jillian's face was terrifying. So sure. So smug. So evil.

"So you think. So She would *have you* think. She has eyes and ears everywhere. Some are decoys, and others know how to be silent and listen and relay what they have seen and heard." She turned to Gavan, "So kill me. I don't mind being one of the faithful who die to do Her will and see the prophecies fulfilled."

"Take her back to her cell," Gavan said as he stood. "Your Holiness, would you please join me in my private quarters?"

The priest inclined his head in agreement.

Once Jillian had been removed from the room, the *Mael'Hivar* lowered their weapons and followed Gavan, Evandar, and Tadaemeric through the winding passages and up to the family quarters.

Maelynn and Samera were waiting in the main drawing room. They had been speaking quietly, but stopped when the men entered.

Andi, Jaed, and Del joined Em and Aria, Samera's *galvana*. Maelynn rose and greeted Tadaemeric, who kissed her cheek lightly before greeting Samera. Once he had asked after the baby, they all sat down.

"I would suggest contacting the Ithram immediately," Tadaemeric said, turning to Gavan. "I know she has broken laws here and should be tried, but, I am sorry to say, the implication that she is a Hathorite extremist fulfilling the commands of their so-called goddess is deeply concerning."

Maelynn and Samera both gasped. Their *galvanas*, who had been getting a whispered account of the meeting from the men, looked equally shocked.

"You mean to say she is working with the Hathorites?" Maelynn asked, her face draining of color.

"It explains why she was trying so hard to get into our meetings," Evandar said to Gavan. Lan had told them she had been pressing him in private. "She was looking for information."

"Lan isn't going to take this well," Samera said. "This will crush him. He loved her so."

Gavan stood and strode to the window, which faced the river and city. "It is hard to forgo the chance to seek justice and avenge lives that have been lost," he said quietly.

"Justice and vengeance are different things, Your Majesty," Tadaemeric reasoned quietly. "And by sending her to the Ithram and allowing him to extract information in ways we cannot—"

Gavan turned to face the priest, eyes blazing. "I can extract information from her."

Tadaemeric inclined his head, accepting the High King's words. "You can. But you can only hurt a body so much before it gives in. The Ithram doesn't need to inflict pain to extract information."

"How do you know this?" Gavan asked, skeptical.

"We are two sides of one coin, the Ithrimir and the priesthood," Tadaemeric said by way of explanation.

Gavan kicked his desk, which moved several inches. "Horseshit." He looked at Tadaemeric. "What do you think she meant? What prophecy did she speak of?"

The priest looked worried at this. "I do not know. This is the first I have heard of a Hathorite prophecy."

"You have heard of other prophecies?" Evandar asked, leaning forward.

The priest inclined his head but did not say anything else on the subject.

Gavan stalked back to the window. The silence that followed was thick with tension.

It was several minutes before he spoke again.

"Evandar, send the message to the Ithram. Tell him we will offer thirty *Mael'Hivar* to go with whatever Masters he picks to escort Jillian Prather to the Isles."

Evandar was quiet for a long moment. "Who will you put in command of that force?"

Gavan turned to face him and Samera. "You," he said to his brother. Samera stilled but did not speak. "I can trust no other to make sure that the Ithram has a full account of her crimes."

Evandar looked at his wife. He would miss the first months of his new daughter's life, leaving his love to bear the burdens and joys alone; that weight sat hard on his heart.

When Samera finally nodded, he let go of the breath he had been holding.

He placed his right fist to his left breast and bowed to his King.

CHAPTER 71

The Goddess Hestia, the Mystic of Hathor
The Temple of Ganna: Hathor
28th of Xavar

Hestia read the missive from Murphy again. The man had gone underground and was being hunted. He had let Morlette and control of Endomir slip through his fingers, and now two-thirds of the Lithonian lords had joined together to support the Raven woman.

He would pay dearly for that mistake, worse than Jardin had twenty years before when he had lost the Raven's father.

She looked down at the consort that had brought the message. "Any word from Servant Jillian?" she demanded.

He bowed his head to the floor and shook it, but something about his posture gave her pause.

Hestia kicked him. "Speak!"

The consort mumbled something to the floor, and she kicked him again.

"A-apologies, Divine One," he stammered. "One of our contacts that lives at the heart of the Blasphemers has sent a message saying that a Master has committed murder in Caeldenon, and someone close to the High King has been injured. The Master is on their way to the Isles with a heavy escort."

Hestia kicked him again, and the cowering man cried out in pain.

"Leave me," she said.

Once the sniveling coward left, Hestia turned to look at the prophecy on the wall again.

So many failures. Was she doomed to fail as well?

She refused.

The male child, she could use him. Priestess Castia was on her way with him now. With the boy at her side... if she removed the

Raven chit… Hestia could take the throne through him. Rule through him.

She had been right all along. The way back to the homeland was through the Fasili line. These failures were just tests of her faith, to see if she would stay true to her goddess.

Hestia would triumph in the end. The Goddess would not let them fail.

CHAPTER 72

Arch Master Lan Coden
White Castle, White City: Caeldenon
29th of Xavar

Lan stood in front of the door that led to the small set of cells in the bowels of White Castle. They were so rarely used that the guard roster had to be moved around. There was usually only a token force, but with Jillian here… there were now forty *Mael'Hivar Naheame* in the small dungeon, along with twenty Masters of the Ithrimir, most brought in from the city.

"Master Lan?" Blood General Hammond said. "Are you here to see the prisoner?"

Lan nodded stiffly. He wore his dark blue dress uniform, and his hair had been tidied as much as possible.

He had taken a leaf out of Gavantar's book and spent a solid day and night shitfaced drunk. Once his brothers had finished doing what they had to, they had joined him, and between them all, they had gone through a keg of beer and several bottles of whiskey.

Maelynn and Samera had told their husbands to stay with Lan— for more than one reason, he was sure.

Hammond opened the outer door to the dungeon and let him pass. Even here, the glittering white stone that the castle had been built from made the cells light and less oppressive than one would usually expect of a dungeon.

There was a large chamber behind the main door, with a round table on one side, and a counter set up to make tea on the other. Four Masters, some in robe and some in tunics and trousers, sat at the table, along with five guards.

Each nodded to Lan; he nodded in return, though he didn't meet any of their gazes. He could feel their pity.

"Down here, Master Lan," Hammond said, leading him to the chamber at the end of the corridor.

Ten *Mael'Hivar* lined both sides of the hall, and two Masters stood outside the chamber. Hammond opened the door, and Lan stepped in.

Four more Masters sat on stools inside the room. None looked at him, or spoke. They were focused on the woman dressed in a pair of plain brown dresses in the Caeldenon fashion.

Her hands were manacled to the table, fingers strapped down, and her feet were tied to the chair legs. White ropes of hardened Air and Energy further bound the blonde woman that he had loved for more than twenty years.

Hammond left the cell, and Jillian looked Lan over for a long moment before saying, "You look like hell."

There was no affection in her voice, nor remorse.

"I can't say you look much better, Jillian," Lan replied.

He did not step closer, but he did notice that one of the Masters had turned his focus to him.

It was to be expected. As her ex-fiancé, he could go one of three ways, and two involved losing his head and attacking—either them or her.

Jillian flexed in her bindings. "I didn't have all the knowledge I needed to complete my mission." She managed to shrug. "It was a miscalculation."

Lan looked her over, disgusted. "So you would have killed Lady Sara first? Before Jane?"

"Wouldn't you?" Jillian tilted her head and looked at him curiously. "I took out the little chits in black with a flick of my hand. Had I known that Lady Sara could touch the Life Source, I would have taken her first. My orders were to kill Jane at all costs, and the old Queen too." She shrugged again. "I will pay for my mistake one way or the other."

"Who will make you pay?"

He wanted to hear if from her. *Needed* to. He had to know.

Jillian eyed him. "If I manage to escape or am rescued, the Mystic… She who is the incarnate form of my goddess. If not, the Goddess Herself will punish me in my next life, but I hope all that I have done in Her service will be weighed against my failures, and cancel them out."

She didn't seem to be distressed that they were talking about torture or death.

"Can I ask you something?" Lan finally said.

Jillian slowly smiled. "Did I ever love you?" she guessed.

Lan nodded.

Her smile widened. "No. Never. You were a pleasant diversion, but an assignment from the start."

Pain lanced through him like a knife. Pain so sharp he felt sick with it. He had been played like a fool for decades.

"We were twenty… when did you convert?" Lan asked; the Masters around him were waiting for an answer too.

"That is none of your affair," Jillian said regally. "You can leave me now. I no longer have to listen to you natter at me, and you, Lan Coden, are a bore."

The Master that had been watching him came to his feet and took Lan's arm. Another Master stepped into the room to take the other's place on the stool.

Lan could hear Jillian laughing as he let the Master steer him out of the dungeons and up a flight of stairs.

They were somewhere in the south wing guest quarters when Lan came to himself.

The Master steered him into a small drawing room and pushed him into a chair before walking to a sideboard and pouring them both a drink.

"Cade Kline," the Master said by way of introduction as he handed Lan his. "She has been a piece of work, trying to rile all of us up in turn. Taunting. Hoping to send one of us over the edge so we end her."

Lan grunted and downed half the glass. "How is that working out for her?"

Kline shrugged. "We rotate out often—we have to. We are restraining her magically, too, so we have to keep our reserves up."

"Has she tried to escape?" Lan asked, looking out the window.

"Three times. Caused some injuries, but all could be healed," Kline said. "We knock her out at night so most of us can rest. It helps. I just wanted to get you out of there before she pushed too many buttons."

He finished his drink and clapped Lan on the shoulder. "Forget her. I know it will be hard, but it will be for the best."

"When does she leave?" Lan asked hoarsely.

Kline hesitated. "We sail on the evening tide. High Prince Evandar will accompany us."

Lan fell silent, and Kline left him alone in the room.

When Lan was alone, he poured himself another drink and knocked it back.

He had been a damn fool.

CHAPTER 73

High Master Tam Gale
Seathor Hall, Port City of Seathor: Lithonia
30th of Xavar

Tam was sitting at the desk in the bedroom that High Lady Lissa Bennings had given him for his stay. It was early, an hour past dawn, but he wanted to get his final thoughts down.

He was organizing the notes he had made in the last war council when a blinking light caught his attention. He looked up to see the red agate pulsing.

He pulled a clean sheet of paper forward and touched the Stone, imbuing it with energy and sending back the code to confirm his identity.

The message came quickly.

QLMC and FPGC,

Attack on LJG and QMM by HM JP. Minor injuries to LJG. QMM has lost part of both legs and is recovering. JP has been sent to Isles. Was working on behalf of Hathorite Goddess. LSP stopped attack. Will send info as it becomes available. Please update as to your position and plans.

Love and best wishes,
Father and Mother

Tam read the letter that had come through the Script Stone given to him by the High King and High Queen before he had left White Castle.

The words went through him like a knife.

He had worked beside Jillian for years and never suspected anything; true, she had never been warm, but some Masters didn't like to form many attachments. But to be a Hathorite? To have tried to kill a child? And poor Mellina... he could not imagine what had been done to her that she had lost her legs.

He read the letter again, and a sentence that hadn't connected before drew his attention.

LSP stopped attack.

Sara's secret, carefully protected for over three decades, was out—or at least, known by the Coden family. Her parents were dead, so her family wouldn't need to worry about a scandal of word spreading, but he would have to tell the Queen.

She's still upset with me over Queen Mellina.

Tam covered his face with his hands for a minute, gathering his strength.

How many times had he delivered such news? How many times had his words brought pain?

He was getting old and tired. He would see Lenathaina on the throne, secure and with a solid advisor at her side, and then, maybe, he could finally retire.

He picked up the letter and made sure he looked the part of Royal Advisor: his robes were clean and pressed, his white hair brushed back from his face. He looked as old and tired as he felt, but nothing could change that.

He knew where he would find her; the whole castle did.

He wasn't surprised to see the practice yards lined four and five deep, as Lenathaina and Lady Ellaemarhie—both dressed in leggings, boots, shirts, and tunics, and with braided hair—went at it hammer and tongs with their swords. To the other side of the yard, the First Prince and Prince Galwyn were doing the same, but all eyes were on Lenathaina.

He had heard the whispers; many were calling her their Warrior Queen.

The crowds made room for him at the front, and he watched as the women continued to spar. Half an hour passed before they wound down and came to a stop.

A page rushed forward and bowed before offering towels to both women to wipe the sweat from their face. The Prince and his man joined them, and the crowds moved forward, eager to speak to their Queen. Tam was glad to see that several of the *Mael'Hivar* were among them and stayed close to the Royal Couple.

He hung back and waited for the Queen to see him. When she did, he jerked his head to the side and walked back into the castle.

Lenathaina found him in the small drawing room that had been given to her for her personal use. Lady Ellaemarhie was with her, as she always was, as were First Prince Gavantar and Prince Galwyn.

"What is it, Master Tam?" she asked, towel still in hand.

He handed her the note and folded his arms inside the sleeves of his robes.

Lenathaina read the message twice before handing it to Gavantar, and whatever fatigue she felt from her morning exercise, she pushed aside. "I will draft a response. I want a detailed report on the condition of my aunt and my cousin as soon as possible."

"I will stand at the ready and send it as soon as possible," Tam replied with a bow of his head.

"LSP?" the Queen asked, as he knew she would.

"Her parents had her privately trained, enough so she could control her abilities," he replied. "I trained her further, with your uncle and aunt's knowledge."

"I see," Lenathaina said, watching him coolly.

It was hard not to fidget under that penetrating stare.

"And it seems to have been a good thing," Gavantar said, laying a hand on her arm. He gave Tam an approving nod.

Tam didn't want to know what the Prince was feeling through their Link.

"Yes," Lenathaina said, her eyes still on Tam.

He could see her wondering what other secrets he had, but after almost three hundred years... he had many. Not all were his to share.

Seeing that he wasn't going to speak further, she turned to a writing desk in the corner and wrote out her reply to the High King and High Queen.

"I am going to bathe," she said when she was finished. "I will meet with you after breakfast to see their reply."

Tam bowed as she left the room.

As he made his way back to his own room, he wondered, after all the secrets he had kept from her, if he would ever regain her trust.

CHAPTER 74

Vera Martique
Clearwater Place, City of Endomir: Lithonia
1ˢᵗ of Minn

Vera, Jack, and Samuel were sitting in the small sitting room, going over the latest exchange from the ambassador. It had been decided that the best way to move messages was to use Jack, who already had a habit of coming often to see Samuel.

Their relationship had caused a minor scandal, but with an army at the gates, two men in love had only caused a blip in the gossip mills.

There was a knock at the door, and Vera tucked away the note before calling, "Enter."

Mallard, the butler, came into the room. "The Lord Regent, High Lord Magne Montgomery, is here to see you, Mistress."

"Bring him in, Mallard," Vera said.

Samuel and Jack rose to leave, but Vera told them, "Stay for a bit."

Both men stayed on their feet, but nodded and then bowed slightly when Magne entered.

He was tall, lean, and muscular, a man who sparred with his men daily. He was bald as an egg, but had recently grown a mustache and beard.

Vera rose, and he kissed her hand before taking a seat. Jack and Sam sat on the edge of a settee and waited in silence.

Magne pulled a note from his pocket and handed it to Vera. "I thank you for the loan of Marie. She has been very helpful in getting rid of the guards who are troublemakers. She would make an excellent secretary." He arched a brow at Vera.

"That would be between you and her, Magne," Vera said, pocketing the note. She would read it in private later. "I have news from the ambassador."

"Oh?" he said, sitting forward. He glanced at the two men, but as Vera was speaking openly, he took them to be part of her team. "And I have news from Seathor."

Magne had sent her a note when Lenathaina had arrived safely, but this had been the first opportunity they had had to meet in person.

"Is the Queen well?"

"She is, and is making plans to advance. I don't have the full scope of it yet, but they plan to draw attention away from Endomir," Magne replied.

"Good. Hopefully Eddening will back down, now that the Queen has arrived," Vera said optimistically.

"Unlikely," Magne said, pulling out his pipe. "I think he is in it for the long haul."

Vera sighed. "The ambassador has had word from Caeldenon that High Master Jillian Prather, who was here as a student with High Master Tam Gale but went to Caeldenon to serve under the High King, was a secret Hathorite agent."

"I'll be damned," Magne said. "Why hasn't the fellow come to me?"

"He plans to call on you later today. We have come to an agreement to share information," Vera said.

"How the hell did that come about?" His dark brown eyes flicked to Samuel and Jack.

"I had information he needed and the means to prove my trustworthiness." Vera nodded to Jack, "And a ready-built go-between."

"Who are you, sir?" Magne said, looking at Jack.

"Jack West." He stood and gave Magne an appropriate bow for a servant to a high lord. "Footman to Lord Jaeryn Lyss, *Marque ah* Rollan and ambassador for His Majesty High King Gavan Coden of Caeldenon."

Magne stood and offered his hand to Jack, who, after a startled glance at Vera—who nodded her encouragement—took it.

The two men shook, and Magne turned to Samuel. "You, I have seen before."

Samuel stood and bowed as well before shaking Magne's hand. "Samuel Thane, Your Grace. I am an employee of Mistress Vera's."

"And Jack is your friend?" Magne asked, taking his seat again.

"My partner," Samuel corrected, laying a hand on Jack's knee to make his meaning clear.

"Been together long?" Magne asked, not at all put off.

"Casually for a year, but we have been exclusive to one another for almost four months," Samuel replied.

"As long as you trust him," Magne said with a friendly smile before turning to Vera. "It might be best for me and the ambassador to pass information through you more often than not. If we are seen meeting regularly, many will believe us to be working together or outright plotting."

"A wise move. Speak to him when you meet today," Vera suggested. "You are known to come and go here, so that won't be shocking."

Magne nodded and rose. "I have a meeting with the Council. There is a lot of tension, with an army outside the gates."

"Send my love to Angela and Beth, please." Vera smiled sadly, and he laid a hand on her shoulder.

He knew of her relationship with the Bennings, but wouldn't say more in front of Samuel and Jack.

"You know where to find me if you want to talk."

Vera squeezed his hand in return and walked him to the door.

CHAPTER 75

High Lord Marc Eddening
The Southern Road, near Nain's Hold: Lithonia
2ⁿᵈ of Minn

The Council meeting yesterday had turned into a shouting match between those high lords who were on the Queen's side, and the ones on his. Parker and Rendon had demanded that their army be allowed into the basin, and Harmon, Vectors, and Maceon had demanded they disperse their troops immediately.

In the end, Montgomery had said they had to remove their force from the gates, or they would be held as traitors.

The silence that had filled the room was deafening.

Marc, Parker, Rendon, and Parr had left the council chamber and adjourned to Marc's house, where they had decided the best move was to leave Endomir and head for Seathor, finding a point to block Lenathaina on the road.

Parr had already sent messages to his estates to begin a muster of his troops. He would meet his men on the march and cut Lenathaina off from the north. She couldn't have a large force at her aid, with all the high lords still in the city. So they could take her and her escort, and force her to abdicate. It would be neat and tidy.

They left as the sun was setting on the city, and camped with their men outside Jasper's Keep. The next time Marc saw Marvin Jasper, the Lord would be kneeling to Marc as his King.

He would forgive those who'd followed the chit; it would be better to heal wounds and move forward than to punish those who had been charmed by the raven-haired beauty.

Marc stepped out of his tent as the camp was coming to life. Around him, his men were breaking their fast and taking the camp apart. Everyone who saw him bowed or saluted.

Most of these men weren't used to being on the march or breaking camp. They were mostly farmers and retainers of Marc, Rendon, and Parker. The makeshift army was led by their house guards. He hoped with some time and practice, they would shape up into a regular army. As it was, it took three hours to break camp and get on the move.

As they passed Nain's Hold, Marc slowed. House guards dressed in Samuel Collins' umber and dark green lined one side of the road, blocking the drive to the Keep. Martin Collins, Lord Samuel's heir, stood at their center. All were armed with rifles, which lay against their shoulders.

Marc gave Martin Collins an ironic salute and rode on.

In time, they would see that he had only done what was needed to secure Lithonia and strengthen her.

CHAPTER 76

Queen Lenathaina Morthan Coden, First Princess of Caeldenon
Seathor Hall, Port City of Seathor: Lithonia
3rd of Minn

Lena rose early but didn't dress for her usual morning sparring session with Ellae. Instead, she donned a dark green riding dress with split skirts in the Lithonian fashion, and buckled on the gold and silver tooled belt that Gavantar had had made to match the scabbard for the sword his mother had given her.

The spell-forged silver filigreed hilt fit her hand perfectly. She had worn the sword often on the ship so she could become accustomed to its weight. Movement was trickier in Lithonian garb.

She hoped that, in time, she could move back and forth between Lithonian and Caeldenon dresses, as she did in White Castle. She had to admit the Caeldenon dresses were far more comfortable.

To finish off her appearance, Sanders braided Lena's hair and coiled it atop her head. She was as ready as she could be for the eight hours of riding they'd planned for the day.

"How do I look?" Lena asked, turning to Sanders.

"Like the Warrior Queen they are calling you, ma'am," Sanders said, giving Lena a last inspection.

Cara Sanders wore a black riding dress, though she would be riding in a carriage with the other Royal maids. She was enjoying her place as senior maid and all the perks that came with it.

Ellae looked Lena over from the corner where she was reading a book. "You will do." She stood and tucked the small volume in her pocket. It had been a gift from High Lady Angela after Ellae had asked questions about the history of the Morthan line. The book was about the last civil war, three hundred years ago. "Ready?"

Lena nodded, and the pair left the room. Cara would finish packing and follow with the baggage train and servants.

They walked down the massive staircase and turned into the dining room, where most of the guests were already eating. As a mark of respect, High Lady Lissa had put Lena in the seat that the high lord of the House would normally occupy.

Everyone rose when she entered the room, but she motioned for them to sit while she made herself a plate at the buffet. When she took her place, Gavantar was already seated on her right, and he took her hand to kiss it after she was settled.

"Good morning." Her husband said with a smile.

The previous night, they had taken full advantage of the last one they'd have in a real bed for a few days, so she was pleasantly sore, and he knew it.

"Good morning, husband." Lena squeezed his fingers before turning to her meal. "Is everything in order?" she asked before she took a bite of eggs.

"As ready as it can be, Your Majesty," Baerik answered as he snagged a roll and put it on Victoria's plate.

She rolled her eyes at Lena, who suppressed a laugh, but began putting jam on the roll.

"I am impressed with General Landgrave and General Hall," Baerik continued. "They have been drilling their men from dawn to dusk for a month, and have put together a decent army for you."

"Lord Forrester-Coden has been kind enough to lend us some of the *Mael'Hivar* to improve the drills and help arrange the companies," General Hall put in gruffly, inclining his gray head toward Baerik. "They have a different way of doing things, but I think we can blend their style with ours and make you a strong force, Your Majesty."

"Those sharp shooters they have are like nothing I have seen before," General Landgrave added. He was a short man, and a little overweight, but he still moved fast. She had seen him sparring in the yards.

"I am glad that you and Lord Forrester-Coden are working well together." Lena smiled at her uncle-in-law. "I have the greatest respect for him. If you can get Under Sect-Commander Mahone on her own, she has quite a few stories about the Lord General."

Baerik blushed and turned back to his breakfast.

*****

An hour later, Lena mounted a black gelding and arranged her riding skirts. She was thankful the split skirts let her ride astride; it was far more comfortable with the sword on her hip.

Settled on her mount and in full regalia, she got many approving looks from the soldiers and generals, while the high ladies and ladies, whose husbands were still in Endomir or just now on the march, watched her in awe—even Angela and Beth, who she had known all her life.

They had all seen her in the practice yards and knew her weapon wasn't for show. She also had a pistol on her belt, and a bow and quiver attached to her saddle. Her dark blue cloak was not pulled closed yet, even though a cold wind came off the bay. She wanted them to see her weapons and her strength, to know that she could lead them.

"Marc Eddening thinks he knows our moves and our plans. He thinks to prevent us from reaching Endomir," Lena said, her voice loud and clear. "But there are seats of power that predate Castle Endomir."

There were cheers from those assembled inside the courtyard; once they quieted, she continued.

"Eddening thought to take Endomir by force and intimidation, and in. my mind, that makes him no better than Morlette. We will show him that the people of Lithonia will not bow to a tyrant!"

The cheers this time echoed off the walls.

A Master stood at the gates, relaying her words to the crowds outside. They added their cheers to those inside the walls.

"Onward, to Hardcastle!" Lena shouted as she flicked her horse's reins and headed for the gates, Gavantar at her side, and Ellae and Galwyn at their backs.

CHAPTER 77

Shan Alanine Fasili
Aboard the Sacred Star: the Indayon Ocean
6th of Minn

Alanine watched the coast of the main island vanish from sight. Cousin Isra had told her she thought the journey to Lithonia would take fifteen days.

Just over a month ago, Alanine had never left the lands of her mother's estates, and now she had not only been to the Imperial City, but she had left Pannarius and been to the Isles of the Ithrimir, and was heading for Lithonia.

She missed her sister already but Nijah had been so happy to explore the Isles with her cousins. She ached for Namar. Her little brother. Before Alanine had left the nursery, he had followed her everywhere, always asking questions. He constant companion. She didn't know if she would ever see him again. She feared if she dwelled over her loss to much, she wouldn't be able to bear it.

Amir came to stand next to her. His mahogany skin had darkened during their time at sea, thanks to his daily sparring sessions with Isra om the deck. He had bold features, deep black eyes, and was heavily muscled. At first, he had intimidated Alanine, but now she found his presence a comfort. "I suppose it is too late to ask if you are sure of your course."

Alanine gave him a wry smile. "I'm afraid so. But I think this is right for me. That way of life…"

She didn't know how to describe it, the segregation of society, of sexes and classes, and the minutia that governed every aspect of her life.

"Every country has its differences," Amir said with understanding, turning to her. "But if you hold firm to who you are here," he laid his hand on his heart. "You will do well. I have no doubt. You are like my Isra, you have a core of steel."

Alanine glowed at his words. But she still felt bad about leaving Nijah alone on the Isles.

She voiced this concern to Amir.

"She would always be in danger, left in Pannarius," he said after a time. "I believe those Hathorites know who and what she is. She is safer on the Isles. As safe as she can be. Perhaps when you decide where to settle... if you go back to River Keep, we will not leave you without a Master by your side."

"And if I don't?" she asked, speaking the question that had been weighing on her mind.

"Even then, we would not leave you on your own," Amir said, putting an arm around her. "Our Mouriani has reached the position of Arch Master. She could come be with you."

"Your eldest, isn't she?" Alanine asked, comforted by his fatherly embrace.

"She is. And much like her mother. And like you," Amir said.

They stood there and watched the shores fade away until all they could see, no matter where they looked, was water.

CHAPTER 78

Samuel Thane
Clearwater Place, City of Endomir: Lithonia
6th of Minn

Samuel had gone downtown to get his favorite tobacco. He could have added it to the shopping list for the household, but it felt good to get out and stretch his legs.

He had spent most of the last ten years walking miles every day, so his new sedentary lifestyle made him twitchy; he found himself making little excuses to go for a walk most days.

Usually his walks were uneventful, but that morning, he rushed back to Mistress Vera with news.

He went straight to her office and knocked on the door, opening as soon as she said, "Enter."

"Light, man!" Mistress Vera looked him over. "What is the matter?"

Samuel caught his breath before saying, "One of the footmen from Havencrest Manor was found dead in an alley this morning."

A few months ago, Samuel would have said murder could never happen in Endomir, but they had now seen four in the last months—though one had been called an execution.

"Maker preserve his soul," Vera said solemnly. "But why murder a footman?"

"Jack can tell you that footmen know a lot about the people they serve." Samuel shrugged. "King Richard is dead, so whoever did it was most likely looking for information about Morlette."

Vera nodded, thinking. Finally, she asked, "How did it happen?"

"That is the oddest part." Samuel took a seat. "There wasn't a mark on the body save a small cut on his finger."

"The man didn't just lay down and die!" Vera glared at Samuel as if he had suggested that. "Not from a tiny cut."

"I was told they had a Master in to look at him, and still, no one knows," Samuel said.

"Has anyone thought to look at Havencrest for Morlette?" Vera asked slowly.

"I heard that they sent someone around to see if anyone had heard from him, but the butler said they hadn't seen Morlette in months. Not up close." Samuel pulled out his pipe and began packing it with tobacco. "But loyal servants might lie."

Vera nodded in agreement. "Keep an eye on the place for anything suspicious."

"I have been doing that since he vanished," Samuel replied.

CHAPTER 79

High Lord Magne Montgomery
Castle Endomir, Endomir: Lithonia
7th of Minn

High Lord Harold Harmon and Lord Marvin Jasper sat across from Magne in his office.

"No news?" Magne asked, lighting the cigar that Marvin had brought with him.

Jasper had a fine stock of Thynnian cigars that he regularly imported, and he shared with those he counted friends.

"No. We have been back to both Morlette House and Havencrest, and all the servants swear they haven't seen him. We even searched both," Harry said, lighting his own cigar. "The butler at Morlette House said he is getting ready to cover everything in dustcloths."

"Havencrest isn't closed down?" Magne asked, leaning forward.

"Most is. Some of the upstairs rooms are still open, but when I asked, I was told that those are the rooms getting a deep clean at the moment." Harry shrugged. "I don't know how these things are done. I could ask Anne."

"Do that," Marvin said, letting out a cloud of smoke. "And I will ask Alice. Might have her come take a stab at talking to the servants. That woman can get just about anyone to open up to her."

Magne felt a spike of jealousy that Marvin had his wife with him. He missed Angela. More than anything he wished that they had been able to grieve together.

He let the barrier down that muted the Link binding them. She was sore, as if she had been riding for many days. He wondered if she had only been on horseback, or had ridden in a carriage too. It had been years since she had spent so much time in the saddle.

He sent a wave of love and pride her way and felt those things in return before muting the Link again.

"We need to find Morlette," Harry said, "I don't think the man is hiding in a cave, so he is either in the city or has managed to get someone to smuggle him out."

"Would anyone help him, though?" Magne asked, leaning forward.

"His man is missing too," Marvin reminded them. "I have a rough likeness of the man that I have distributed, but he still may have slipped by."

"I won't give up yet," Magne said. "He may be laying low until we call of the search."

Both men nodded.

"I don't know that he could cause much trouble," Harry said, "But I sure do want to get my hands on the bastard."

"A lot of people do," Magne snorted. "And that is the problem. There are some that would slit his throat and leave him in the streets. I want him to pay."

Marvin looked him over. "You would do more than slit his throat, and none of us would stop you."

Magne's hands were shaking.

He had thought long and hard about what he'd do if he had the choice, but deciding what happened to Morlette wasn't his job. It was the Queen's.

CHAPTER 80

Dowager Queen Mellina Morthan
Trahelion Manor, Providence of Denon: Caeldenon
7th and 8th of Minn

Sara still took daily walks, and now that her abilities were known, Master Braxton had taken up her training where Master Tam had left off. He had contacted the Ithram, who had given official permission for her continued studies, stating she was far too old to be an apprentice, especially in light of the fact that Master Braxton felt she could pass her Master's test with very little study. There had been a lightly veiled suggestion that if she could pass the tests to become a journeyman, that could be arranged.

Sara had confessed to Mellina that she wanted to visit the Isles someday, just to see what they were like, but for now, she was happy with her life the way it was.

It seemed the Ithram was equally content to leave Sara loose, as long as a Master had an eye on her. The lessons meant that Sara spent less time with her, so Mellina had to find new ways to fill her hours. She was glad that she had Jane to keep her company.

Jane was with Mellina every moment that the Dowager High Queen allowed. Arrysanna and Mellina agreed that the little girl needed to return to her studies and spend time with the other little girls, but Jane still took breakfast and tea with Mellina, and dinner too, as Mellina insisted she be carried out to enjoy dinner with the rest of the household.

She refused to hide herself away and dwell on her many losses.

At night, Jane curled up in bed with Mellina, who read to the child until she fell asleep. Sometimes, Sara or one of the other women would carry Jane back to her bed, and sometimes, Mellina let her sleep there, comforted by her presence.

Would Garrett and Richard have been different, if I had given them the same love and affection?

Perhaps if she could have seen past her own hurt pride and losses, she would have seen the damaged boys they were *before* they became damaged men with power.

Nothing for it, now. What's done is done.

At least she had done better with Brandon. Her sweet boy. Her baby. He was safe in the Isles, learning to be a Master of the Ithrimir. He would outlive them all.

One of the male black-clad warriors came to carry Mellina to dinner, as he usually did. She wore a light gray evening gown that covered the stumps of her legs.

The bandages had finally come off the day before. The skin was still tender, so Sara had cut several sets of stockings, refashioning them into something that would cover Mellina's legs and keep them warm.

Another of the *Mael'Hivar* opened the door to the drawing room, and she was carried in and set into a chair.

"Good evening, Mellina dear," the Dowager said once she had made herself comfortable.

Mellina smiled in return.

"You didn't get to spend much time with the family while visiting White Castle," Arrysanna continued, "but I think you met my granddaughter?"

High Princess Aeleonna Coden had arrived midafternoon, according to Sara.

High Princess Aeleonna gave a small curtsy before taking the seat next to Mellina and taking her hand. "We were so sorry to hear of your injuries, but everyone at home has said that you were so brave." She pulled a small velvet envelope from her pocket. "Papa wanted to come and give this to you himself, but with everything…"

"Yes, a murderous High Master is a lot to deal with," Mellina said.

Aeleonna smiled back. "I am just glad she was found out before she became my aunt."

313

"How is your uncle holding up?" the Dowager asked. "He hasn't responded to my letter or my message through the Stone."

Aeleonna didn't release Mellina's hand, or the envelope she held in the other, but turned to her grandmother. "Better than one might expect, Gran, but he is feeling like a fool."

The Dowager sighed but didn't say anything else.

Aeleonna turned back to Mellina and handed her the envelope. Mellina opened it and pulled out a medal on a red ribbon, a golden shield embossed with a rose.

"What is this for?" she asked nervously, looking at the Princess.

"It is the Shield of the Realm, the medal awarded to those who act selflessly in defense of others," Aeleonna said before pulling out a vellum scroll and passing it to her. "It comes with this."

Jane came to stand beside Mellina to admire the medal, and Mellina opened the scroll, bewildered. A large gold wax seal with the Caeldenon crest was affixed to a red, white, gold, and purple ribbon at the bottom. She heard the Dowager and the other Caeldenon lords and ladies do likewise commenting on the medal as well.

Mellina had to read the document twice before she took it in.

Gavan Dominaris Coden, High King of Caeldenon and Shield of the Realm, hereby creates Dowager Queen Mellina Morthan the Marquess 'ah Shael, a hereditary title. She will be a direct vassal of the High King and will be granted all the Rights and Privileges accorded a Marquess. Queen Mellina has one year to name her chosen heir and to claim her seat in the House and her Home, Shael House, located in the Providence of Denon.

By Order of
High King Gavan D. Coden
1st of Minn, the year 1001

"Oh, Aunt Mellina!" Jane exclaimed as she read the document. "Soon, you will have as many titles as cousin Lenathaina." She giggled.

"We can't have that," the Dowager said with a smile. "So, what has he done?"

Mellina handed Jane the parchment, which she took to the Dowager with solemnity—as much as a ten-year-old girl could muster. "Aunt Mellina is a *Marquess*!"

Aeleonna handed Mellina another envelope while everyone was distracted with the letter of patent. "Mother and Papa asked me to give this to you as well, to read in private. I also have some things to bring to your room later."

She looked at Jane and then back to Mellina. "I cannot imagine the pain of an unfaithful husband or having to deal with the consequences of that infidelity, but I can say that you did a wonderful thing."

Mellina squeezed the young woman's hand. She was incredibly beautiful, with amber skin and silver hair and eyes. She had heard that High Prince Evandar's son was after her, and she could see why. "Thank you."

The Dowager had the letter of patent taken to Mellina's room, and everyone drank a toast in her honor before they moved to the dining room. There, tender roast beef was served with glazed carrots, and potatoes mashed with butter and cream.

Jane sat beside her, and Mellina watched as the little girl ate her meal and chatted with Cressa and Nyelle. The girls were planning to take a ride to sketch the next day, and they invited Aeleonna, who, it turned out, was a talented painter.

"You should show Aeleonna the samples you are looking at for your rooms here," the Dowager said to Mellina.

"Which rooms has she been given, Gran?" Aeleonna asked, taking a bite of her carrots.

"Your great-grandmother's old suite. I think I shall rename it the Shael Suite," the Dowager said, taking a sip of her wine. "Better than the High Queen Zephier Suite."

Aeleonna hid a smile. The Dowager's distaste for her dead mother-in-law was well-known. "I would love to see what you are doing," she told Mellina. "And, of course, if you need help with Shael House when the time comes, I would be pleased to help you there as well."

"If you want to come to my rooms tomorrow, I would love to get your opinion. Arrysanna refuses to help, and Sara finds herself busy." She smiled at Sara, who blushed. Mellina knew that she felt guilty for about not spending more time with her. "And Seryl can't hold onto a decision for more than a day," she teased the young woman.

"I do think that the green would be best for the furnishing," Seryl protested. "I said so twice!"

Mellina turned to Aeleonna, who was smiling. "She also said the same of blue and violet, in turn."

"I will come after breakfast and be the deciding vote," Aeleonna promised.

*****

Mellina had been too tired the night before to face whatever Gavan and Maelynn Coden had to say in the missive Aeleonna had given her. She had stayed up late, enjoying the company, and had only left the gathering long enough to get Jane to sleep.

She was slow to wake and took her breakfast in bed. Once Jane left for her lesson, Mellina pulled out the letter from the High King and Queen.

5ᵗʰ of Minn, the Year 1001

Dear Mellina,

In light of what you have done for dear Jane, Gavan and I thought that it would be appropriate to honor you. It also gave us the excuse to provide you a place of safety.

We are so sorry that someone we trusted did this to you, but also so proud of your courage and quick thinking. Nothing can bring back what you have lost — or make up for our failing to keep you safe, as we promised Lenathaina we would — but at least now, no matter what happens in Lithonia, you have a home of your own. A place to make your own. Let us know when you have settled on an heir, and if there is anything that we can do to assist you, when it is time for you to move. The property is a small one, but has a decent income and is near Rose Hall, where Mother Arrysanna spends most of her time.

317

Aeleonna has a second present from us. Should any adjustments be needed, she will send us a message, and we will have the craftsman come deal with them directly.

Our best wishes to you,

Maelynn and Gavan Coden

Mellina tucked the letter into her nightstand and sat quietly for a moment. Even if Lena pardoned her, Mellina felt she would never be fully welcomed into Lithonian society again. At least here, she thought that most people would accept her actions.

She had just finished dressing, with the help of her maid, Lyle, when High Princess Aeleonna knocked on the door. Seryl let her into the sitting room, and the female *Mael'Hivar* assigned to her that day, Micah, carried Mellina in to meet her.

Micah was moving to set her on an armchair, but Aeleonna had risen and was laying a hand on a plushily padded mahogany chair that had wheels.

At Mellina's nod, Micah set her in the new chair, and Seryl helped arrange her skirts.

"Father had it made for you. Mother thought the dark gray would go with most things you would wear," Aeleonna said, stroking the soft material that the chair was upholstered with. "And you can either have someone push you, or use the wheels to move yourself."

Mellina touched the metal wheels. The chair was shaped like an armchair with an elevated leg rest, and the seat was angled so Mellina wouldn't slip out, even though she couldn't use her legs to keep her stable.

Master Braxton came in once a day to help her exercise her legs so she didn't lose muscle, but at the moment, she had to wait for someone to carry or move her when she wanted to change positions or go to another room. She hadn't been outside yet.

"Is it comfortable?" Aeleonna asked anxiously.

"Very," Mellina said. Her throat was tight with emotion. "I am very grateful for all your parents have done for me."

"Shall we take it for a test drive?" the silver-haired young woman suggested.

Mellina nodded, and Micah moved behind her and began pushing; Seryl opened the door to the suite, and Mellina was pushed out of the sitting room and down the hall.

She didn't feel at all jostled; it was far better than being carried from place to place.

"Where to, Your Majesty?" Micah asked.

"Where is the Dowager High Queen?" Mellina asked.

"She will be in the day drawing room, doing her embroidery," Seryl supplied.

"Very well. That is where we will go," Mellina said, smoothing her skirts. Her voice was trembling with emotion. Joy, sorrow, regret and thankfulness all battled for the upper hand.

I will have to write the High King and Queen to express my thanks for giving back some of my freedom.

CHAPTER 81

High Queen Maelynn Coden
White Castle, White City: Caeldenon
8ᵗʰ of Minn

"We never suspected her," Gavan said as he took Fadean from Samera so she could button her dress up again. He took a cloth from her and put the baby over his shoulder and began patting her back in a practiced manner. "Who is to say there aren't more Masters that have converted?"

Fadean let out a large belch, almost in agreement with her uncle.

"Not just Masters," Samera said as she finished adjusting herself. "It could be anyone."

Gavan settled into a more comfortable position and laid the baby on his chest. Fadean's groping fingers found his warrior's braid and clamped on. She settled, and Samera took a sandwich from the tray and sat across from Gavan.

"But why?" Maelynn asked as she poured everyone a fresh cup of tea. "We have always assumed they were only looking for more land or resources. If that is so, why would they go to the trouble of putting spies in our home, or ordering the murder of a child?"

"I have been thinking on that as well," Gavan said as he rubbed Fadean's back. She was a good baby and usually slept shortly after she ate. Her Uncle Gavan was one of her favorite beds. "It has been some time since anyone has tried to send a missive to Hathor."

"Because they set our ships on fire," Samera retorted with irony.

"But *why*?" Maelynn asked as she passed out the tea and sat down. "None of it makes sense."

"Do you really expect fanatical zealots to make sense, Mae?" Gavan asked as he bent down and laid the baby in her sleeping basket.

"It would make a nice change of pace," Maelynn replied tersely.

"What about those women?" Samera asked between bites. She had already regained her figure but was eating often since she was nursing the baby herself.

"Which women? There are lots of women," Gavan murmured, taking a sandwich for himself.

Samera rolled her eyes. "The ones taken at the Battle of Keltonmere." She didn't call him dense, but her tone heavily implied it.

Maelynn hid a smile.

"Oh yes, those women," he said, ignoring her tone. "What about them?"

"Why don't we have a few of them brought around for a nice chat?" Samera said. "If they really have changed sides, we might be able to learn a bit about the Hathorites. Couldn't hurt."

"Unless one is a secret magi," Gavan scoffed as he grabbed another sandwich. "Hopefully Lan can join us. If not, then Jacean Greer."

Maelynn nodded at the suggestion. "Jacean is a talented fighter, both with a blade and with his Gift." He was also the Master they employed to oversee the training of the Red Shields and Gold Swords.

"So… I can arrange it?" Samera asked.

"Yes, but I want to be there too." Gavan met her gaze.

Samera yawned, and smiled at her brother-in-law, "If you must."

Maelynn said, "Go get some sleep. We can take her to the nanny if she wakes up."

"Are you sure?" her sister-in-law asked, but she was already standing.

"Get on with you," Gavan said gruffly. "Fadean and I get on perfectly."

Samera kissed his cheek. "All the children get on with you… until they start talking back."

"Even then, they follow me about." He chuckled.

Samera left, shaking her head.

Once she had gone, Maelynn settled herself on the settee with Gavan, who wrapped an arm around her.

"Are you sure you don't want another of those?" He nodded to the baby in her basket.

"I know you would love one, but I am just fine with the six we have, plus Galwyn, Fenora, and Jaemi," Maelynn said. "But we can enjoy this one on the side."

CHAPTER 82

Edwin Murphy

City of Endomir, Endomir: Lithonia

9th of Minn

Selwyn Mathers had recognized Edwin in the Blue Hound Pub. Killing him had been necessary, but before he did that, he had found a quiet place to interrogate the man.

Morlette wasn't made for roughing it; he had been pampered his whole life. It had been eighteen days since he had vanished from Castle Endomir, so Edwin was sure he had found someplace to lay low. Someone to hide him. But he didn't have many friends, so Edwin was sure that Morlette was either in his new home, Morlette House, or in Havencrest Manor.

The staff at Morlette House was new and didn't have much loyalty to Morlette yet. Havencrest Manor, though... many knew and respected him, because Morlette had protected them from Richard.

Edwin had watched the manor a few times but hadn't seen sign of the jumped-up lordling. Morlette abandoning his post was going to cost Edwin.

Before I leave the city, I am going to pay that little shit back.

Mathers, with some coaxing, had revealed that Morlette was indeed in the house and keeping to his private rooms. Only the cook, housekeeper, and butler were allowed in. The few times that someone had come to see if he was there, the cook had hidden him in the root cellar.

Thanks to the things that the Mystic had taught Edwin, his questioning hadn't left a mark on the footman. A Master would be able to tell that he had been killed by magic, but not *how*.

A nice parting gift to the city of ingrates who had always looked down on Edwin: fear.

He penned a note to the Lord Regent and dropped it at the post office. He wished he could stay to watch Morlette be taken in, but he needed to get out of the city before anyone saw Selwyn Mathers' double walking around.

He had cut the man's finger and taken some of his blood—it was needed to make the transformation. He had been quick, so it wouldn't be a perfect likeness, but near enough. It's not like he would be able to leave the city looking like Edwin Murphy... he was too well known.

No, he would have to wear this face until he got back to Hathor. Just to be safe.

CHAPTER 83

High Lady Beth Bennings
twenty miles south of Hardcastle: Lithonia
9ᵗʰ of Minn

Beth and Angela rode next to one another, not far behind the Queen. Lenathaina had ridden all day every day, with her eye-catching sword on one hip and a beautifully made pistol on the other. A bow and arrow hung from the pommel of her saddle in front of her right knee and more than once she had notched an arrow and taken down a bird while still riding. She was impressive and commanding. She was strong and powerful. The men were in awe of her.

High Prince Gavantar was impressive himself, but that he and the *Duc 'ah* Kilmerian bowed to the Queen and asked her advice and took her orders made an impression on the Lithonian generals and soldiers. And somehow, the woman that was a shadow to the Queen, the tall, silver-blonde woman that Lena affectionately called Ellae, looked less the guard that she was and more an extension of the powerful Queen.

"I can't put my finger on it," Angela said, again.

This was a conversation they'd had often since Lena had returned to them.

"It can't just be marrying him," Beth said, again. "Something changed her."

Angela nodded.

The pair were silent for a time before Lady Rachel Malick dropped back. Rachel, the *Ducessa*, and Princess Fenora always rode with or just behind Lenathaina. A she-wolf pack.

"Lady Rachel," Beth said. "To what do we owe the pleasure?"

"The Queen would like to invite you to a council after dinner," Rachel said, keeping pace with them.

Beth noted that Princess Fenora, the *Duc,* and the *Ducessa* had likewise dropped back, as well as a few of the *Mael'Hivar* officers.

Angela and Beth were the only High Houses represented, but all their vassals either had wives or another family member leading their House guard, and had soldiers among the army that trailed after the Queen or scouted ahead. Sending high-ranking people to invite them to the council was a wise move.

"We serve at her pleasure," Angela said, "and will be happy to attend the council."

"Tomorrow is an important day," Beth replied. "It is a smart to meet beforehand."

Rachel inclined her head.

Beth thought the honey-haired woman was another who had changed. She had always been at Lenathaina's side, her constant companion and advisor. But there were sharp edges now that hadn't been there when she'd left Lithonia only four months ago.

What happened to the women who had left Endomir?

All three of them seemed to have aged; Lena and Rachel most of all, but Victoria had left as a young woman and returned married to a *Duc* and was now the sister-in-law of the High King.

There was something they weren't being told, and Beth didn't like it.

"What a pretty bracelet," Angela said, nodding to the blue ribbon clasped around Rachel's wrist.

They had only seen it because Rachel had raised her hand to push back her hood.

The air was frigid, even though the sun was shining, but the warmth and light were welcome, as the last few days had been damp and miserable.

The blue ribbon of the bracelet had a pattern of red interlaced that didn't match the dark green riding dress the lady-in-waiting wore, so Beth figured it must have some other significance.

Rachel blushed. "It is a Caeldenonian courting bracelet. It signifies that I haven't yet accepted a proposal, but I am considering my suitor seriously."

Beth smiled at that. "It seems all three of you went to Caeldenon and found happiness."

Something dark crossed Rachel's face, and she was quiet for a long time before turning back to them. "It was a journey that changed me in more ways than I could have imagined, but yes, I found love and happiness."

She twitched her reins and pulled her horse out of line. "I will let the Queen know that you will be at the council."

She nudged her horse forward and vanished into the knot of black-clad warriors that surrounded the Queen and First Prince.

"Curiouser and curiouser," Angela muttered.

"Isn't it?" Beth replied.

*****

Lena sat at a camp table in the middle of a large pavilion tent. The thin scar on her neck drew Beth's eye again.

She had asked about it once already and received only a sharp look.

Beth surveyed the tent that had been erected for the meeting. The Caeldenon contingent had brought more than warriors and horses: they had brought the knowledge of long campaigns and the quick setup and breakdown of camps. This was what the *Mael'Hivar* lived and trained for: war.

Beth and Angela were seated on folding camp stools as a sign of respect for their ranks and positions. Angela was still the acting lady marshal, and Beth, the admiral. Around the tent the representatives for the Houses that traveled with them stood with the captains of their forces and the *Mael'Hivar* commanders.

The First Prince and the *Duc* sat with Lena, Angela, and Beth. A woman with copper dark skin and cropped, red hair stood next to Prince Galwyn, having a quiet conversation.

Beth had spoken to Commander Mahone a few times and liked the woman, though she seemed to have a sharpness to her.

Lord Edward Proudmourn, who was Angela's brother-in-law and the last of the Proudmourn brothers, had command of his eldest brother's men. Lord Deverry, the head of the House, was in Endomir supporting Magne, so David, the middle brother, had been left in charge of Southwind, the family seat. Lady Cynna Payne, wife of Lord Nicholas, was leading her husband's men, having left her daughter-in-law and daughter in charge of their family seat, the Stone.

She was the eldest of the nobility on the road with them at seventy-seven, and she didn't let any of them forget it. She had been offered—but had refused—a chair. On the other end of the spectrum, Lord Soren Prather and his wife Lady Wren were the youngest, next to Lena herself.

Lord Mark Highland had sent his mother Lady Mary, and Lord Joseph Southernby had sent his widowed sister, Lady Ella Malick, who was mother to Lady Rachel.

Rachel had grown up in fosterage at Endomir, as Lady Ella had taken a long time to come to terms with the death of her husband, who had been the right hand of Prince Matthew Morthan. Ella and Rachel had danced around one another in polite conversation, but had spent little real time together.

Lady Kern Lorvette, Morlette's uncle, had sent his wife Lady Kendra in his stead. Kendra was sour-faced and rarely came to the city, but seemed pleased to have an honored place among this company; it made Beth wonder if staying away from the city had been her choice.

"The messengers that I sent to the Steward of Hardcastle and the city council of Dale have returned," Lena said, putting two envelopes on the table. "Lord Gerard Rythan has written out his pledge of fealty and promises to give it in person when I arrive, and the mayor and Council have done likewise."

"Gerald is a good lad and a smart one," Lady Cynna Payne said. "You needn't worry about him, Your Majesty. The Rythans have always served your family well."

Lena inclined her head to the old lady with a small smile. "Thank you, Lady Payne."

She set the letters aside and stood. Every seated person in the room did likewise.

"I am less concerned about our reception and more concerned about defending our position once we have taken command of the castle and city," she explained, looking down at the map.

Victoria pulled a notebook from her pocket, along with a pen.

Beth hadn't known the young woman long, but her studious approach to the conflict hadn't surprised either herself or Angela.

"Your Majesty?" Lord Baerik ventured. "Might I suggest putting the *Zandair Gelines* and the *Lynene 'ah Hanal* on the castle walls?"

"There are five of the Daughters and five sharpshooters ma'am," Victoria supplied. "Perhaps two shifts of three and have the night watch at four?"

"You do not want to rely solely on the *Mael'Hivar,* Your Majesty," Rachel added before Beth got a chance. "A healthy mix of Lithonian soldiers should be included in your personal guard as well."

Beth and Angela shared a look, impressed and proud of how these young women had grown.

"There is a garrison of two hundred Lithonian soldiers sworn to the throne in Dale, Your Majesty," the nineteen-year-old Lady Wren Prather reported. She was a tiny thing with pale blonde hair and light blue eyes.

She blushed when most of the eyes in the room turned to her. "Lord Gerard Rythan is my grandfather. My father, Lord Farran, has command of the guard."

Beth saw Victoria flip a few pages in her notebook and make a note. She really was an asset to Lena.

"Thank you for that information, Lady Prather. We will make sure that your father and his men have their place in the guard and defense of the city," Lena said, inclining her head to the young woman.

Wren's blush deepened, and she sat down.

"What of the army, Your Majesty?" General Hall asked. "How would you like us placed?"

Beth knew that Generals Hall and Landgrave had been working closely with Lord Baerik, and thought the question was more for the lords, ladies, and their men so she wasn't surprised when the Queen said, "Lord Baerik?"

"We will divide into three forces, one to the north of the city, one to the east, and the last to the west," Lord Baerik said, "General Hall will be in command to the east, and General Landgrave to the west."

"And to the north?" Lady Cynna asked.

"I had hoped that Lord Edward would take command there, for the time being?" Lena looked at the middle-aged man with thinning, brown hair.

Lord Edward Proudmourn bowed low. "It would be my honor, Your Majesty."

"Well-played," Angela whispered to Beth.

Being the youngest son and second youngest of five children, Edward often felt overlooked by his siblings. By singling him out, Lena had tied him to her more firmly.

"I will leave the four of you to divide the men," Lena said to Baerik, Edward, and the two generals. "Lady Wren, if you could walk with me?" she asked the young woman. "I confess I have only been to Hardcastle a few times and am not very familiar with it. I would like to know what to expect as far as accommodations."

Lena led the procession with the wispy blonde at her side and Ellae at her back. Lady Rachel and Princess Fenora must have been given other tasks, as the two women slipped off together. Victoria left with one of the *Mael'Hivar*, a dark-haired woman with black eyes and olive skin of a height with the *Ducessa*. Beth had noted that the woman was often in Victoria's company.

Beth and Angela excused themselves and headed back through the camp to find their tents, which were next to each other.

"It won't be easy," Angela said quietly, "but I do believe, with those young women at the helm, we will make it through this."

Beth nodded. "Lena has been raised to be a leader, a ruler. She is wise enough to know that she doesn't have all the answers, and shrewd enough to look deeper into the information she is given, even by trusted sources."

"And her ladies are smart and resourceful, and she uses them well," Angela added. "They know this isn't a game. It isn't a court intrigue."

"I just hope that we can end this quickly and with as little bloodshed as possible," Beth said. "Let us take off Morlette's head and be done with it."

"Let me rip out his heart first," Angela growled.

They finished their walk in silence.

CHAPTER 84

High Lord Garrett Morlette
Havencrest Manor, City of Endomir: Lithonia
9th of Minn

Matilda, the cook, had brought Garrett his dinner and, at his insistence, ate hers with him in the small sitting area of his bedchamber. They had left the door open to preserve her reputation, even though she was at least sixty, with children and grandchildren, and she and his nurse had practically raised him.

He had little company or interaction. The housekeeper, Mrs. Jenkins, did the cleaning herself, preferring to keep the maids out of his rooms. The butler brought the firewood, and Matilda brought his meals. The whole household knew he was there, but since the death of Selwyn, the footman, it had been agreed by Garrett and Barnes, the butler, that the less he was seen, the better.

Barnes and Mrs. Jenkins were trying to find ways to get him out of Endomir, now that the gates were open again. He wouldn't be safe in Havencrest forever.

After Matilda left, Garrett changed into his pajamas and dressing gown and sat by the fire with a glass of sherry and a novel, *The Affair*. It had been a favorite of Lenathaina's, and for some reason, the reminder of her, and of her approach to the city, was comforting.

Better to turn myself in to her if I can't get free then to fall into Montgomery's hands.

Some time later, he had dozed off in the chair, sherry half drunk and his book on his chest.

"Master Garrett!" Someone was shaking him, a woman, her voice frantic and scared. "Oh, wake up, Master Garrett."

He opened his eyes to see Matilda. She had on her nightcap and a faded dressing gown. "What is it, Matilda?"

The door to his room flung open, and Matilda screeched and stood in front of him.

"You can't have him! You can't have my boy!"

"Stand aside, mistress," commanded a guard dressed in Morthan blue and green.

Captain Reming.

Garrett had put him in prison for refusing to follow his orders.

This isn't going to go well.

He could see many other guards in the hallway, and none that had been in his pocket.

"He is a good boy," Matilda wailed. "He just went wrong. He needs help! Never had anyone there for him. Just leave him to me, and I will see him right."

Garrett laid a hand on her shoulder. He could see the steel in Reming's eyes. "It's okay, Matilda. Captain Reming will see me safely to my destination." He looked at the fair-haired man. "Won't you, sir?"

"Aye, mistress." Reming turned a kind eye to the plump cook. "Just taking a ride up to the castle for a talk with the Lord Regent."

Matilda turned to Garrett and gave him a fierce hug. "You let me know how you are, Master Garrett. Maybe the Lord Regent will let me visit?" She turned to look at the captain.

"I am sure chaperoned visits will be allowed."

'For now,' hung in the air.

The captain took Matilda by the arm gently and led her into the hall. Garrett could hear her sobs as she was steered away. When the captain came back in, Garrett straightened his back.

"Where has she been taken?"

"The cook and the rest of the staff will be held here until the Lord Regent decides what to do with them," Captain Reming said. "And you will be his guest at the castle until the Queen arrives."

Garrett bowed his head. "Am I allowed to change and pack?"

Reming looked as if he would say no for a moment, but finally nodded.

Four guards were posted in the room to supervise Garrett as he changed and packed the same things as when he'd gone into hiding. The rest of his clothing was still at the castle. The place where he had briefly ruled. The place where he would now be a prisoner.

*****

Garrett was taken by carriage to Castle Endomir in the small hours of the morning, but the commotion and presence of an entire troop of Morthan House guards, along with a contingent of Endomirian soldiers—High Lord Harold Harmon and Lord Marvin Jasper with ten men of their own—had drawn attention. Garrett could see servants huddled in the cold in the spaces between houses, and their employers standing in the windows.

He waved. What else was there to do?

Montgomery was waiting for him in his office, dressed in a fresh suit but looking like he hadn't slept. He motioned for Garrett to take a seat.

"This is High Master Simon Montaz," the Regent said, gesturing to a dark-haired Master in the corner. "If you so much as blink wrong, he will have you trussed up like a hog in seconds."

Garrett inclined his head in acceptance of those words, and left his hands on his knees, visible.

So far, this was going better than he might have hoped.

"If I were a weaker man, I would kill you here and now," Montgomery continued. "Be glad that my wife isn't here."

There didn't seem to be much to say to that, so Garrett remained silent.

The Lord Regent watched him for a long moment and then said, "Why did you do it? Charles groomed you for so long to be the right hand to the throne, and Queen Lenathaina would have used you. So *why*?"

Garrett contemplated his words before saying, "I wanted to be first for once. The best loved, the most trusted. The chosen child. I was tired of coming second or third or last in the affections of those who should have loved me."

Montgomery shook his head, and Garret had to admit that the look of disgust the man gave him was well-earned. "Have you figured it out at last?"

Garrett looked down at his hands, at the ring that had been on his father's hand most of Garrett's life. The large emerald was set in gold with an embossed acorn to each side. He pulled it off and set it on the desk before meeting Montgomery's eyes.

"Lenathaina was born to be a leader. She is strong... stronger than me." He paused. "I was never meant to lead. Only to help. To follow."

Montgomery was watching him, waiting.

"I never meant for your son to die." His voice cracked.

Montgomery flinched as if he had been struck. He looked away while he composed himself before he asked, "And Benjamin Bennings?"

Garrett looked down at his hands again, now bare, and drew a long breath. "I thought... if I took one of you, one who had defied me so blatantly, the others would fall in line. Then, I thought if I could get you all to fall in line, that I could do it. Make us a strong and great nation again."

Montgomery clenched his jaw. "And now?"

"I know I was a fool with bad advisors," Garrett replied quietly.

"Who were your advisors?" the Regent asked, pulling a sheet of parchment forward as he picked up his pen.

Garrett listed them off. "Edwin Murphy—my former secretary—High Lord Ellis Parker, and High Lord Blake Rendon. Rendon and Parker provided the letter and the will that I used as a pretense to take the throne."

Montgomery met his gaze. "Did you believe they were real?"

Garrett shook his head. "I knew they were fake. I just wanted..."

"What wasn't yours?" the High Lord finished.

Garrett nodded.

"Will you write out a statement tomorrow, with the details of your dealings with Parker and Rendon?"

Garrett nodded again. "I will."

"Then I think we have nothing else to say to one another for now." Montgomery stood.

"Where will I be held?" Garrett asked, not daring to move.

"In the Nursery Keep." The Lord Regent gave him a sour smile. "Master Simon will come tomorrow to witness your confession."

Garrett inclined his head, and Montgomery left the office, leaving him with the Master at his back.

It was fitting, he supposed, that he would be held in the same place he had kept his own prisoners.

CHAPTER 85

High Lord Marc Eddening
Downsworth Hall, near Seathor: Lithonia
10th of Minn

Marc sat at a table in the great hall of Downsworth Hall, home of Lord Ainsley Dorn, with Rendon and Parker, and several generals and lesser lords while the camp outside was broken down. Dorn had hosted the high lords, lords and higher-ranking officers in his small castle the night before.

When they had arrived, Lady Geillis, Lord Ainsley's wife, had informed them that Queen Lenathaina's party had passed three days before. She didn't seem too upset about it. In fact, Lady Geillis had slowly looked Marc up and down, then given him the slightest curtsy possible before welcoming him, reluctantly, into her home. It was clear that she thought her husband was misguided and that she supported Lenathaina.

The men had stayed up late into the night drinking the Ainsley's wine and discussing their next move, but they were still at odds.

"I really think gathering a larger force and heading back to Endomir is our best option," Rendon said yet again. "Endomir is the capital, and holding it will mean a lot."

"We won't get past Jasper's Keep," Parker said. His pasty complexion was chapped from the cold winds, and he was irritable from the days on horseback.

After Marc had declared he would ride at the head of his own army, Parker and Rendon had felt shamed out of their plush carriages.

"We won't," Marc agreed. "As long as that woman is on Lithonian soil, Montgomery and Jasper's Keep will stand."

He took a drink of his tea as the rest mulled that over. Then he continued.

"The Caeldenonian King might be interested in having a foothold here, but I don't think he will fund an all-out war on this side of the water while still dealing with the Hathorites."

And Marc knew he would be dealing with them very soon.

Parker and Dorn both nodded, and Dorn said, "In the end, I think more of us want to avoid becoming just another providence of Caeldenon. Lenathaina is a smart and well-trained young woman, but she isn't suited for the throne. She is too young and too inexperienced. We need a strong leader. Why the laws were ever changed to allow a woman to rule is beyond me."

There were many murmurs of agreement.

Marc knew he held sway over many of these men simply because they didn't want to bow their heads to a woman. It wasn't the strongest position, but he would show them in time that his cock wasn't the only thing that made him superior to the Morthan Princess.

She would still be that; he would let her keep her title. After all, she was the daughter of a prince and the niece of a king.

But Lenathaina *would* curtsy to him before this war was over. He couldn't kill her... he would lose the alliance with Caeldenon, but he could convince the High King that the loss of Lithonia wasn't worth the loss of the alliance and all that the two men could accomplish together. He had met the man at the wedding—he was sensible, if a bit rough. The High King would see the right way and order his men down, and the Princess would have no choice.

For now, he needed a base to operate from.

"Verto stands empty," Marc said. It was the estate that Garrett had been given when he became a high lord. To Marc's knowledge, the boy had never set foot on the estate.

All eyes turned to him.

"A token force that has barely met, let alone served under, the high lord they owe fealty to," he explained.

"You don't think Morlette went there?" Parker asked, leaning forward.

"I don't think he got out of Endomir," he replied. "If he lives, he is somewhere in the basin."

"Using Verto as a base would be wise," Rendon considered, nodding. "Halfway between Jasper's Keep and Hardcastle. We could move whatever direction we needed to quickly."

Marc stood, and so did every man at the table, as if he were already king.

"Ready your men," he commanded. "First, we take Verto… then we start cutting the Princess off from those who should have stood with us."

"Grey and Wallace," Rendon said bitterly.

"And Long," Parr added with a grimace.

"If they don't fall into line, we will deal with them," Marc promised. "Any estates left over will be given to those who showed the most loyalty."

The men around the table all bowed their heads before leaving to get their soldiers ready.

It was a start.

CHAPTER 86

Lady Victoria Forrester-Coden, Ducessa 'ah Kilmerian
Hardcastle, the City of Dale: Lithonia
10th of Minn

Baerik grabbed Tori by the waist and swung her down from the black mare's back. *Danon*, which meant justice in the Old Tongue, had come with them from Caeldenon, a gift from Mother Arrysanna. She'd wanted to be sure that Tori had a sure-footed mount.

Tori smiled up at her husband before taking his offered arm.

Like the Queen, Tori, Rachel, and Fenora all rode armed. Each of them had a short sword on one hip and a pistol on the other.

Tori also had her throwing knives strapped to her leg. She used the ebony-hilted weapons that Baerik's first wife had once owned; Hira's parents had suggested it when they learned of the planned campaign, wanting their new daughter—for in their way, they had taken Tori into their family—to be able to protect herself.

The Steward of Hardcastle, who oversaw the former capital for the ruler of Lithonia, stood at the top of the steps in front of the great, ebony, wood doors of the massive limestone castle.

It was a thing of sprawling beauty, set on top of a hill and somehow built into the side of it. The castle was essentially three large keeps that melded into one another.

The section of the castle on top of the hill was five stories high, with two additional floors under the peaked slatestone roof. Two additional sections of the castle were built on lower elevations so that the upper floor of the first section, which was three stories, connected to the lower floor of the second section. Likewise, the upper two floors of the second section, which was four stories, connected to the lower floors on the main part of the castle.

The stair-stepped look, along with the turrets that flanked each level, made Hardcastle visible for miles. It put Endomir to shame, truthfully.

Lord Gerard Rythan and his wife Lady Davina were flanked by a variety of children and grandchildren, ranging in age from their mid-twenties to a young boy just out of small clothes. No doubt there were a few still in the nursery.

They all bowed and curtsied as the Queen dismounted. She wore a dark green riding dress, and her midnight hair was piled atop her head in a mass of coiled braids. The dark colors set off her violet eyes and contrasted her sandy skin well. She was an exotic thing of beauty, and the sword and pistol at her side made her look like a mythical warrior queen.

Lord Rythan and his family looked at her in awe.

Lena had become accustomed to this reception since returning to Lithonia. She came forward, Ellae one step behind her, and offered her hand, which Lord Rythan took and bowed over.

Lady Wren Prather joined the Queen and made introductions. The poor young woman was bright red from all the attention, but did her job well.

They were escorted into the bastion, the bottom of the three keeps, which was where official receptions and offices were kept, along with apartments for visiting dignitaries. It was little used these days, but the Rythan family had done their duty and kept the rooms pristine—though some of the furnishings were a century out of style.

"Your Majesty," Lord Rythan said as he led them into a drawing room that was at least forty feet long and twenty wide. It was set into the old-style conversation areas, small groups of chairs or settees scattered down the length of the room to provoke intimate conversations. "We are so pleased that you have decided to make Hardcastle your home until you can retake Endomir. I hope that the welcome provided by the mayor and city council was warm."

It had been long-winded for such a cold day, in Tori's opinion. They had been greeted at the city gates with multiple speeches and then led through streets lined with cheering citizens. While the welcome was encouraging, the slow procession had left Tori with numb fingers and toes and a desire to plant herself in front of the blazing hearth, but she held her ground next to her Queen as Rythan spoke.

"It was a very warm welcome," Lena said with a polite smile. "It has been a long time since I was in Hardcastle. I forgot how large it is."

"I have taken the liberty of having the royal suite prepared for you," Lady Davina Rythan said, steering the Queen to a settee. She was an older woman, like her husband. Both had gray hair and the wrinkled faces of people who had lived well and smiled often. But Lady Rythan was shorter than her husband, and he was a bit wider than his wife. "But first, we must get you warmed up."

At some hidden signal, servants entered the room, and mugs of steaming liquid were passed around. The nobility that had traveled with the Queen and their generals and upper officers were being entertained by the various Rythan children. Lena barely had a chance to sip her drink between questions and introductions.

Baerik turned to Lord Rythan and said, "Lady Prather informs me that there are barracks in the city for the Lithonian soldiers that guard Dale but there are also barracks for the King's Guard here in the castle grounds?"

"There are, Your Grace," Rythan nodded. Baerik had been introduced to him upon arrival. "The barracks of the King's Guard house four hundred soldiers and their commanders. There are three buildings. I currently use the smallest for the Morthan House Guard that is under my command here."

"There are Morthan guards here?" Lena asked. She had been engaged in conversation with High Ladies Beth Bennings and Angela Montgomery and Lady Davina, but hearing her maiden name must have caught her attention. "How many?"

"One hundred, ma'am." Lord Rythan said with a small bow. "And they and their commander," he inclined his head toward his son Lord Jarod, "Are at your disposal, of course. They are, after all, your men."

Lena turned to Lord Jarod. "I would be pleased if you and Lord Baerik would come to an understanding about my personal guard, Lord Jarod. I must have some of the *Mael'Hivar,* but would be pleased if some of the men under your command could be added to their number."

Lord Jarod, a man in his late forties but who looked much like his daughter, Lady Gwen, bowed deeply. "It would be an honor to work with the *Duc* to protect you, Your Majesty."

"Well-played," Baerik whispered in Tori's ear; she nodded her agreement.

"Dinner is at eight," Lady Davina said, "if that suits, ma'am?"

She turned to the Queen, who nodded.

Lady Davina was taking it in stride that she was no longer the ranking lady of the house.

"But for now, I am sure that you would like to see your rooms and freshen up," the Lady intimated.

"We would," Lena said as she set her cup down. "And perhaps you might give me a tour tomorrow?"

Lady Davina smiled. "It would be my pleasure, though you had best set aside the day for it." She laughed, "Hardcastle is large and she has many secrets. Your rooms are in the Aerie, Your Majesty. I have arranged rooms for your court there as well."

The two women began walking to the sitting room door, Ellae at their heels.

*****

An hour later Diason, Tori's maid, and Jorin, Baerik's manservant, were unpacking their trunks in a pair of dressing closets while Tori and Baerik sipped tea in a well-appointed sitting room.

"I am glad we have rooms close to Gavantar and Lenathaina," Baerik said. "This place is a maze."

"This is a very nice apartment," Tori said as she looked at the oil painting on the wall. "I think that might be Queen Andrea Ryne."

Baerik followed her gaze. The woman in the painting had dark brown hair and blue eyes and was dressed in red velvet with a jeweled belt. "The last Ryne Queen, wasn't she?"

His store of obscure facts still amazed Tori.

She nodded, and Baerik stood to walk around the room. They had a sitting room, small dining room, bedroom, two dressing closets, and a second small bedroom to themselves.

"The rooms are a sign of respect." He looked down at Tori. "I worried that my birth might get us snubbed."

"Rank means much," Tori said, smiling at him. "And most will just ignore what they think of as barbaric customs."

Baerik leaned down to kiss her neck before growling in her ear. "I am glad we have a proper bed again so I can reacquaint you with my barbaric ways."

He scooped her up, she squealed with delight... and someone knocked on the door.

Baerik growled again and set her on her feet before crossing the room and flinging the door open.

Fenora arched an eyebrow at Tori's flushed face and Baerik's wild eyes. "The Queen has news. Come." She turned on her heel and walked down the corridor, trusting them to follow.

Baerik grabbed his jacket from the back of the chair he had been sitting in and pulled it on once more. He had worn the dark gray Caeldenonian military uniform since they arrived in Lithonia—save for formal dinners, when he and Gavantar donned their whites.

Tori straightened her skirts, and the pair left their apartment and caught up with Fenora, who had been purposely moving slow.

"Where have they put you and Rachel?" Tori asked once she was abreast with the mahogany-haired woman.

Fenora nodded to a door as they passed. "Between you and the Queen. Our apartment has two bedrooms." It was left unsaid that only one would be used. "The Queen has had a small dining room cleared of furnishings to make a practice area for us to spar in. It is beastly cold here, so I am glad we have a place indoors to exercise. I thought you were all being funny when you told me to pack woolen underthings."

"Tell me you did, Fenora!" Tori said.

Baerik was laughing; the look on Fenora's face was enough to say that she had not.

Tori shook her head. "I am sure that Lady Davina can recommend a seamstress."

She linked arms with Fenora as they walked the rest of the way down the corridor.

The royal suite made the apartment that Tori and Baerik shared look tiny. *Mael'Hivar* flanked the outer doors, and there were four more inside the apartment, stationed at various doorways that led to a variety of rooms.

Fenora took them to a sitting room that had a desk, several cushioned chairs, and two settees. Baerik bowed, and Tori and Fenora curtsied, first to the Queen and then to the Prince.

"Have a seat," Lena said from one of the settees.

Gavantar sat beside her, while Ellae and Galwyn were in a corner, having a whispered conversation. Fenora joined Rachel on the other settee.

Tori couldn't quite gauge Lena's emotions as she and Baerik sat down.

Master Tam was seated at the desk. He handed Master Ellis Braithwaite, one of his apprentices, two sheets of paper, and Braithwaite took them to the Queen with a small bow.

Lena read the first aloud. "*Morlette in custody. Was at Havencrest. Confession to follow but states that Parker and Rendon provided the documents that he used to take throne. MM.*"

"That is good news," Rachel said to Lena. "We have him off the throne and can ride to Endomir."

"Rendon and Parker are currently with Eddening, standing between us and Endomir with an army," Lena reminded her.

"They are in the minority," Rachel pressed. "Surely they understand that they cannot win."

"I don't think they do." Lena handed her the second note.

"*Lord Lyss has been approached by Eddening to inform HKG that when Eddening becomes king, he will honor the treaty signed by the late Charles Morthan,*" Rachel read, shock filling her voice. "That bloody bastard."

PART THREE

Late Autumn and Winter, the Year One Thousand and One and One Thousand and Two, A.C.

CHAPTER 87

Lord Owen Eddening
Verto, Southern Region: Lithonia
13th of Minn

Owen sullenly sat in his father's study—or really, Garrett Morlette's study—as his father outlined his plan.

"The Mystic would like you to go to Hathor," Father said as he leaned back in his chair.

"Why?" Owen asked.

"To seal our alliance," Father said. "This is important. You will have an honored place in Her court."

"Father, I don't like this. Any of it," Owen said. "You know I don't support your war."

"I will never understand why you like that woman so much," Father said, sounding disgusted. "Is it because she wouldn't have you?"

"I didn't want the Queen." Owen drew out the title, and his father's face twisted. "She is my friend and has never been more."

Father stood and placed his hands on the desk, leaning forward. "I don't care if you think she is the rightful heir, she isn't what we need, and she is in the way of destiny." His voice was low and menacing. "I will rule on behalf of the Mystic until She comes, and then I will rule at her side. You will go to Her as a token of my promise."

"I won't go to that woman," Owen protested, coming to his feet.

"You will give Her the respect She deserves," Father growled. "And for once in your life, you will do as you are told, or I will put you aside for your brother."

"The law won't let you," Owen said defiantly.

"Boy, soon I will be the law!" Father roared.

"You will be a puppet," Owen hissed. "At the beck and call of a madwoman."

Father rounded the desk and pulled his arm back to slap Owen, but he caught his father's hand.

Father yanked away. "Don't push me, boy. She will rule this country sooner or later, with me by her side. If you play your cards right, you will have an honored place. Stepson to the Queen, brother to the next ruler."

Owen shook his head in disgust. "Send Edward if you want. He has always been your puppet, but I won't go." He turned on his heel and moved to leave, but his father got the last word.

"She has ways of changing minds," Father called after him. "But if you truly won't go, then you won't leave my side. You'll be just as confined as you were under Morlette."

Owen hunched his shoulders and kicked the door closed behind himself.

I have to get away.

CHAPTER 88

High Queen Maelynn Coden
White Castle, White City: Caeldenon
14th of Minn

Blood General Henrik Lyss stood in front of Maelynn, Gavan, and Samera. "I don't like it."

"I don't like a lot of things, Henrik, but I have learned not to argue with my wife," Gavan said. The expression on his face said he wished he could agree with his old friend, but he knew better than to try.

"We will have their backs, sir," Emerlise said.

She was standing next to the hearth, looking as if she wanted to argue too. Again.

She and Maelynn had gone at it hammer and tongs that morning.

Aria nodded her agreement and laid a hand on Samera's shoulder.

"Then I want ten of *naheames* in the room," Henrik said, sounding defeated.

"Five," Maelynn said, and Samera nodded.

"Give it up, Henrik," Gavan said as he lit his pipe. "Make yourself comfortable."

Henrik was nearly sulking as he sat down and pulled out his pipe.

Once both men were settled, Maelynn and Samera left the room with Em and Aria in tow.

When they reached the door to the room where their interview would take place, Em said, "Are you two sure about this?"

"These women have already shown a reluctance to open up or socialize with the male students in their training program. Being questioned by men or having them present is only going to put them off," Samera said.

Maelynn nodded. "Besides, you two will be there, and you would never let us get in over our heads."

The two *galvanas* exchanged looks, snorted, and pointedly ignored looking at Maelynn and Samera.

Samera said, "There was that time with the wine…"

"And the boar hunt…" Maelynn laughed.

"Alright, you two," Aria said as she opened the door.

The four of them stepped into the small sitting room where two women in gray pants and tunics were waiting, along with five female *Mael'Hivar Naheames* and High Master Geillis Kane, who was dressed in a non-descript pair of green and brown dresses.

The two Hathorite women didn't seem concerned by the guard, but as soon as they saw Maelynn and Samera, they prostrated themselves.

"That isn't necessary," Maelynn told them. "Get up please."

The two women, one with black hair and eyes and the other with red hair and gray eyes, stood with hesitation. One of the *naheame* stepped forward to stand beside them and bowed to Maelynn and Samera. The two young women copied her, seeming relieved to have some formal way to respond to royalty.

Maelynn smiled kindly and took a seat on a settee; Samera sat beside her, and they motioned for the women to sit.

The *naheame* next to them nodded encouragingly, and finally, both women sat down on the other settee.

"You are both *draedin?*" Maelynn asked. Draedin were initiates who hadn't taken their vows.

The two women nodded.

"Your names are Ara and Jal?" Samera asked.

Again, they nodded.

"Blood General Lyss said that you might be willing to speak to us," Maelynn said. "We are trying to understand what your people want so we can come to an understanding. Perhaps end the fighting."

The two women exchanged a look, and then the dark-haired one spoke.

"You will never end the fighting until She has what She wants." Her voice was melodic with odd inflections. "She will sacrifice us all to get it."

"She? Your Goddess?" Maelynn asked.

The redhead spoke. "They call Her so, and She and Her priestesses can do many things, and the magi under them." Her voice was melodic too, though it shook with fear.

Samera looked at Master Geillis and nodded.

The Master stepped forward, her skirts snapping with each step. She was tall, with ebony skin and black hair that was coiled in sleek braids atop her head. Her dark brown eyes rested on the young women as she held her hands out, and red flames appeared above them. The flames shifted to black and green and blue.

The women recoiled in terror, and the redhead covered her face.

"Blasphemers!" the dark-haired young woman cried.

The redhead looked at the woman with the flames in her hand and shook her head. "No, Jal. She is what they call Ithrimir." The fear left her as she watched Master Geillis. "She is not making us grovel. She is not making us kiss the dirt at her feet. She serves the High Queen."

Master Geillis inclined her head to the young woman, who must be Ara. "Masters of the Ithrimir are servants of the people. I choose to serve under the High King and Queen."

"What do you do?" Jal asked.

Master Geillis sat down in one of the chairs and looked at the young women. "I maintain this castle, for it was made with the aid of the Gift, and any artifacts that were crafted by Ithrimirian craftsmen."

Ara looked around the room as if the walls themselves might perform magic.

Jal turned to Maelynn, "They live a long time, Her and Her priestesses, but my mother's mother remembered the blood days when the new Mystic came to power."

"The blood days?" Samera asked.

"The daughters of the old Goddess wage war among themselves to see who will take their mother's place," Ara explained. "And they do not care who dies."

"What does this Mystic want?" Maelynn asked. "Why does she attack? Why did you all come to Keltonmere?"

"The city we took?" Ara asked. "We called it Neve Hal."

"Mostly, we were to be a distraction from the real work, but the magi and the priestesses hoped we could make a foothold here," Jal said. "A place to spread the word of our Mystic and the everlasting life that is given to all who faithfully worship She Who Was, Is, and Will Always Be."

Maelynn and Samera exchanged a look.

"What is the real work?" Maelynn asked.

"Lithonia," Ara said.

"The Promised Land," Jal added. "We were to keep you distracted while others disrupt Lithonia."

"The Promised Land?" Samera asked. "Why is Lithonia the Promised Land?"

"It is one of the prophecies given by the goddesses," Jal said, nodding. "We are taught them from birth—the primary ones and, depending on our station, others.

"Ara and I were of the lowest station, fit to be wives of warriors and to give them sons." This was said with old bitterness. "Assigned so at birth."

"Is this why you chose the path you are on now?" Samera asked.

Maelynn could tell that some of her wariness about the Hathorite women was fading.

"Never before have we had a choice," Ara said. "Our husbands were chosen for us. They chose for us to come on the colony ship. Had we not had babes that were still suckling, we would have been made to fight even though we had no training."

"What of your children?" Maelynn asked.

"They would have been taken from us when they were weaned and assigned a station. Raised to be whatever the priestesses decided they were destined to be," Jal said. "I have had three taken from me.

At least I know Ari will be raised in a place where he can choose what he wants to be."

"And my Sari won't be forced to churn out babes until she dies of it," Ara said.

Jal rested a hand on her friend's knee. "The last one nearly killed Ara. They almost cut it from her."

"Jal saved me," Ara said, looking at her friend before turning back to Maelynn and Samera. "We owe them nothing, for they don't care if we live or die. Only that we bend to their will."

She drew a breath. "The first prophecy is this: *When we attain the Promised Land, the Chosen People will be Free.*"

"There is debate among the lower stations if we are part of the Chosen," Jal scowled. "We are mostly those that were in Hathor before the migration of the Goddess and the Faithful.

"The other prophecy is: *The path Homeward lies in the roots of the Oaken Heart. The Branch that Flourishes From the Ashes of Fire and Death is the true Ruler of Lithonia and will Unite the Lands and Bring a Lasting Peace.*"

"So she wants Lithonia," Samera inferred. "But not Caeldenon?"

"She wants the world." Jal clarified, meeting Samera's gaze. "Lithonia is just where she will start. The biggest prize."

"But why?" Maelynn asked. "Why does she want Lithonia so badly?"

"When the followers of Hathor and Hestia were driven from Pannarius and Lithonia," Samera recalled, "Lithonian Masters took down their ships with extreme prejudice. The wars there were brutal on both sides."

"There is more to it," Jal said.

"The first Mystic was of the House of Ryne," Ara said. "We are taught Her lineage. The current Mystic believes She is the true heir. If She can unite with the one from the prophecy, the one born from the ashes…"

"The war in Lithonia…" Maelynn said. "She is behind it."

"She has had servants there for forty years, working to crack their foundations. Now she has done it."

"Maker preserve us," Samera whispered.

Maelynn rose and took Jal and Ara's hands. "I cannot thank you enough."

"We owe you our lives." Jal bowed her head to kiss Maelynn's hand.

"Whatever we can do to help," Ara added, also kissing Maelynn's hand.

"They are good students," the *naheame* who had helped them earlier said. "All the women who have come to us are like them. They were little more than slaves. Jal and Ara have worked the hardest and are progressing well."

"Let me know when they are ready to graduate." Maelynn said, looking at the young women. "They will be offered a place in the Red Shields. I would be honored to have such strong women at my back."

The *naheame* nodded as she smiled at her charges. "Yes, Your Majesty." She saluted Maelynn with her right hand over her left breast. "I wondered if I could show them the city before we return to the compound?"

"Of course. I will make arrangements to have you housed here. Let them have a week to see the city and enjoy themselves," Maelynn said.

"Perhaps take them to a play," Samera said. "I know there are several good ones on right now."

"And they are welcome to come spar with us in the mornings," Emerlise spoke up. "We come down at six."

The two young women looked overwhelmed but nodded their thanks.

Maelynn and Samera left them with the *naheame*, while Master Geillis followed them. They returned to the sitting room where Gavan and Henrik were waiting, and Maelynn resisted pouring herself a drink—only because she knew Samera was not drinking while she nursed.

The nanny brought Fadean in, and Samera sat down to feed the baby while Maelynn recounted the conversation with Ara and Jal for her husband.

Both men listened in silence.

She finished with her offer to the young women and the information that she had let them spend a week in the city.

"They will have a place if they want it," Gavan said. "And perhaps they will agree to meet with me so I can offer my thanks for this information."

"So this Mystic thinks we won't be able to help Lithonia if we are protecting our borders?" Henrik said. "She underestimates us."

Maelynn nodded. "We need to get this information to Lenathaina and Gavantar."

"It is too much for the Stones," Samera said, and Master Geillis nodded.

"Send Aeleonna or Merra," Gavan said.

"Merra," Maelynn said. "Aeleonna has requested to stay at Trahelion Manor to help Queen Mellina."

"And to be near Taemos," Samera added. Fadean cooed and kicked her feet.

"Mother did say that she is spending a lot of time with Queen Mellina," Gavan said, "And we can trust her to keep an eye on them."

Maelynn nodded. "Merra would enjoy the chance to travel, anyway. She liked Lithonia."

Henrik sighed. "She will need a guard too. Shall I pull some from the Red Shields?"

"I think Merra should have the choice. We will meet with her and decide from there. If she chooses the Red Shields, I will let you know," Maelynn said.

"Very well." Henrik rose and bowed to all three of them. "I will go make arrangements for the *naheame* and the *draedin* to stay here for the next week."

Master Geillis rose and bowed her head to each of them as well. "With your permission, I need to compile a report to send to the Ithram and Council."

"Of course. Thank you for your help, Master Geillis," Maelynn said.

Once they had left, Samera said, "I think some time on her own will do her good."

"And a chance to see that woman again," Gavan muttered.

"Woman?" Samera asked, intrigued.

"She met someone," Maelynn explained. "They have been writing to one another. But she needs a chance to get out of her sister's shadow. Gavantar will give her room to grow and fly safely, and Baerik will keep an eye on her."

"It may be time to consider that Merra isn't the marrying type," Samera said. "Pushing her into a marriage will only diminish her. We have enough heirs between us."

She met Gavan's gaze. "She needs to hear from you that she won't be a disappointment if she finds her own path."

Gavan grunted. "You are right. You usually are."

Maelynn and Samera shared a smile.

"Well, we have a lot to do and not much time to do it." Samera said, lifting the baby over her shoulder to burp her.

"All my chicks are leaving the nest. Only four of them remain, and it won't be long before Jaemi has to decide his path," Gavan said morosely, looking longingly at Fadean.

Samera stood and put the baby in his arms. "We will have this one for a while yet, and I am sure Evandar will share her."

Gavan cooed at the baby. "You won't leave your Uncle Gavan, will you."

Maelynn and Samera exchanged another smile before moving to the desk to begin writing the letter to Lenathaina and Gavantar that Merra would deliver, leaving Gavan happily talking to Fadean about all the adventures they would have.

CHAPTER 89

High Lord Garrett Morlette
Castle Endomir, Endomir: Lithonia
14th of Minn

Five guards escorted Garrett from the room that was his prison in the Nursery Keep to the council chamber in the main castle.

Magne Montgomery sat at the head of the table, with Randal Bennings to his right and Harold Harmon to his left. Derrick Maceon and Caleb Vectors flanked the other two men.

Only half the Council was present, with Rendon, Parker, Parr, and Eddening missing. And of course, Lenathaina as the head of House Morthan.

Garrett thought it was a foregone conclusion that he no longer had a place.

"Have a seat, Morlette," Montgomery said, gesturing to the other end of the table.

Garrett bowed his head and sat down, placing the folder that he had brought in front him.

"You have already given me a verbal confession, but I understand you have your written one ready?" the Regent asked.

"I do. As well as some letters and other documents." Garrett held up the folder, and one of the guards took it to Montgomery.

"You can wait outside," he said to the guards as he opened the folder.

Garrett was silent as the men ringing the table, his former equals, passed around his four-page confession, which detailed Parker and Rendon's parts in his plans, as well as Murphy's. Also among the contents were the letters that Rendon and Parker had provided. Detailed accountings of his conversations with all three men.

357

He didn't think he could save himself; it was far too late for that. But he hadn't gotten here on his own, so he wasn't going to go down alone.

"How do we know that you are telling the truth here?" Caleb Vectors asked as he put down the page he was reading.

"I am responsible for the deaths of Benjamin Bennings and Derek Montgomery," Garrett said, avoiding looking at Magne Montgomery and Randal Bennings. The grief and rage in both men's expressions was too painful for him. "And many other crimes. I know that, at best, I will spend the rest of my days in Foregate, and at worst, the Queen will have my head."

He sighed. "I didn't create all of this mess. If my brother had been kept from the throne... well, who knows how things would have gone? But I made it a lot worse from greed and because for once, I wanted to be the one everyone looked to for salvation. The one with the answers."

Montgomery shook his head. "Not all born to the throne are made for it, and not all that are made for the throne are born to it. It is better to use the damn skills the Maker gave you than to take what you have no right nor ability to hold."

"You were given a bad hand, lad," Harry Harmon said, looking almost, but not quite, sympathetic. "But it was your choice how to play it, and now you have to pay the price. I am glad you see that and aren't making excuses."

Garrett inclined his head.

"I will make copies of these and send them to the Queen and await her orders," Montgomery said in dismissal.

Garrett rose and bowed to the assembled High Lords before letting himself out.

The guards returned him to his rooms in the Nursery Keep, where he would stay until his cousin decided what to do with him.

CHAPTER 90

High Prince Evandar Coden
Aboard the Rose Queen, Indayon Ocean
15ᵗʰ of Minn

Evandar made it a point to check on the prisoner daily to ensure that she was adequately looked after. She had tried to escape twice, though where she would go in the middle of the Indayon Ocean was beyond him.

Arch Master Cade Kline, who was in charge of those who had come with Evandar to see Jillian to the Isles, thought that she was trying to provoke them into killing her so she didn't have to face the Ithram. Evandar thought he had a point there.

When he entered the cabin where Jillian was being held, Deldemar at his side, he found that she was in a talkative mood.

"Ah, it is the man who would have been my brother-in-law."

"Hello, Jillian," Evandar said. "I just wanted to tell you we are almost halfway to the Isles."

Her expression faltered for a moment before she straightened her back. "If you turn the ship around, I will give you a list of the agents that I know are operating in Caeldenon."

"If you wanted to make a deal, you would have done so with the High King."

Evandar leaned against the wall. Even though she was bound to a chair by both cloth ropes and magical ones, and the chair was, in turn, bolted to the floor, he didn't plan on getting any closer than he was now.

The cabin was spacious enough to also allow four Masters room to observe the prisoner without being too close to her. It was one of them who spoke next.

"She has had time to consider what will be done to her when the Ithram is through with her," Master Janduin said.

"What is that?" Evandar asked.

"At the least, she will be cut off from the Life Source," Master Janduin said as he watched Jillian. "After that, she will be executed, if she is lucky."

"If she is lucky?" Evandar was watching Jillian as well, and could see that she was struggling for composure.

"To have lived so long with the abilities she has had, and then to have them taken..." Janduin said. "Few in our histories have had the Gift removed, but none have lived for more than ten years after, and all have lost their minds before that. But after what she tried to do to the little girl and the Lithonian Dowager, and what she did to those guards..."

Evandar glanced at the Master's face and saw disgust and rage battling with one another.

"It is too late for turning around, Jillian," Evandar said to her. "You will have to face whatever consequences are coming your way."

She met his gaze, her eyes blazing. "There are agents in White Castle. With your precious wife and children. Turn us around now, and I will give you their names."

Ice rolled down Evandar's spine.

He almost turned to give the order, but then Janduin met his gaze. The Master arched an eyebrow as if to ask if Evandar really believed her.

He took a deep breath and left the room.

Jillian called after him, "Think of little Fadean, Evandar!"

Whatever she might have said after that was cut off by the Masters in the room with her.

It wasn't the first time that Jillian had been gagged, and the Maker knew it wouldn't be the last. He no longer cared; whatever pity he might have had left for her was gone.

CHAPTER 91

Mael'Hivar Galvana Lady Ellaemarhie Lindal
Hardcastle, the City of Dale: Lithonia
17ᵗʰ of Minn

Lena was pacing the study as Fenora and Rachel took turns reading Morlette's confession and the documents that had come with it. Ellae sat in the corner with Victoria. The pair of them exchanged glances as they waited for the explosion.

"So, Parker and Rendon set Garrett up in hopes of having a puppet king, and when that didn't work, they turned to Eddening?" Lena's voice had a sharp edge. She sat down at her desk.

The room was silent for a long moment, and Lena smacked the desk with the palm of her hand. "If the idiot had used his brain for five minutes…"

"We might still be fighting a war," Rachel said with a sigh. "Too many of them are reluctant to let a woman rule—but look at the mess they've made without you."

Lena snorted. "Well, I can't try him until this war is over."

"Let him stew in the Nursery Keep," Tori chimed in. "It would serve him right."

"It would," Rachel agreed, "and there's little else you can do right now. Although, we need to get on with these appointments. I know you are content to let High Lady Montgomery keep her post as Lady Marshal. She has been working well with the *Mael'Hivar* and the *Duc* and the Lithonian armies."

"The *Mael'Hivar* are having an easier time with her command than most of the Lithonian generals," Tori scoffed as she stood. She poured each of them a fresh cup of tea.

"It will be good for them," Fenora said as she added honey to hers and Rachel's tea. "Have you thought any more on Lady

Davina's offer to find you a secretary, ma'am?" Her gaze moved to Lena.

"I have, but I confess that I am hesitant," Lena said. "Lord and Lady Rythan have been model retainers, but I want to be sure whoever I choose is my creature to their bones."

"Any idea on how to achieve that?" Fenora asked.

"Yes, actually," Lena said with a smile. She and Rachel exchanged one of those looks in which they had a conversation without words, and Rachel nodded.

"What are you going to do about Rendon and Parker?" Tori asked.

Lena lifted her chin. "I am going to crush them."

CHAPTER 92

High Lord Randal Bennings
Castle Endomir, Endomir: Lithonia
20ᵗʰ of Minn

Randal sat at his father's desk in the Council wing of Castle Endomir. His desk now.

He just couldn't get used to that. All his life, this room had been his father's office when the House and Council were in session. Bennings Place had been his parents' home in Endomir, and Seathor Hall had been their House seat. Now... it was all his, and Mother only had a dower house in the country and a suite in the houses he owned.

Father had left her with all he could, but by law, the bulk of the family fortune had passed to Randal, and he was responsible for maintaining his family.

They deserved better, his family. They deserved to have a man who wasn't rash enough to break free from a prison. Randal's escape had been the excuse Morlette had needed to search Bennings Place and from there, find proof of his treason. Randal had done that. His father's blood and Derek's was on his hands.

There was nothing he could do about that now, save do the best job he could, both on the Council and in managing his family affairs.

Randal was about to break from his work for dinner when someone knocked on his door.

"Enter!"

Stephen and Travis Montgomery came in and took seats in front of his desk.

Stephen asked, "Any news about Morlette? We heard there was a messenger from the Queen this morning."

"Your father didn't tell you?" Randal asked.

Their relationship had changed a bit in the last weeks, with Randal's sudden elevation to high lord. In addition, Magne had been keeping his boys close, even having them moved to the castle, since he was still acting as Lord Regent of Endomir.

Some of the younger men still met for cards while their fathers worked in either the Council or the House, the Montgomery boys among them, but others had been sent back to their family estates, either for safety or to begin gathering those men who owed their families allegiance.

"Father left the meeting and went to the Nursery Keep to speak with Morlette," Travis explained.

"Ah." Randal leaned back in his chair. "Well, it isn't any secret. The Queen wishes Morlette to be held in the Nursery Keep until she has put down the rebellion and been crowned. At that point, he can have his trial and be sentenced."

"Do you think she will pardon him in the end? He is her cousin after all," Stephen said sullenly.

"Considering his actions sent this country into a civil war, no, I don't think so," Randal said. "She might be able to commute it to life in prison instead of execution, but I think that is as far as she would try to go." He looked at both men. "But you know her as well as I do, so you should have known that."

Travis sighed in frustration. "I wish I could just go over there and kill him myself. It is what he deserves."

"But you aren't a murderer," Randal said quietly.

Travis grunted and stood, then began pacing the room. "Father is keeping us here like children. I want to join Mother and the Queen."

"He is worried and grieving," Randal soothed. "He wants you close because he needs you here. And travel is dangerous, even by train."

"None of the couriers have been molested," Stephen pointed out.

"Yet," Randal countered. "But none of them have been a prize, either. You are the son of the Lord Regent and have already been kidnapped once. It is understandable that your father wants you close just now."

"But he is allowing my mother to sit in the middle of a war camp," Travis said as he continued pacing.

"She is hardly in the middle of a camp." Randal suppressed the urge to rub the bridge of his nose.

This wasn't the first time they'd had similar conversations, but it was the first time they had tried this particular excuse.

"She is inside the castle, surrounded by soldiers," he continued, "and the castle is inside the city walls. The war camps are outside those walls—yet another layer of protection."

"Now that you are a high lord, you are all common sense," Stephen grumbled. "It wasn't that way two months ago."

The words came out harshly, with more than a hint of blame. Stephen looked shocked at himself, and Randal could see his friend regretted them instantly, but there was no calling them back.

Travis stopped pacing and turned to look at the pair of them.

Randal slumped in his chair. "No, it wasn't. But don't think I don't regret it every day."

He looked around the office that his father should be sitting in, and then back to his friends. "I am to blame for your brother and my father's deaths. Maybe not as much as Morlette, but still. We could have sat safe in the keep and ridden it out, but I was determined to get out so my father could be free to move against the Usurper."

He worked his jaw, and his eyes grew intense. "But before you put all the blame on me and Morlette, remember that you *asked* to come with me."

Both men looked as if they had been struck.

It was the first time in the last two months that Randal had voiced his feelings. He had let them make sly comments and dealt with their resentment, but he was sick of it.

Finally, Stephen let out a long breath. "You're right. We are all to blame. Even Derek."

He held up a hand to Travis, who looked like he would burst. "Derek chose to come with us, same as you. Same as me."

Travis began pacing again. He was quiet for a long moment, and the older boys let him stew.

Stephen gave Randal a look that managed to convey how sorry he was, and Randal shrugged his acceptance.

When Travis finally sat back down, he said, "You are right, and I have been an ass."

Randal stood and went to the sideboard where he poured each of them a stiff measure of whiskey. Once he had taken his seat again, he said, "I know that you want to take action. Let me speak to your father—I think you can do more around here than just sit and play cards."

Stephen gazed down into his glass for a minute before he could bring himself to look at Randal again. When he did, there were tears in his eyes. "Thank you."

Travis had already downed his whiskey. "Anything would be better than being locked up here."

*****

Randal joined Magne, Caleb Vectors, and Harry Harmon for dinner at the castle, as he did most nights. Stephen and Travis were there, as well as Harold's second son, Nate.

Most nights, Randal returned to his family home late, but sometimes, he stayed in the room that Magne had set aside for him at the castle. Before dinner, he had sent a note to Kern, his butler, that he would be staying at the late that night.

After the port had been served and the cigars smoked, Randal turned to Magne and Harry. "Might I have a word before you retire?"

Magne nodded, and the younger men rose to leave. Caleb went to put out his cigar, but Randal waved for him to stay seated.

Once he was sure his friends were gone, he said, "The younger men need something to do. They can't continue to stew in their juices while their friends are off at their estates preparing for war, or already sitting in war camps on one side or the other."

Magne took another draw off his cigar. "What do you suggest?"

Randal turned to Mange. "Have Harmon train them. Every one of them has some level of experience with sword and pistols, but if we are going to war, they could use a good bit more. Set them to drilling. Train them as officers. Put them on watches. Let them be useful."

Harry snorted and took a drink of his port as he watched Randal. Finally, he said, "They may not like you for the suggestion once they get to the end of a day of training."

Randal shook his head. "I think you will find that many of them need a place to vent their emotions."

He avoided looking at Magne, but he sensed the other man stiffen and it was clear the Lord Regent understood what Randal was saying.

"It isn't a bad idea, Harry," Magne said after a moment. "Better than them sitting up here drinking and gambling all day. I am just sorry I didn't think of it."

"Alright. I will make an announcement tomorrow that all peers wanting to train as officers are welcome," Harry said. "We have already recruited some of the farm lads, and men from the city. But we will need more officers."

Caleb looked at Randal. "Your father would have been proud."

Randal nodded his thanks, and the men around the table seemed to understand that he couldn't speak, lest he lose control of his own emotions.

CHAPTER 93

Shan Alanine Fasili
Seathor Hall, the Port City of Seathor: Lithonia
21ˢᵗ of Minn

Alanine stepped off the ship with Cousin Isra at her side. Her cloak and wrap dress were no match for the icy winds coming off the bay. Her teeth chattered as she clutched the thin material around herself.

"We must take you to a seamstress, cousin," Amir said to her. "We should have thought of it sooner."

His voice was just loud enough to catch Isra's attention.

"We didn't have time in the Isles, and anything we would have found in the Imperial City wouldn't have suited anyway," Isra said. "We should be able to find appropriate material here."

"Masters." A pair of older men dressed in dark blue uniforms and wrapped in black cloaks approached and bowed.

Behind them were a pair of younger men with trays around their necks, complete with inkwells and ledgers. Four guards were with them, but they looked bored, as if this task were one that rarely required their full attention.

Alanine, Isra and Amir had been speaking Pannarian, but switched to Common when the men approached.

"Gentlemen." Cousins Isra and Amir inclined their heads as they pulled out their credentials. Cousin Isra had Alanine's, so she was free to look around as the officials took down their details.

It was obvious they recognized Cousin Isra's name, for their party was quickly escorted to the harbor master's office, where they were served tea next to a roaring hearth.

The harbor master, who had introduced himself as Mr. Greg Baker, asked, "What brings you to Lithonia? Normally we would not pry, but with the war…" he trailed off.

"Of course, Mr. Baker," Cousin Amir said. "Our young cousin, *Shan* Alanine Fasili, has come to offer her support to her cousin, Queen Lenathaina. We are acquainted with Her Majesty and the First Prince, and volunteered to escort the *Shan* to meet her."

Mr. Baker, a short, trim man with short, light brown hair turned his green gaze on Alanine. "I can send word to Seathor Hall, *Shan* Fasili. The Queen was in residence there until a few weeks ago. High Lady Lissa is in residence now."

Cousin Isra frowned. "I thought High Lord Benjamin Bennings' wife was named Beth."

Baker replied to Alanine's tall, dark-haired cousin with a grim expression. "High Lord Benjamin Bennings was murdered by the usurper Morlette. His widow, High Lady Beth, is with the Queen, so their daughter-in-law Lissa has remained behind to run the estate."

"May he find peace in the halls of the Maker, and may his soul dwell forever in honor and glory," Cousin Amir said solemnly.

Alanine might previously have been shocked to hear Amir honor the Maker, but she had learned that both her cousins had respect for the traditions of others.

Baker murmured, "Amen," spoke to one of his aides. "Please go to Her Grace and inform her of her waiting guests."

Once the aide had left, he addressed the Masters and Alanine. "Have you traveled far, my lady?"

"I have, sir," she said, uncomfortable with being the focus of conversation. "I have never been this far north. I confess the cold weather has been a shock."

Baker smiled. "I hope you adjust quickly."

The next hour passed with small talk. Alanine answered questions and contributed to the conversation where she could, but situations like these were a reminder of the extent that her education and training had been neglected. She felt like she was drowning.

When the aide returned, he had another Master with him. This man was tall and thin, with cropped, dark red hair and gray eyes.

Cousins Isra and Amir rose, and the other Master inclined his head in respect. They returned the gesture, and Isra held out her hand. "Arch Master Nathan Zane, it is good to see you again."

"Arch Master Isra Hameen-Palin," Master Nathan greeted as he bowed over her hand. Once he released it, he shook hands with Amir. "And Arch Master Amir Hameen-Palin." He smiled at the man as if they were old friends before his gaze settled on Alanine. "And this must be *Shan* Alanine Fasili."

Isra had spent much time with Alanine on the ship, teaching her the protocols of the Lithonian court. It felt odd to offer this strange man her hand, and odder to have his lips touch her knuckles lightly, but Isra smiled in approval, and Amir practically beamed.

"I am pleased to meet you, Master Nathan," Alanine said.

Master Nathan's eyes lingered on her for a long moment, and Alanine blushed. Cousin Isra cleared her throat, causing Master Nathan to jump before tearing his gaze from Alanine's.

Amir chuckled, and Nathan blushed before saying, "I am pleased to meet you as well, my lady. I am here on behalf of High Lady Lissa Bennings to invite you to stay at Seathor Hall before you continue your journey north."

"North?" Cousin Isra asked.

Master Nathan turned to address her. "Her Majesty, Queen Lenathaina, has been informed that her cousin is here, and has invited *Shan* Fasili to come stay with her at Hardcastle."

"I would be honored," Alanine replied.

When they left the harbor master's office, they were directed to a dark blue lacquered carriage. Master Nathan helped Alanine in before going with Amir to get their belongings from the ship.

While they had been traveling, Isra and Amir had both worn fleece-lined leggings and tunics, but this morning, Isra had donned a pair of green dresses in the Caeldenon fashion, and Amir, a gray suit, with trousers tucked into knee-high boots, and a jacket that was fitted to the waist and flared out at the hips.

Isra arranged her skirts and looked at Alanine across the carriage. "You will have to become accustomed to that and decide how to deal with it."

What?" Alanine asked, but her blush gave away that she knew exactly what her cousin was talking about.

"Men looking at you. Reacting to you," Isra said anyway. "In Lithonia, men will flirt and openly admire you. The women are taught from a young age how to handle themselves, but I have little experience with this."

Isra rarely discussed her youth on the Isles, so Alanine took the chance to ask.

"How did you and Amir meet?"

Isra smiled. "We were Acolytes together. All students are taught physical combat. When he found out that my mother was the Empress, he began to take it easy on me in the practice yards." She chuckled. "When he would not fight back properly, I decided to pummel him into the ground. Eventually, he got tired of being teased by the others, and fought back. He earned my respect, and we began spending time together outside our lessons."

Before Alanine could respond, Cousin Amir and Master Nathan climbed into the carriage.

She realized that, just three months ago, being alone with three Masters of the Ithrimir would have been terrifying. The path that her parents' deaths had set her on had changed her in so many ways already, and she knew she was only at the beginning of it.

Can I ever return to River Keep and the life that awaits me there, and if I do not... what kind of life can I make for myself?

She let the Masters speak among themselves, and watched through the glass windows of the carriage as they rode through the city. Women with baskets on their arms walked from shop to shop or browsed the stalls that lined the sidewalks. As the carriage ventured up the hill, toward the towering castle that lay behind a beautiful gray stone wall, the shops gave way to large houses and parks.

When they pulled up in front of the castle, the massive oak doors opened, and Master Nathan helped Alanine down.

"Welcome to Seathor Hall, *Shan* Fasili."

CHAPTER 94

Vera Martique
Clearwater Place, City of Endomir: Lithonia
22ⁿᵈ of Minn

Vera was at the dining room table with Samuel and Jack. Marie had taken the post of secretary to Magne with Vera's blessing. It wasn't exactly a step up, but a step into a different circle. Vera lived in the world of spies and mistresses and secrets, but now she was under the protection of the Lord Regent.

His choice of a woman for a secretary had been met with shocked whispers, but the speed in which Marie had sorted out the mess of papers left by Morlette and his secretary, and the efficiency that she brought to the Lord Regent's schedule, had impressed many.

Mallard, Vera's butler, was serving breakfast when one of the footmen came in and spoke quietly to him.

Mallard turned to Vera. "Mistress, there is a messenger here from the Queen. Shall I show him in?"

"By all means. And set a place for him," Vera mused as she spread marmalade on a scone.

A few minutes later, the footman ushered in a dark-haired young man who was red-faced with cold but dressed in a well-made suit. He was of middling height and moderately handsome.

The messenger walked to Vera's side and bowed formally. "Mistress Martique, Her Majesty Queen Lenathaina sends her regards and best wishes for your health." He took her hand and kissed it.

Vera arched an eyebrow. "That is kind of her."

He smiled and released her hand. "I am Lord Alexander Rythan, grandson of the Lord Steward of Hardcastle."

"Have a seat, Lord Alexander," Vera invited, indicating the chair to her left.

Mallard quickly set another place at the table and poured the young lord a cup of strong tea.

"I am sure that the Queen did not send you all this way to give me her regards," Vera ventured as she took a sip of her tea.

Lord Alexander studied Samuel and Jack before his brown eyes shifted to Vera. "Perhaps we can discuss that in private?"

She nodded in acknowledgment, and they changed the topic to the state of Endomir and the Queen's reception in the City of Dale and Hardcastle.

After breakfast, Jack left to go back to the embassy; it was his half-day, so he had chosen to take the morning off and stay the night before. When he was gone, Samuel went to his own office, and Vera took Lord Alexander to her study.

"Are you sure you don't wish to change and have a rest?" Vera gestured to a plush chair in front of the hearth. "For you to arrive so early, you must have left Jasper's Keep before dawn."

"Actually, my train got into Hartford late last night. I got a room in the city and came through the gates of the keep as soon as they opened," Lord Alexander explained.

"Your errand must be very important," Vera said, "for you to travel with such haste."

"It is." Lord Alexander pulled an envelope from his pocket and handed it to her.

Vera opened the letter and read.

Cousin,

First, I thank you for all that you have done in my service these last months. Your tireless work on behalf of the Crown will not be forgotten.

I have yet another request from you, however: I am in need of a secretary. We had to leave our gandine behind to see to our affairs in Caeldenon, so I have been using my ladies in turn, but I need someone dedicated to the cause.

I trust no one more than you to provide me with a suitable candidate who cannot be turned against me. Someone who could act as my eyes and ears on top of dealing with other matters would be a bonus.
If I had my way, I would bring you to Hardcastle, but the position is beneath you, and your talents are needed in Endomir.

On a personal note, I am sorry for your loss. I know that you and Benjamin were close, and he meant much to you. I hope in time, you and Beth will be able to comfort one another in your shared sorrow.

I look forward to the day we can see one another again.

All my love and thanks,
Lena

Vera's eyes watered slightly. It meant a lot to her that Lena had remembered Benjamin in her letter. More than that, the letter had been a personal one instead of a political move.

She folded the note and looked at Lord Alexander, who was watching her.

"I have another packet of letters for you," he said as he slipped a vellum-wrapped package from his pocket. "These are personal in nature, I was told."

Vera tucked the packet into her pocket and looked back to the young lordling. "Why did the Queen send you?"

"My family has pledged itself to her service, and she could not spare any of the men that she brought with her," Lord Alexander said. "And while her ladies all volunteered, the Queen would not be parted from them, so I offered to come.

"I have to visit the Lord Regent, as well, but was told to come to you first." He arched an eyebrow at her as if asking why she was so important.

"Do you have a place to stay while you are in the city?" she asked.

Lord Alexander smiled at the change of topic. "My family has a house here, but I would hate to have it opened just for me. I thought to get a room at my Club."

"Nonsense. You can stay here. I would like to know more about those who are serving the Queen at Hardcastle," Vera said as she came to her feet. "I think I have just the man to send to the Queen. I will speak to him today. When do you plan to return to her?"

"I hope to spend no more than two days here. There is much to be done, and I would like to be on hand to help my father and grandfather," Lord Alexander said as he stood. He bowed formally. "Should you require anything of me, I am pleased to be your most humble servant."

Vera took him back to the sitting room and told the housekeeper to prepare rooms for the young lord before she went to Samuel's office and let herself in.

"Mistress Vera," Samuel greeted as he placed the paper he had been working on in a folder. A good habit, she noted. One never knew when prying eyes were about. "Are you finished with our visitor?"

"For now. He is going to clean up before he goes to see the Lord Regent," she explained as she sat down. "I have offered him a room while he is in Endomir."

"He seems a like a decent chap." Samuel linked his hands behind his head and leaned back in his chair. "How long will he be here?"

"Long enough for you to pack," Vera said. "How do you feel about being secretary to the Queen?"

Samuel's mouth dropped open, and he sat forward. "Me?"

"I don't see anyone else in the room." She gave him an ironic smile. "I think you would do a fine job."

"Is she coming here?" Samuel asked, letting the idea sink in.

"I do not know her future plans, but for now, she is setting up her base in Hardcastle," Vera said. "I know it will mean being away from Jack for a while, but it's a good opportunity."

Samuel nodded and looked toward the window. "He won't like it. I won't either."

"Think about it and talk to Jack," Vera advised as she stood.

Samuel nodded again absentmindedly, and she left him to his thoughts.

It was a big decision, but one that could give him powerful protectors.

It seems all my chicks are leaving the nest.

Vera wondered how much longer she would be able to go on. She felt so alone. She ached for Benjamin. She ached for Beth. Work that had once given her joy now drained her.

Perhaps it was time to retire.

CHAPTER 95

The Goddess Hestia, the Mystic of Hathor
The Temple of Ganna: Hathor
23ʳᵈ of Minn

Hestia was reclined on a low sofa, wearing scarlet, form-hugging robes that were embroidered with golden sigils. Two female acolytes knelt in the far corner, waiting to do her bidding, and Kaleck sat on a low stool at her side. He was there not only as a member of the Consortium, but as protection.

Priestess Castia entered the chamber and pushed the boy she'd brought with her to his knees before prostrating herself before Hestia.

"Your Holiness," Castia said, her forehead still pressed to the floor. "I have returned with the boy."

Hestia looked the young man over. He was on his knees, staring at her in awe. He had deep black eyes and tawny skin. Something of Jardin, his real father, showed through in his features.

Even if his mother wasn't of the pure blood, he was still half Hathorite—enough for her purposes—and the Lithonian blood, the Morthan blood in his veins, was priceless.

"Namar, is it?" Hestia asked in soothing tones. "Come to me." She held out a long-fingered, ebony hand that glittered with gold and rubies.

Namar hesitated, but Kaleck rose and walked to him.

"Come now. I will show you how to make your obedience to Her Holiness."

Kaleck knelt, his red-trimmed, open-front, gray robes flaring behind him. Beneath those, he wore trousers, high, soft boots, and a tunic, all in dark gray. His eyes met Hestia's before he lowered his forehead to the carpeted floor.

Namar copied his movements, and the pair rose.

"You may leave, Castia," Hestia said to the waiting priestess.

A look of defiance crossed her face, and for a moment, Hestia thought she would refuse.

Castia was one of those rare children born to the original inhabitants of this land. Her parents had been of the third station; in all, there were six stations or ranks among those who were not born in the temples.

Castia had been surrendered to the Temple of Ratheon when she was seven, but her blood was not pure enough for her to breed. Instead, she served Hestia out in the world. However, her resentment of her station had grown lately.

At last, Castia bowed her head to the floor again and left.

Kaleck helped Namar get settled next to Hestia before he resumed his place on the stool.

Hestia looked the boy over. His weeks at sea had left a mark: his braids had grown out, and his scalp was flaky. He had been hastily bathed, but was in need of some care and attention and a nice long soak in a bath.

"Did you have the freedom of the ship while you traveled?" she asked.

Namar shook his head, still in awe of her.

Hestia looked a Kaleck, whose face was set in a frown, then back to the boy. "Would you like to take a trip to the baths?"

Namar swallowed hard and asked, "Why am I here?"

"What did Castia tell you?" Hestia asked in turn.

"That my father would have wanted me free of the blasphemers and my elder sister had summoned them to come take me away." Namar's voice was quivering, and there were tears in his eyes. "But Alanine would never do that, and Cousin Isra was nice when she stayed with us."

It was obvious that trying to speak badly about the only family the boy had known wouldn't be a wise idea, so she took a different tack.

"Did you know, child, that your father was one of my servants?"

Namar nodded. "Papa taught me all about you. He told me that he had seen you in person four times and that he hoped to see you again." His lip trembled. "But he is dead now."

"Let me tell you something," Hestia said as she stroked his cheek. "He is with my mother in her Halls, and he dines in splendor and is dressed in garments of red and gold. I have seen him and spoken with him when I have visited her there in my sleep, and he wanted us to save you so you could become a great man in my service. A Magi of renown."

"You have seen my Papa?" Namar asked.

"I have, and when I visit my mother's Halls tonight, I will tell him you have arrived safely and that soon, you will begin your training."

"Will I ever see my sisters again?" Namar asked hesitantly.

"I will do my best to bring them here so we can keep you all safe," Hestia said as she put an arm around him. "For now, this is Kaleck. He is the father of the children of my body, and he has offered to act as your foster father, to help you settle in to the temple, and to oversee your training."

Namar turned to Kaleck, who had come to his feet.

"First, I think we should get you to the baths," Kaleck said. "If you wish to keep your hair braided, you can, but we must tend to it." Kaleck's own hair flowed to his shoulders in tight curls.

Namar looked from him to Hestia.

She stroked his cheek again. "Kaleck will take good care of you, and then the three of us can have dinner in my rooms."

Namar nodded, and Kaleck gave him a reassuring smile, and the pair left.

*****

That evening, Kaleck brought Namar for the evening meal. Hestia had changed into a sleep shift and her scarlet dressing gown. Kaleck and Namar both wore dressing gowns over sleep pants and loose shirts.

They had a Pannarian dish of lamb simmered in a tomato cream sauce with lots of spices, served over rice. Thick slices of buttery flatbread accompanied it. The familiar food seemed to soothe Namar, and he settled down to eat a hearty meal.

When they finished, Kaleck poured them each a large glass of wine, and they settled on the low couches in Hestia's private rooms.

It didn't take young Namar long to become drunk. Hestia and Kaleck coaxed him into her bedroom, and once he lay in the bed, his dressing gown discarded, Hestia and Kaleck disrobed and began the dance they had perfected over many years.

He made love to her as the drunk boy watched, and soon, they had coaxed Namar out of his clothes, and they were a tangled mess of naked limbs and sweaty bodies.

Then Namar was well and truly hers.

CHAPTER 96

Samuel Thane
Clearwater Place, City of Endomir: Lithonia
23rd and 24th of Minn

Samuel put the small leather box that held his spare cravat pins and cufflinks in his trunk before closing it. He looked around the room to make sure that he had everything he planned to take with him, and then finally turned to Jack.

He was leaning against the door, his brandy-colored eyes on the floor.

Samuel crossed the room and took him in his arms. "I will be back."

"I know," Jack said, his face against Samuel's shoulder. "Just don't go falling for one of those Caeldenonian soldiers," he joked feebly.

"Not on your life," Samuel promised as he leaned back to look at him. "You're stuck with me good and proper. Maybe I can get you a job with the Queen."

"What, me? Work for the Queen?" Jack laughed. "You daft bugger. I am not good enough for all that."

Samuel kissed him. "You are more than good enough."

Jack blushed and picked up Samuel's satchel and the polished walnut lap desk that Mistress Vera had given him. It had a lock and a supple leather strap so he could carry it over his shoulder—suited for a secretary to someone who would be on the move often.

Samuel kissed Jack once more before they went downstairs.

When they arrived in the drawing room, they both bowed to Vera and then to Lord Alexander. Technically, it should have been the other way around, but Lord Alexander seemed to understand how much the Queen valued Vera and didn't make a fuss.

"I hope to see you soon, Samuel," Vera said as she kissed his cheek. "Give my regards to the Queen."

Samuel smiled at her and shook Jack's hand before he followed Lord Alexander out. He didn't look back.

The pain and longing he would see on his lover's face would shatter him if he did.

*****

The trip was dull and uneventful, though Lord Alexander was good company. He didn't seem to put much stock into rank. They played cards through most of the journey from Hartford to Dale, and when they stepped off the train, the young lord made sure that Samuel's things got loaded onto the carriage that was waiting for them.

Dale was a large city, bigger than Endomir, but it was the castle that took his breath away. The way it was built into the hill was a marvel.

Lord Alexander chuckled when he noticed Samuel gaping. "I am still in awe of it myself, and I grew up here."

"It makes you wonder why the Morthans ever left," Samuel murmured. "This place is magnificent."

"I think they saw it as weak after Jonathan Morthan was able to starve the city. While you could besiege Endomir, it would be hard to starve it. The basin is full of farms, and the woods are teeming with game."

Lord Alexander climbed out of the carriage and turned to Samuel. "The footmen will take your things to your rooms. If you will come with me?"

The trek through the many levels of Hardcastle seemed to take ages; the halls and corridors were bustling with people. As they walked through the different parts of the castle, Lord Alexander threw around words like *Bastion, Midhold* and *Aerie*.

Samuel was going to need a map to navigate this place.

"I don't know how anyone could think this place weak," he said as they climbed yet another staircase. "Anyone who didn't know the way could get lost for days."

Lord Alexander smiled as they approached a new set of doors. "This is the Aerie, also known as the Royal Residence."

Four guards flanked the doors. Two were dressed in the familiar Morthan livery, and two were dressed in black with gold swords on their breasts and arms.

The Morthan men saluted Lord Alexander, while the men in black inclined their heads in a show of respect.

"Lord Alexander Rythan and Mr. Samuel Thane for Her Majesty Queen Lenathaina," he said formally.

The guards opened the ornate doors and stepped aside.

They continued their trek for several minutes before turning into a new wing that was teeming with activity. A tall man with golden skin who Samuel recognized as the Prince came out of a room flanked by two men, one with honey skin and mahogany hair, and another with ocher skin and curling black hair.

The last man had to be the most beautiful creature that Samuel had ever seen. He had to shake himself from a fog.

The men stopped, and Lord Alexander and Samuel bowed.

"May I introduce His Royal Highness Gavantar Coden, the First Prince of Caeldenon, His Highness, Prince Galwyn Tearhall of Cael, and His Grace Lord Baerik Forrester-Coden, the *Duc 'ah* Kilmerian?" Alexander gestured to each man as he gave their name and title before turning to Samuel. "My Prince, this is Mr. Samuel Thane, who was sent by Mistress Vera Martique as a candidate for the post of secretary to Her Majesty Queen Lenathaina."

"I am not sure if that will please or sadden Tori," the *Duc* said with a laugh. "Though I imagine Her Majesty will keep her close by, even if someone else is wielding the Queen's pen."

"I hope I am not taking anyone's place, Your Grace," Samuel said. *Maker, but the man is beautiful.*

"My uncle jests," the Prince said. "The Queen's ladies have been taking it in turn to fill the post of secretary, but the *Ducessa* and the Queen can often be found working late into the evening together."

"Ah, then I am sure that I will have the pleasure of getting to know Her Grace well," Samuel said.

"So we mustn't keep her waiting," the Prince said. "We are off to check the camps, but the Queen and her ladies are in the study."

Lord Alexander and Samuel bowed, and the three men continued down the hall.

The door to the apartment that the men had left was flanked by more guards, but one of the black-clad ones here was a woman.

Once they had been admitted, Lord Alexander explained, "There are several women soldiers here. You are in for a bit of a shock."

Samuel nodded but didn't reply. He was trying to memorize the layout of the apartment, for surely if the Queen took him on, he would be here often.

They passed several doors and more than a few guards, both those in the Morthan blue and the Caeldenon black, until they finally reached their destination.

When they were finally brought into the room, Samuel and Lord Alexander found themselves outnumbered. Seven women sat at various tasks around the space.

Both men bowed, and the Queen smiled politely.

"I take it your errand was a success, Lord Alexander?" the Queen asked.

"I believe so, Your Majesty." Lord Alexander turned to Samuel. "Allow me to introduce Her Royal Majesty Queen Lenathaina Morthan Coden, First Princess of Caeldenon. Ma'am, this is Mr. Samuel Thane."

The Queen rose, and so did every other woman in the room. She extended her hand to Samuel, who took it and bowed.

"A pleasure to meet you, Mr. Thane." She turned to the other man. "Thank you, Lord Alexander."

It was a clear but polite dismissal.

Once the young lord had left, she turned back to Samuel. "How long have you worked with Mistress Martique, Mr. Thane?"

"Five years, Your Majesty," Samuel replied as he released her hand. "She sends her regards." He pulled out the thick packet of letters that Mistress Vera had given him for the Queen, and handed it over.

"Five years?" one of the women said, and he would have bet his best boots that she was the Dowager High Lady Bennings. "You must be one of her agents, then."

Samuel's mouth nearly fell open. "Uh…"

Another woman, this one with chestnut hair, laughed. "We have all known Vera for a long time, lad, so we know her business."

"Yes, well, I was an agent for a while, but more recently, I have worked in the house side of things." Samuel felt the heat rise in his face.

The Queen sat down at her desk and gestured for him to sit as well. The other women resumed their seats, but all eyes were on Samuel.

"So you were given a promotion?" Her Majesty asked.

"Yes, ma'am," Samuel said as he set his satchel on the floor beside him. "Mistress Vera thought my various talents would be of use to you."

"She was right, of course," the Queen said. "And if you have worked for Vera that long, she has thoroughly investigated you. I will take you on a trial basis, and if things work out, it will become a permanent posting. Is that agreeable?"

"I think you should read Mistress Vera's letter, Your Majesty, before you make any firm offers," Samuel said. "In case anything in there would change your mind."

He and Mistress Vera had discussed the matter, and both agreed that his past might at some point come to haunt him. It would be better for the Queen to know it from them first.

The Queen arched a black brow and opened the packet Samuel had given her. The letter from Mistress Vera was on the top. She opened it and read it.

All the while, the gazes of the women in the room flicked from him to the Queen and back again.

At last, a small smile curved her mouth, and she handed one of the three pages to the honey-blonde woman beside her. She read it and laughed before handing it to a woman that looked like the female version of Prince Galwyn, who also smiled.

As the letter rounded the room and each woman either smiled or sighed or laughed, Samuel felt his color rise even more. He was about to storm out, when the Queen turned her smile on him.

"Please feel free to use the royal courier to write to your young man. I will send instructions so your letters are delivered."

"Y-you mean you don't mind, Your Majesty? I worried that it would, uh, reflect b-badly on you," Samuel stammered.

"One can't help who they love," the Queen replied. "And even if they could, it should not matter. Love is love. Now then. Would you like to see your room or your office first?"

CHAPTER 97

Queen Lenathaina Morthan Coden, First Princess of Caeldenon
Hardcastle, the City of Dale: Lithonia
28th of Minn

Gavantar kissed Lena's collarbone before he untied the laces of her nightdress.

She moaned and stretched. "This is a nice way to wake up."

She felt his mouth curve against her skin as his lips moved downward to the top slope of her breast. He suckled the skin lightly, and she felt the tension leave her body.

"I woke and couldn't sleep," Gavantar murmured. "I hope you don't mind keeping me company."

"Not at all," Lena gasped as his mouth closed on her nipple.

Her hand tangled in his hair as he set to work with his mouth, first at one breast and then the other, while his hand busied itself between her legs.

When she was moaning and quivering beneath him, he sat up and looked down at her. She smiled up at him. She could see more of him now as the sunlight shown through the gap in the curtains and made his skin glow. Golden. That was the word that always came to mind when she looked at her husband.

It must be past dawn.

"Perhaps we should finish this later," Gavantar murmured. "I know you will want to get to your workout…"

"Damn my workout." Lena sat up, pulled off her nightdress, and tossed it to the floor. "Unless you would rather go wave your sword at Galwyn?" she challenged.

Gavantar gave her a wolfish grin, and his sleep pants joined her nightdress on the floor.

Lena pushed him onto his back and straddled him, hovering for a moment, teasing him.

"Lenathaina," he growled, his hands on her hips. He arched up, seeking.

She bent down and kissed him thoroughly before she lowered herself, letting him slide into her. He groaned into her mouth as her hips rocked against his.

They were very late to breakfast.

*****

Master Tam entered after luncheon the study with Braithwaite, who was carrying a folder. "Your Majesty."

Both men bowed, and Braithwaite handed the folder to Lena. "I have had word from the Greys."

Lena took the folder and opened it. Inside was a Script Stone message.

Parker's men have besieged us. We cannot leave our keep by land, and the winter storms prevent us from leaving by sea. We are well-stocked for winter. As soon as the storms pass, we will abandon Maynard and come to your aid. Please send Jane our love.

Your servant,
Gerald Grey

"Damn Parker," Lena said as she handed the note to Rachel. "Thane, where is that letter from Harry?"

Samuel Thane was sitting at a desk across the room from Lena, smartly dressed in a crisp, black suit. He quickly sorted through the letters before him. Once he found the one he was looking for, he brought it over and handed it to her.

"Thank you, Thane." Lena handed the letter to Master Tam. "The short of it is Edward Long got a message to his daughter saying that he is likewise besieged. As you know, his daughter is Carrie

Harmon, Harry's sister-in-law. Harry sent that to me through the royal courier."

"They are trying to block as many of your allies as they can." Master Tam frowned as he handed back the letter. "We don't have the forces yet to break the siege. The Greys could get to Harmon's by hugging the coast if they feel it safe now, and the Longs could do the same to Black Hall if Norrington isn't patrolling the coast south of them. I believe if you ask High Lord Harmon and High Lady Montgomery, they will offer shelter."

"Considering High Lord Harmon's forces won't be able to march until spring, I am sure that they would be happy to have whatever forces the Greys could bring, ma'am," Rachel added from her seat beside Thane.

The pair of them had been working through some of the official correspondence to create a filing system. Thane, it turned out, was quite the organizer. He also didn't get his dander up over working with and under so many women.

It wasn't surprising, after his years working for Vera, but it was still out of the ordinary for men of Lithonia.

"I will write to Harry and speak to Angela," Lena said with a sigh. "Why Marc Eddening is persisting in this is beyond me."

"Because he's an idiot. You are a young woman, married to a man who comes from fertile stock," Tori said with a smile. "Once you and the Prince get down to the business of starting your family, Eddening will just get shoved farther and farther from the throne. But honestly… I never thought he would go this far for power."

"*I* am not surprised," Rachel snorted. "He has always been a grasping little shit. Begging your pardon, ma'am. I do know he is your distant cousin."

"He is a vile toad," Lena growled. "There are many reasons that I have never had a familial relationship with him. Owen, on the other hand, is a charming young man."

"You never would have married him, though," Rachel smirked.

"Of course not. Besides not being attracted to him, I had no intention of tying myself to Marc's family," she said. "But I have always gotten a queer feeling from Marc. He makes me feel uneasy."

"One that his wife shared, I think," Tori replied. "There have been a lot of rumors over the years."

"Be that as it may," Tam said. "He has amassed enough support to be a large problem. At some point, we really need to discuss what will be done with the traitors."

"I know. But I am not ready yet, Tam. When it is time, I will meet with you and the other members of the Council to consider it," Lena said. "Any word on my other cousin?"

She had been messaged as soon as *Shan* Alanine Fasili had arrived in Seathor. If the girl were not with Masters Isra and Amir, Lena would have been leery about letting her come to Hardcastle, but she owed the Masters a great debt and didn't think they would bring the *Shan* here if the young woman meant her harm.

"They have left Seathor," Tam reported. "The snows will slow them down, but with two Masters at her side, I do not believe any will attempt to halt her."

"Please let me know if you get any updates," Lena said.

Tam bowed formally and excused himself.

"He is looking tired," Rachel said thoughtfully after the Master left.

Lena was staring at the door as if it could give her all the answers in the world.

She turned back to her friends, and there were unshed tears in her eyes. "I am not sure how much longer I will have his counsel and aid, and I do not know what I will do without it."

Fenora stood and moved to Lena's side. Resting her hand on the Queen's shoulder, she said, "As with all things… you will find a way through."

KRISTINA GRUELL

CHAPTER 98

Princess Fenora Tearhall
Hardcastle, the City of Dale: Lithonia
31ˢᵗ of Minn and 1ˢᵗ of Charn

Fenora and Rachel left their apartment shortly before midnight and went to the Queen's rooms. Fenora had a black scarf in her hand, as that was the color for mourning in Caeldenon, and Rachel had a gray one to honor her Lithonian upbringing.

When they entered the cavernous apartment, they found most of the immediate court there: the Queen, the Prince, Tori and her husband—and of course, their *Mael'Hivar*—as well as High Lady Montgomery, the Dowager High Lady Bennings with her oldest daughter, Master Tam and his apprentices, and Samuel Thane.

Fenora and Rachel curtsied to the Queen and Prince and the *Duc* and *Ducessa* before joining the party.

"I have had word from my parents," Gavantar said. "Merra is coming. Father said she had information too delicate to pass through the Stones. She leaves in the morning."

"That seems ominous," Fenora replied.

"I did like High Princess Merra when we were in Caeldenon. I wish I had gotten to know her better," Rachel said to the Prince.

"We will have to keep an eye on her. Merra is a wild thing… She will love the chance to go to war." Gavantar took a healthy sip of wine.

Just before midnight, they left the apartment and went down to the royal temple, which was connected to the aerie. Lady Rythan had informed Fenora, with much joy, that it would be the first time in over one hundred years that a member of the Royal Family would observe the Night of Reflection there. She had gone to much trouble to make sure that there were plenty of fresh beeswax candles, rosemary, lilies, and, in honor of those from Caeldenon, snowdrops.

392

Pine boughs had been placed on every windowsill. Rich scents filled the air.

The Queen, the Prince, the *Duc,* and the *Ducessa* all sat in the front row, Galwyn and Ellae with them. Fenora and Rachel sat behind them with the rest of their immediate household, including Thane. The rest of the court was arrayed in the other rows and seats by rank, but the Rythans had a place of pride in the first row, to the right of the Queen.

She had made it clear that they would retain their place as Steward of Hardcastle no matter what came, for the place was big enough that she could never manage it alone.

High Priest Lyle gave a long sermon—overly long, in Fenora's opinion. He most likely hadn't had this grand of an audience in some time. When it was over, everyone stood and took candles from the baskets waiting at the end of each row, and acolytes came with tapers to allow the attendees to light them. Fenora noticed that Lena had four, as she took two herself, one for each of her parents.

Several altars had been set up along the sides of the walls, with racks to hold candles. Everyone placed their lit candle or candles in the racks and honored their dead before moving out of the temple room and toward the large drawing room on the main floor of the Aerie. The Queen and those with her had gone first, but Fenora and Rachel lingered when they placed their candles, taking time to pray together for each of their loved ones.

Whether it was fate or planned, Fenora could not say, but Lady Ella Malick, Rachel's mother, chose to join them at their altar. She placed a candle and said a silent prayer. Fenora and Rachel exchanged a look and then retreated a few steps to give her privacy, but felt that leaving altogether would be rude.

Lady Ella finished and turned and smiled when she found them waiting for her. She curtsied to Fenora and then held out a tentative hand to Rachel. "Hello, daughter. I was hoping we would get a chance to speak this evening."

"Good evening, Mother." Rachel took the offered hand, but Fenora didn't need a Link to know that she was uncomfortable.

When Rachel was one year old, Lady Ella had taken the late King Charles' offer to have her daughter raised in the nursery alongside the royal children, as the woman was too bowed down with grief to give a newborn love. Rachel's first memory of her mother was Lady Ella crying in the Nursery Keep at Endomir because Rachel looked too much like her father.

Rachel had told Fenora that she saw her family socially during the season and once a year for a formal visit at the castle. The relationship was frosty at best.

"I wondered if I might sit with you at the party. Perhaps I can share some memories of your father with you?" Lady Ella's voice shook, but Fenora thought the offer genuine.

"I do not think the Queen would mind," Rachel said, trying to sound cordial but not too friendly. "I will, of course, be in attendance on her."

Fenora touched Rachel's back lightly in support. She knew this was tough for her darling girl.

"If the Queen would not mind..." Lady Ella trailed off.

"I am sure she would not," Fenora said as she slipped her arm through Rachel's and smiled at Lady Ella. "Tonight is a night to cherish the family we have."

Lady Ella gave Fenora a grateful smile and fell in beside them. "I understand that you are Prince Gavantar's foster sister?"

"I am," Fenora said. "And Prince Galwyn, his *thane*, is my twin brother."

"Anyone with eyes could see that," Lady Ella said with a smile. "You favor one another in a striking manner."

Fenora returned the smile and covertly squeezed Rachel's arm.

The Queen was holding court next to one of the two large hearths in the drawing room. Small clusters of chairs and settees were arranged throughout, and footmen in Morthan livery—a dark gray suit with a crisp white shirt and a sapphire vest—were circling the room with finger foods and steaming cups of mulled wine and hot cider.

Fenora, Rachel, and Lady Ella curtsied to the Queen, who invited Lady Ella to sit down.

"I am sure that your aunt and uncle have told you many stories of your parents, Your Majesty, but I have some of my own," Lady Ella said shyly.

Lena arched an eyebrow. "I would love to hear them. I know that Lord Andrew was close with my father. They trained together at the academy, did they not?"

"They did, ma'am. Lord Andrew and I married while he was there. Prince Matthew and Princess Nikkana married just a month later, and we were honored with an invitation to some of the private receptions in the days after," Lady Ella said.

"I didn't know that," Rachel said quietly.

Lady Ella turned to her daughter with a sad smile. "And that is my fault. It took me a long time to be able to speak of your father."

"What changed?" Rachel asked.

Lady Ella hesitated. Every eye in their small party was on her.

"Our new Master consulted with some of his colleagues after examining me. He said that I suffered from depression. It took some time, but they found a blend of herbs, and he began brewing a tincture for me. That was about a year ago. Between that and conversations with our priest exploring my grief and guilt, I have begun healing. I didn't know how to put it in a letter...."

Rachel watched her mother for a long moment before she finally nodded. Fenora could tell that she was processing.

Lena, always in tune with Rachel's feelings, drew Lady Ella's attention away from her daughter to give Rachel time to compose herself. "I find it rather brave of you to share that. Thank you."

Lady Ella blushed, and Gavantar interjected, "I would like to hear stories of Prince Matthew. Lena has told me a few, but it would be nice to hear one from someone who knew him."

The next few hours passed with everyone sharing stories of those who had passed into the Maker's Halls. There were some tears but more laughter. Eventually, Rachel relaxed enough that Lady Ella told stories of her husband and Prince Matthew's academy antics and pranks.

Near five in the morning, they all moved to the dining room, where strong tea and coffee was served alongside a hearty breakfast, after which the Queen announced that she didn't want to see anyone until dinner.

The members of the court began to drift off in ones and twos, most to go find their beds but a few, like the *Duc,* went to check on other things.

Fenora kissed her brother's cheek and bid Lena and Gavantar a good night. Rachel and Lena embraced, and then Gavantar kissed her cheek, Tori gave her a tight hug, and Galwyn squeezed her hand.

They slipped out of the room arm in arm, and headed up to their apartment, but just after they took their second turn, they heard a voice call out.

"Rachel?"

They paused and turned to see Lady Ella hurrying to catch up with them. Rachel gave her mother a tentative smile, and Fenora moved to release her arm so she could step away and give them privacy, but Rachel would not let her go.

"Yes, Mother?"

"I wondered if we could talk a little more?" Lady Ella asked.

Rachel looked to Fenora, who nodded; Lady Ella didn't miss the gesture, but did not seem affronted.

"You could join us for tea in our apartment," Rachel offered.

Lady Ella smiled. "I would like that. I did not realize that you shared…"

"Princess Fenora and I share many things," Rachel replied coolly.

Lady Ella inclined her head in acceptance of this, though she seemed confused by the arrangement.

They saw a bleary-eyed footman, and Fenora requested tea for three. He gave her a small bow and opened a door to the servants' passage, while Rachel opened the door to the opulent apartment and let them in.

Lady Ella, who was on one of the lower levels of the aerie and had not been in the royal wing before, took a few minutes to look around the sitting room. This one had been furnished with several paintings done by Queen Nelia Morthan when she was still a Rythan princess. They were a mix of watercolors that all depicted the landscape around Dale and Hardcastle; she had talent.

"Your rooms are close to the Queen, then?" Lady Ella asked as she sat in one of the wing-backed chairs while Fenora and Rachel settled themselves on a settee.

"Yes. Hers is just one door down. She likes to keep us close," Rachel said.

"I am glad that you two have such a tight bond," Lady Ella said quietly.

Rachel hesitated, but finally said, "We had a lot in common. We both lost our parents because of the battle of Harmon's Island."

Lady Ella was silent for a long time before she replied. "You did, but I hope you will allow me the chance to try and rebuild what we have lost."

There was an awkward silence for a few moments.

"My own mother died shortly after my youngest brother was born," Femora murmured. "My father had died a few months before, and after Jaemi was born, she fell into a deep sadness. I wish that she had been able to get help."

Rachel relaxed a little, and Lady Ella turned her attention to Fenora. "I am sorry that you lost your parents so young, Your Highness. I can't imagine. It seems many of your generation did."

"The battles and skirmishes between our peoples and the Hathorites have cost many children their parents, and many parents their children. I hope someday we can finally have peace between our people," Fenora replied.

"Will Uncle Joseph be coming to take command of his men?" Rachel asked her mother.

"Yes, after the spring thaw. I expect I will return to the abbey then," Lady Ella said. "But if I do, could I write to you more often?"

Fenora knew that Rachel got quarterly letters from Lady Ella now, and they were mostly accountings of Lord Southernby's children and the doings on his estate. Very dry and formal.

Rachel nodded her acceptance, and Lady Ella smiled. "I will let the two of you get to bed, I know you young women rise early. I have heard of your sword fights. You lead quite a different life than I ever could have imagined for a young woman."

"But it is a happy one," Rachel said. "I have work and friends and a world that I belong to. I am happy."

Lady Ella's eyes misted slightly, and she looked from Rachel to Fenora. "I can see that, and that makes me happy."

She rose, and Rachel and Fenora did as well.

She hesitated before asking Rachel, "Might I give you a hug?"

Rachel nodded, and Fenora stepped back and allowed them a moment.

When they broke the embrace, both Rachel and Lady Ella had tears in their eyes.

Lady Ella embraced Fenora briefly and whispered, "Thank you."

After she had gone, Fenora and Rachel helped one another undress and change into their nightclothes before washing their faces and brushing their teeth. Once they climbed into their bed and Rachel had settled her head on Fenora's chest, Fenora spoke.

"Are you alright?"

Rachel was quiet for a few minutes. "I think I am."

CHAPTER 99

High Lord Marc Eddening
Verto, Southern Region: Lithonia
3rd of Charn

Marc sat in a private sitting room, sipping sherry with Ellis Parker and Blake Rendon. The pair was nattering on again about being stuck for the next few months and the support that was flooding in to Hardcastle.

Marc had to admit he never thought that Princess Lenathaina would take advantage of the old capital. It was a smart move.

Something I should have thought of.

He had received a missive from the Mystic that morning; one of the plans she had put into motion had yielded its fruit. Once the storms passed, She would be ready to send him aid.

It was time to fully bring Rendon and Parker to his side of things.

"Gentlemen," Marc said, "we have allies that are more powerful than any the Princess could bring to the table."

They exchanged a look and then Rendon shifted uncomfortably. "What allies are those?"

Marc studied his nails for a moment, letting the moment draw itself out. The skin around his cuticles was cracking from the cold— that didn't look very kingly, but better than a man who could barely walk down a hall without having to pause to catch his breath.

"I have been in contact with the Hathorite leader," he finally revealed.

The stunned silence that followed was as thick as the fog in Endomir in the spring.

Parker downed his sherry and said, "You must be joking. No one is in contact with the Hathorites unless they are fighting them."

"I am not," Marc said. "Do you know your history well, gentlemen?"

"I know what I needed to know to graduate university," Rendon said. "What good is history? There is nothing to learn from studying the past."

Marc snorted. "Did you know that the Hathorites were refugees from Lithonia and Pannarius? When the Maker's priests claimed Lithonia, those who followed the one that they called the Red Goddess were killed or exiled. Later, some of their fellows from Pannarius joined them. They are now led by one who goes through a ritual so that She and the Goddess are one."

"That is preposterous," Rendon said.

Parker leaned forward and looked at Marc. "I am more interested in how you know this and why you are telling us."

"Because the Mystic has offered her aid in this war," Marc said. "She and Her people will come in force for Lithonia soon, but if we partner with Her instead of fight against Her, we will be just one step below Her. She will be our Goddess, and we will rule our parts of Lithonia in Her name."

Parker and Rendon looked at him, shock plain on their faces.

Rendon said, "You're joking, aren't you?"

"I am not," Marc said. He rose and went to the door and called his secretary in.

Ken Rider wasn't much to look at: thin, with light brown hair and dark eyes, he was of average height. Most wouldn't look at him twice.

Marc nodded to Rider, and Rider turned to Rendon. "Might I have a drop of your blood, Your Grace?"

Rendon looked at Marc for a long moment before he pulled a pen knife from his pocket. He pricked his finger and held it out to Rider, who delicately wiped his finger across Rendon's before putting it into his mouth and sucking the blood off.

Before Parker and Rendon could react, Rider closed his eyes. His face began to twist, he looked as if he was in agony, and then…

his features melted, and the buttons on his shirt began to strain and pop open.

Marc had seen it before, but it was still something that curdled his stomach.

The minutes stretched on as Rider's body changed. He grew shorter and more muscular, like a man used to sparring. His hair got shorter and turned gray, and his eyes turned blue.

In short, he was a copy of Blake Rendon.

"Maker preserve us," Parker whispered as he looked from the real Rendon to the copy.

"Not the Maker," Marc corrected him. "May the Goddess ever favor us."

He nodded to Rider again, who began to reverse the process. Several minutes later, he excused the man and closed the door.

He poured Rendon and Parker another drink and sat back down. "To the Mystic and her priestesses, that was a parlor trick. She has the power to help us deliver Lithonia from Lenathaina and into the future—a future not controlled by Masters or the priests. One in which our children won't be taken to another country if they have the Gift. Instead, they will be taken to Her and then they will be free to return to us and use their Gift to honor their families."

"You want to sell Lithonia to a woman who thinks she is a goddess?" Rendon asked.

Parker was looking at the door that Rider had walked through not that long ago. "I don't know about you, Blake, but I have never seen a Master do anything like that."

"Ellis, you can't seriously be considering this?" Rendon asked, turning to his friend.

"Think about it," Parker pressed, "If this Mystic takes over, neither of us could be tried for the Morlette business. We would be set above the others... and Eddening says we will really be ruling for her."

"She will divide the country into regions, and we will each rule one under her. Like kings, all of us," Marc said, his voice pitched low.

"Under a woman?" Rendon asked, sounding hesitant but interested.

"Under a Goddess," Marc countered. "And she will give you servants, like she has given me Rider. Men with powers that rival the Masters of the Ithrimir, but without their restrictions."

"What do we have to do?" Parker asked.

"Swear a blood oath to her," Marc replied. "Rider can perform the ceremony."

"When?" Rendon asked as he tossed back the last of his sherry.

"At the dark of the moon. Three days from now," Marc said, looking from one man to the other.

Rendon and Parker exchanged a look before turning back to Marc.

"Alright," Parker agreed. "Arrange it."

Marc smiled. "She will reward us above all other Lithonians."

CHAPTER 100

High Lord Magne Montgomery
Castle Endomir, Endomir: Lithonia
6th of Charn

Magne sat in his office, reading over the latest reports from the north, where Eddening and his followers were currently pinning any supporters of the Queen that they could. The storm that had blown through the day before was not helping anyone.

Marie Adley came in with a stack of letters and sat them on Magne's desk. "Can I get you anything, Your Grace? Some tea?"

"Order some for both of us and we can get through this pile," Magne said, waving at the tottering tower of paper on his desk.

*One would think the snow would mean **less** paperwork, but somehow that always finds its way through.*

Marie returned twenty minutes later with a tea cart. Not only was there a steaming pot of fragrant black tea, but there was a basket of rolls, bowls, and a large, covered dish. When she lifted the lid, the scent of roasted chicken and carrots filled the air.

"It looks like we might be here a while," she said.

"I think so, Marie," Magne agreed as he moved from his desk to the table that was usually used for small luncheons or meetings.

Marie set their places and served them both a hearty helping of the soup, which had a thick, rich broth.

"I got a letter from Mr. Thane in the last packet from Hardcastle," she said as she sat down.

The messenger had arrived just two hours before the snow had begun falling.

Magne was still working his way through his share of letters, reports, and documents. "How is Mr. Thane settling in?"

"Quite well," Marie said as she poured their tea.

Her dark hair was pinned up, save her maiden's lock. She had one of those faces that was hard to read most of the time. He enjoyed her company. She reminded him of his daughters: headstrong, intelligent, and cunning.

There had been some grumbling about him giving the post to a woman, but her ability to not let the nobility that visited his offices fluster her and the way she looked down her nose at those who tried to flirt with or dismiss her, as if they were all naughty schoolboys who needed a smack, had earned her a begrudging level of respect.

Her efficiency had quickly elevated that respect in most, and now she encountered few issues inside or outside the castle.

"I am glad. The Queen needs a reliable person in the posting," Magne said.

They ate their luncheon in quiet companionship. Once they had finished, Marie left the tea service on the table, but put the rest of the dishes on the cart and took it back to the servants' passage.

By the time she came back, Magne had moved the stacks of correspondence to the table. They settled themselves and got to work.

Half an hour later, they had laid out all the messages of the north, both those sent by mundane methods and those relayed via Script Stone.

"It looks like the rebels that were flanking the Greys didn't pack up in time. They are snowed in their camps outside the Keep." Marie handed him a message. "Lord Grey doesn't seem inclined to let them in."

"A smart man," Magne said as he read the account. "It appears as if those who were besieging the Longs read the weather and broke their siege. Not that it matters. Earie Point is behind a mountain range with only one passage in or out. Even if it is not snowed in, Long isn't getting a force through there."

"Are you and your lady going to give them shelter if the weather clears enough for them to leave by ship?" Marie asked.

"Of course. I have already sent word to my brother, who is manning the castle now." Magne put the message on the stack that they had already gone through and saw Marie make a note.

He didn't bother trying to read it. Her notes were in a shorthand that only she understood, but somehow when she came back with her reports, they were rich in detail. He was glad that she had consented to take the post on permanently.

"From what I am reading here, I think that the north is blocked off until the thaw," Marie said. "We haven't had snows this bad in a few years. Fitting that it happens when we are fighting a civil war." The sarcasm was thick in her voice.

Magne snorted. "This year has been one for the books all around."

"Not the good books," Marie muttered.

"No," Magne agreed soberly as he looked around the office. "King Charles was always going to leave us far too soon, but the rest... Richard should have never taken the throne, and poor Maratha should have never been betrothed, let alone married to him. And Queen Mellina..."

"What about her?" Marie asked. "I heard that she was in Caeldenon, recovering from her many losses." She sounded skeptical.

"She is, or so I have been told. It makes sense that she would have gone to the Queen, but that she left before Richard and Maratha's funerals..." Magne was sure he hadn't gotten the whole story there, and wondered if he would. "Don't repeat this, but she was attacked."

"Attacked?" Marie put her pen down. "By whom?"

"High Master Jillian Prather," Magne answered, lowering his voice. "The Queen sent me a message. Queen Mellina lost part of both legs protecting little Lady Jane Grey."

"That is awful," Marie said. "And the poor child, to have seen that. Are they really safe there, or should they be brought back to Lithonia?"

"Is anyone safe anywhere, Marie?"

CHAPTER 101

*Dowager Queen Mellina Morthan, Marquess 'ah Shael
Trahelion Manor, Providence of Denon: Caeldenon
7ᵗʰ of Charn*

Mellina sat in her wheeled mahogany chair in the library with High Master Anton Brown, a Lithonian man with graying brown hair and dark green eyes.

"It is understandable that Lady Jane has been distracted of late, though your newly regained freedom seems to have lightened her mood," the Master said. "Is she sleeping well?"

Mellina shook her head. "She still struggles, though it is better than a month ago. In the first weeks after the incident, she hardly slept at all, and when she did, she woke often, screaming."

"Poor child," Master Anton said. "I have been taking walks with her and encouraging her to talk."

"I appreciate your care for her," Mellina said. "How are her studies?"

Master Anton was the children's teacher. In the Dowager's house, not only were the noble girls taught, but all the staff's children as well.

"Lady Jane is very bright. It is clear that her grandparents made sure she was diligent with her studies." He gave Mellina and understanding smile. "She is far more advanced with her studies in history compared to the other students. I would like to have some lessons with her in the morning before I start with the other children—after breakfast, perhaps, if the Dowager is willing to let her out of her needlework lessons."

"That is another area she is already accomplished in, and the Dowager values education, so I am sure she would be happy to allow Jane the chance to broaden her mind," Mellina said.

"Excellent. I will let you make the arrangements," Master Anton said.

"Not willing to challenge the Dowager's schedule?" Mellina teased with a smile.

Master Anton blushed. "You, Your Majesty, can get whatever you wish from her these days, and I am glad that you have formed a good friendship. The rest of us know to tread with caution. Her Majesty is sharp-witted and sharp-tongued, and it doesn't do to get on the wrong side of her."

"Why do you continue in this post if that is how you feel?" Mellina asked.

Master Anton hesitated before giving her a frank look. "Many of the noble and royal houses leave the education of servants to the village schools, which are often underserved. Did you know that the school in Meadborrow, the village by Rose Hall, is overseen and funded by the Dowager? She is implementing the same funding at the village school here. Her Majesty values education highly, and she has been kind enough to take my advice on a number of occasions."

This revelation, after having spent so much time with Arrysanna, wasn't shocking.

"I will speak with her this afternoon and send a note."

"Thank you, Your Majesty." Master Anton gave her a small bow from his seat.

Mellina hesitated and then asked, "Would you mind if I sat in on her lessons? I was always fascinated with history, but my education was focused elsewhere. I knew Lithonian history well, but for the rest of the world…"

"It would be an honor to have you as a pupil, ma'am," Master Anton said with a smile.

Despite Mellina being a prisoner in name—if not in fact—for the first time in her life, she felt as if she were taking control of the path she was on. She felt empowered. She felt like she could make a life that was what she wanted.

Well, once Lenathaina can put me on trial.

Even if she had to pay with her life for her crimes, her last months would be spent as the woman she wanted to be instead of who others decided she would be.

CHAPTER 102

Lady Victoria Forrester-Coden, Ducessa 'ah Kilmerian Hardcastle, the City of Dale: Lithonia
8th of Charn

The snow was thick on the ground, and the air had a sharp bite to it. Tori and Baerik had gone for a ride to check the camps, as they did every few days, and she was chilled through.

"Next time, you should stay at the castle, my love," Baerik said as he helped her off the back of her black mare, Danon.

"Nonsense. Other than when we go to bed, these rides are the closest we get to alone time. I enjoy our talks and inspecting the camps. I am learning so much."

Ten *Mael'Hivar*, General Hall, and ten of his men were dismounting around them, but Tori's words were still true.

With all the preparations for the coming conflict, Tori and Baerik were constantly at work. She spent much time with Queen Lenathaina and Baerik was in constant meetings with the First Prince and the Lithonian generals. By the time they fell into their bed at night, they were exhausted.

"You are frozen through," Baerik chided as he took her in his arms. "Let's get you inside."

"We are supposed to report to the Queen," Tori reminded her husband as she took his offered arm. "And I have a letter from my mother. They are coming here!"

"You must slow down, *cimminaria,*" Baerik said. "We will be consumed by this war for months, if not longer. Pushing yourself beyond your abilities now only means you will have less to give later."

"You are so annoying when you speak sense." She sighed as they entered the heavily carved doors to Hardcastle. "I do wonder if the designers intended this place to be so difficult to navigate that intruders would simply give up."

"It was a different time, when it was built," Baerik said as they let a maid and footman remove their cloaks and outer wrappings. She knew that, before long, those garments would be back in their respective closets. "Tealaran in Meldenon was built in the same timeframe, and it is an ostentatious warren of rooms and corridors. At least Hardcastle is pleasant to look at, inside and out."

"True. I just wish there were a shortcut between the front door and the Aerie. It takes ages to get there," Tori complained.

Baerik chuckled, and they continued to make their way to the Queen's rooms.

When they entered the Queen and First Prince's apartments, the page ran to announce them. Before they had reached Lenathaina's study, both she and the Prince had emerged, with their *Mael'Hivar* and Princess Fenora and Lady Rachel behind them.

Tori curtsied and Baerik bowed before they greeted the Queen and the Prince.

"Was your tour of the camps informative?" Gavantar asked as he shook his uncle's hand.

"I think so," Baerik said. "General Hall had some observations we should discuss."

Lena led them into the drawing room, where High Lady Angela Montgomery and the Dowager High Lady Beth Bennings were already engaged in conversation with Captain Townsend. All three rose and bowed or curtsied to the Royal Couple.

"Lord Prather wishes to know if you have any word on his cousin, Your Majesty," Captain Townsend said as Queen Lenathaina sat down.

The First Prince, Baerik, and Galwyn were standing near the hearth with General Hall, each man lighting a pipe or cigar. Tori looked at her husband, just because she could, before turning her attention back to the Queen.

"Master Tam was informed that she has arrived in the Isles and has been formally charged," Lena said. "But I think I will pass that on myself." She turned to Samuel Thane, who had followed them in and set himself in the corner with his traveling desk. "Send a note down and invite them for dinner tonight."

"Yes, ma'am," Thane said as he set himself to the task.

He had fit in nicely; the servants had taken to him, and he had already begun bringing Lena bits of information.

"General Hall, you had some recommendations?" The Queen glanced at the group of men by the hearth.

"Right now, each of the lords are treating their men as theirs," General Hall said as he looked at her. "We need a unified structure. We have a few regular army officers here, and you are our commander. Every lord or lady leading here, of course, needs to retain some of their personal guards, but those men that they have gathered to come fight in your name need to be here to *serve* in your name."

"You want me to authorize you to enlist any man willing, and to require each lord here to provide support?" Lena asked.

Hall bowed his head. "Yes, ma'am."

"Open the books, General Hall. I will find the money to pay them." Lena sighed. "Samuel…"

"I will draft a proclamation for your approval directly," Thane said as he sealed the note that he had written to the Prathers, and pulled out a fresh sheet of parchment.

Before Lena could respond, Master Tam came into the room, a *Mael'Hivar* at his heels.

"Your Majesty, Parker's men have taken Maynard Keep. He has Lord and Lady Grey."

"Damn him!" The Queen came to her feet. "Any word on what they want?"

"They want Jane Grey." Tam handed her a scrap of paper. "Lord Grey had his Master send me a message as soon as the keep was taken. He says under *no* circumstances are you to let them have Jane—even if they threaten to kill him and Lady Grey."

Rachel gasped. "They wouldn't."

411

Lena told her friend, "After these pasts months, I have no idea what anyone would do anymore."

CHAPTER 103

High Prince Evandar Coden
Ensley and Leanaire Hall, Isle Aratama: Isles of the Ithrimir
10th of Charn

Evandar stepped off the ship, Deldemar Lynn at his side.

His *Mael'Hivar Thane* had not left him once on this long journey. At White Castle, he had his own room in the antechamber of Evandar and Samera's private chambers, as he did here on the ship, but he had insisted on sleeping in the same room as his *thane*, refusing to believe that Jillian couldn't escape from her jailors.

Not that Deldemar could do much against a trained Master of the Ithrimir—and one with training from the Hathorite magi, at that—but all the same, he insisted on being Evandar's last line of defense, even in a hopeless situation.

They were greeted by a delegation of Masters, adepts and journeymen, when they disembarked. Among those was a familiar face that he had last seen just over two years before.

Evandar greeted the ranking Masters before folding his nephew, Ederic Coden, into his arms. Once he had done that, he leaned back to really look at him. "Aren't you a sight for sore eyes?"

Ederic had begun the slowing. Evandar remembered the first time he had realized that Lan looked younger than he did. Now his nephew looked closer to his younger brothers' ages than he did his sixteen years.

"My teachers let me have the afternoon off so I could meet your ship," Ederic said. "I am sure I will have to make up my lessons later, but it is worth it."

He, like Merra, was a true blending of his parents: copper-skinned with auburn hair, though he had bright blue eyes. He was tall and lanky, like a colt.

"I will give them my thanks personally," Evandar said. "I was loaded down with gifts and letters before I came."

"How is Uncle Lan?" Ederic asked, concern clear in his voice. He sounded much older his years.

"Not good," Evandar admitted. "He is taking it pretty hard."

"Your Highness?" High Master Stuart Vern interrupted. "If we could get the prisoner off the ship?"

"Of course." Evandar turned to the *Mael'Hivar* commander at his side. He had been in charge of the Mael'Hivar forces that had accompanied Evandar. "Blood Commander Pagent, could you please inform Arch Master Kline that we are ready for the prisoner?"

Pagent saluted Evandar and headed back up the brow to relay the orders.

Evandar turned back to the High Master and asked, "What will be done with her?"

Vern hesitated. "She will be interrogated and tried for her crimes. I do not know what will happen after. Did she give you any trouble on the way?"

Evandar nodded. "She tried to convince me to turn the ship around. She claims there is another spy at White Castle, and assured me she would reveal who they were if we turned back."

"I take it you did not believe her?"

"She may be speaking truthfully, but she deserves to die for her crimes. Two women are dead and another maimed for life. The Dowager Queen Mellina will never walk again, but if Jillian Prather had her way, both she and Lady Jane Grey would be dead," Evandar said. "And who else would have died by her hand? My brothers? My wife? I would run her through with a sword this very minute if I could."

Vern arched an eyebrow at the vehemence behind Evandar's words but nodded. "She has betrayed us all and cast suspicion on every Masters of the Ithrimir. You may trust that the Ithram and his Council will see justice done, Your Highness."

"The High King has requested that I stay until the conclusion of events here," Evandar said.

"His Majesty relayed that to us, and rooms have been prepared for you in Leanaire Hall. Your nephew may stay with you, if you wish. No one will mind if he uses this opportunity to enjoy some time with family." Master Vern smiled at Ederic, who beamed back. "But he will still have lessons and his studies to attend to."

Ederic bowed his head. "Of course, High Master."

Any further talk was interrupted by the host of Masters escorting Jillian Prather from her cabin on the ship. Her hands were bound with iron cuffs, and her hair was done in a simple braid. She wore a plain gray dress, but she held her head high as she walked down the brow.

She gave Evandar an imperious look before turning to address High Master Vern. "I hope adequate chambers have been prepared for me. Until formal charges have been laid by the Ithram and his Council, I should be treated as a High Master with the privileges afforded to that rank."

High Master Vern was an older man, not wrinkled, but with wings of gray at his temples. He was shorter than Jillian but powerfully built, with dark brown skin. He smiled up at her before pulling a scroll from his pocket. "You have been charged with murder and treason, Mistress Prather. You will be confined in the Depths until your trial is concluded."

Jillian faltered for a moment, some of her bravado slipping away. "What proof do you have?"

"Statements from the Dowager Queen Mellina and Lady Sara Parten have been sent from Trahelion Manor," Master Vern reported. "And signed copies are being brought by courier ship. Finally, the contents of your rooms and office were transported by His Highness," he inclined his head toward Evandar, "and we will surely find some interesting items there."

Jillian turned toward Evandar, her eyes blazing.

He was sure that if she'd had the ability to use the Gift, he would be a dead man.

*****

415

Ithram Taran Havensgrad sat on a white marble chair that could only be described as a throne. Above his head was a square containing a white diamond with a silver 'I' inside it. The square was made up of colored triangles, one for each of the eight mirs.

The Ithram's hair was pure white, and his ebony skin was wrinkled, but his gray eyes were bright. He inclined his head toward Evandar and Deldemar but did not rise. "Your Highness, I am honored by your presence. It has been some time since we were last graced by a member of your family who did not belong to the Ithrimir."

Deldemar and Evandar bowed, but the latter only slightly.

"I am sorry that such disturbing events are the cause of my visit, but I thank you for your hospitality," Evandar said.

"You are welcome here as long as you like, Your Highness. And I hope you enjoy your time with Adept Coden. I am told he is a bright pupil."

"I will convey that to his parents. They will be pleased to hear it." Evandar replied.

"We will sort through Jillian Prather's personal items before our first interrogation. I will let you know what the results are," the Ithram said.

"I would like to be there when she is interrogated," Evandar requested firmly.

The Ithram hesitated before finally nodding. "Of course, Your Highness. I will make sure you are apprised of our plans regarding the prisoner."

Evandar knew a dismissal when he heard one.

He made his farewells and he and Deldemar returned to their apartment in the lower levels of the diamond-shaped tower that served as the residence and offices of the Ithram and his council.

CHAPTER 104

Lord Owen Eddening
Verto, Southern Region: Lithonia
11th of Charn

Owen sat in his father's study while Rendon and Parker debated the next step. His father was watching both men over steepled fingers.

When Parker finished sputtering on about his proposed plan using the Greys against the 'Princess', Father spoke up.

"She isn't going to move to save them. They are nothing to her. She likes them, but she isn't going to risk anything to save two old people with little influence or power." He stood and walked to the window. "She is too comfortable."

"We can't storm Hardcastle," Rendon said. "They are too well fortified."

"We need to draw her out," Parker replied.

"No. I think we need to go to her," Father said. "What do you say, Rider?"

Owen shifted uncomfortably. Even before his father had revealed that Rider was someone sent to him by the Hathorite goddess, the man had made Owen's skin crawl. There was something odd about him, something unnatural.

"I think I can pay a quiet visit to the castle," Rider said with a bow of his head.

Owen stood. "Father, you can't☐"

"Quiet, boy!" His father turned a steely gaze on him. "Sit and know your place."

Owen clamped his mouth shut and sat down.

Fine, he would stay quiet. He would stay quiet so he could learn their plans and hopefully get word to Queen Lenathaina.

417

"Do you mean to have your man take out the Princess?" Rendon asked, trying sound nonchalant and failing.

"If he can get to her without being seen, yes," Father said. "But there is one man she counts on. If he is removed, I believe she will crumble."

Rider's smile in response to his father's statement sent a chill up Owen's spine.

Maker preserve him. Maker preserve us all.

He had to get out of here.

CHAPTER 105

Shan Alanine Fasili
Hardcastle, the City of Dale: Lithonia
13ᵗʰ of Charn

Alanine, Isra, and Amir had spent a week as the guests of High Lady Lissa Bennings while they'd had warmer clothes made for Alanine.

Her cousins had packed proper clothes for themselves when they had stopped at the Isles to leave Nijah there. It seemed they had accumulated an eccentric and varied wardrobe in their many years of travel.

Since speed was essential in their undertaking so they could venture north to the Queen as soon as possible, Isra had stuck to basic patterns and designs for Alanine's garments. Much to the shock of High Lady Bennings and the seamstress, her cousin had ordered a tunic and trousers in a soft, pale green wool for her to ride in.

"You haven't ridden before, and the few lessons you have had won't prepare you for riding for days," Isra had reasoned while Alanine was getting fitted. *"Best not to fight with skirts."*

That had shut the seamstress up.

Wool and heavy linen petticoats, shifts, nightdresses, pantlets, and silk stockings were also ordered, along with a pair of black, heeled slippers and supple leather boots. A velvet evening gown in dark red and a day dress in teal silk rounded out her hasty wardrobe.

Now, after more than a week in the saddle, riding through snow—and even camping in it, when there wasn't a castle or village nearby—she was more than ready to be done with her horse. Not that the horse was bad, but her body ached fiercely.

Even as tired and sore as Alanine was, her thirst to know more about Lithonia couldn't be satisfied. She'd peppered Isra and Amir with questions from dawn to dusk the first few days, until the pair had finally decided to take turns educating her on the history of the nation she found herself seeking refuge in.

As they rode through the streets of the city of Dale, Amir spoke in the Common tongue. Isra rode in front of them, leading one of the two pack horses that they had brought with them. Amir had the other.

"Before Jonathan Morthan married Princess Nelia after the civil war, Hardcastle and Dale were the capitals of Lithonia."

"Why did the capital move?" Alanine asked as she watched shopkeepers close up their stores for the night.

"Morthan wanted a more fortified position. He didn't want to chance being besieged himself and getting cut off from their food supply. You notice that Queen Lenathaina has surrounded Dale with her own troops? It prevents Eddening from blocking her access to the farms and such."

Amir went on to explain, "Endomir is surrounded by mountains with only one way in or out. The Bowl, as they call it, is mostly self-sustaining. There are many farms and even a forest to hunt in."

"Then why didn't the Queen go there?" Alanine wondered aloud.

"From what High Lady Bennings told me," Isra replied, "High Lord Eddening's forces are between the Queen and the current capital. She is well placed here, I think, and it was much easier for us to get to her at Hardcastle versus Endomir."

Any reply that Alanine might have made was silenced by the sight that unfolded as they crested the hill.

The massive limestone castle that had been on the horizon as they approached the city had been momentarily hidden as they'd wound their way through the streets of Dale, but as they came upon the open gates, it seemed to magnify. It was all there was to her world now. It was everything.

"Hardcastle," Amir said unnecessarily.

Ten guards flanked the gates, most of them in dark blue, but two were in black, and one of those black-clad soldiers was a woman.

"What is your business here?" one of the men in dark blue asked.

Isra pulled her horse to a stop. "I come at the invitation of Queen Lenathaina Morthan Coden," she said in an imperious tone. "With her cousin, Lady Alanine Fasili, *Shan* of River Keep in Pannarius and the great-great-granddaughter of Charles Morthan the First."

It appeared that they had been warned of her impending arrival, for it didn't take long for Alanine and her party to be escorted inside. For once in her life, Alanine was the important one, and the Masters with her—the sister to the Empress of Pannaria, and her husband—were second and third in line.

The Lord and Lady Rythan, the Steward of Hardcastle and his wife, greeted Alanine personally shortly after she, along with Isra and Amir, had been shown into a drawing room on the first floor of the massive castle.

What shocked Alanine most was the fact that she was greeted first.

"Lady Fasili," Lord Rythan said, bowing his head. His lady curtsied before the pair approached her. "I welcome you to Hardcastle. Queen Lenathaina said that you would be joining us here, and I am honored to be the first to welcome you."

Lady Rythan offered her arm, which Alanine took after Isra nodded her reassurance. "We will escort you up to the royal residence along with your Masters. You must tell us if you need them to be housed with or near you, or if we can house them near the rest of the Masters in residence. I must admit, they almost have a colony to themselves in the Midhold."

"Midhold?" Alanine asked, confused.

"Hardcastle is broken up into three levels or keeps," Lord Rythan supplied. "The Bastion, which is this keep, Midhold, which is the next one—that's where Lady Rythan, myself, and our family, as well as many of the servitors required to run the royal household live—and the Aerie, where the Queen and her household reside."

"Oh," Alanine said. After a moment of silence, she decided, "Master Isra and Amir should stay with me. She is also a distant cousin of Queen Lenathaina, after all."

Isra shot her a glare, but was treated with almost the same level of courtesy after that.

They were led through several levels of staircases and corridors, the Rythans giving brief histories of the various keeps that seemed to have been built both atop and in connection to one another, until they reached the Aerie.

The hallways and corridors were busier here than they had been in the keeps below. Men in uniforms moved brusquely, and even a few women in Lithonian day dresses weaved through the halls.

The crossed paths with many people but only stopped once to converse.

"Lady Forrester-Coden," Lady Rythan said. She curtsied, and Lord Rythan bowed.

Lady Forrester-Coden, a woman that looked to be Alanine's age, nodded in greeting to Lord and Lady Rythan before she caught sight of Isra and Amir.

"Master Isra," the brown-haired woman said as she held out her hand to Alanine's cousin. "The Queen told me you would be coming."

Isra took the young woman's offered hand and bowed over it slightly. "Lady Forrester-Coden, is it?" Her cousin had what could only be described as a cheeky grin. "I assume you snagged the *Duc 'ah* Kilmerian."

The young woman blushed. "We snagged one another."

"I have been traveling, but I haven't seen announcements in any of the papers. I take it this was a recent development?" Isra arched an eyebrow.

Lady Forrester-Coden waved a hand as if brushing the topic aside. "We haven't announced it yet. I hope to speak to my parents before the news gets out."

"Oh-ho!" Amir said as he took the Lady's hand and bowed over it himself. "I think there is an interesting story here."

"Perhaps the *Duc* and I will share it with you in private, but I think that the Queen is anxious to see her cousin."

Lady Forrester-Coden turned her green gaze to Alanine then. It wasn't unfriendly, but there was some reservation there.

Alanine hesitated but decided that a curtsy would be a good idea, considering the deference her cousins had shown this woman.

The Lady gave her a small smile and offered her hand. Alanine mimicked what Isra had done, taking the Lady's fingers in hers and squeezing them lightly.

"I understand that you haven't spent much time in court circles," the Lady said. "The Queen has already asked her other ladies and I to help you." She offered an arm, which Alanine took. "Come along. I will take you to meet her."

Alanine let the others chatter around her as they walked the maze of corridors.

Soldiers in blue uniforms were everywhere, and as they reached the floor that the Queen resided on, the presence of the black-clad soldiers grew.

Four guards flanked the ornate doors at the end of the corridor, two dressed in blue and two in black. The two in black saluted Lady Forrester-Coden before they admitted the party.

They entered a new hallway. Some of the doors they passed were open, and Alanine saw a reception room and a dining room. Her head was spinning with the size of both the castle and the Queen's apartment.

Finally, they came to another door, and the Lady addressed the guard outside. "*Shan* Alanine Fasili and Arch Masters Isra and Amir Hameen-Palin for Queen Lenathaina."

The black-clad guard nodded and led their party in before announcing Alanine, Isra, and Amir. It seemed that Lady Forrester-Coden and Lord and Lady Rythan needed no introduction.

Queen Lenathaina was... not what she expected. Alanine knew she was only a few years older, but the raven-haired woman with sandy brown skin and violet eyes had a *presence*—almost as much as her cousin, the Empress, may the Light ever favor her.

The Queen rose, and Isra and Amir both bowed their heads lightly. Despite the fact that she wore trousers, Alanine followed Lady Rythan's lead and curtsied deeply.

"*Shan* Fasili," Queen Lenathaina said as she offered her hand. "I am pleased that you would come all this way to meet me."

Alanine took her hand as she had Lady Forrester-Coden's, and bowed over it. "Thank you for seeing me, Your Majesty."

"Let us sit," the Queen said.

It was then that Alanine noticed how many people were in the drawing room.

Two other women, one fair-skinned with honey-blonde hair and another with skin like aged honey and mahogany hair, took seats near the hearth. A man that looked much like the second woman stood by the window, but he was dressed in black like some of the soldiers. With him was a woman with a golden braid. A man with skin the color of fresh-tilled earth and black hair, and another with golden hair and skin stood in front of a settee across from where Queen Lenathaina now sat. Another man with dark brown hair and gray eyes took a seat at a desk in the corner.

The addition of six more bodies made the room slightly crowded.

Seeing that Alanine was uncomfortable, the Queen gestured to the seat beside her. "You can sit here," she said before turning to the honey-blonde woman. "Rachel, could you order tea?"

"Of course, ma'am." Rachel rose and left the room.

The golden man moved to greet Isra and Amir, and the man with mahogany hair followed suit.

The Queen caught Alanine's attention. "The message from Master Isra said that you've had some difficulties. Perhaps you can join me for a private conversation after dinner?" She gestured to the busy room. "Discretion does not come easy, with this lot around."

Alanine smiled shyly and nodded. "Yes, I would like that, Your Majesty."

*****

Master Isra helped Alanine change into the dark red evening gown and arranged her beaded braids into an intricate coil atop her head in a style that mixed the Pannarian and Lithonian fashions. She even left two of the braids down and draped them over her right shoulder.

"Why did you not pin those up?" Alanine asked Isra's reflection.

"Unmarried young women leave what they call a maiden's lock over their shoulder. Right for unattached, and left for those betrothed. When in Lithonian dress, perhaps you should follow this custom, yes?"

Alanine nodded to her cousin, "Yes. I think that makes sense."

Isra wore a gown in the Pannarian fashion but in thicker fabrics than Alanine had ever seen at home. It was a dark green velvet wrap dress secured with a black belt under her breasts. Her hair had been pinned up as well.

When they left Alanine's chamber and entered the sitting room to the apartment they had been given to share, they found Amir admiring a painting. He was dressed in a pair of flowing trousers and a belted tunic in shades of deep green and brown, his beaded braids tied back with a brown ribbon.

"Ready, my heart and my little cousin?" he asked as he offered them each an arm.

They encircled his with their own, and Amir steered them out of the apartment and down two staircases.

"How do you know where to go? This place is so... big," Alanine said, taking in the gilt trim and the paintings and sculptures that lined the halls.

"The First Prince came while you two were bathing and dressing, and gave me a tour," Amir replied. "He showed me the room that has been set aside for sparring and training," he said to Isra, "and invited me to join him and the *Duc* in the morning."

"Good. I get tired of beating you," Isra said with a smile.

They arrived in a much larger drawing room, but it was filled to bursting with men and women in gowns and suits and sparkling jewels. They were announced by a footman in black livery with a sapphire vest.

Every eye in the room fixed on Alanine.

First Prince Gavantar Coden, who Alanine had met that afternoon, led Queen Lenathaina through the crowds, their black-clad guard at their heels.

"You look lovely, *Shan* Fasili," the Prince said as Alanine curtsied to Queen Lenathaina and then to him.

"Thank you, My Prince." Alanine could feel the heat rising in her cheeks. She still found it odd to have men openly compliment her.

The next hour and a half passed in a dizzying swirl of drinks, introductions, and a heavy meal with at least twenty people. When the meal was over, the Queen, the Prince, and the two black-clad guards who followed them everywhere led Isra, Amir, and Alanine to the drawing room in the Queen's apartments.

The Royal Couple sat on one settee, and Isra and Amir on the other with Alanine between them. The two figures in black sat in chairs by the hearth, where they would have a good view of the guests.

"Before we begin, Your Majesty, I would like to apologize for the actions of the man who was posing as my father," Alanine said with a trembling voice.

"Posing as your father?" the Prince asked.

"You saw the man's face melt," interjected the man who had been introduced to her as *Mael'Hivar Thane* Galwyn—who was, confusingly, a prince himself. "I suppose her father originally bore the face the man used as his mask before he died."

"Indeed," Isra said, taking the burden of the telling from Alanine. "Amir and I went through the personal effects of the man who stole his likeness. From what we found there, we've determined that he killed Consort Arian Fasili thirteen or fourteen years ago. That means the two younger Fasili children were his, but Alanine is the daughter of the true Arian Fasili."

"How can you be sure?" the Queen asked Isra.

"We think we met the man who killed the true Consort," Amir said. "He accompanied *Shan* Maevis to the wedding of our niece and was introduced as Arian's companion. It isn't unusual for the husbands of noblewomen to have a male companion to pass their time with. Usually someone of a lower rank.

"I spoke to the man, though when he found out I was a Master, he began avoiding me." Amir shrugged. "It happens, but thinking back on it, his behavior was odd. He didn't fear me… it was more a loathing."

"At the time, Arian was unwell, his skin ashen and yellow-tinged," Isra recalled. "I offered to examine him, but he preferred to put his trust in the wise women. His outward symptoms were much the same as we later saw in *Shan* Maevis. Alanine was three then." She smiled at her young cousin. "I remember playing with her in the gardens."

Alanine started at that. She hadn't realized Isra had known her so long.

"Where are Alanine's siblings now? They might be the children of this mysterious man, but they are *Shan* Maevis' too and should be looked after," the Queen said, looking from Alanine to Isra.

Alanine felt the tears roll silently down her cheeks.

Amir put his arm around her, and Isra took her hand.

The Queen and the Prince exchanged a look.

"What is it?" the Prince asked.

"Nijah, Alanine's younger sister, is with my children on the Isles of Ithrimir, taken there for her safety. My sister the Empress, may the Light ever favor her, would have taken her in, but we agreed, under the circumstances, that it would be best for the child to be surrounded by Masters that could protect her."

"Under what circumstances?" the Queen asked, her eyes resting on Alanine.

"My brother was taken by the Hathorites," Alanine whispered.

A stunned silence filled the room.

Several moments passed before Isra finally said, "Namar was taken from River Keep on the twenty-fourth of Minn. Less than a week before that, a woman I believe to be a priestess of the Hathorite goddess visited Alanine. My cousin wrote to me and asked me to come, but I was too late. This woman revealed that Namar had the Gift and his father had been training him. She wanted to live with Alanine so she could further train the boy and keep him safe from me. So the woman kidnapped him."

"Oh…" The Queen stood and crossed the room to kneel before Alanine. "My dear."

She opened her arms, and Alanine slid off the settee and into the waiting embrace of her cousin.

CHAPTER 106

Prisoner Jillian Prather
Leanaire Hall, Isle Aratama: Isles of the Ithrimir
15th of Charn

Jillian sat in her cell, dressed in a plain gray robe.

Three times a day, she was given meals and taken to the water closet. Twice a day, she was escorted for short walks through the halls of the prison below Leanaire Hall, one of the three towers housing the administration and teaching arm of the Masters of the Ithrimir.

The Ithram and the Council were also in Leanaire. Her trial had taken place here over the last week, once her interrogation had ended.

She had refused to give over anything voluntarily. Thankfully, the nature of the network meant that she had few names to give when they finally forced a potion down her throat that gave her no choice but to answer truthfully. When asked if there were other Hathorite spies, she had said yes but since she didn't know their names, she could not be forced to give them up.

They already had all the evidence they needed. Queen Mellina Coden and Lady Sara Parten had both sent testimony, and some of the things among her own belongings had damned her as well.

The Ithram and the Council had taken their time debating on her punishment, but the day before, she had finally been summoned.

Ithram Taran Havensgrad sat with two members from each of the eight Mirs on a raised dais. A third member of each of those Mirs stood watch over her.

"We will give you one last chance to confess your crimes and repent before the Maker," the Ithram said.

Jillian sneered. "I won't repent to a god that does nothing for his people."

Several members of the Council glared down at her.

"Then we are left with no choice, child," the Ithram intoned. "Jillian Prather, you are stripped of the rank High Master. Tomorrow at dawn, you will be taken to the hospital ward, where your barrier to touch the Life Force will be sealed."

"Will my execution follow that same hour?" Jillian asked, trying and failing to be fearless.

The smile the Ithram gave her was chilling.

"No," he said coolly. "You will be sent to one of looms to live out your remaining days spinning cloth and watching others imbue it with the magic you will never again be able to touch."

"No! I demand to die!" she wailed.

I am ready to die for my Goddess, but not to live without her Blessing!

"You no longer have a choice in anything, Jillian," High Master Parana Intion said. He was the head of the White Mir, the healers, and disappointment showed clearly on his face. "You have proven that you aren't capable of making rational decisions."

"I had no choice in confessing!" Jillian spat out.

"You had a choice in serving your Mystic," High Master Lirian Rainier, Head of the Blue Mir, replied, looking down her nose at Jillian. "You can contemplate that as you work off your debts. You have taken lives, two that we know of but possibly more. You have given information to the enemy. By your own confession, you were responsible for the kidnapping of the heir to Lithonia, and you would have murdered Lady Jane Grey and the Dowager Queen Mellina."

Master Lirian pinned her with a level stare. "How many more crimes have you committed? How many lives have you shattered?" The old woman leaned back in her chair. "Death is too good for you."

Jillian was then returned to her cell, where she passed a sleepless night.

At dawn, she had a visitor.

High Prince Evandar Coden sat in a chair across the room from her, leaving a good six feet between them, even though she was bound to her chair. His *Mael'Hivar Thane,* Deldemar, stood behind him.

"Do you have any messages you wish me to deliver?" he asked.

She looked away for a time before turning back to him. "I was fond of Lan. Tell him that. It wasn't all duty."

It was Evandar's turn to look away. When he finally met her gaze again, he asked, "Why?"

"Power," Jillian said simply. "The ability to use my Blessing as I saw fit, without nannies and rules."

Deldemar looked disgusted with her.

Jillian didn't care.

He is nothing.

Evandar shook his head. "Laws and rules aren't there to deny you. They are meant to keep the whole of society safe."

"Believe what you want, princeling," Jillian sneered.

Evandar left her then. Shortly after, the Arch Masters that were guarding her escorted her to the hospital ward.

The Ithram and the entire Council sat in the observation deck of the procedure room. Evandar and his *thane* were there as well. Usually, the deck was filled with students and young Masters, watching as spells or techniques that they had only read about were put into practice.

Jillian was strapped to a padded table, and the gaslamps were turned up. The room was bright as day. Four Masters in white robes stood around her. One administered a sleeping draught—the only mercy she was shown.

The world went black.

*****

Jillian was broken.

That thing that had defined her for so long was gone. She was alone in a chamber, tucked into a bed. She hadn't been alone since she was captured.

She pushed the covers back and sat up. With her eyes closed, she reached for that place inside herself, the barrier through which she could touch the Life Force and use it to do great and terrible things.

But it was sealed. She felt empty. Hollow. As if some vital part of herself had been cut out. She was only a shadow of what she had been.

Jillian pulled at her hair, screaming, wailing. Grieving for her loss.

The door crashed open. White robes swirled around her as four Masters entered her chamber. She scratched and clawed at them until they pinned her to the bed. Liquid was poured into her mouth.

The blackness came for her again.

CHAPTER 107

Lady Victoria Forrester-Coden, Ducessa 'ah Kilmerian
Hardcastle, the City of Dale: Lithonia
26th of Morin

"In the last two months, the men who've joined the Lithonian Army have begun to resemble soldiers, Your Majesty," General Hall said to Lenathaina before he took a sip of his tea. "I do wish that you would come down to the camps again. Last time, it really boosted their spirits."

"I have a meeting this afternoon with some of the high lords and high ladies," the Queen mused before turning to Samuel Thane. "But schedule an afternoon off next week so I can review my troops."

"Consider it done, ma'am," Thane said.

"Let me know what day you decide on," Baerik said. "Hall and I will arrange it. The men will like that."

"I will, *Duc*," Lena said. "Thank you."

Tori and Baerik left the Queen and went down to courtyard and mounted up. They took ten *Mael'Hivar* with them, and five Lithonian soldiers, and rode to the southwestern camp where General Landgrave had command.

"I look forward to the return of the warmer weather," Baerik said as they followed the well-marked path.

There had been a lot of traffic in the last months, almost creating a road between Dale and the camp.

Tori nodded. "I am glad the snow has melted, but the mud…" She looked around her. "It's horrendous."

Baerik laughed. "You could stay in the castle."

"I have the best of both worlds. I get to come with you to the camps and speak with the commanders and lords and ladies, and bring the gossip back to the Queen, and work with her on next steps. That's better than being cooped up all the time," she scoffed.

433

"I won't complain." Her husband grinned at her. "You are a sight prettier, hen, than this lot," he jerked his head at the *Mael'Hivar* and soldiers around them.

Stalvar Lynn, the *Mael'Hivar Naheame* that Tori was sure Baerik would take as his *thane* any day now, snorted.

Naheame Salmeara Jinn, who had become a close friend of Tori's, held up a fist, and the soldiers halted their horses.

Tori knew better than to ask why they had stopped. She slowed her breathing and tried to listen over the sound of her pounding heart.

Images flashed in her mind of another ride on a beach in Caeldenon... The day that she and Rachel had lost their innocence, and Lenathaina had been kidnapped.

She wasn't sure if the sound of galloping horses she heard was a memory or happening in the present until Baerik turned to Salmeara and said, "Stay close to her."

He turned his horse out of line, and three of the *naheame* formed a knot around Tori.

"Lynn!" she called to the silver-haired man with teak skin.

"I have him, Your Grace!" Lynn shouted as he dug his heels into his horse's flanks.

Salmeara edged closer to Tori. "Don't panic yet."

She nodded, and the five of them held their place.

A few minutes later, Baerik and Lynn rode back with their soldiers. One of the men peeled off to the west at a gallop.

"The camp is closer than the city," Baerik panted. "Ride hard!" He shouted to them all.

As much as she wanted to look back as she rode, she kept her eyes on Baerik's back. She could hear whoever was chasing them.

One of the *naheame* behind her called out, "Rear guard, stand and hold!"

Shots rang out.

Tori gripped her reins tighter. Something whizzed past her head, and she pressed her face to Danon's neck. The black mare whinnied.

Baerik looked back briefly to make sure she was on his roan's tail. Whatever he saw behind her made him spur his horse on faster.

The guard that had left their party had warned the camp. Lines of soldiers were forming with shields, pikes, and rifles.

They rode through the gap and dismounted.

Baerik pulled Tori into a fierce embrace. "Are you alright?"

"Yes," she panted.

"Good. Get to the center of camp," he ordered before turning to greet General Landgrave.

"I will not," Tori countered. She could feel Salmeara at her back, along with two other female *naheame*. "I am not a delicate flower to be coddled. I am perfectly capable of defending myself, Baerik Forrester-Coden, and you won't send me away."

General Landgrave's mouth fell open, and the soldiers standing with him awaiting orders looked from her to Baerik and back again.

Baerik rubbed his hand over his face. "You have your knives?"

Tori patted her thigh, then she pushed her cloak over her shoulders so it trailed behind her like a train, revealing the short sword and pistol she wore on her belt.

"Stay with the commanders," he said before turning back to the general.

"But surely the *Ducessa* should not be exposed to ☐"

The sound of gunfire interrupted the rest of Landgrave's sentence, and everyone turned.

Tori saw at last what they had been running from. At least one hundred soldiers were dismounting and forming ranks. The rear guard that had slowed them down rode through the line and dismounted. She could see that two of them were injured.

"Half our men are on patrols," Landgrave grumbled to Baerik.

Baerik met Tori's eyes before he turned back to the general. "We have been training our men hard. They can handle this."

Landgrave saluted Baerik and began issuing orders.

Tori went to the wounded men. *Naheame* Jarvin saluted her as one of his comrades held a handkerchief on his leg.

Memories of Glenn's shattered leg on that rocky beach swam before her, and for a moment, Jarvin was Glenn.

Pull yourself together.

She took over holding pressure on Jarvin's leg and sent the other *naheame* to get the doctors. Once they had arrived, she wiped her hands on her own handkerchief and turned to survey the action.

The two opposing sides were steadily exchanging fire.

Salmeara twitched beside her.

"Anxious to join the fighting?" Tori asked her.

Salmeara arched a dark brow at her. "Hoping the fighting doesn't get too close because I know I won't be able to keep you out of it."

Tori's reply was cut off by a shout from the rear of the camp.

"Another force is cutting through the south lines!"

"You had to say something," Tori muttered as she pulled her pistol from its holster and began the process of loading it.

The gunpowder went in first, and then a small bit of cloth, followed by the ball. She removed the ramrod from its holder and tamped the ball down before putting the rod back, loading the priming pan, and locking down the frizzen.

She did all of this with quick, economical movements that had been honed over months of practice. After all... when the snows were at their deepest, there had been little to do but hone her combat skills and make love to her husband.

She had set about mastering both tasks with equal enthusiasm.

When she looked up, she saw that the Lithonian soldiers standing near her were staring at her with a mix of shock and awe.

"Fifteen seconds, I swear it," said a pockmarked lad with straw-colored hair.

"Nah... ten," a young man with dark brown hair challenged. "Anyone have a watch? We can time her next time."

"Next time, you better have your own guns loaded," Tori said darkly as she turned to the south.

Baerik came to her side, along with all the uninjured *Mael'Hivar*—Jarvin and the second man were chivying the surgeons to tie their bandages in place so they could join the line too. And several Lithonian soldiers joined their ranks and began loading their guns.

Baerik looked down and her and pulled her into a quick embrace, kissing her hard on the mouth before setting her down and loading his rifle.

Men in Rendon's gray and moss green moved through the tents, heading their way. Tori raised her pistol at the same time that the soldiers around her raised their guns and fired.

The next half hour passed in a blur of reloading and firing her pistol until her ears were ringing and her head throbbed, until at last, Rendon's men broke and ran, leaving their dead behind.

By then, part of the front lines had broken, and Tori and Baerik turned to the west.

She shoved her pistol back in its holster and pulled out her sword.

Salmeara gave her a long look.

"I am out of shot," Tori said.

"Me too," the dark-haired woman replied. She had also traded her pistol for a sword. "So much for a dull ride through the countryside."

Tori stifled a laugh.

Four men broke through the line together. Baerik took one down with a well-placed shot between the eyes, and then thrust his rifle into Tori's hand before pulling out his own sword. Stalvar and another *naheame* advanced.

Tori sheathed her blade and reloaded the rifle. She wasn't as fast with it as she was her pistol, but she was fast enough.

As the next group broke through the lines, she lifted the rifle to her shoulder and took two steady breaths before firing.

The shot wasn't as clean as Baerik's—she had caught him in the cheek—but it dropped him all the same, and then she put down the rifle, knowing she wouldn't have it loaded before the advancing soldiers were on her.

Salmeara and *Naheame* Hearissa were to her right and left. Both women had their swords in hand as four men came their way.

Tori knew what they saw: two women in uniforms and another in a riding dress. What could three women do against four men?

In a smooth motion, Tori pulled a throwing knife from the sheath strapped to her leg and threw it. The hilted blade firmly lodged in the throat of the man in the lead.

His three companions faltered for a moment before continuing forward.

Tori threw two more knives. One missed, but the other took a man in the shoulder.

He yanked out the blade and tossed it to the ground.

Taking a deep breath, she pulled out her sword once more. She looked at the women to her right and left; they nodded to one another, and then stood firmly as the three men, also armed with swords, fell on them.

CHAPTER 108

The Man formerly known as Edwin Murphy
The Temple of Ganna: Hathor
28th of Morin

Even with his stolen face, Edwin had been careful as he traveled south.

He had traveled through the pass south of Jasper's Keep and taken a packet boat to Greenwich Island. On the south end of the island, near Sounton Hall, there was a port town called Bayberry. He waited there two weeks before he saw a ship with the sigil scratched into the hull that indicated it was part of the network that served the Mystic.

To anyone else, the symbol would look like scratches in the paint, or an oddly flowing mane of curly hair on a figurehead, but those who knew what they were looking for would see the three interlocking circles, the center one with a line through it, and would know what it meant. This ship was bound for Hathor.

Edwin had met the captain, a Pannarian woman, and given the appropriate handshake. When she took him below to her cabin, he revealed the tattoo that marked him as one of the Chosen.

The journey had been a roundabout one. The captain had other stops to make along the northern coast of Lithonia before turning north for Hathor. But in one of the port towns, he had learned that Morlette had been captured, Princess Lenathaina—now styling herself Queen Lenathaina—was in Hardcastle, and Eddening was in Verto.

They have made a mess of it all.

He had arrived at the Temple of Ganna the night before and had promptly gone through the cleansing ceremony before being shown to barracks where the Chosen were quartered. A bath, fresh robes, and the freedom to return to his true self had gone a long way toward making him feel relaxed and whole.

He looked into the mirror and saw the strong, bold features he had been born with: his shock of black hair and pale green eyes. He was taller now that he had shed his previous form, and his body was muscular.

Edwin adjusted the open-fronted, black robes over his black trousers and shirt before he left his chamber. In the halls of the barracks, he passed other men dressed as he was. Most had plain robes, but some were edged in embroidered sigils marking them as high-ranking.

He made his way out of the barracks, across the courtyard, and into the temple proper. It took some time to get through all the checkpoints, but he eventually entered the Mystic's outer offices, where he took a seat on a low couch to await her pleasure.

Some time passed before he was allowed in. When he was admitted, he prostrated himself until he heard Her deep, melodic voice bid him to rise.

"Braeden," the Mystic said from Her low couch. "I am disappointed in you."

When did I last hear my true name?

"I beg your forgiveness, your Holiness," Braeden replied. He knelt before Her but did not meet Her gaze. "The boy proved difficult to control."

"Too difficult for you, that is certain. Perhaps another would have done a better job."

He could feel Her eyes on him, but he didn't flinch as he replied, "Your ultimate goal has been achieved, Lithonia is more unstable than she has ever been. The time is now. Let me to continue serving you in this mission."

She was quiet for so long that he was tempted to look up, but to look upon Her without invitation would not do.

"I think you can still be of use," the Mystic finally said. "In fact... I believe I know where I will send you next."

"I live to serve, Your Holiness," he breathed.

"Good. You will return to Lithonia," She said.

Braeden felt Her fingertips under his chin, and She lifted it so that he looked into Her dark eyes.

"But with a new face, I think." Her smile was chilling.

CHAPTER 109

High Queen Maelynn Coden
White Castle, White City: Caeldenon
1st of Nane

Across the room, Maelynn watched Emerlise poured herself a glass of brandy before she and Aria sat down on one of the sofas. They had a comb and a wooden box filled with spools of black and colored threads. The pair were taking advantage of the late evening meeting to redo their warriors' braids.

While it was possible to do the sometimes-complex patterns of colored thread on oneself, it was much easier to do it to someone else—Em had told Maelynn so when they had first bonded.

Maelynn often performed the service for her *galvana,* and knew Samera did the same for Aria, but with baby Fadean's needs and her own work, Samera was falling into bed exhausted more often than not. So upon seeing the state of her friend's braid, Em had gone to her room to get the supplies to tidy it up.

"As much as I would like to, I can't exactly use the excuse of this attack on Baerik and Victoria to send more aid to Hardcastle, since he is there himself as aid to Lenathaina," Gavan said as he burped Fadean after her most recent feeding.

Samera finished straightening her clothing. "With the information that Evandar sent, we almost have enough to send them reinforcements because of the Hathorite threat."

"*Almost,*" Maelynn clarified. "But not enough. Yes, we have testimony from Jillian, and there was that business with the man who kidnapped Lenathaina, but that isn't well-known. If it were…"

"Then many in Lithonia might question the usefulness of our alliance if we couldn't keep her safe when she was just a princess here," Samera finished. "Want me to take her, Gavan?"

"I will play with her until Nanny comes to steal her away." Gavan cooed at the baby.

Fadean, who was six and a half months old now, laughed at her uncle and reached for his warrior's braid, which had a multitude of colored threads, including gold and silver shimmerthread, which sparkled when the light from the gaslamps hit it right.

"I am glad that Evandar will be coming home soon," Samera sighed as she looked at her daughter.

Maelynn was too. Fadean had only been a little more than two months old when he had left. At that age, infants grew so fast. He was missing so much.

"Me too," Gavan said. "We have much to do." He gave his sister-in-law a smile that said he understood her other reasoning. "I have already begun looking into our available ships, and have called in three of our warships to make sure they are in good order. It has spread our patrols thin, but there is no help for it. I need to make sure they are all fighting-fit."

"A wise move," Jaedinar said from the stones table. He and Andamar had been having a quiet game.

"And Blood General Olind has been discreetly calculating how many *Mael'Hivar* we can take without leaving us vulnerable, when the need arises," Gavan said.

"Will we need to bring some of the regular army soldiers?" Maelynn asked.

Her husband paused to tickle Fadean. "We aren't sure yet, but if we do, I will have to write each king and ask for one of their generals as well. It will be a tangled mess. I am hoping we can manage with the blood-sworn alone."

"If this gets much worse, we may need every man we can get," Samera warned.

Someone knocked, and Andi rose and crossed the room.

Gavan scowled when Nanny came in. She curtsied before crossing the room to scoop up Fadean.

"Give your uncle a kiss, Princess, and then we will see about your bath," Nanny said to the baby.

Gavan kissed Fadean's cheek, and Samera rose to do the same. Now that the baby was sleeping through the night, Samera left her with Nanny after her last feeding so she could get quality sleep.

Maelynn hid a smile at the wistful expression on both Samera's and Gavan's faces.

Once the door closed, she said, "It might be a good idea to have the kings here for a council and inform them of the severity of the threat. Even if we don't need them, they all need to be aware that there may be spies in their midst. Jillian wasn't the only operative for the Hathorite woman, of that we are sure."

"Wise counsel, as always, my heart," Gavan praised. He took her hand and kissed her fingers lightly. "I will see it done."

CHAPTER 110

Lady Victoria Forrester-Coden, Ducessa 'ah Kilmerian
Hardcastle, the City of Dale: Lithonia
2nd of Nane

The day of reckoning had come.

Tori had greeted her parents briefly before they had gone on to a private audience with the Queen. She waited for them now in one of Lena's drawing rooms.

When they returned, Tori ran into her father's arms. "Papa!" she cried.

He caught her and buried his face in her hair. She felt him shudder as he fought to suppress his emotions.

Her mother greeted her next, taking her hands and looking her over as if she were some exotic creature she had never seen before.

Tori wondered if she should have worn Lithonian dress for this meeting, but she had decided to show them who and what she had become. She was truly a woman of two countries now.

Mother took in her hair, which was loose but held back from her face with the jeweled combs Baerik had given her for her birthday. She wore a blue dress over green in silks embroidered with green leaves, and her black boots were made of fine tooled leather.

"Your time away seems to have agreed with you, daughter," Papa said, breaking the silence.

Tori's sister, Jaina, was looking her over too. "The perks of being a lady-in-waiting in Caeldenon are substantial," she said acerbically.

"Leave your sister alone," Papa chided as he led Tori to the sofa. They sat down, him to one side and her mother to the other. "I heard that you were visiting the camps on behalf of the Queen when they were attacked?"

"We worried for you when the Queen told us you had been in the thick of it." Mother's voice quavered as she traced the embroidery that edged the slit on the side of Tori's overdress.

Tori laid her hand over her mother's. "I am not the same girl I was when I left here," she said gently. "I have had teachers and instructors."

Jaina snorted. "Instructors in what? Are you saying you were part of the fighting?"

"She was," a voice said from the door.

They all rose and curtsied to the Queen and the First Prince. Baerik, Ellaemarhie, and Galwyn were with them too.

"Victoria was part of the contingent that was inspecting the camps," Lena explained. "As she is Lithonian by birth, many of the lords and ladies know her. She has been a valuable asset in gathering information and helping the Caeldenonian and Lithonian generals and lords come together. I regret that she was tangled up in a conflict, but she acquitted herself well, I am told."

"But she is just a child, Your Majesty," Mother protested, wringing her hands.

Tori had never seen her so distraught.

"She is a woman grown, Latasha," Papa said gently. "And a fine one at that." He turned to the Queen. "I thank you for your care of her, Your Majesty."

"Victoria is more than capable of caring for herself now," Lena said as she crossed the room. "I am grateful for such a companion and comrade at my side during these trying times."

"You intend to stay here while your generals continue the muster, or will you move to Endomir?" Papa asked as they all sat down.

"We are still formulating our strategies," Lena said, "But whatever happens, I hope that Victoria will continue to serve at my side."

"Of course, Your Majesty," Tori said, bowing her head.

Too late, she realized she had given only a slight bow, as was suitable for a *ducessa* to a queen or first princess.

Her parents noticed but said nothing.

"I believe there is a family matter that needs to be discussed," the Queen said after an awkward silence. "Lady Jaina will wait outside."

After a glance at their parents, her sister sullenly left the room.

The Wallaces then turned to the Queen, waiting, but it was the Prince who spoke first.

"We spent some time with my grandmother after we arrived in Caeldenon."

No need to explain the circumstances of that, thankfully.

"During that time, Lady Victoria took lessons with my uncle, Lord Baerik Forrester-Coden." Gavantar said.

Papa and Mother both looked at Baerik. Finally, her Papa said, "What kind of lessons?"

"I taught her how to use throwing knives, a dagger, a sword, and later, a pistol. She already knew the short bow, but she honed that skill as well," Baerik said. Whatever nerves he felt were not showing. "She was and continues to be an excellent student and is proving to be a capable warrior."

"A warrior?" Mother asked, her voice rising several octaves. "You can't be serious!" She belatedly added, "My Lord."

"My uncle is the *Duc 'ah* Kilmerian," the Prince said offhandedly. "He is my grandfather's son by his second wife."

"His, uh..." Papa looked from Baerik to Prince Gavantar.

"In Caeldenon, some men, only with the permission of their wives, choose to take a *kessiana*, which is a second wife," the Queen said. "The children of that union are acknowledged and have rights and privileges as such. The *Duc 'ah* Kilmerian is the son of the late High King's *kessiana* and was also adopted by the Dowager High Queen when his mother died. He was created a *duc* at birth, and it is a title that will pass to his eldest son when he dies."

Papa and Mother sat in stunned silence until Baerik spoke, continuing the earlier conversation. "Victoria took down three men and injured four more during the confrontation at the camps. I can confidently say that she is a warrior, and a skilled one at that."

Mother's jaw dropped, and Papa laid his hand over Tori's, squeezing it.

"She has never failed to master a skill she set out to learn," Papa smiled. "But I do not see why the Queen thought this was a family matter. I am proud to know that she has served her liege lady well, though this is not the way that Lithonian girls are brought up."

"While Baerik was teaching me," Tori began, looking at her father. "We became close."

"You cannot call a *duc* by his first name, Victoria!" Mother hissed.

"I see," Papa said, looking down at Tori.

"I have given my permission and my blessing," the Queen said quietly.

"For what?" Mother said, looking from Tori to the Queen to Papa.

"They wish to wed, Latasha," Papa said with a small smile. "Our little warrior scholar has always forged her own path. It doesn't surprise me that she should make such a match."

Mother looked at Baerik again. "Is this true, *Duc*?"

"Yes, Lady Latasha, but, uh…" for once, Tori's husband was at a loss for words.

"They only wish to be blessed in your family's grove, to honor the Lithonian traditions," Prince Gavantar said blandly.

Papa's head whipped around, and his gaze bore into Baerik. "I see."

The Queen and the Prince rose and the rest of them followed.

"My father has given his blessing as well," Prince Gavantar said. "And a handsome wedding present to the new *Ducessa*, but as my wife said, this is a family matter, and we will leave you to discuss it."

He clapped Baerik on the shoulder and whispered, "Good luck." Before retreating with the Queen and their *Mael'Hivar*.

Tori thought Mother would faint, but Papa nodded, his gaze shifting to the Prince and Queen as they made their leave. Once they were gone, Tori moved to Baerik's side and took his hand so they faced her parents together.

"You are wed, then?" Papa asked.

Mother collapsed onto the sofa muttering, "*Ducessa*?"

With Papa only being a lord, the chances of any of her daughters marrying a high lord, or even a second or third son of one, were slim. And here Tori stood, wife of one of the most powerful men in Caeldenon, as well as a lady-in-waiting to the new Lithonian Queen.

"We are wed according to Caeldenonian law and custom," Baerik said. "Though Victoria wishes to be blessed in your family's grove, as my nephew said. We have discussed Linking, but have yet to come to a decision on that."

"I see. And what sort of ceremony was had without consulting us?" Papa asked brusquely, sitting next to Mother.

Tori and Baerik took up the opposite sofa, still holding hands. "We exchanged blood vows in the presence of my adoptive mother, the Dowager High Queen, and had a private family ceremony at White Castle with the blessing of Queen Lenathaina—whom, as you pointed out earlier, is Victoria's liege lady—as well as my brother, the High King of Caeldenon."

Mother's face drained at the mention of blood vows.

No need to mention the handfasting or anything else that came before the ceremony with the High King...

"And we registered our union at the Royal Registry Offices," Baerik continued. "Victoria is recognized as the *Ducessa 'ah* Kilmerian in Caeldenon, and is received at court as the sister-in-law to the High King."

"So, you wish my blessing and a blessing from a priest at our family home?" Papa asked.

"I understand that according to Lithonian law, our marriage is already binding, but Victoria wishes to also honor the customs of her birth country, and I support her in that." Baerik met Papa's gaze. "And I would not like Victoria and I to start our life together by quarreling with you."

Papa nodded. "You have made no mention of a dowry."

"Since we entered into this union without negotiating one first, it would not be right to ask for one now," Baerik replied. "In fact, the opposite is true. If you would like recompense for the wrong that I have done in taking your daughter as my wife without your blessing, I will freely give it."

Papa was stunned into silence for a long moment. "I don't think that will be necessary." Finally, he turned to Tori. "You are happy with him, daughter?"

Tori could not help but smile; she looked up at her husband, and Baerik brought her hand to his lips and kissed it lightly.

She turned back to the man who raised her. "I am very happy, Papa."

"Then we will arrange the blessing with all haste. Though I don't know when we can return to our estate..."

Blushing, Mother said, "I assume you live as man and wife now?"

"We do," Baerik said. "But she isn't with child."

Papa made a strangled sound; Lithonian men didn't speak of such things.

Baerik tactfully ignored it and went on. "We decided to wait until after things were settled, both with the Lithonian throne and with you, before we had more children."

"More?" Mother squeaked.

"Baerik has a daughter by his late wife," Tori said gently. "I have adopted her in the Caeldenonian custom."

"Well, then," Mother said, genuinely smiling. "A granddaughter. Is she here?"

"She is with my mother," Baerik said. "This was not a journey for children. But I hope you can meet her soon."

Papa stood, and the rest of them followed.

"I am not saying that I am pleased with how you two have managed things," he said gruffly. "But if Victoria is happy and you treat her well, then I will give my blessing, and gladly."

"Thank you, Papa." She crossed the room to kiss his cheek.

"You'll have to deal with Gates on your own—he has been in a state," Papa said, wrapping his arms around her. "But you've made something of yourself, my girl, and made a splendid match in the process. I am proud of you."

Gates was their butler and Tori had always been his favorite.

Tori hugged her father back, basking in his approval.

CHAPTER 111

Mael'Hivar Galvana Lady Ellaemarhie Lindal
Hardcastle, the City of Dale: Lithonia
4th of Nane

Ellesmerra Coden was best described as a force of nature. When Merra arrived at Hardcastle, it was almost as if a storm blew in.

Merra had brought with her, for some reason she did not explain, Lady Jane Bennings, the second daughter and third child of the Dowager High Lady Beth and her late husband. Isma, Merra's *galvana,* was silent on the matter.

"Sister," Merra said as she kissed Lena's cheek before she curtsied. "And brother, dear." She performed the same gestures to Gavantar before allowing Lady Jane to step forward and curtsy. She linked her arm with the young woman.

Jane Bennings was a carbon copy of her mother, with red-blonde hair, golden brown eyes, and ample curves.

"Lady Jane," Lena said as she offered her hand to the young woman, who shyly kissed it. "Your mother didn't tell me you were coming."

The young woman blushed. "She didn't know. I didn't think the matter worthy of a Script Stone message."

"I asked her to come," Merra interjected. "I knew that you and your ladies would be busy, and of course, I will help where I can, but I wanted to have a friend of my own, and Lady Jane and I got on very well when I was here for your wedding. You do not mind, do you, sister?"

Lenathaina hesitated before saying, "No, I don't. But you should inform your mother that you are here. I believe there is a spare room in her apartment."

"Or she could stay with me," Merra said casually. "I am sure that the Dowager High Lady and Lady Anne are quite busy."

Gavantar and Lenathaina exchanged a look before Lena turned to Samuel Thane. "Could you please ask Lady Rythan to arrange rooms for High Princess Merra and Lady Jane?"

Thane bowed and excused himself from the room and its tense atmosphere.

"I will go find my mother, with your permission, Your Majesty." Lady Jane's distress at being the center of the drama was clear.

Lena nodded, and the young woman was off like a shot, leaving Lena, Gavantar, Merra, and their *galvanas* and *thane* alone.

Galwyn, Ellae, and Isma busied themselves with pouring tea and filling their plates with the dainty sandwiches and cakes that the Lithonians preferred for their mid-afternoon meal, but there was no escaping the tension for them.

"I do not understand why you brought Lady Jane without messaging," Lena said as she added a small dollop of honey to her tea.

"I didn't think you would mind," Merra replied defensively.

"It isn't that I mind, I just would have liked to have been informed. It is distressing enough that you traveled with such a small guard in war time, but Lady Jane would have been a prime catch for the opposition." Lenathaina's vexation was clear. "They would have let *you* go on your way, or would have risked your father getting into the thick of it, but Jane is Lithonian and they would have tried to use her to get to her brother."

Merra paled. "I didn't think of that."

Gavantar snorted. "Obviously."

"You are both here and safe," Lena said. Ellae could tell she was trying to brush off her irritation. "Tell me what message was so important that your parents sent you into the middle of a civil war to deliver it."

Merra pulled a stack of letters from the satchel she had carried into the drawing room with her. "Mother wrote out a report. You can read it later, but the gist of it is this: Jillian Prather wasn't the only Master or agent of the Hathorite goddess. She said there were more, so Mother and Aunt Samera met with some of the Hathorite women

453

from Keltonmere to get information. The end goal of the Hathorites has always been Lithonia."

"What do you mean the 'end goal'?" Lena asked warily.

Merra shrugged. "They think that Lithonia is their homeland and that they are destined to take it back. They have a lot of prophecies about it."

"They aren't the only ones," a familiar voice said from the doorway.

They turned to see Master Tam flanked by his apprentices.

All three men bowed to Lenathaina and, at her nod, entered the room.

"What is this?" Lena asked.

"It is not surprising that the Hathorites have prophecies of their own." The old man sighed and sat next to his young Queen. "Only those born with the Gift seem to have the ability to see things beyond the veil. I, thankfully, have only done so once, and it was a draining and terrifying experience."

"When was this?" Lena asked as she took his hand.

"When I was twenty-seven," the white-haired Master said as he met her gaze. "It was that prophecy that decided my life's work, and I will say no more about it now. Someday, you may come to know it, for it is recorded in the Ithram's repository."

Lena looked at Tam for a long moment before she turned back to Merra. "Did these women tell their prophecies to your mother?"

"Two were shared with my mother and aunt," Merra said as she pulled a folder from the satchel. "The first was, '*When we attain the Promised Land the Chosen People will be Free.*' The women seemed to think it was something to do with the Hathorites or those who serve them."

"Why do they think Lithonia is their promised land?" Gavantar asked.

"Some of them came from here," Lena told him. "They were part of a group of zealots over a thousand years ago who murdered those who didn't follow their goddess. They were put on ships and told to leave our shores and never return."

How diluted has that history become? Ellae wondered.

"And the second?" Lena asked Merra.

"The path Homeward lies in the roots of the Oaken Heart. The Branch that Flourishes From the Ashes of Fire and Death is the true Ruler of Lithonia and will Unite the Lands and Bring a Lasting Peace," Merra replied.

Master Tam gasped.

"What is it?" Lena turned back to him.

"I must write the Ithram," he whispered.

"Why?" Gavantar asked, looking at the old man in concern. Master Tam's pale skin had lost what little color it had.

The old man met Lenathaina's gaze. "There is a prophecy with similar wording in the repository. I cannot recall it, but I know there are differences. It has long been debated what and who it means, but I think…" He trailed off.

After a moment, young Master Braithwaite came to his mentor's aid. "Master, let me take you to get something to eat."

Master Kareen joined his fellow student, his beaded braids clicking. "He hasn't been sleeping much, Your Majesty."

"Go rest, Tam. There is plenty of time to write to the Ithram," Lena said uneasily.

Tam laid his hand on Lena's cheek and looked into her eyes. *"Born from the ashes, on a day of blood and fire."*

The room stilled. Ellae felt as if icy water had been poured down her back.

"What…" The power of speech seemed to have been taken from Lena, for she could not continue.

Master Tam's watery blue gaze held Lenathaina's. "Those words were spoken over you on the day we laid your parents to rest."

CHAPTER 112

The Dowager High Lady Beth Bennings
Hardcastle, the City of Dale: Lithonia
4ᵗʰ of Nane

Beth and Angela were strolling in the gardens after their tea. Beth's appetite was finally returning, as was Angela's. The last months had been trying for both of them, but now that Lenathaina had secured Hardcastle, even with the skirmishes, they were both hopeful that the end of the war was in sight.

The attack on the camp, during which the young *Ducessa 'ah* Kilmerian had distinguished herself, had been the first. In the last eight days, three patrols had been ambushed and another camp attacked.

Marc Eddening was getting impatient.

The two women exited the hedge maze that they had decided to explore, arm in arm, and came across a pair of figures. Beth thought she was seeing double; it took her a moment to realize that it was not a trick of her eyes or imagination, and that she was in fact looking at *two* of her daughters, both dressed in shades of blue.

Anne and Jane curtsied to their mother and her best friend. Anne's lips were pursed, and Jane looked guilty.

"Hello, Mother."

CHAPTER 113

The Goddess Hestia, the Mystic of Hathor
The Temple of Ganna: Hathor
7th of Nane

Kaleck and Namar sat on a rug before the low couch in Hestia's apartment as they passed several balls of water between them. One finally quavered and fell to the floor, splashing both of them.

Namar looked at Hestia sheepishly.

Hestia smiled. "You have not been able to use your abilities openly. Now that you can, your control will grow rapidly."

"I will do my best," he said eagerly.

"I am very proud of his progress," Kaleck said as he laid his hand on the boy's shoulder.

Namar beamed.

"All of your instructors are happy with your work," Hestia said as she held out a hand in invitation. Namar joined her on the couch, and he cuddled up to her in a way that few in the temple would. "You are already caught up to the other young men your age."

"I hope that I soon surpass them. I want to make you happy." Namar was blushing now.

Kaleck met her gaze over Namar's head.

"You please me greatly," Hestia said. "So much that I wonder if you would like to stay with me sometimes, as Kaleck does."

"Stay with you?" Namar asked.

Hestia stroked his cheek. "In your veins flows the blood of the Morthans, the rulers of Lithonia. I have the blood of an ancient and powerful line. Together, we have the power to rule Lithonia and more. Our children could rule the world."

"Our children?" Namar asked, his tongue licking suddenly dry lips.

Kaleck smiled at her. He knew he would always be first in her heart.

"Our children," Hestia whispered. She bent her head and brushed her lips across his. "I will make you a great man, Namar. My consort. My king. Would you like that?"

Namar's face was flushed. "More than anything."

CHAPTER 114

High Master Tam Gale
Hardcastle, the City of Dale: Lithonia
10ᵗʰ of Nane

Tam covered a yawn that made his eyes water and decided it was finally time to close the anatomy book he was using to teach Ellis and Babak the structure of a human heart.

"Ready to call it a night, sir?" Babak asked.

"That I am, lad," Tam replied as he stood.

His old bones were aching something fierce, but that was to be expected for someone who would be three hundred and ninety-eight in a month's time.

"I will clean up here, and Ellis can walk you back to the apartment," Babak offered.

Tam snorted. "You boys make a fuss over nothing."

It was Ellis' turn to snort. "You aren't as spry as you think you are, old man."

"I can still teach you two a lesson when needed," Tam grumbled.

Ellis and Babak laughed as Ellis gathered Tam's belongings, and Babak set about straightening up the room.

Hardcastle had been built in the days when the upper nobility often took apartments with the king—for a small fee—and thus had a complex for Masters either employed by the king or serving the high lords in residence. In recent years, it had been used to house Masters visiting Dale or working in the hospital. Thus, the complex of rooms set aside for the Masters boasted a magnificent library that was perfect for training young minds.

"I was wondering about the heart, Master," Ellis said as they walked down the corridor. "And the barrier for those who can use the Gift."

"Ah!" Tam said with a grin as he suddenly felt more alert. "Many Masters wonder about it as well. What are your thoughts?"

"It seems that the barrier is less in the physical world and more in the metaphysical world," Ellis said slowly. "If you were to cut open the body of a Master—after death, of course□"

"It wouldn't do to cut it open before death," Tam said with a laugh.

Ellis blushed. "Quite. However, I don't think there would be any physical structure, but rather, I think the barrier exists on another plane of being." He looked at Tam, waiting to see if his teacher would dismiss his theory.

"You are, of course, correct, Ellis." Tam reached out to squeeze his arm. "I would suggest that you and Babak spend some time in examination of one another's barrier to further understand it."

Ellis nodded, thoughtful. "Babak and I have discussed my theory, and he agrees. I think he would be willing to do the exercise. We might try this evening."

"Don't stay up too late," Tam said. "We have a meeting with the Queen in the morning."

"I appreciate her willingness to allow Babak and I in her meetings with you. It has been quite an education. Once I attain Arch Master, I may apply to become a counselor."

"I think you would make a fine counselor, Ellis." Tam patted the boy on his shoulder. "And a Master that is both a healer and a counselor would be highly sought after. You would have your pick of postings."

Ellis smiled as he opened the door to the apartment that they shared. He held out his palm, and a ball of light appeared there. Before he could cross the room to turn on the gaslamps, another light filled the room.

A ball of flame hurtled toward Tam, who pushed Ellis out of the way as he dove to the ground.

"If you cooperate, I will make it painless, old man." A thin man with light brown hair stepped out of the shadows. With a flick of his hand, he closed the door behind Tam and Ellis.

Tam came to his feet slowly but with purpose. He felt more than saw Ellis rising beside him.

Ellis erected a shield, and Tam opened himself to the Life Force.

The man grinned and crafted another ball of fire. He threw it, and Ellis caught it with his shield. The ball shattered, spraying droplets of flame around them, which Tam quickly put out by drawing the energy from the fire into himself.

"A neat trick, old man," Brown Hair said.

"I have a few more," Tam replied as he made a white rope of crackling energy.

The man grinned, and in his hands, another rope appeared. This one was black, though, and seemed to suck the light from the room.

Tam swung his rope in an arch and threw it at the man, but Brown Hair caught the white rope with his black one.

Tam's rope crackled, and he felt his own Life Force being sucked from him through his connection with the rope. He let it fizzle out of existence.

"Run, Ellis! Get help!" Tam bellowed before he fashioned a lightning bolt and threw it at the man.

Brown Hair dodged aside, and the lightning struck the fireplace, charring the white stone black.

Tam could feel his energy fading. Whatever that black rope had been made of, it had taken a lot from him. More than he could spare.

He heard the door close behind him and Ellis' voice calling for help.

"Give it up and let me take you quietly," Brown Hair whispered as he advanced.

"I won't let you pass. You won't get to her," Tam said hoarsely.

The man cocked his head. "Do you really think I am here alone?"

The door burst open behind Tam just as the man threw his black rope again. It burned as it touched Tam's skin. As his vision faded and the energy flowed from his body in a river, he saw three ropes of pure white flash past him.

And then... there was nothing.

CHAPTER 115

Prisoner Jillian Prather
Leanaire Hall, Isle Aratama: Isles of the Ithrimir
10th of Nane

Jillian stepped out of the shower in the bathing complex and donned the gray trousers and tunic that were now her uniform before she returned to her room.

The space was a huge step down from the apartment she had in the keep where most of the White Masters lived on the Isles. She now had a narrow bed with a lumpy mattress and a faded blanket, a chest for the few possessions and books they had deemed appropriate for a prisoner, a wardrobe filled with clothing in the same dull gray that she wore now, and a small bedside table that held a gaslamp. There was also a threadbare rug before a small hearth.

She took her brush out of her trunk and sat down on her bed to brush out her hair, and that was when she saw it—a folded sheet of paper under the corner of the rug.

She set her brush on the bed and crossed the room to pick up the note. With trembling fingers, she opened it.

Prather,
You may not be as useful as you once were, but even a broken tool can be mended and refashioned for a new purpose. Stand by for further instructions.

It was written in the familiar code that she had used to write her reports, one she had memorized long ago.

She pressed the sheet of paper to her heart and took a long, shuddering breath. She had not been abandoned.

Jillian read the note through three more times before she finally made herself turn to the banked hearth. She added a log to the smoldering embers and stoked the fire until it was blazing. Then, with almost loving affection, she laid the note on the flames and watched it burn.

CHAPTER 116

Queen Lenathaina Morthan Coden, First Princess of Caeldenon
Hardcastle, the City of Dale: Lithonia
10th of Nane

Lena was in her study with only Ellae for company. It was late. She had stayed in the drawing room after dinner for a long time, talking to Alanine over coffee.

Lena and Master Isra had talked many times since the girl had arrived at court, and Lena had come to the conclusion that the young woman would have a chance at a better life in Lithonia. She had expressed an interest in the university in Dale, and had already begun taking private lessons with the various Masters in residence at Hardcastle.

Further, Master Isra believed she would be safer in a place where Masters of the Ithrimir could live openly and protect her.

Since Alanine was eighteen and unwed, with no living parents, Lena could officially make her cousin her ward to give her a place at court. Samuel and Master Tam had worked up a document that would make all of this official, and had finished it just before dinner.

Lena wanted to look it over once before bed, as she planned to present it to Alanine and Master Isra the next day. She was so absorbed in the task that she didn't hear the door open.

"Get down, Lena!" Ellae shouted.

Lena rolled under her desk without a thought, and heard the sounds of a clash. She peeked over the edge of the desk and saw Ellae and a man in Morthan livery fighting over a pistol.

Damnation!

She didn't have her sword on her; the only weapons in the room were Ellae's and the man's.

While the pair were occupied with one another, Lena rounded the desk to put space between her and the attacker. She heard the gun go off, and though Ellae grunted, the *naheame* didn't let go of the pistol.

Lena saw blood pouring from her *galvana's* shoulder, and pulled Ellae's sword from its sheath.

The man released his hold on the gun, and Ellae fell backward and he turned to Lena.

The man grinned. "I have heard that you like to think yourself a warrior." He pulled a dagger from a sheath hidden under his livery coat. "It is one thing to play around with other women, pretending to spar, and another to face a man with live steel. Give over, Princess, and I will make it easy. I will even leave your friend here alive. If someone comes quick enough."

Lena fell into a stance with Ellae's sword across her body, standing between her *galvana* and the intruder. "Where did you get that uniform?"

"From one of your servants. But you won't be around to mourn him." He pulled out a second blade so he had one dagger in each hand, and advanced.

Lena lunged forward and slashed at the man. He crossed his blades, caught her sword, and twisted, trying to disarm her, but Lena pulled back and disengaged her sword from the daggers.

A few seconds later, she slashed again, and he danced back. She pressed her advance and jabbed at his arm.

He growled in pain. "I am done playing with you."

He rushed her, and she slashed again, slicing her blade across his thigh. He screamed and plunged his dagger into her side.

Searing pain brought the world into focus, and she saw the door to the study open behind the man. She dropped the sword □she no longer had the strength to hold it□ and stumbled back, clutching her side.

Ellae had gotten to her feet. Her hands were covered in blood, but she picked up her sword.

The man grinned at her... and then grunted as if he had been struck.

CHAPTER 117

Samuel Thane, Secretary to the Queen
Hardcastle, the City of Dale: Lithonia
10ᵗʰ of Nane

Samuel had gotten a letter from Jack in the post that afternoon, but had left it in the study when duty called. He had already read it once, but he wanted to read it again before he wrote him back.

When he left the drawing room, earlier that evening, both the Queen and the Prince had already excused themselves, so he assumed they had gone to bed.

The guards nodded at him as he entered the apartment. He walked through the silent halls and the maze of corridors and let himself into the study that he shared with the Queen.

The scene that greeted him was horrific.

Lady Ellaemarhie was struggling to get to her feet with one bloody hand over her shoulder, and a man with a dagger was grappling with the Queen.

Samuel could see both women were in pain.

He crossed the room while pulling his dagger from the sheath on his belt, enraged that anyone would assault his lady like this. He stabbed the stranger in the back, taking him in the kidney—just like the Prince had taught him.

He wondered if the Prince had foreseen a situation like this.

The man grunted, and Samuel saw Lady Ellaemarhie pick up her sword. He took a step back, and with a howl of rage and pain, the warrior woman swung her sword, and the man crumpled to the ground. His head bounced across the floor in the opposite direction.

Samuel stepped over the body and pulled his handkerchief from his pocket, then looked from one woman to the other, trying to gauge who needed help more urgently.

"Bind her damn wound!" Lady Ellaemarhie shouted at him as she pulled her own handkerchief out and pressed it to her shoulder.

Samuel guided the Queen into a chair and pressed the cloth to her side. Almost immediately, it was soaked through.

Footsteps sounded in the hallway, and the warrior woman raised her sword and moved between the Queen and the door. Samuel kept his hand on the Queen's wound as he turned to see the First Prince and Prince Galwyn come in.

"Damnation!" the Prince said. He looked both enraged and terrified.

Samuel moved aside enough for the First Prince to get close to the Queen, while continuing to keep pressure on the wound. He could see Prince Galwyn tending to Lady Ellaemarhie as four more *Mael'Hivar* entered the room.

"Should we send for Master Tam?" Samuel asked.

The two princes exchanged a look.

"Send for Babak or Ellis or one of the other Masters who can heal," Prince Galwyn said to one of the *Mael'Hivar*.

"Why not Tam?" the Queen asked. Samuel could hear the pain in her voice.

"He was attacked too," the First Prince said. "He lives for now, but he is very weak."

"His attacker?" she asked.

"Captured, I am told. He said he wasn't alone, so we came to check on you. And then I felt your fear and pain and we ran for it."

The First Prince pulled out his own handkerchief and handed it to Samuel, who put it on top of his own. The Queen's gaze had turned glassy. The Prince's hands were shaking and panic was gaining the upper hand in his expression.

"She is losing blood too fast," Samuel said. His heart was pounding.

We might lose her.

The Prince looked around the room and grabbed a shawl from the back of the Queen's chair, handing it to Samuel before kneeling beside his wife. "Lena, can you hear me?"

The Queen grunted and tried to focus on her husband.

"Stay with me, love. Stay awake," the Prince he pleaded.

Samuel could hear the fear in his voice.

The minutes ticked by slowly. The First Prince spoke quietly to the Queen as she faded in and out. Prince Galwyn and Lady Ellaemarhie argued; she wanted to come to the Queen, but he wouldn't let her move, as he held pressure on her wound like Sam was doing for Her Majesty.

After what seemed an eternity, Master Ellis Braithwaite came into the room with another Master that Samuel didn't know but had seen around the castle.

"You take the warrior," the other Master said to Ellis.

Ellis moved toward Lady Ellaemarhie, and the other Master, a dark-skinned man with closely cropped hair and dark eyes, moved toward the Queen. He knelt beside her, and Samuel moved his hands.

The Master ripped open her gown. "Damn corset kept this from being worse, but it will make this harder." He unhooked the corset and hastily draped the bloody shawl over the Queen to preserve her modesty before he laid his hands on the wound.

Samuel looked across the room to see Ellis working on Lady Ellaemarhie.

Several minutes passed before the Master that was working on the Queen stood. "She needs something to eat and her bed, but she will be alright. The blade nicked a blood vessel, that is why she lost so much blood." He looked down at her. "She was lucky."

Ellis was cursing on the other side of the room. "Master Braden, if you are done with the Queen, I could use your help. This ball is stuck."

Samuel saw that Lady Ellaemarhie was biting a strip of leather while Master Ellis held a pair of silver instruments.

The Master who had worked on the Queen crossed the room, and the pair bent over the warrior woman together.

"Should we get the Queen to her bed?" Samuel asked the Prince.

"I won't leave her," the Queen murmured. "And Gavantar won't leave Galwyn. We stay."

The Prince rested his hand on the her shoulder and turned his gaze to the gathering on the other side of the study.

Samuel looked down at the Queen, and she met his gaze. "I will fetch your dressing gown, then, Your Majesty."

"Thank you, Mr. Thane," she said, squeezing his hand.

Samuel squeezed back. "It my pleasure to serve you, Your Majesty."

CHAPTER 118

Arch Master Lily Morthan

Shell Cottage on Isle Mortaria and the City of Sounton and Leanaire Hall, Isle Aratama: Isles of the Ithrimir

11ᵗʰ and 12ᵗʰ of Nane

Lily's home on Isle Mortaria was situated on a hill that overlooked the sea. Every room at the back of the house had one or more sets of double doors that could be opened to let the sea breeze in, thus her ivory skin had long ago tanned.

It washer habit to rise before dawn and have her tea on the porch, allowing her loose, brown hair to blow in the wind while the sun rose over the water. Since her mother had come to stay, Rowan Morthan often joined her in this.

"I got a letter from Lenathaina yesterday," Mother said as she sipped her tea.

Lily warily asked, "How is she?"

Her resistance to engage in conversation about the war that was raging in the nation of her birth irritated her mother, but Lily refused to get involved in what amounted to a family squabble. First her brother's son had tried to take what wasn't his, and now her cousin, Marc, was doing the same thing. All because they didn't want to be ruled by a woman.

The toxicity of Lithonian culture was the main reason she had stayed away so long. Lily knew the moment she showed an interest, she would be sucked in. Tam had been trying to lure her for years; he wanted her to follow him as advisor to the throne. But Lily didn't think she was made for that life.

Standing in the shadows and watching generation after generation of my family die...

"Alanine Fasili has joined her at Hardcastle," Mother informed her. "It seems the boy was kidnapped, so that answers that mystery."

472

A few months before, Nijah, the youngest of the Fasili children, had arrived on the Isles. Brandon had told them so when they saw him for one of their weekly visits. Lily knew Mouriani Hameen-Palin, the daughter of Arch Masters Amir and Isra Hameen-Palin and the cousin—as Lily was a distant cousin—of Nijah. Lily and Mouriani had been friends for a long time so she sought her out. Lily had casually asked why the young girl had come to stay without her siblings, but Mouriani had quickly changed the subject.

"The boy was kidnapped?" Lily asked as she sat forward.

"By a Hathorite priestess," Mother looked troubled. "Lenathaina plans to offer Alanine a home."

"Even after…" Lily shook her head. Tam had told her of Lenathaina's abduction, but she hadn't shared that with her mother. But that family had caused enough trouble. Some poisoned fruit a dozen years back and meddling in the House of Lords ten years ago "After all the drama that the Fasilis have caused?"

Mother gave her a sharp look, as if she sensed Lily was holding something back, but she was saved from having to deflect by the maid.

"Master Lily?" Danielle ventured as she walked through the open doors.

"Yes?" Lily replied.

"One of your Stones is flashing," the dark-haired woman said.

Lily sighed and excused herself.

A message this early in the morning didn't bode well.

*****

Three hours later, Lily, her mother, and her mother's maid, Hawkins, stepped off the ferry in Sounton, the town on the southern shore of Aratama, the main island of the Isles of the Ithrimir.

As soon as Lily received the message from the Ithram's offices that Lenathaina and Tam had been attacked, she and her mother quickly dressed and began the journey to Leanaire Hall.

Very little information had been given through the Stones, other than both lived, though Tam was not doing well.

"I don't know why they couldn't have given you more information," Mother said for at least the third time.

"We will find out soon enough," Lily replied as she went to the taxi stand and ordered a carriage.

While the driver and his assistant loaded their luggage, she walked over to a row of stalls and got hand pies, aged cheese, and fruit for the journey. They could eat lunch on the road and hopefully avoid making too many stops before nightfall.

Lily purchased a basket and bought a few stone bottles of cider as well before she returned to the carriage.

Mother looked at the food and then up at Lily.

"It is honest food, Mother. I don't have time to order a silver-service picnic." Lily handed the food to Hawkins. "Haste, not comfort and your queenly sensibilities, matters here."

"Honestly, Lily, sometimes I think you resent having been born into royalty," Mother grumbled as she climbed into the carriage.

Lily followed and smoothed the dark blue skirts of her traveling dress before she met her mother's eyes. "I resent those who can't look outside the confines of their station in life to see the world around them as it truly is. I resent those who don't use their privilege for the betterment of the less fortunate."

Mother looked at her, and for a moment, Lily's breath caught.

Mother had such an inner strength that it was easy to forget all she had lived through. The loss of her husband and three of her four children, one not quite eight years old when she died, and then Matthew and Nikkana and, more recently, Charles. Plus all the babes that Mellina had tried and failed to bring into the world, and finally, Richard.

Her fair skin was deeply wrinkled, and her hair, which had been more brown than gray just a few months ago, was almost completely silver now. Her pale blue eyes were shadowed, just as Lily imagined hers must be.

Lily took a slow, deep breath. "I am sorry, Mother. My fear and frustration got the upper hand. I should not have snapped at you."

Hawkins nodded her approval. She had been Mother's maid since the queen and the maid had been girls.

Mother gave her a shrewd look. "Many would call someone who preaches about others needing to use their privilege for the greater good, while hiding themselves away in a cottage on an island far from any that might need her, a hypocrite. You might consider what *you* could do for the world, if you came out of hiding and lived in it." She turned her face to the window, signaling that she was done with the conversation.

Lily felt guilt gaining the upper hand. She looked out her own window, avoiding Hawkins' gaze.

The day passed mostly in silence. Lily read one of the books she had brought with her. *The Travels of Miriam Gore* had long been a favorite, and it always brought her comfort when she needed it most.

They got to their inn, the Prancing Pony, late, and went to bed after a cold supper, only to rise early the next morning. The innkeeper's wife packed a lunch basket for them, and they returned to their carriage.

With luck, they would be at Leanaire Hall by teatime.

*****

"The Ithram will see you now, Queen Rowan and Arch Master Morthan."

Lily had been so lost in her own thoughts that the voice of the Steward startled her. She rose and offered her mother an arm, and the pair of them walked into the private study of Ithram Taran Havensgrad together.

Ithram Havensgrad wore white trousers and a tunic, with sandals of soft, white leather. He was old, his ebony skin wrinkled, and his hair white.

That he was meeting with them in his private rooms while casually dressed was an honor. In all Lily's years on the Isles, she had only met with him privately a handful of times, but never in his rooms.

She bowed from the shoulders to greet him. Her mother inclined her head.

The Ithram crossed the room and inclined his head to her mother in return before taking her hand and leading her to a sofa. "My dear Queen Rowan. I wish that we were meeting again under better circumstances."

While it was Lily's first time in these apartments, it was not her mother's. She had been invited to dinner parties many times over the years when she would visit.

"Ithram Havensgrad," Mother said as she sat down. "What news of my granddaughter and cousin?"

"Queen Lenathaina," Havensgrad began, "is recovering from her injury. She was stabbed, but the wound has been healed. She is still weak from blood loss, but is otherwise well. So is the other woman that was injured with her."

"And Tam?" Mother asked, fear clear in her voice.

Havensgrad hesitated.

"Sir?" Lily asked, her voice unsteady.

"The attacker was a Hathorite. The spell he used against High Master Tam Gale seems to have done some serious damage." Havensgrad looked from Mother to Lily. "High Master Braden James is the ranking healer in Hardcastle, after Master Tam. He has messaged that Master Tam is stable for now, but he fears that he will never regain his full strength."

"And the Hathorite?" Lily asked.

Havensgrad was holding her mother's hand in an overly familiar way that Lily decided to ignore. "He took his own life with some sort of poison."

"Poor Tam…" Mother pulled a handkerchief from her pocket and wiped her eyes.

"He will not be able to serve the Lithonian throne for some time, if ever," Havensgrad said, his eyes resting on Lily.

She recalled that, just moments before, he had referred to her niece as 'Queen Lenathaina'.

"You recognize her, then?" Lily asked.

Previously, Havensgrad and the Council had refused to take a side.

What has changed?

The Ithram nodded. "How many of these Hathorite attacks have there been? Your sister-in-law and the Lady Jane Grey. Queen Lenathaina has been attacked twice now. Their raids and skirmishes in northern Caeldenon and Lithonia have been more frequent in recent years…

"Lithonia needs stability for whatever is coming. High Lord Morlette has signed his confession, and legally, the Council and I feel that High Lord Eddening has no right to the throne. With Morlette dealt with, there is no denying that Lenathaina is the rightful ruler of Lithonia."

She understood what he was getting at.

"The Hathorites are coming for her."

Lily felt it in her bones. She had read the letters from the Caeldenon High King; more than that, she had spent many years in study of the Repository. She only had clearance to access the fifth level, but she was in study to become a High Master, which would give her leave to access the sixth. The history of the Hathorite War were there, or most of them, along with some of the prophecies that had come to pass and others that had not.

The Ithram released her mother's hand and walked to the desk that sat in front of a bank of windows. He returned with a blue lacquered box and handed it to Lily.

With trembling fingers, Lily opened it. Inside, she found two tightly rolled scrolls and a large, square opal with a diamond carved into the top. She looked up at the Ithram.

"Too long have you hidden," he murmured. "Too long have you avoided your destiny." The Ithram knelt before her. "You have been invited to sit your exams for High Master three times?"

Wordlessly, Lily nodded.

"You are afraid of what you will find when you continue your research." It was a statement, not a question. "It is time. You will sit your exams, and then you will go to your niece. Whatever truths you find, I trust you will be strong enough to face them."

"What are you speaking of, Taran?" Mother asked him, but he kept his eyes on Lily.

"You will know when it is time to open these." He touched the scrolls. One was wrapped in blue thread, and the other in green. "The blue refers to the Queen, I think."

"And the green?" Lily asked.

"No one is sure, but if anyone can figure it out, I believe it is you," Havensgrad replied. "Will you do it? Will you take your exams and go to Lithonia?"

Lily drew a shuddering breath and nodded.

CHAPTER 119

Princess Fenora Tearhall
Hardcastle, the City of Dale: Lithonia
12th of Nane

The body of one of the Aerie footmen had been found the day after the attack, hidden away in a cupboard in one of the servants' passages. His name had been Victor Watson.

The Queen had received his parents and sisters in her personal drawing room, even though High Master Braden James had suggested she stay in bed. Fenora and Rachel had sat with Lena and Gavantar while they comforted the grieving family.

Victor had lay in state for a day and a night in the great hall of Hardcastle before his funeral in the temple. His parents had taken most of his ashes to put in their family vault, but some had been left with the Queen to inter in the vault of the Defenders of Hardcastle, which had not been used in over three hundred years.

To be laid to rest there was truly a great honor.

After the funeral, Lena and Gavantar had gone to spend some time at Master Tam's sickbed. They were all taking it in turns to keep him company.

It was Fenora and Rachel's turn, so they left their apartment to relieve the Queen.

Master Ellis Braithwaite was in the sitting room, head in his hands, and Master Babak Kareen sat next to him, looking lost. When Rachel and Fenora entered the room, both men moved to stand, but Rachel waved for them to stay seated.

"How is he?" Rachel asked, laying a hand on Ellis's shoulder.

"Master Braden says the end is here." Ellis fumbled for a handkerchief, but when he couldn't find one, Rachel pulled hers from her pocket and handed it to him. "He had us say our goodbyes and come out here."

Rachel let out shaky breath.

Babak took her other hand and squeezed it. "You should go in. There isn't much time."

Rachel nodded and looked at Fenora. The pair of them clasped hands and walked into the next room.

Master Braden and Gavantar stood by the window with Galwyn, speaking quietly. Ellae stood a few feet behind Lena, who was sitting on the bed next to Tam, holding his hand.

Fenora felt Rachel's hand slip from hers as she moved across the room to sit on the other side of the old Master's bed. Fenora stood beside her, mimicking Ellae's stance. A silent guard.

The Queen smiled at Rachel, her cheeks blotchy and tear-stained. "I was about to send for you."

"Ellis said..." Rachel let the sentence trail off.

Lena nodded.

Rachel looked down at Master Tam, whose breathing was labored. "Master Tam, can you hear me?"

He opened his eyes and looked up at her, blinking slowly.

"You needn't worry," she said quietly. "I will be with her. To the end."

Master Tam blinked again, his breath coming in raspy gasps.

"There are other Masters here—loyal men and women. She will be alright."

Fenora could hear the pain in Rachel's voice, and laid a hand on her shoulder.

"You can go now, Tam," Lena said. She leaned forward and pressed a kiss to his brow. "I will be alright. You have given me all the tools I need to see this through."

"From the ashes," Tam gasped, his eyes on Lena. His voice was strong, sure. The room almost seemed electrified. *"The ember that with spark the fire is born. She burns from within. A flame that will cleanse the world."*

Master Braden frantically looked for a pen and paper.

"Tam?" Lena asked, confused.

"I will tell your mother and father," he wheezed, "that you are a woman—" He paused, struggling for breath. "To be proud of."

Lena choked on a sob.

Master Tam's labored breathing stopped, and the only sound in the room was the scratching of Braden's pen.

*****

Fenora and Rachel had gone to Lena's apartment and consoled the Queen for some time. When High Lady Montgomery and the Dowager High Lady Bennings came, the younger ladies excused themselves and went to their own apartment.

As soon as Fenora closed the door, Rachel collapsed onto a settee and began weeping. Fenora sat next to her and pulled out her handkerchief, remembering that Rachel had given hers to Ellis Braithwaite.

A short time later, someone knocked at the door. Fenora rose to answer it, intending to send whoever it was away unless they had been sent by the Queen. Instead, she found Lady Ella Malick, along with a maid and a tea cart.

Lady Ella gave Fenora a slight curtsy, the greeting appropriate for a woman of her station to visiting royalty.

"How can I help you, Lady Ella?" Fenora asked, not unkindly.

"I hoped to come give some comfort to Rachel. I know, having grown up with Master Tam, she will feel his loss." The Lady seemed uncomfortable but determined.

Fenora glanced over her shoulder to see Rachel wiping her face. She nodded at Fenora and stood, moving to look out the window so the maid would not see her face.

Once Lady Ella and the tea cart were inside, Fenora dismissed the maid and moved to Rachel's side.

She put an arm tenderly around her lover and said in a soothing voice, "Your mother has brought tea and some food. You haven't eaten since luncheon, and it is almost ten in the evening."

When Fenora had coaxed Rachel back to the settee, she turned to face Lady Ella, but the look of dawning reality and understanding the woman wore halted Fenora's thoughts.

Silence filled the room for several moments. Fenora thought the beating of her heart must be so loud that everyone could hear it.

"'You share many things,'" Lady Ella finally murmured, quoting the conversation from the Night of Reflection almost two and a half months ago, when she had asked about Rachel and Fenora sharing an apartment.

Rachel drew a sharp breath before she nodded.

Lady Ella sat, stunned.

Fenora did the only thing a well-bred woman could do in an awkward situation. "Would anyone like tea?"

She poured tea without waiting for a response, automatically adding one lump of sugar and a splash of milk to Rachel's tea before handing it to her.

Something crossed Lady Ella's face as she watched this simple thing, and Fenora understood what she must be thinking.

Fenora knew how Rachel liked her tea. The pair had taken tea together often enough that Fenora didn't need to ask. Fenora knew more about Rachel than her own mother did, and demonstrated that with this simple act.

"How do you take your tea, Lady Ella?" Fenora asked with a measure of sympathy as she poured a cup for her.

"Uh, milk please. No sugar," the Lady replied, still dazed.

When they all had a cup of tea, and the platters of sandwiches—and one of cakes—had been passed around, Lady Ella finally found her voice.

"You are together, then?"

Rachel said, "We are," and took a sip of tea, laying her other hand on Fenora's knee.

Fenora felt a thrill run though her as she laid her hand on top of Rachel's.

"And the Queen?" Lady Ella asked, her voice an octave higher.

"Knows and approves," Rachel replied.

"It isn't terribly uncommon in Caeldenon," Fenora said gently, "as long as a line is secure. However, neither of us have the need to provide heirs for a title. Love is love, and I love your daughter. We both wish to dedicate our lives to serving the Queen and First Prince, and one another."

Lady Ella drew a quavering breath. "You will marry?"

Rachel hesitated and looked at Fenora, who nodded.

"Eventually," Rachel answered.

Lady Ella put her teacup down.

A moment passed, and then another. Fenora wondered if the woman would get up and leave, but instead, she said something surprising.

"Will you let me come to your wedding?" Love and fear both made her voice tremble.

Rachel was crying again, but this time, her tears were happy ones. She nodded. "We will… Mother."

CHAPTER 120

High Lord Marc Eddening
Verto, Southern Region: Lithonia
14ᵗʰ of Nane

Marc crumpled the note and tossed it into the hearth with a curse.

"What is it, Father?" Owen asked.

The boy had been reclusive at best, and at worst, outright insolent. Marc was setting him up to rule as consort of a goddess, to be a king! But the boy acted like he was being asked to murder puppies, rather than gifted with being one of the most powerful men in the world.

If only Marc had come into the Mystic's service as a young man, *he* could have been her consort, but she made it clear that she wanted an untouched man.

It was almost absurd to imagine a world where a man's virtue meant more than a woman's… but Owen wouldn't be the only one to gain power through the Mystic.

"Our men died in the attempt on the chit," Marc grumbled. "Master Tam was wounded and died two days ago, but Princess Lenathaina is alive and well."

Owen gave a sigh of relief.

"Boy, you are going to have to learn where your loyalties lie," Marc roared as he crossed the room and yanked his son out of his chair by his shirt. "And it isn't with her, do you hear me?" He shook him, hard.

"What are you going to do?" Owen asked, laughing. "Without your lapdog to instill fear and awe into the others, how long will you hold them?" He sobered and met his father's glare. "I know Lenathaina. You haven't weakened her. She will take her anger deep inside, and it will strengthen her resolve."

Marc pushed the boy away, and Owen stumbled backward before drawing himself up.

"The others will still follow me. They have seen what one Magi can do on his own," Marc sneered at his son. "Wait until I have twelve of them."

Owen paled and croaked, "Twelve?"

"The Mystic is sending twelve of her best Magi to me," Marc replied as he stepped closer to his eldest child. "And with those twelve, I will be able to do great and terrible things. None will stand in my way then. Not Lenathaina, and certainly not you."

He had sent a contingent of men and servants south to meet magi already, but he didn't tell the boy that.

"Father, you can't seriously want to set those kind of people loose in Lithonia?"

Marc leaned forward. "I will do what I must to secure the future of this family and to take the power that is rightfully mine."

There was a hint of pleading in Owen's voice as he protested, "But, Father□"

"Out of my sight, you spineless puppy! You'd better find some guts before the Mystic meets you." Marc leaned back. "Her other consort has arrived at Her Holy Temple. You need to go Hathor now. No more of this petulant nonsense, it is time to do your duty and marry."

"I won't," Owen said hoarsely.

"Go pack your things," Marc ordered, disgusted with his son. "You leave tomorrow."

After Owen left, Marc turned to the window. With his hands clasped behind his back, he watched his men drilling in the yard. The sloping expanse of lawn had been turned into an army camp.

He had hoped, with time, more of the lords would come to his side, but it seemed that the lines had been clearly drawn.

For now.

When the Mystic's Magi arrived, they would see where the real power truly was.

CHAPTER 121

First Prince Gavantar Coden
Hardcastle , the City of Dale: Lithonia
14th of Nane

High Master Tam Gale received a funeral fit for a prince. High Priest Lyle had spent time with Lenathaina talking about the Master's life, and had spoken with many of the lords and ladies that had known him. High Lord Montgomery had sent his own thoughts about the Master via Script Stone.

He had wanted to come, but everyone agreed that it wouldn't be wise for him to leave Endomir. As it stood, Lena or her people held the two great seats of power, and they couldn't chance losing that advantage.

When the ceremony was over, Masters Ellis Braithwaite and Babak Kareen stood at either end of the altar where Master Tam lay in ceremonial white robes. They met one another's eyes and lowered their hands to touch their beloved teacher. A flash of blinding white light ran down Tam's body, and when it faded, only ashes were left.

Beside Gavantar, Lena choked back a sob and wiped her tears away. The rest of the mourners were dismissed, and Gavantar and Lena held hands as the priests collected the Master's ashes into a polished wooden box.

Gavantar knew that there was a grove of trees at Hardcastle. This one mixed trees of oak, elder, silver birch, hawthorn, rowan, hazel, and even a few willow by the stream that flowed through the center of the grove.

He had asked Lena why there wasn't just one kind of tree, and she had said that the first Morthan king was the one who'd started the fashion of picking one tree for a grove, and that some families kept to the old ways, letting the deceased or their next of kin decide what kind they would be buried under. Others had vaults where the ashes of loved ones were stored, like in Caeldenon.

"Will you bury him here?" Gavantar asked.

Lena shook her head. "When this is over, I will take him back to Endomir. His parents' ashes were buried there, and all the people he loved and served and gave his life to are there. He deserves to rest among them."

"I think he would like that," Gavantar replied as he turned to kiss her temple.

Galwyn and Ellae were a few feet away, giving them privacy, but when the priests approached, he felt them at his back.

"Your Majesty, I am so sorry for your loss," High Priest Lyle said as he handed the polished oak box to Lena. "If there is anything I can do, send for me. No matter the hour."

"Thank you, Your Holiness," Lena replied as she wrapped her arms around the box. "You have been very kind through all of this, and I won't forget it."

Lyle bowed his head and excused himself.

Gavantar and Lena left the temple and went back to their apartment. She placed the box in one of the unused bedrooms and locked the door herself. When they finally went to the drawing room, they found the intimate members of their court waiting for them.

Rachel took Lena into her arms, and Baerik shook Gavantar's hand. The women had ordered an informal luncheon, so they drew Lena into the dining room to eat.

Alanine was on the edge of things, still nervous. Gavantar crossed the room and spoke to her quietly.

"I know that this is quite different from how things are done in Pannarius."

"Yes, Your Highness," Alanine said. "At home, only the immediate family would be part of the burial rites... and a priestess. And of course, we bury our dead after three days of ritual ceremonies."

Gavantar nodded. "Yes, I remember something about that from my lessons as a child."

The young woman wrinkled her nose. "I am terribly jealous of your education, sir."

"I hear that you are getting caught up," Galwyn joined in as he took cups of tea from a sideboard and handed them to Gavantar and Alanine. "There are rumors you have been taking archery lessons."

"I have been, Prince Galwyn." Alanine blushed. "It is quite freeing to be able to choose what I want to learn. The Queen has been generous with providing teachers and tutors in every subject I have thought to ask about, and even to suggest some I've never considered."

"That sounds like Lenathaina," Gavantar said with a smile.

"I am happy to do whatever I can to help her," Alanine said. "I only wish that I could change things that happened in the past."

Galwyn laid a hand on her shoulder. "You aren't responsible for the actions of others."

"No," Alanine replied. "But if I had spoken to my cousin about that Hathorite woman sooner, my brother and sister might both be here with me—or at least, both safe on the Isles. That is my shame, and I will carry it with me all my life."

"You couldn't have known what would happen." Galwyn squeezed her shoulder before removing his hand. She had tensed up for a moment. It was obvious that she was still getting used to being so near men. "You did the best you could and sent for Master Isra. I know that all that can be done will be done to get your brother back once Lithonia has been secured."

"You have my word on that," Gavantar added.

"And mine," another voice said.

They all turned to Lenathaina. Gavantar and Galwyn bowed, and Alanine curtsied.

"The Hathorites have been moving in the shadows for far too long," Lenathaina said, her voice thick with emotion. "They have kidnapped, raided, and terrorized, and it will end now. I will put this rebellion down, and then this Hathorite woman will see the wrath that she has brought upon herself."

CHAPTER 122

Lord Owen Eddening

Verto, Southern Region and Hardcastle, the City of Dale: Lithonia

14ᵗʰ – 17ᵗʰ of Nane

The house was quiet. So quiet that Owen worried that every one of his footsteps sounded like the crashing of a boulder to his own ears as he crept down the halls and down the servants' passages.

He wore black trousers and a jacket, with riding boots and a cloak. He had a pistol and a dagger on his belt, but had left his sword behind, fearing it would make it harder to move stealthily. He had skipped dinner with his father and had gone down to the kitchens to order a simple meal. While there, he had spent a few minutes chatting with a maid.

None of the servants here were his father's; they had no loyalty to him.

When the maid had brought his dinner, she had also delivered a basket of apples, hard cheese, nuts, and flatbread. He had told her that he planned to stay up late to pack, and to write letters to his mother and sister, and that he needed snacks to keep him going.

Owen had stowed all of her offerings into a satchel, along with a pair of clean clothes, a bit of soap and a razor, his brush, and a clean handkerchief. His father kept his purse strings tight, but Owen had a little money—not much, but Maker willing, it would get him where he was going. Along with the satchel, he had his bedroll, and that was it.

He wasn't stupid enough to try to go to the stables; those would be heavily guarded. Thankfully, he wasn't the only son on this estate that thought his father was on the wrong side of things.

Owen came out of the house through the kitchens and crept around the garden wall. With his back to the cold, damp stone, he slowed his breathing and listened to the patrols as they passed.

Once three pairs of guards had come and gone and he knew the pattern, he edged out. Staying low and close to the stone wall, he ran the length of the wall toward the barns.

The smell of shit and piss filled the air. Owen covered his mouth as he ran, but the reek still cramped his stomach, which was already knotted with fear.

His boot hit a slick of cow shit, and he slipped, letting out a whoop of surprise. He silently cursed himself and ran for the side of the barn that was drenched in shadows.

Just as Owen put his back to the stone wall, he heard someone shout.

"Oi! Who goes there?"

"Relax, Sergeant," replied a voice with a lazy but cultured drawl.

Frederick Gordon, son and heir to Lord John Gordon, passed within two feet of Owen, fastening his trousers.

"Sorry, milord," the guard said. "Heard a skelloch. Dinnt see anyone, did you?"

"Just the dairy maid that I was giving a good swive," Frederick said. "If you will excuse me, I would like to enjoy a bit more fun before I head back to my tent."

Owen could just imagine Fred arching an eyebrow as if the guard were the one in the wrong.

"Yes, milord. Of course." The guard bowed before hurrying off in the other direction.

Frederick waited until he was out of sight before jerking his head toward Owen and then turning back the way he had come.

Past the barn and the milking sheds, a pair of horses were saddled and tied to a fence.

"Thanks, Fred. I owe you one," Owen said as he tied his bedroll to the back of the saddle and tucked the satchel into one of the saddle bags. He saw that Fred had managed to get him some supplies as well.

"I only wish I was going with you, but it will be easier for you to get away if I cause a diversion." Fred clapped him on the back. "Tell the Queen that not all of us who ride on this side of the war do so of our own free will."

"I will. Take care of yourself." Owen shook his friend's hand and mounted up.

The pair rode down the path a bit before two other riders came out of a stand of trees and fell in beside them, putting Owen in the center of the pack. He knew them to be Jack Norrington and Lyle Avery.

Just before they reached the guard post at the entry of the camp, a shot went off in the distance, the bullet flying high over their heads.

"Attack!" Fred yelled. "We're under attack!" He turned to the guards, who were standing at the ready. "After them!" To Owen, he said, "Rouse the camp!"

Owen dug his knees into the sides of the borrowed mare, and wheeled past the guards and into the camp. As he rode down the center path, he yelled over and over, "We are under attack!"

Those men who were still awake armed themselves and headed to the entrance of the camp. The poor buggers that had been in their beds came out of their tents dazed, some still pulling on their trousers or boots.

No one noticed as Owen hit the eastern edge of the camp and kept riding, into the countryside. He just hoped his friends managed to pull off the ruse without getting caught. Owen turned to the northeast and rode through the night.

The sun was rising over the hills as he turned into the Tornald Forest. He pushed on for another hour until he found a clearing large enough to tether his mare.

Fred had included some oats and a nosebag among the supplies he'd provided, so Owen watered the mare in a stream and filled the bag with oats.

As soon as she had finished eating, he lay down on the ground with his bedroll and fell asleep.

*****

The sun was just passed its zenith when the horse nudged Owen awake. He watered her again and let her graze a bit. He wished he could take off the saddle and give her a real rest, but there wasn't time; his father would have men looking for him already.

While the mare grazed, Owen had a simple meal of apples, cheese, and flatbread, and put some nuts in his jacket pocket to eat while he rode.

When they'd both had their fill, Owen broke their meager camp, and pulled out his compass to check his bearings.

In a few more miles, he would need to turn south.

The day passed uneventfully. He stayed well inside the tree line and kept the mare going at a steady but not taxing pace, stopping every few hours to water her and stretch his own legs. He made camp when he could no longer safely ride.

Though it was almost spring, there was still a chill in the air, and most mornings, there was a layer of frost on the ground. Owen gathered deadwood and made himself a fire, which he used to warm his flatbread, all the while wishing for a hot cup of tea and some roast chicken.

Once the mare had had her dinner, Owen banked the fire, curled up as close as he dared, and fell asleep.

*****

"Hey, you." A booted foot nudged Owen in the side.

He woke with a start and rolled over to see he was surrounded by men in blue uniforms. Four rifles were pointed at him.

He held his hands up.

Lord Soren Prather dismounted from his horse and came to stand over Owen. It wasn't that long ago that they had been attending classes together at university in Endomir, but the man looked as if he had aged years in the past months.

"Spying, Eddening?" Soren sneered. He was tall, blond, and thin, with blue eyes, though he had developed a more muscular build since Owen saw him last, and gained a scar over his right eye.

"Bringing information, if you must know." Owen untangled himself from the bedroll and came to his feet, trying to ignore the rifles aimed at him.

"Information?" Soren asked, skeptical.

"Search me and take my weapons if you like, but take me to my cousin." Owen lifted his arms so they could easily take the dagger. The pistol lay next to his bedroll.

Soren nodded, and one of the soldiers picked up the pistol before taking the dagger off Owen's belt.

"The *Duc* is due in camp this afternoon, Lord Prather," reported a man with lieutenant's bars on his coat. "He can decide what to do with him."

It was then that Owen noticed Soren had captain's bars.

"The *Duc*?" Owen asked.

"The *Duc 'ah* Kilmerian, uncle-in-law to the Queen," Soren replied. "He and the *Ducessa* visit the camps for the Queen often. Try anything with him and he will deal with you swiftly and effectively." He turned back to his men. "Break his camp and let's head back."

Two of the soldiers kept their rifles on Owen while the rest checked his saddle bags and saw to his horse.

Soren said, "I assume you are willing to give me your word that you won't try to run?"

"Of course, Prather," Owen said. "Anything to get away from my father."

Soren arched a fair brow but nodded.

They rode into the bustling camp shortly after noon. Owen was taken to a command tent where he was presented to a fair-skinned, slightly overweight, graying man in a blue military uniform with two stars on his epaulets. Also in the tent was a very tall man with ocher skin, curling black hair, and gray eyes. His eyes matched the unfamiliar gray uniform covering his slender-hipped but well-muscled figure.

A woman in a dark blue Caeldenon overdress and leggings sat next to a brazier. She looked familiar, with her light brown hair, ivory skin, and dark green eyes.

Owen glanced at her, then returned his attention to the general before his eyes jerked back to her. "Lady Victoria?" he gasped.

"You may address her as '*Ducessa*,'" the tall man said gruffly. "Unless she gives you leave to address her less formally."

"Don't scare him, Baerik," Lady Victoria scolded as she stood and crossed the tent.

She offered Owen her hand, which he kissed formally, still in a daze.

"I wed while I was in Caeldenon," she explained. "We didn't announce it because I wanted to tell my parents in person. This is my husband Baerik Forrester-Coden, the *Duc 'ah* Kilmerian."

Owen bowed slightly. "*Duc*."

"And this is Lord Owen Eddening, cousin to the Queen," she said to her husband.

"And son to High Lord Marc Eddening," the general growled.

"Not by choice," Owen countered. "I escaped my father two days ago to come give warning to the Queen."

"Well, we were headed back to the castle, so you can come with us," the *Duc* said, looking him over.

An hour later, Owen, the *Duc* and *Ducessa*, ten black-clad soldiers—a few of whom were women, he noted with some shock—and ten Lithonian soldiers left the camp.

The *Duc* kept a steady pace, and just under two hours later, according to Owen's pocket watch, they rode into Dale. As they traveled upward through the city, Hardcastle loomed above them.

When they entered the courtyard and dismounted, the *Duc* dismissed all but four of the black-clad soldiers, and a messenger was sent ahead of the arriving party.

When they reached the Queen's apartment, quite the audience was assembled. It was teatime, so platters of cakes and sandwiches sat on a sideboard, and the fragrant smell of tea filled the air.

There were at least twenty people in the spacious drawing room, but Owen only had eyes for his cousin.

He turned to the Forrester-Coden, who had been given his weapons, and asked, "Might I have my dagger, *Duc*?"

The man turned to the Queen, who nodded. Somewhat warily, he pulled the dagger from his belt and handed it to Owen.

One of the black-clad women, this one with a golden braid over her shoulder, stepped forward to stand next to the Queen.

Owen crossed the room and knelt before them. He kissed the tang of the blade and then offered his cousin, his Queen, the hilt. "I swear by my hope of life everlasting, on my honor, that I will faithfully serve you as my liege and Queen. Never shall I raise my hand in rebellion, and if I do, I ask you to pierce my heart with this blade."

Lenathaina let out a long breath. She took the dagger and kissed it as Owen had done, and then returned it to him. "I accept your pledge, and promise to always treat you and yours with fairness and justice, cousin."

Some of the tension left the room.

While still kneeling before the woman who had been both kin and friend for all of his life, Owen said, "Your Majesty, I regret to inform you that my father was behind the attack on yourself and Master Tam. He is in league with the Hathorites."

CHAPTER 123

The Goddess Hestia, the Mystic of Hathor
The Temple of Ganna: Hathor
17th of Nane

Hestia read the missive again before crumpling it in her fist and tossing it into the blazing hearth.

"What is it?" Kaleck asked from the low couch.

"Eddening has lost one of the Chosen and an assassin, and now his son has run off as well." Hestia poured herself a glass of wine and rubbed an ebony hand over her bald head. "He is making a bloody mess of this."

"What will you do?" Kaleck asked as he rose and walked to her side, stroking her back through her form-fitting, crimson robes.

"I have already sent him more Chosen, but I believe he needs a reminder of who is in charge—and the cost of failure." She took a sip of her blood-red wine. "I think I will send Niadthyr soon, if progress is not made. This is taking longer than I had hoped, and Eddening makes too many excuses."

"You think it wise to send her?" Kaleck asked, unease clear in his voice.

"Do you question me?" Hestia asked sharply.

"Never, Your Holiness." His tone changed from a lover conversing with his mate to submissiveness in an instant.

As it should.

"Explain yourself," she commanded.

"Priestess Niadthyr is among your most skilled generals. I would not want her talents wasted when she could be better used commanding the forces around you, Your Holiness," Kaleck said quietly.

Hestia put her glass down and turned to him. "You are worried for me," she replied.

"I know that the prophecies say this is our destiny, but already, so much has gone wrong." Kaleck's gaze rested on the floor. "Perhaps we have misinterpreted them."

Hestia was quiet for a long moment.

"All things are possible," she said at last. "But in this, I am sure: the prophecies say that the Lasting Peace cannot come until Hathor's children reunite in the homeland. What else could it mean but that I, the Goddess Incarnate, daughter of Hathor, take the sons of the Morthan line as my husbands? One, a follower of the Maker, most assuredly of his bloodline. The other, a child with the blood of my line, and all three of us, me, Namar and Owen, with the blood of the Morthans. The three of us together... two heirs of the Morthan line and me. You know the secrets of my line. Why the daughters of the first Goddess and every one that came after were carefully guarded. Why our lines must remain pure."

Kaleck bowed his head. "Yes, Your Holiness. But what of the third... of the other Goddess?"

"She has never mattered. Our Goddess and the Maker have always been the two at the center of it all. Lithonia is our birthright," Hestia said. "I will give Eddening a little more time, and if he is not successful, then I will send Niadthyr with a contingent of the bloodlinked." She stroked her Consort's cheek. "I can't play my hand too early. If the Caeldenon High King knows what part we play in the Lithonian war, he will have reason to come to their aid. I need Lithonia under control before I treat with him."

Kaleck nodded his agreement. "As you say, Your Holiness."

"How is Namar coming along?" she asked.

Something crossed Kaleck's face.

Jealousy, perhaps?

"His powers grow rapidly. Soon he will be able to face the Trials—another three months, maybe," Kaleck replied stiffly. "Jardin did well with him."

Hestia's fingers trailed down his neck, and he shuddered. "You know that once I have taken him as my mate, you will have to leave my bed until I have birthed his child?"

Kaleck swallowed hard. "I know my duty and I know my place."

"Good. Come to my bed now," Hestia purred. "For tonight, *that* is your place."

CHAPTER 124

Shan Alanine Fasili
Outside the City of Dale: Lithonia
25ᵗʰ of Nane

Alanine wore a dark green riding dress with split skirts, calfskin gloves, tooled leather boots, and a matching velvet cloak trimmed with silver fox fur. Her braids had been piled atop her head in an elaborate configuration, with three of the braids left down over her right shoulder as a maiden's lock.

Beside her, Owen Eddening wore a well-made suit of fine wool with a dark gray silk vest.

Queen Lenathaina, resplendent in a sapphire silk riding dress with her sword on her hip, rode in front of them with the First Prince, who had donned his military uniform. They were of course accompanied by their two *Mael'Hivar*.

A platform had been erected outside the walls of the city, and gathered there was every soldier that wasn't needed to patrol or guard the camps, as well as many of the inhabitants of the city, and all the lords and ladies in residence.

Twenty *Mael'Hivar* stood in front of the platform. They saluted the Queen and First Prince when the Royal Couple approached.

Gavantar bowed to his wife and stood to the side as she climbed the steps of the platform.

Owen gave Alanine a tight smile and offered her his arm.

He is still wary of me.

The pair followed their cousin, taking position behind her, next to Ellaemarhie, the Queen's protectoress.

Silence fell as Lenathaina looked over the crowd, her hand on the sword at her hip. She let it draw out until a stillness fell over them.

Master Braden stood nearby, his hands moving in a complex pattern. A clear, shimmering disk appeared before Lenathaina, and he nodded.

"Good people of Lithonia..." She spoke into the disk, her voice loud enough that even those in the back could hear her clearly. "We face a threat unlike anything this country has seen in over a thousand years. I am not speaking of Marc Eddening and his cohorts, or any of the people who have tried so hard to keep me from my birthright. I speak of the Hathorites."

The stillness broke, and some in the crowd shifted and murmured to one another. Lenathaina spoke over them.

"They have long moved in the shadows, influencing events, taking what isn't theirs," the Queen said. "They poison minds, promise wealth and power. They kidnap those who might either get in their way or prove useful. I know this is true, for one of their agents kidnapped *me*."

Shouts and cries of dismay rose.

Lenathaina held up her hand, and quiet descended once again. "I was beaten, tortured, and held prisoner. My husband and his men, with the help of these Masters," she gestured to cousin Isra and Amir. "Came to my aid."

Both Arch Masters gave a small bow of their heads in acknowledgment.

"Later cousin Namar Fasili, brother of Lady Alanine Fasili, *Shan* of River Keep, was taken by a Hathorite priestess," the Queen said.

The crowd was stunned into silence. Alanine could see shock on many of their faces.

Lenathaina's voice shook slightly as she continued.

"High Master Tam Gale, who devoted his life to my family, was killed because Marc Eddening thought the loss of my trusted friend and mentor would shake me enough that I would lose my courage." Her voice was hoarse with emotion. "He sent a Hathorite Magi and an assassin into Hardcastle. He had Tam Gale *killed,* and his assassin tried to kill me. If not for my *galvana* and my secretary, my blood would be on his hands. As Tam Gale's blood is on his hands!"

The crowd was nodding along with her. Calls of *"Yes"* and *"Traitor!"* rang out. Some audience members were looking at Owen, who stood stiff with fear.

"I promise you now," the Queen intoned. "I will not let the Lithonian people fall under the yoke of a tyrant!"

The crowd began cheering her, even the lords and ladies.

"I will not let my people be subjugated by a woman content to sit behind her temple walls while she sends her lackeys out to do her bidding!"

The cheers swelled.

"My cousins and I stand together." Lenathaina held out her hands, and Owen came forward on her right, and Alanine to her left. They took her hands, and she raised them high. "The three of us stand before you, united by blood and oath."

The noise was deafening.

"We are *Lithonians*!" Lenathaina shouted. "We are strong! Rich or poor, young or old, I will not sit safe behind castle walls. I will ride *with* you. Together, we will stand in the face of greed, corruption and evil."

She released their hands and stepped forward, alone. "I will give my life," she said quietly. The crowds stilled, leaning in so as to hear every word. "To protect my country and my people. Will you stand with me?"

The force of the cheers pushed Alanine back a step. Owen gripped her arm to steady her.

Lenathaina stood as more than a figurehead. She was one of the people. The mother of a nation. A warrior queen. She pulled her sword from its sheathe and raised it into the air, the sapphire catching the light of the sun blazed.

"For Lithonia!"

EPILOGUE

High Lord Marc Eddening
Verto, Southern Region: Lithonia
30th of Nane

Marc stood on the steps of Verto as the twelve magi dressed in black trousers and vests with open, billowing robes dismounted from their horses. He had sent an escort of fifty men to the city of Moriah, on the southwestern coast of Lithonia, along with a handful of servants to see to their needs.

They came up the steps to meet him, and bowed their heads slightly.

One tall and powerfully built man with sandy skin and bright blue eyes stepped forward. His brown hair was shorn so less than half an inch stuck up. "I am Harridan, senior of the Chosen here." His voice was melodic and raspy all at once. "Rooms have been prepared, yes?"

"They have," Marc said. "By what title should you be addressed?"

"You southlanders are all the same," Harridan said as he eyed their host with scrutiny. "You all put so much stock into titles given by others instead of the honors you earn yourself." He shook his head as if disgusted. "You may call us magi."

"Very well, Magi Harridan," Marc said uncomfortably. "My servants will show you to your rooms. We dine at half past seven."

Harridan inclined his head, and the twelve men swept past Marc, most barely looking at him.

*****

At the dinner table, the magi were interspersed between the lords who had sworn fealty to Marc. Most of the lords seemed uncomfortable with this arrangement, but Rendon made an attempt at bravado by engaging with the fellow to his left.

"I wonder, how did you get that mark on your forehead, Magi Franklin?" Blake asked as he took a bite of his roast pork. "I assumed your lot would be like the Masters of the Ithrimir and could heal most things."

The short but sturdy red-haired magi glowered at Rendon. "Do not compare us to the blasphemers!"

"They do not know our ways yet, Franklin," Harridan said superiorly as he speared a carrot with his fork. "We will... *educate* them."

The room stilled for a moment, and then Franklin nodded and turned back to Rendon.

"Men who are honored to see the Goddess in person receive a cut on their forehead so all can see that they have been in Her divine presence. Only the Consortium, those who serve as mates to the Goddess and Her priestesses, may normally see Her. Other men must be purified before seeing Her, and that is only if they have been summoned for that honor."

He gestured to Harridan. "As you may notice, Harridan has seen Her three times."

Rendon guffawed. "How do you *see* a bleeding *goddess*?"

Marc heard Blake's voice catch, and watched as the man clutched at his throat and began to choke and gasp for breath, slowly rising into the air until his feet were dangling a few inches off the ground. Marc nearly jumped when the other man's chair fell backward.

Franklin tilted his head and watched Rendon's face turn purple.

"You have made your point," Harridan said idly as he took another bite.

Whatever Franklin had been doing, he stopped, and Rendon crumpled to the ground.

Parker hurried to his side.

"Can your Masters do that?" Franklin asked Marc, his tone condescending.

"No. They are bound by archaic rules that favor the weak over the strong," Marc replied. "I will follow the Mystic and Her teachings. Through Her Holiness, we will find the path to power, and through that power, we will create our own form of peace."

*****

High Master Lily Morthan
Aboard the White Raven, the Indayon Sea
30th of Nane

Lily Morthan leaned against the rail of the *White Raven,* near the figurehead. She wondered who had thought to adorn the white-robed woman with golden wings and flowing, blonde hair.

It was one of the ships that the Ithram commanded, and he had pulled it away from its intended destination to deliver her to Lithonia. The Council had agreed on the importance of her journey, so her own Mir had rushed through the celebrations and ceremonies that surrounded her being elevated to High Master.

There were many scholars, but fewer and fewer dedicated themselves to becoming High Masters. Most took on the Mir as a secondary specialty to another and never took it farther than becoming an Arch Master.

High Master Ardent Rythan had been so proud of her that he had commissioned several dresses and robes, paid for by the Mir's coffers, to proclaim her status.

Lily glanced down at the rust orange dress, cut in the Lithonian fashion and trimmed with black lace and embroidery, and vowed to do her Mir proud.

She watched the horizon as the sun set. Soon, she would walk in the lands of her forefathers and foremothers, and begin to unravel the secrets of her family. Secrets that just might help her understand the two prophecies she carried with her.

She touched the leather case that rested in her pocket. She had already read one of the rolls of parchment within and committed it to memory. The one that had been tied with blue thread…

*****

The Secret Prophecies
7th Level of the Ithram's Repository
Recorded: 21st of Xavar, 730

Wars will ravage Redolan and the lands will burn. Who shall save us from fire and damnation? They shall be born and raised in the Oaken Heart. Forged in fire. Tried and tested. They will be our only hope.

THE END

*****

Pre-order book three of the In Blood and Fire *series,* The Flame Within *today!*

To find out more about the world of Redolan and future books, visit www.KristinaGruell.com.

Other Books by Kristina Gruell:
From the Ashes, book one of the In Blood and Fire Series

APPENDICES
THE CAST

Castle Endomir, home of the Morthan Family
- King Garrett Morlette, bastard son of the late King Charles Morthan also called the Usurper
- Edwin Murphy, secretary to King Garrett

The Exiled Court of Queen Lenathaina Morthan Coden of Lithonia:
- Queen Lenathaina Morthan Coden and her husband, First Prince Gavantar Coden of Caeldenon
  - Prince Galwyn Tearhall, Mael'Hivar Thane of Gavantar
  - Lady Ellaemarhie Lindal, Mael'Hivar Galvana of Lenathaina
- Lady Jane Grey, Lenathaina's bastard cousin and ward
- Lady Rachel Malick, lady in waiting to Queen Lenathaina
- Lady Maratha Vectors, lady in waiting to Queen Lenathaina
- Lady Victoria Forrester-Coden, *Ducessa ah'* Kilmerian and lady in waiting to Queen Lenathaina
  - Her husband, Lord Baerik Forrester-Coden, *Duc 'ah* Kilmerian and their daughter, Lady Cressa
- High Master Tam Gale of the Ithrimir, Advisor and Healer to the Royal family the Queen and a distant relation.
  - Masters Babak Kareen and Ellis Braithwaite, his students

Noble Families and Members of the Lithonian Court
- The Vassals of the Morthan Family
  - Lord Marvin and Lady Anne (Vectors) Jasper
    - Numerous children and relations

- o Lord Samuel and Lady Allis (Parr) Collins
  - Their children: Lady Annabeth and her husband, Lord David Proudmourn; Lord Andrew and his wife, Lady Andrice. Grandchildren: Lord Michael Proudmourn, Lord Eric and Lady Nikka Collins
  - Deceased brother, Lord Eric, and his wife, Lady Leann (Wallace) Collins, also deceased: their daughters, Dowager Queen Mellina Morthan and Princess Nikkana Morthan
- High Lord Benjamin and High Lady Beth (Rendon) Bennings
  - o Their children: Lord Randal and his wife, Lady Lissa; Ladies Anne, Jane, Mary and Sara; Lord James
  - o Master Nathan Zane, Advisor to HL Bennings
    - Their Vassals: Payne, Prather, Proudmourn
- High Lord Caleb and High Lady Giselle (Eddening) Vectors
  - o Their Children: Lord Jon, Lady Maratha, Lady Cynthia, Lord Markus
    - Their Vassals: Crawford, Moore, Howard
- High Lord Montgomery and High Lady Angela (Rendon)
  - o Their children, Lords Stephen, Derek and Travis; Ladies Henrietta and Claire; Adept Adeline
    - Their Vassals: Lorvette, Highland, Southernby
- High Lord Ellis and High Lady Leanne (Vectors) Parker
  - o Children: Lord Jared and his wife, Lady Ellen (Malick) and their son, Jacob; Lord Michael and his wife, Lady Bree (Long), and their daughter, Lady Janna
    - Their Vassals: Malic, Grey, Cromby
- High Lord Derrick and High Lady Corrine (Greene) Maceon

- o   Their children: Lord Albert, Lord Arden, Lady Cynna, Lady Lucy
  - ▪ Their Vassals: Parten, Greene, Broome
- High Lord Mitchel and High Lady Janet (Dorn) Parr
  - o   Their children, Lord Gerald, Lord Joshua, Lord Brent, Lady Gwen; assorted spouses and grandchildren
    - ▪ Their Vassals: Long, Norrington, Dale
- High Lord Blake Rendon, wife deceased
  - o   His children: Lord Harrison, Lady Gia Proudmourn, Lord Gerald; assorted grandchildren, bastards
  - o   His brother, Lord Jarrod and his wife, Erin, their daughter, High Lady Beth Bennings
  - o   His brother, Lord Roger and his wife, Nancy, their daughter High Lady Angela Montgomery
    - ▪ His Vassals: Wallace, Dorn, Gregory
- High Lord Marc and High Lady Ann (Bennings) Eddening
  - o   Their children: Lord Marc, Lord Edward, Lady Anna, Lord Macin
    - ▪ His Vassals: Harewood, Gordon, Avery
- High Lord Harold and Lady Anne (Maceon) Harmon
  - o   Their children: Lord Harold, Lady Eloisa, Lord Nate
  - o   His mother, High Lady Eloise
    - ▪ His Vassals: Fraser, Kent, Harmon (oldest son)
- Lord Gerald and Lady Hanna Grey
  - o   Various issue, daughter Lady Joan (deceased) and her daughter, Lady Jane, bastard of King Charles
- Lord Garn and Lady Latasha Wallace
  - o   Their children: Lord Garran, Lady Jaina, Lady Victoria, Lord Derrick and Lord Samuel

City of Endomir, Lithonia:

- Vera Martique, Information Dealer

- o   Marie Rowan, Vera's assistant
- o   Samuel Thane, Lamp Lighter and Spy for Vera
- o   Jack West, an informant and footman to the Caeldenon Embassy

White Castle, Court of Caeldenon:

- High King Gavan and Queen Maelynn (Ederic) Coden
  - ▪ Jaedinar and Andamar Broughton, Mael'Hivar Thanes to HK Gavan
  - ▪ Emerlise Elfinder of Andolin, Mael'Hivar Galvana to HQ Maelynn
  - o First Prince Gavantar Coden and Queen Lenathaina Morthan Coden, exiled ruler of Lithonia
    - ▪ Prince Galwyn Tearhall, Mael'Hivar Thane of Gavantar
    - ▪ Lady Ellaemarhie Lindal, Mael'Hivar Galvana of Lenathaina
  - o High Princess Aeleonna Coden
    - ▪ Darane J'all Mael'Hivar Galvana to Princess Aeleonna
  - o High Princess Ellesmerra Coden, called Merra
    - ▪ Isma Andara Mael'Hivar Galvana to Princess Merra
  - o High Prince Ederic Coden, ward of the Masters of the Ithrimir and living with them
  - o High Princes Landon and Evandar Coden, twins
  - o High Princess Lyssa Coden
- Arch Master Lan Coden
- High Prince Evandar (First Advisor to the HK) and Princess Samera (Emberskye) Coden
    - ▪ Deldemar Lynn, Mael'Hivar Thane to Prince Evandar
    - ▪ Aria Emberskye. Mael'Hivar Galvana to Princess Samera
  - o Prince Taemos

- Narrin Linhere, Mael'Hivar Thane to Lord Taemos
  - Princess Lithe
  - Prince Takanar

- Princess Fenora Tearhall of Cael; ward of the High King
- Prince Jaeminderiel of Cael, called Jaemi, ward of the High King
- Lord Kieran Rainsmere, Gandine to First Prince Gavantar and First Princess Lenathaina
- Blood General Riland, Commander of the Gold Swords, Guard of the First Prince

At Trahelion Manor:
- Dowager High Queen Arrysanna (Mycium), mother to the High King
  - Warder
- Lady Cressa Forrester-Coden, the Dowager's granddaughter
- Lady Jane Grey, cousin and ward of Queen Lenathaina
- Dowager Queen Mellina Morthan
- Lady Sara Parten, Queen Mellina's lady in waiting

At River Keep:
Their children, Alanine, Namar and Nijah
- Shan Alanine Fasili
  - Her siblings, Namar and Nijah
- Princess Lynear Palin, niece of the Empress of Pannarius
- Sevinc Dal, Hassana to Shan Alanine

At Hardcastle:
- Lord Gerard Rythan, the Steward of Hardcastle, and his wife Lady Davina
  - Lord Jarod Rythan, Captain of the Guard
  - Lord Alexander Rythan, grandson of the Lord Steward

- o   Various other relations

At the Isles of the Ithrimir
- Ithram Taran Havensgrad
    - o   High Master Parana Intion, Head of the White Mir
    - o   High Master Lirian Rainier, Head of the Blue Mir
    - o   High Master Stuart Vern
    - o   Arch Master Cade Kline
    - o   Arch Master Lily Morthan
        - ▪   Her mother, the Dowager Queen Rowan Morthan
        - ▪   Danielle, her housekeeper
    - o   Mouriani Hameen-Palin, daughter of Arch Masters Isra and Amir Hameen-Palin
    - o   Adept Lan Coden

A Note on Caeldenon:

Members of the Royal family, once they reach a certain age, choose a dedicated bodyguard. This person is referred to as Brother or Sister and their title (depending on their gender) is Mael'Hivar Thane or Mael'Hivar Galvana

A note on Pannarius:

Pannarius is a matriarchal society. Men take the names of their wives and have little legal rights.

CALENDAR AND DATES

There are twelve months in the year, three weeks in a month and ten days in a week. The current calendar was adopted by all countries after the Consolidation of Caeldenon and is referred to as A.C.

The Months and Major Holidays

- Ando
  - Wellspring, the celebration of the new year, 1st of Ando
- Morin
- Nane
  - Spring Feast (Lithonia), Awakening Festival (Caeldenon and Thynn), Rite of Life (Pannarius): 1st
- Zulin
- Youn
- Julas
  - First day of Summer, Feast of the longest day (Lithonia), Feast of Light (Caeldenon), Fire Festival (Pannarius): 1st
- Caro
  - Consolidation Day (Caeldenon, the anniversary of the founding of the United Kingdom): 18th
- Jinda
  - Harvest Night (Lithonia): 30th
- Rison
  - Autumn Festival (Caeldenon), First day of Autumn: 1st
- Xavar
  - Battle of Two Rivers anniversary, when Morthan Family took the throne (Lithonia): 14th
- Minn
- Charn

- o Night of Reflection (Lithonia), Commemoration (Caeldenon), First Day of Winter: 1st
- o Highpoint (Day of celebration and gift giving for followers of the Maker): 30th

ACKNOWLEDGEMENTS

Michael, you have been my rock. My best friend. My everything. Thank you for your love and support. So many times I wondered if I could do this but you wouldn't let me quit. You are always here for me. Beside me. Encouraging me. I love you.

Joey, Manny, and Serenity: I love you all so much. Even when you are driving me crazy.

My parents, Mark and Sabrina Klis and my bonus dad, Chris Wiggins. You have been some of my biggest cheerleaders. Thank you.

Aunt Susan, my partner in crime.

The Ladies of FBS: Sally Ross, Michelle Schwartz, Robyn Bennett, Misty Dawn Seidel and Kenzie Whyte, Kathy Jones, Wilma Collins, Margaret Banks, Beth Gourbiere, Soup Fick, Judy Henrickson, Maryrose Serac. For your continued love and support.

Matt Zupka, you are one of the most important people in my life. Thank you for all that you do and all that you are.

And Leanda Zupka, you are a gem among women.

Rosina Lippi, you continue to be a wonderful friend. I am thankful for our chats.

Malorie and Jill Cooper, thank you for continuing to be there for me and teach me. You are true friends.

Jen McDonnell, you have become a true friend. You are an editing superhero.

Samantha Lane, there are so many things I could say. Your friendship is priceless. I love how well we work together.

Odd Magne Wegner and Angela Montgomery: you continue to inspire me. Your love and support mean more than I can say.

Corinne Alton, I don't know what I would do without you.

And to so many more… thank you to everyone who has walked with me on this journey.

ABOUT KRISTINA

Kristina was born in Midlothian, Texas, a former farming community in North Texas. Growing up she rode horses, participated in FFA, danced and read voraciously. After a car accident left her wheelchair bound for eight months and continuing health issues limited her previously active lifestyle, she turned to books and online play-by-post role playing in the early days of AOL chatrooms. Her original stories and first novel attempt were background for her online characters; eventually she began writing and telling stories to entertain her friends.

She has spent the last several years doing social media support for authors and filmmakers as well as ghost writing blog posts and promotional material for entrepreneurs while following her Naval Officer husband around the country. Now that he has retired, they have returned to Texas to raise their three children and finally spend time with their extended family. Their busy household includes two cats, three dogs and an amazing Aunt.

She loved dogs and cats, enjoys a good glass of wine or whiskey in the evenings and is a tea snob. She spends her spare time reading, running play-by-post role playing games, building elaborate Lego sets and playing World of Warcraft (where she met her husband, because she is that geeky).

Her life is chaotic but she wouldn't have it any other way.